To Isaac, with love

Contents

Preface   Ray Bradbury   1

Second Preface: The Nonmetallic Isaac *or* It's a Wonderful Life   Ben Bova   3

Strip-Runner   Pamela Sargent   7

The Asenion Solution   Robert Silverberg   41

Murder in the Urth Degree   Edward Wellen   57

Trantor Falls   Harry Turtledove   75

Dilemma   Connie Willis   95

Maureen Birnbaum After Dark   George Alec Effinger   115

Balance   Mike Resnick   135

The Present Eternal   Barry N. Malzberg   141

PAPPI   Sheila Finch   153

The Reunion at the Mile-High   Frederik Pohl   173

Plato's Cave   Poul Anderson   187

Foundation's Conscience   George Zebrowski   217

Carhunters of the Concrete Prairie   Robert Sheckley   225

The Overheard Conversation   Edward D. Hoch   273

Blot   Hal Clement   281

The Fourth Law of Robotics   Harry Harrison   307

The Originist   Orson Scott Card   321

Afterword: A Word or Two from Janet   Janet Jeppson Asimov   397

Afterword: Fifty Years   Isaac Asimov   401

Preface

by Ray Bradbury

One of my favorite stories as a child was the one about the little boy who got a magical porridge machine functioning so wildly that it inundated the town with three feet of porridge.

In order to walk from one house to the other, or head down-street, one had to head out with a large spoon, eating one's way to destinations near or far.

A delightful concept, save that I imagined tomato soup and a thick slush of crackers. Going on a journey and making a feast, all in one!

I imagine the name of the little boy in that tale should have been Isaac Asimov. For it seems to me that since first we met at the First World Science Fiction Convention in New York City the first week in July 1939, Isaac has been journeying and feasting through life, now at the Astronomical tables, now in a spread of other sciences, now in religion, and again in literature over a great span of time. One could call him a jackdaw, but that wouldn't be correct. Jackdaws focus on and snatch bright objects of no particular weight. Isaac is in the mountain-moving business, but he does not move but eat them. Hand him a book and a few hours later, like that above-mentioned porridge, Isaac comes tunneling out the far side, still hungry. Is there a body of literature he hasn't taken on? I severely doubt it.

And now here, with this book, we have Asimov's honorary sons and daughters. Their machines may not run amok and inundate a city, but they are producing, nevertheless, and looking to Papa Asimov and us for approval, which will not be withheld.

To say more would be to call attention to my comparable size, a mole next to a fortress or a force of nature. I would add only a final note. People have said Isaac is a workaholic. Nonsense. He has gone mad with love in ten dozen territories. And there are a few dozen virgin territories left out there. There will be few such virgins left, when Isaac departs earth and arrives Up There to write twenty-five new books of the Bible. And that's only the first week!

One night two years ago, I dreamed I was Isaac Asimov. Arising the next day, it was noon before my wife convinced me that I should not run for President.

Bless you, Isaac. Bless you, Isaac's children, found herein.

February 21, 1989

The Nonmetallic Isaac or
It's a Wonderful Life

by Ben Bova

Astrophysicists (to start with a scientific word) classify the universe into three chemical categories: hydrogen, helium, and metals.

The first two are the lightest of all the hundred-some known elements. Anything heavier than helium, the astrophysicists blithely call "metals." Hydrogen and helium make up roughly ninety-eight percent of the universe's composition. To an astrophysicist, the universe consists of a lot of hydrogen, a considerable amount of helium, and a smattering of metals.

Now, although Isaac Asimov is known throughout this planet (and possibly others, we just don't know yet) as a writer of science fiction, when you consider his entire output of written material—all the four-hundred-and-counting books and the myriads of articles, columns, limericks, and whatnots—his science fiction is actually a small percentage of the total. As far as Asimov's production is concerned, science fiction tales are his "metals." Science *fact* is his mettle.

It is the "nonmetallic" Asimov that I want to praise.

Remember the classic movie *It's a Wonderful Life!*? The one where an angel shows suicidal James Stewart what his hometown would be like if Jimmie's character had never been born?

Think of what our home planet would be like if Isaac Asimov had never turned his mind and hand to writing about science.

We narrowly missed such a fate. There was a moment in time when a youthful Isaac faced a critical career choice: go on as a researcher or plunge full-time into writing. He chose writing and the world is extremely happy with the result.

Knowing that science fiction, in those primeval days, could not support a wife and family, Isaac chose to write about science fact and to make that his career, rather than biomedical research.

But suppose he had not?

Suppose, faced with that career choice, Isaac had opted for the steady, if unspectacular, career of a medium-level research scientist who wrote occasional science fiction stories as a hobby.

We would still have the substantial oeuvre of his science fiction tales that this anthology celebrates. We would still have "Nightfall" and "The Ugly Little Boy," the original Foundation trilogy and novels such as *Pebble in the Sky*. We would, to return to the metaphor we started with, still have Isaac's "metallic" output.

But we would not have his hydrogen and helium, the huge number of books that are nonfiction, mainly books about science, although there are some marvelous histories, annotations of various works of literature, and lecherous limericks in there, too.

If Isaac had toiled away his years as a full-time biomedical researcher and part-time science fiction writer, we would never have seen all those marvelous science books. Probably a full generation of scientists would have chosen other careers, because they would never have been turned on to science by the books that Isaac did not write. Progress in all fields of the physical sciences would have slowed, perhaps disastrously.

Millions of people all over the world would have been denied the pleasure of learning that they *could* understand the principles of physics, mathematics, astronomy, geology, chemistry, the workings of the human body, the intricacies of the human brain—because the books from which they learned and received such pleasures would never have been written.

Entire publishing houses would have gone into bankruptcy, no doubt, without the steady, sure income that Isaac's science books have generated for them over the decades. And will continue to generate for untold decades to come. The wood pulp and paper industry would be in a chronic state of depression if Isaac had not turned out all those hundreds of books and thousands of articles. Canada might have become a Third World nation, save for Dr. Isaac Asimov.

To make it more personal, I would have never started to write popularizations of science if it had not been for Isaac's works—and for his personal encouragement and guidance. The gods themselves are the only ones who know how many writers have been helped by Isaac, either by reading his books or by asking him for help with science problems that had them stumped.

Blighted careers, ruined corporations, benighted people wandering in search of an enlightenment that they cannot find— that is what the world would be like if Isaac had not poured his great energies and greater heart into nonfiction books about science.

A final word about a word: popularization.

In the mouths of certain critics (including some professional scientists) "popularization" is a term of opprobrium, somewhat akin to the sneering "pulp literature" that is still sometimes slung at science fiction. "Popularizations" of science are regarded, by those slandering bastards, as beneath the consideration of dignified persons.

Such critics regard themselves as among the elite, and they disdain "popularizations" of science with the same lofty pigheadedness that George III displayed toward his American subjects.

To explain science is probably the most vital task any writer can attempt in today's complex, technology-driven society. To explain science so well, so entertainingly, that ordinary men and women all over the world clamor for your books—that is worthy of a Nobel Prize. Too bad Alfred Nobel never thought about the need to explain science to the masses. I'm certain he would have created a special prize for it.

Isaac Asimov writes about science (and everything else) so superbly well that it looks easy. He can take any subject under the sun and write about it so lucidly and understandably that any literate person can grasp the subject with hardly any strain at all.

For this incredible talent he is sometimes dismissed as "a

mere popularizer." As I have offered in the past, I offer now; anyone who thinks that what Isaac does is easy is welcome to try it. I know I have, with some degree of success. But easy it is not!

Thanks be to the forces that shape this universe, Isaac decided *not* to be a full-time researcher. He became a full-time writer instead. While he is famous for writing science fiction, his "nonmetallic" output of science fact is far larger and far more important—if that word can be applied to writing—than his deservedly admired and awarded fiction.

If all this adds up to the conclusion that Isaac Asimov is a star, well, by heaven, he is! One of the brightest, too.

Strip-Runner

by Pamela Sargent

The three boys caught up with Amy just as she reached the strips. "Barone-Stein," one boy shouted to her. She did not recognize any of them, but they obviously knew who she was.

"We want a run," the smallest boy said, speaking softly so that the people passing them could not hear the challenge. "You can lead and pick the point."

"Done," she said quickly. "C–254th, Riverdale localway intersection."

The boys frowned. Maybe they had expected a longer run. They seemed young; the tallest one could not be more than eleven. Amy leaned over and rolled up the cuffs of her pants a little. She could shake all of them before they reached the destination she had named.

More people passed and stepped onto the nearest strip. The moving gray bands stretched endlessly to either side of her, carrying their human cargo through the City. The strip closest to her was moving at a bit over three kilometers an hour; most of its passengers at the moment were elderly people or small children practicing a few dance steps where there was space. Next to it, another strip moved at over five kilometers an hour; in the distance, on the fastest strip, the passengers were a multicolored blur. All the strips carried a steady stream of people, but the evening rush hour would not start for a couple of hours. The boys had challenged her during a slower period, which meant they weren't that sure of themselves; they would not risk a run through mobs of commuters.

"Let's go," Amy said. She stepped on the strip; the boys got on behind her. Ahead, people were stepping to the adjoining strip, slowly making their way toward the fastest-moving strip that ran alongside the localway platform. Advertisements flashed around her through the even, phosphorescent light, offering clothing, the latest book-films, exotic beverages, and yet another hyperwave drama about a Spacer's adventures on Earth. Above her, light-worms and bright arrows gleamed steadily with directions for the City's millions: THIS WAY TO JERSEY SECTIONS; FOLLOW ARROW TO LONG ISLAND. The noise was constant. Voices rose and fell around her as the strip hummed softly under her feet; she could dimly hear the whistle of the localway.

Amy walked up the strip, darted past a knot of people, then crossed to the next strip, bending her knees slightly to allow for the increase in speed. She did not look back, knowing the boys were still behind her. She took a breath, quickly stepped to the next strip, ran along it toward the passengers up ahead, and then jumped to the fourth strip. She pivoted, jumped to the third strip again, then rapidly crossed three strips in succession.

Running the strips was a lot like dancing. She kept up the rhythm as she leaped to the right, leaned into the wind, then jumped to the slower strip on her left. Amy grinned as a man shook his head at her. The timid ways of most riders were not for her. Others shrank from the freedom the gray bands offered, content to remain part of a channeled stream. They seemed deaf to the music of the strips and the song that beckoned to her.

Amy glanced back; she had already lost one of the boys. Moving to the left edge of the strip, she feinted, then jumped to her right, pushed past a startled woman, and continued along the strips until she reached the fastest one.

Her left arm was up, to shield her from the wind; this strip, like the localway, was moving at nearly thirty-eight kilometers an hour. The localway was a constantly moving platform, with poles for boarding and clear shields placed at intervals to protect riders from the wind. Amy grabbed a pole and swung herself aboard.

There was just enough room for her to squeeze past the standing passengers. The two remaining boys had followed her onto the localway; a woman muttered angrily as Amy shoved past her to the other side.

She jumped down to the strip below, which was also moving at the localway's speed, hauled herself aboard the platform once more, then leaped back to the strip. One boy was still with her, a few paces behind. His companion must have hesitated a little, not expecting her to leap to the strip again so soon. Any good strip-runner would have expected it; no runner stayed on a localway or expressway very long. She jumped to a slower strip, counted to herself, leaped back to the faster strip, counted again, then grabbed a pole, bounded onto the localway, pushed past more people to the opposite side, and launched herself at the strip below, her back to the wind, her legs shooting out into a split. Usually she disdained such moves at the height of a run, but could not resist showing her skill this time.

She landed about a meter in front of a scowling man. "Crazy kids!" he shouted. "Ought to report you—" She turned toward the wind and stepped to the strip on her left, bracing herself against the deceleration as the angry man was swept by her on the faster strip, then looked back. The third boy was nowhere to be seen among the stream of people behind her.

Too easy, she thought. She had shaken them all even before reaching the intersection that led to the Concourse Sector. She would go on to the destination, so that the boys, when they got there, could issue another challenge if they wished. She doubted that they would; she would have just enough time to make her way home afterward.

They should have known better. They weren't good enough runners to keep up with Amy Barone-Stein. She had lost Kiyoshi Harris, one of the best strip-runners in the City, on a two-hour run to the end of Brooklyn, and had reached Queens alone on another run after shaking off Bradley Ohaer's gang. She smiled as she recalled how angry Bradley had been, beaten by a girl. Few girls ran the strips, and she was better than any of the others at the game. For over a year now, no one she challenged had ever managed to shake her off; when she led, nobody could keep up with her. She was the best girl strip-runner in New York City, maybe in all of Earth's Cities.

No, she told herself as she crossed the strips to the expressway intersection. She was simply the best.

Amy's home was in a Kingsbridge subsection. Her feeling of triumph had faded by the time she reached the elevator banks that led to her level; she was not that anxious to get home. Throngs of people moved along the street between the high metallic walls that enclosed some of the City's millions. All of Earth's Cities were like New York, where people had burrowed into the ground and walled themselves in; they were safe inside the Cities, protected from the emptiness of the Outside.

Amy pushed her way into an elevator. A wedding party was aboard, the groom in a dark ruffled tunic and pants, the bride in a short white dress with her hands around a bouquet of flowers made of recycled paper. The people with them were holding bottles and packages of rations clearly meant for the reception. The couple smiled at Amy; she murmured her congratulations as the elevator stopped at her level.

She sprinted down the hall until she came to a large double door with glowing letters that said PERSONAL—WOMEN. Under the sign, smaller letters said SUBSECTIONS 2H–2N; there was also a number to call in case anyone lost a key. Amy unzipped her pocket, took out a thin aluminum strip, and slipped it into the key slot.

The door opened. Several women were in the pleasant rose-colored antechamber, talking as they combed their hair and sprayed on makeup by the wall of mirrors. They did not greet Amy, so she said nothing to them. Her father, like most men, found it astonishing that women felt free to speak to one another in such a place. No man would ever address another in the Men's Personals; even glancing at someone there was considered extremely offensive. Men would never stand around gossiping in a Personal's antechamber, but things were not quite as free here as her father thought. Women would never speak to anyone who clearly preferred privacy, or greet a new subsection resident here until they knew her better.

Amy stood by a mirror and smoothed down her short, dark curls, then entered the common stalls. A long row of toilets, with thin partitions but no doors, lined one wall; a row of sinks faced them on the other side of the room.

A young woman was kneeling next to one toilet, where a small child sat on a training seat; Amy could not help noticing that the child was a boy. That was allowed, until a boy was four and old enough to go to a Men's Personal by himself or with his father, an experience that had to be traumatic the first time around. She thought of what it must be like for a little boy, leaving the easier, warmer atmosphere of his mother's Personal for the men's, where even looking in someone else's direction was taboo. Some said the custom arose because of the need to preserve some privacy in the midst of others, but psychologists also claimed that the taboo grew out of the male's need to separate himself from his mother. No wonder men behaved as they did in their Personals. They would not only be infringing on another's privacy if they behaved otherwise, but would also be displaying an inappropriate regression to childhood.

Amy kept her eyes down, ignoring the other women and girls in the common stalls until she reached the rows of shower heads. Two women were entering the private stalls in the back. Amy's mother had been allowed a private stall some years ago, a privilege her husband had earned for both of them after a promotion, but Amy was not allowed to use it. Other parents might have granted such permission, but hers were stricter; they did not want their daughter getting too used to privileges she had not earned for herself.

She would take her shower now, and put her clothes in the laundry slot to be cleaned; the Personal would be more crowded after dinner. Amy sighed; that wasn't the only reason to linger here. Her mother would have received the message from Mr. Liang by now. Amy was afraid to go home and face her.

Four women were leaving the apartment as Amy approached. She greeted them absently, and nodded when they asked if she was doing well in school. These were her mother's more intellectual friends, the ones who discussed sociology and settled the City's political problems among themselves before moving on to the essential business of tips for stretching quota allowances and advice on child-rearing.

Amy's mother stepped back as she entered; the door closed. Amy had reached the middle of the spacious living room before her mother spoke. "Where are you going, dear?"

"Er—to my room."

"I think you'd better sit down. We have something to discuss."

Amy moved toward one of the chairs and sat down. The living room was over five meters long, with two chairs, a small couch, and an imitation leather ottoman. The apartment had two other rooms as well, and her parents even had the use of a sink in their bedroom, thanks to her father's Civil Service rating. They both had a lot to protect, which meant that they would scold her even more for her failures.

"You took longer than usual getting home," her mother said as she sat down on the couch across from Amy.

"I had to shower. Uh, shouldn't we be getting ready to go to supper? Father'll probably be home any minute."

"He told me he'd be late, so we're not eating in the section kitchen tonight."

Amy bit her lip, sorry for once that her family was allowed four meals a week in their own apartment. Her parents wouldn't have been able to harp at her at the section kitchen's long tables in the midst of all the diners there.

"Anyway," her mother continued, "I felt sure you'd want to speak to me alone, before your father comes home."

"Oh." Amy stared at the blue carpet. "What about?"

"You know what about. I had a message from your guidance counselor, Mr. Liang. I know he told you he'd be speaking to me."

"Oh." Amy tried to sound unconcerned. "That."

"He says your grades won't be good at the end of the quarter." Her mother's dark eyes narrowed. "If they don't improve soon, he's going to invite me there for a conference, and that's not all." She leaned back against the couch. "He also says you've been seen running the strips."

Amy started. "Who told him that?"

"Oh, Amy. I'm sure he has ways of finding out. Is it true?"

"Um."

"Well, is it? That's even more serious than your grades. Do you want a police officer picking you up? Did you even stop to think about the accidents you might cause, or that you could be seriously injured? You know what your father said the first time he heard about your strip-running."

Amy bowed her head. That had been over two years ago, and he had lectured her for hours, but had remained unaware of her activities since then. I'm the best, she thought; every runner in the City knows about me. She wanted to shout it and force her mother to acknowledge the achievement, but kept silent.

"It's a stupid, dangerous game, Amy. A few boys are killed every year running the strips, and passengers are hurt as well. You're fourteen now—I thought you were more mature. I can't believe—"

"I haven't been running the strips," Amy said. "I mean, I haven't made a run in a while." Not since a couple of hours ago, she added silently to herself, and that wasn't a real run, so I'm not really lying. She felt just a bit guilty; she didn't like to lie.

"And your grades—"

Amy seized at the chance to avoid the more hazardous topic of strip-racing. "I know they're worse. I know I can do better, but what difference does it make?"

"Don't you want to do well? You used to be one of the best math students in your school, and your science teacher always praised—"

"So what?" Amy could not restrain herself any longer. "What good is it? What am I ever going to use it for?"

"You have to do well if you want to be admitted to a college level. Your father's status may make it easier for you to get in, but you won't last if you're not well prepared."

"And then what? Unless I'm a genius, or a lot better than any of the boys, they'll just push me into dietetics courses or social relations or child psychology so I'll be a good mother someday, or else train me to program computers until I get married. I'll just end up doing nothing anyway, so why should I try?"

"Nothing?" Her mother's olive-skinned face was calm, but her voice shook a little. "Is what I do nothing, looking after you and your father? Is rearing a child and making a pleasant home for a husband nothing?"

"I didn't mean nothing, but why does it have to be everything? You wanted more once—you know you did. You—you—"

Her mother was gazing at her impassively. Amy jumped up and fled to her room.

She lay on her narrow bed, glaring up at the soft glow of the ceiling. Her mother should have been the first to understand. Amy knew how she once had felt, but lately, she seemed to have forgotten her old dreams.

Amy's mother, Alysha Barone, was something of a Medievalist. That wasn't odd; a lot of people were. They got together to talk about old ways and historical book-films and the times when Earth had been humanity's only home. They dwelled nostalgically on ancient periods when people had lived Outside instead of huddling together inside the Cities, when Earth was the only world and the Spacers did not exist.

Not that any of them could actually live Outside, without walls, breathing unfiltered air filled with microorganisms that bred disease and eating unprocessed food that had grown in dirt; Amy shuddered at the thought. Better to leave the Outside to the robots that worked the mines and tended the crops the Cities demanded. Better to live as they did, whatever the problems, and avoid the pathological ways of the Spacers, those descendants of the Earthpeople who had settled other planets long ago. They could not follow Spacer customs anyway. In a world of billions, resources could not be wasted on private houses, spacious gardens and grounds, and all the rest. Alysha Barone, despite her somewhat Medievalist views, would not be capable of leaving this City except to travel, safely enclosed, to another.

Her mother had, however, clung to a few ancient customs, with the encouragement of a few mildly unconventional friends. Alysha Barone had insisted on keeping her own name after her marriage to Ricardo Stein, and he had agreed when she asked that Amy be given both their names. The couple had been given permission to have their first child during their first year of marriage, thanks to their Genetics Values ratings, but Amy had not been born until four years later. Both Alysha and Ricardo had been statisticians in New York's Department of Human Resources; it made sense to work for a promotion, gain more privileges, and save more of their quota allowances before having a child. They had ignored the chiding of their own parents and the friends who had accused them of being just a little antisocial.

Amy knew the story well, having heard most of it from her disapproving grandmother Barone. The two had each risen to a C–4 rating before Alysha became pregnant; even then, astonishingly, they had discussed which of them should give up the Department job. Only the most antisocial of couples would have tried to keep two such coveted positions. There were too many unclassified people without work, on subsistence with no chance to rise, and others who had been relegated to labor in the City yeast farm levels after losing jobs to robots. Her parents' colleagues would have made their lives miserable if they both stayed with the Department; their superiors would have blocked any promotions, perhaps even found a way to demote them. Someone also had to look after Amy. The infant could not be left in the subsection nursery all day, and both grandmothers had refused to encourage any antisocial activity by offering to stay with the baby.

So Alysha had given up her job. Her husband might be willing to care for a baby, but he could not nurse the child, and nursing saved on rations. Ricardo had won another promotion a few years after Amy's birth, and they had moved from their two-room place in the Van Cortlandt Section to this apartment. Now Amy's father was a C–6, with a private stall in the Men's Personal, a functioning sink in his room, larger quota allowances for entertainment, and the right to eat four meals a week at home.

Her parents would have been foolish to give up a chance at all that. How useless it would have been for Alysha to hope for her position at the Department; they would have risked everything in the end.

The door opened; her mother came inside. Amy sat up. Her small bed took up most of the room; there was no other place to sit, and Alysha clearly wanted to talk.

Her mother seated herself, then draped an arm over Amy's shoulders. "I know how you feel," she said.

Amy shook her head. "No, you don't."

Her mother hugged her more tightly. "I felt that way myself once, but couldn't see that I'd be any better off not trying at all. You should learn what you can, Amy, and not just so that you'll be able to help your own children with their schoolwork. Learning will give you pleasure later, something you'll carry inside yourself that no one can take from you. Things may change, and then—"

"They'll never change. I wish— Things were better in the old days."

"No, they weren't," her mother responded. "They were better for a few people and very bad for a lot of others. I may affect a few Medievalisms, but I also know how people fought and starved and suffered long ago, and the Cities are better than that. No one starves, and we can, generally speaking, go about our business without fearing violence, but that requires cooperation—we couldn't live, crowded together as we are, any other way. We have to get along, and that often means giving up what we might want so that everyone at least has something. Still—"

"I get the point," Amy said bitterly. "Civism is good. The Cities are the height of human civilization." She imitated the pompous manner of her history teacher as she spoke. "And if I can't get along and be grateful for what I've got, I'm just a pathological antisocial individualist."

Her mother was silent for a long time, then said, "There are more robots taking jobs away from people inside the Cities. The population keeps growing, and that means people will eventually have even less—we could see something close to starvation again. The Cities can't expand much more, and that means less space for each of us. People may lash out at an occasional robot now, since they're the most convenient targets for expressing resentment, but if we start lashing out at one another—" She paused. "Something has to give way. Even that small band of people who hope the Spacers will eventually let them leave Earth to settle another world know that."

Amy said, "They're silly."

"Most would say so."

Amy frowned. She knew about those people; they occasionally went Outside to play at being farmers or some such thing. She could not imagine how they stood it, or what good it did them. A City detective named Elijah Baley was the tiny band's leader; maybe he thought the Spacers would help him. He had recently returned from one of their worlds, where they had asked him to help them solve a crime; maybe he thought Spacers could be his friends.

Amy knew better. The Spacers had only used him. She thought of the Spacer characters she had seen in hyperwave and book-film adventures. They were all tall, handsome, tanned, bronze-haired people with eyes as cold as those of the legions of robots that served them. In the dramas, they might be friendly to or even love some Earthpeople, but in reality they despised the people of the Cities. They would never allow Earthfolk to contaminate their worlds or the others in this galaxy. They might use an Earthman such as Baley, but would only discard him afterward.

"What I'm trying to say," Alysha said softly, "is that change may come. Whatever disruptions it brings, it may also present opportunities, but only to people who are ready to seize them." Amy tensed a little; this was the most antisocial statement she had ever heard from her mother. "It would be better if you were prepared for that and developed whatever talents might be useful. When I worked for the Department, I knew what the statistics were implying—it's impossible for even the most determined bureaucrat to hide the whole truth. I could see—but I've said enough."

"Mother—" Amy swallowed. "Are you going to tell Father what Mr. Liang said?"

Alysha plucked at her long, dark hair, looking distressed. "I really should. I'll have to if I'm called in for a conference, and then Rick will wonder why I didn't mention it earlier. I won't if you promise you'll work harder."

Amy sighed with relief. "I promise." She hoped she could keep that vow.

"Then I'll leave you to your studying. You have a little time before Rick gets home."

The door closed behind Alysha. Amy reached for her viewer and stretched out. Nothing would change, no matter what her mother said. Whatever Amy did, sooner or later she would, as her friend Debora Lister put it, wind up at the end of the line. She would be pushed to the end of the line when her teachers began to hint that certain studies would be more useful for a girl. She would be forced back again when college advisers pointed out that it was selfish to take a place in certain classes, since she would not use such specialized training for a lifetime, as a boy would. If she moved up the line then, she would only be pushed back later, when she married and had her own children.

She could, of course, choose not to marry, but such a life

would be a lonely one. No matter what such women achieved, people muttered about how antisocial they were and pitied them, which was probably preferable to outright resentment. She would have to live in one of the alcoves allotted to single people unless she was lucky enough to find a congenial companion and get permission for both of them to share a room.

Alysha had wound up at the end of the line long ago, although later than most, and she had a loving husband to console her, which was a good thing. Even couples who hated each other would not willingly separate, lose status, and be forced into smaller quarters. Of course Alysha would hope that Amy might move up the line; she had nothing else in life except her husband and daughter.

A fair number of women were like Alysha. Sublimated antisocial individualism—that was what a textbook-film Amy had scanned in the school library called it. Many women lived through their children, then their grandchildren, hoping they would rise yet knowing that there were limits on their ambitions. Their transferred hopes would keep them going, but they would also be aware that too much individual glory would only create hard feelings in others. That was one reason her parents refused to flaunt the privileges they had earned and used them reluctantly, with a faintly apologetic air.

Men had different problems, which probably seemed just as troublesome to them. Some men cracked under the strain of having a family's status resting entirely on them. The psychologists had terms for that syndrome, too.

Amy saw what lay ahead only too clearly. Perhaps she shouldn't have viewed those book-films on psychology and sociology, which were meant for adult specialists. Her parents would eventually have the second child they were allowed; except for tending to Amy and her father, and being sociable in ways that eased relations with neighbors and her husband's colleagues, there was little else for Alysha to do. Small wonder many women even had children to whom they weren't entitled. When Amy was grown, her mother would be waiting for the inevitable grandchildren, and transfer her hopes to them. What a delusion it all was, pretending that your children wouldn't be swallowed by the hives of the City while knowing that this was the way it had to be.

Happy families, as the saying went, made for a better City; mothers and wives could go about their business feeling they were performing their civic duty. Amy's mother would cling to her, and then to her children, and—

If this was how knowing a lot made people feel, maybe it was better to be ignorant, to settle for what couldn't be changed.

She folded her arms over her chest. She still had one accomplishment, and no one could take it from her; she was the best strip-runner in the City. She wouldn't give that up, not until she was too old and too slow to race, and maybe that day would never come. If she made a mistake and died during a run, at least she'd be gone before she came to the end of the line. Her parents could have another child, maybe two, and the loss of one life would make no difference in a steel hive that held so many. She could even tell herself that she was making room for someone who would not mind being lost in the swarm.

The psychology texts had terms for such notions, all of which made her feelings sound like a disease. Perhaps they were, but that was yet another reason not to care about what happened to her on the strips.

"Amy Barone-Stein," the hall monitor said, "a person is looking for you."

Amy glared up at the grayish robotic face, a parody of a human being's. She did not care for robots, and this one, with its flat eyes and weirdly moving mouth, looked more idiotic than most. "What is it?" she asked.

"Someone outside wishes to speak to you," the robot said, "and has asked me to bring you there."

"Well, who is it?"

"She told me to give you her name if I were asked, or if you told me that you did not want to meet her. It is Shakira Lewes."

Amy's mouth dropped open. Debora Lister moved closer to her and nudged her in the ribs. Shakira Lewes had not run the strips in years, but Amy had heard of her. Kiyoshi Harris claimed she was the best female runner he had ever seen, and her last run, when she had led three gangs from Brooklyn to Yonkers and lost them all, was still legendary.

She *was* the best, Amy told herself; I'm the best now.

"Oh, Amy," Debora said. "Are you going to talk to her?"

"Might as well."

"You'll miss the Chess Club meeting," the blond girl said.

"Then I'll miss it."

"I'm coming with you," Debora said. "I've got to see this."

"Miss Lewes requested the presence of Amy Barone-Stein," the robot said. "She did not say—"

"Oh, stuff it," Amy said. The robot's eyes widened a little in what might have been bewilderment. "She didn't say I couldn't bring a friend, did she?"

"No, she did not."

"Then lead us to her."

The robot turned, leading them past a line in front of a Personal, then through the throngs of students crowding the hall. Amy wondered how Shakira Lewes had made the robot do her bidding. Technically, the hall monitors weren't supposed to fetch students from the school levels except for an emergency, but this robot was probably too stupid to tell that it was being deceived. The robot's back was erect as it marched along on its stiff legs. Damned robots, she thought, taking jobs from people. The hall monitors had once been human beings.

By the time she and Debora reached the elevator banks, a small crowd of boys and girls was following them. They all clambered aboard after the robot and dropped toward the street level. When they emerged from the school, Amy saw more boys clustered around a tall, dark-skinned woman with short black hair.

"Ooh," Debora whispered. "Maybe she wants to challenge you." Amy shook her head and motioned at the robot's back. A robot could not harm a human being or, through inaction, allow a human being to come to harm; to this creature's simple positronic brain, possible harm would certainly include strip-racing.

"Amy Barone-Stein," the robot said in its toneless voice. "This is Shakira Lewes."

The boys stepped back as Amy approached. The woman was slender enough for a runner, if a bit too tall; most runners, like Amy, were short and slight, able to squeeze into even the smallest gaps between passengers during a run. Shakira Lewes had a perfect, fine-boned face; she looked a lot like an actress in a historical drama about Africa Amy had recently viewed. She wore a red shirt and black pants that made her long legs seem even longer. The boys were staring intently at her. None of them had ever looked at Amy that way, not even after hearing about her run against Bradley Ohaer's gang.

"You may leave us," Shakira said to the robot. The hall monitor turned and went back inside. The woman sounded as arrogant as a Spacer; Amy looked up at her, filled with admiration and hatred. "I've heard about you," Shakira continued. "I'd like to talk to you."

Amy stuck out her chin. "What about?"

"Alone, if we could." Alone meant walking among the crowds, standing on a strip or localway to talk, or, if one was lucky, finding an unoccupied chair or bench somewhere.

Amy said, "If you've got something to tell me, say it here."

"She's going to challenge," someone said behind Amy; she looked around. Luis Horton was with the group; he'd been mad at her ever since she beat him on a long run up to the Yonkers Sector. "She's going to challenge," Luis repeated. "Maybe Amy can't take her."

Amy said, "I can take any runner in New York."

Shakira frowned. "I said I wanted to talk. I didn't say anything about running."

"Afraid?" another boy asked.

Shakira's face grew grimmer. Amy saw where this was leading; the others expected a challenge. Normally, she would have demanded one herself, but something felt wrong. It didn't make sense for this woman, who surely had better things to do, to come looking for a run against Amy, whatever her fame. Shakira had to be out of practice, and would risk much graver consequences as an adult offender if she were caught by the police. Yet what else could she want Amy for? Perhaps something illegal—some illicit enterprise where a boy or girl who could easily shake off a police pursuit might be useful.

Amy shrugged. "Come on, guys. Anybody can see she's too old to run the strips now."

"I'm old, all right," Shakira said. "I'm nearly twenty-one."

"Lewes isn't scared," Luis muttered then. "Amy is."

Amy's cheeks burned. They were all watching her now; she even imagined that the crowds passing by were looking at her, witnesses to her shame. "I'm not afraid of anything," she said. "Make your run, Shakira Lewes—you won't lose me. From here to the Sheepshead Bay localway intersection—unless you're too old to make that long a run."

Shakira was silent.

"Now! Or are you just too old and tired to try?"

The woman's large dark eyes glittered. "You're on. I'll do it."

A boy hooted. Even Debora, who would never run the strips herself, was flushed with anticipation. Amy was suddenly furious with them all. She wasn't ready for this run; she realized now that she had been hoping Shakira would back down. If the woman actually beat her, she would never live it down, while if Amy won, the others would simply assume Shakira was past her prime. She had risked too much on this challenge, and still didn't know what Shakira wanted with her.

"Let's go," Amy said.

"Just a minute." The woman raised an arm. "This is one on one, between you and me—and I still want to talk to you later."

"Talk to me after I beat you," Amy said without much conviction, then followed Shakira toward the nearest strip.

Shakira strode along the gray bands, moving to the faster strips at a speed only a little more rapid than usual. Amy kept close. Most of the boys and girls had already headed for the expressway; they would greet the victor at the Sheepshead Bay destination. Luis and two of his friends were following to study a little of Shakira's skill before joining the others. There were still some gaps between passengers, but the strips were already getting more crowded.

Shakira showed her moves, increasing the pace. She did a side shuffle, striding steadily, then moving to an adjacent strip without breaking her pace; Amy followed. She did a Popovich, named after the runner who had perfected it, leaping from side to side between two strips before bounding from the second one to a third. She even managed to pull off a dervish. Turning to face Amy, she leaped into the air and made a complete turn before landing gracefully on a slower strip; a dervish was dangerous even on slow strips.

She was good, but Amy knew the moves. Show-off, she thought; the woman was only trying to intimidate her. Flashy moves were more likely to draw attention, as well as wearing out a runner too soon. She followed Shakira onto a localway, then swung off after her, leaving the boys behind. She had caught Shakira's rhythm, but remained wary and alert; some runners could lull a follower into their pace before doing the unexpected.

They danced across the strips toward an expressway. The crowds were thick on the strip next to the expressway platform. Shakira reached for a pole and swung herself up; Amy grabbed the next pole. The woman's long legs swung around, never touching the floor and barely missing a passenger, and then she was back on the strip, her back to the wind as she grinned up at Amy.

Amy gripped her pole, about to follow when a few people suddenly stepped to the strip just below her. She caught a glimpse of startled faces as her legs swung toward them; there was just enough space for a landing. A woman swayed on the strip; a man grabbed her by the arm. Amy knew in an instant that she could not risk a leap. Shakira turned, ran past more commuters, stepped to her left, and was gone.

Amy hung on to the pole; the wind tore at her legs. She hauled herself aboard, numbed by the abruptness of her defeat. She had lost before they even reached lower Manhattan; tears stung her eyes.

Someone shoved her; passengers surrounded her. "Damn runners!" a man shouted. Other riders crowded around her; a fist knocked her to the floor. "Get the police!" a woman cried. Fingers grabbed Amy by the hair; a foot kicked her in the knee. She covered her head with her arms, no longer caring what happened to her; she had lost.

A plainclothesman, a C–6 with seat privileges on the expressway's upper level, got Amy away from the crowd before she was beaten too badly and took her to City Hall. Police headquarters were in the higher levels of the structure; Amy supposed that she would be turned over to an officer and booked. Instead, the detective led her through a large common room filled with people and desks to a corner desk with a railing around it.

She sat at the desk, feeling miserable and alone, as the plainclothesman took her name, entered it in the desk computer, called up more information, then placed a call to her father on the communo. "You're in luck," the man said when he had finished his call. "Your father hasn't left work yet, so he'll just come over here from his level and take you home."

She peered up at him. "You mean you aren't going to keep me here?"

The detective glowered at her. He was a big man, with a bald head, thick mustache, and brown skin nearly as dark as Shakira's. "Don't think I haven't considered detaining you. I shouldn't even be wasting my time with you—I have a very low tolerance for reckless kids who don't care about anyone else's safety. You could have started a riot on that expressway—maybe I should have left you to the tender mercies of that mob. Do you know what can happen to you now, girl?"

"No," she mumbled, although she could guess.

"For starters, a hearing in juvenile court. You could get a few months in Youth Offenders' Level, or you might get lucky and be sentenced to help out in a hospital a few days a week. You'd get lots of chances to see accident victims there." He pulled at his mustache. "That might do you some good. Maybe you'll be there when they bring in some dead strip-runner who wasn't quick enough. You can watch his parents cry when the hospital makes the Ritual of Request before they take any usable organs from the corpse. And you'll have deep trouble if you ever misbehave again."

Amy squeezed her eyes shut. "Stay here," the man said, even though she hardly had a choice, with the common room so filled with police. She sat there alone, wallowing in her despair until the detective returned with a cup of tea; he did not offer anything to her.

He sat down behind the desk. "Will you give me the names of any runners with you?"

She shook her head violently. Much as she hated Shakira, she would not sink that low.

"I didn't think you would. You're not doing them any favor, you know. If they meet with accidents or end up hurting somebody else, I hope you can live with yourself."

The detective worked at his desk computer in silence until Amy's father arrived. She glanced at his pale, grim face and looked away quickly. The formality of an introduction took only a moment before the plainclothesman began to lecture Ricardo Stein on his daughter's offense, peppering his tirade with statistics on accidents caused by strip-runners and the number of deaths the game had resulted in this year. "If I hadn't been on that expressway," the man concluded, "the girl might have been badly roughed up—not that she didn't deserve it."

Her father said, "I understand, Mr. Dubois."

"She needs to learn a lesson."

"I agree." Ricardo shook back his thick brown hair. "I'll go along with any sentence she gets. Her mother and I won't go out of our way to defend her, and we probably share some of the blame for not bringing her up better and supervising her more. You can be certain there'll be no repetition of such behavior."

"I imagine you'll see to that, Mr. Stein—a solid citizen like you." Mr. Dubois leaned back in his chair. "So I'll do you and your wife a favor, and let Amy here off with a warning. She's only fourteen, and this is her first offense—the first time she's been caught, anyway—and Youth Offenders' Level is crowded enough as it is. But she's in our records now, and if she's picked up again for anything, she goes into detention until her hearing, at which point she'll likely get a stiff sentence."

"I'm grateful to you," Amy's father said.

"Listen to me, girl." Mr. Dubois rested his arms on the desk. "Don't think you can lie low for a bit and then start strip-running again. We know who you are now, and you'll be easy to spot. Not many girls run the strips." He glanced at her father. "I think I can count on you to keep her in line. Wouldn't do your status any good to have a criminal in the family."

"You can count on me, Mr. Dubois."

Amy's father did not speak to her all the way home. That was a bad sign; he was never that silent unless he was enraged. He left her outside the Women's Personal and went on to the apartment.

She dawdled as long as she dared inside the Personal, then dragged herself down the hall, filled with dread, wondering what her parents would do to her. They would have discussed the whole affair by now, and her mother had probably mentioned the guidance counselor's earlier message.

They were both sitting on the couch when she entered; there was no use appealing to her mother for some mercy. The two rarely disagreed or argued in front of her, and in a matter this important, they would present a united front.

She inched her way to a chair and sat down. She would not be beaten; her parents did not believe in physical punishment. A beating, even with all the bruises the expressway riders had already left on her, might have been better than having to endure her father's harsh accusations and talk about how humiliating her offense was for all of them. She hadn't thought of them at all, of how upset they would have been if she were injured. She hadn't thought about how her pathological display of individualism might damage Ricardo's reputation at work, or her mother's among their neighbors. She hadn't considered how such a blot on her record might affect her own chances later, or reflected on the danger she had posed to commuters. She hadn't thought of the bad example she was setting for younger children, and had completely ignored her father's earlier warning about such activity.

By the time her father had finished his lecture, repeating most of his points several times, it was too late to go to the section kitchen. Her mother sighed as she folded their small table out of the wall and plugged in the plate warmer; her father grumbled about missing the chicken the section kitchen was to serve that night. They had been saving their fourth meal at home this week for Saturday, when Ricardo's parents were to visit with a few of their own rations; Amy had ruined those plans, too.

Amy pulled the ottoman over to the table and sat down as her mother sprinkled a few spices she had saved over the food. Her father took a call over the communo, barked a few words at its screen, then hung up. "That was Debora Lister." He moved the two chairs to the table, then seated himself. "I told her you couldn't talk."

Amy poked at her zymobeef and broccolettes listlessly. Just as well, she thought. Debora would only be calling to tell her what had happened when Shakira showed up, alone and triumphant, at Sheepshead Bay.

"You won't be taking any calls from your friends for a while," her father continued. "I'll notify the principal at school that you're not to leave school levels except to go directly home, and a monitor will note when you leave, so don't think you can wander around during the return trip. When you're not in school, you'll stay here except for going to meals with us or to the Personal. And in your free time, when you're not studying, you'll prepare a report for me on the dangers of strip-running. You shouldn't find the data hard to come by, and you'll present it to me in a week." Ricardo took a breath. "And if I even hear that you've been running the strips again, I'll turn you in to the police myself and demand a hearing for you."

"Eat your food, Amy," her mother said; it was the first time she had spoken.

"I'm not hungry."

"You'd better—it's all we have left of home rations for this week."

She forced herself to eat. Her father finished his food and propped his elbows on the table. "There's something I still don't understand," he said wearily. "Why, Amy? Why would you do such a thing? I thought you had more sense. Why would you risk it?"

She could bear no more. "I'm the best." She stood up and kicked back the ottoman. "I'm the best strip-runner in the City! That's all I'll ever do, it's all anybody will remember about me! I was the best, and now they've taken it away!"

Her father's gray eyes widened. "You're not sounding very repentant, young lady."

"I'm sorry I lost! I'm sorry I was caught! I'm sorry you had to come and get me, but I'm not sorry about anything else!"

"Go to your room!" he shouted. "If I hear any more talk like that, I *will* raise a hand to you!"

Alysha reached across the table and grabbed his upraised arm s Amy fled to her room.

Her life was over. Amy could not view matters any other way. The story had made the rounds quickly. She had lost to Shakira Lewes and been picked up by the police; Luis Horton was doing his best to spread the news. A hall monitor noted the times she left the school levels and reminded her, right in front of other students, that she was expected to go straight home; a few boys and girls always snickered.

She greeted questions from her friends, even Debora, with a scowl, and soon no one was speaking to her outside of class. Nobody dared to bring up the run, or to tell her what the Lewes woman had said when she arrived at the destination. There was the inevitable conference with Mr. Liang and her mother, and an additional embarrassment when the guidance counselor learned about the report she was preparing for her father. She delivered the report over the school's public address screens, forced by Mr. Liang and the principal to repudiate the game; she cringed inwardly whenever she thought of how the students who had viewed her image must be laughing at her. Time inside the Youth Offenders' Level couldn't have been much worse.

After three weeks, her parents eased up a little. Amy still had to come home directly from school, but they allowed her to do schoolwork with friends in the subsection after supper. News of her downfall had been replaced by gossip about Luis Horton's successful run to the edge of Queens against Tom Jandow's gang. Her friends were again speaking to her, but knew enough not to mention Shakira Lewes.

She was ruined, and it was all that woman's fault. She dreaded the daily journeys along the strips, when she sometimes glimpsed other runners and recalled what she had lost. She could no longer hear the music of the strips, the rhythmic song in their humming that urged her to race. She was already at the end of the line; the last bit of freedom she would ever know was gone. She would become only another speck inside the caves of steel, her past glory forgotten.

Amy left the elevator at her floor with Debora, then suddenly stiffened with shock. Down the hall, Shakira Lewes was loitering outside the Women's Personal.

"What's she doing here?" the blond girl asked.

"I don't know."

"I never told you," Debora said, "but when she finished the run, she—"

"I don't want to hear about it." Amy took out her key when they reached the door, determined to ignore the woman. Hanging around outside a Personal was the crudest sort of behavior.

"Hello, Amy," Shakira said.

"Haven't you caused enough trouble?" Amy snapped. "You don't belong here."

"But we never had our talk. This is the first chance I've had to find you, and I was pretty sure you'd be stopping here after school."

Amy gritted her teeth. "Now I can't even go and take a piss in peace."

Shakira said, "I want to talk to you." She lowered her voice as three women left the Personal. "Tonight, after supper, alone."

Amy's fingers tightened around her key. "Why should I talk to you?"

Shakira shrugged. "I'll be at the Hempstead G-level, at the end of the Long Island Expressway. Get off and cross the strips to G-20th Street. I'll be standing in front of a store called Tad's Antiques—think you can find it?"

Amy felt insulted. "I know my way around. But I don't know why I should bother."

"Then don't. I'll be there by seven and I'll wait until nine. If you don't show up, that's your business, and I won't pester you again, but you might be interested in what I have to tell you." Shakira turned and walked toward the elevator before Amy could reply.

Debora pulled her away from the Personal door. "Are you going?" she asked.

"Yes. I've got to find out what she wants."

"But your parents told you not to leave the subsection. If any of their friends see you—"

"I'm going anyway. I have to go." She would settle matters with the young woman one way or another.

"To the edge of the City?" Debora whispered.

"She can't do anything to me on the street with people around. Deb, you have to cover for me. I can tell my parents I'll be at your place. I don't think they'll call to check, but if they do, tell them I went to the Personal."

"If my father doesn't get to the communo first."

"I'll just have to take the chance," Amy said.

Debora let out her breath. "She may want to challenge you again. What'll you do?"

"I'll worry about that when I get there." She had already made her decision. If Shakira wanted another run, she couldn't refuse, and she'd make sure some of the boys she knew were waiting at the destination as witnesses. Whatever the risk, it was a chance to restore her lost honor.

* * *

Amy was on G-20th Street by seven-thirty. Shakira, as she had promised, was waiting in front of the antique store, which had an old-fashioned flat sign in script. There weren't many stores in the shabby neighborhood, where the high metallic walls of the residence levels seemed duller than most, and no more than a few hundred people in the street. Amy felt apprehensive. Sections like this one were the worst in the City; only badly off citizens would live here, so close to the Outside.

Shakira was gazing at an attractive display of old plastic cutlery and cups in the store window. Inside the store, the owner had made one concession to modern times; a robot was waiting on the line of customers. "Didn't take you long to get here," the woman murmured.

"I shouldn't be here at all," Amy said. "I'm not supposed to leave my subsection, but my parents think I'm with a friend." For once, they hadn't asked too many questions, and had even seemed a little relieved that she would be gone for the evening. "I told them I'd be back by ten-thirty, so say what you have to say."

"I didn't want to make that run, but you insisted, and I still have my pride." Shakira looped her fingers around her belt. "Then, once I was running, old habits took over. Maybe I wanted to see if I still had my reflexes."

"You must have had a good time bragging about it later."

"I didn't brag," Shakira said. "I just met the kids and told them to go home. I said it was tough shaking you, and that you were one of the best runners who ever tailed me."

Amy's lip curled. "How nice of you, Shakira. You still beat me."

"I saw what happened, why you didn't jump back on the strip. Some runners would have risked it anyway, even with less room than you had. They would have jumped, and if a couple of people got knocked off the strip, too bad. I'm glad you aren't that antisocial."

"What do you want with me, anyway?" Amy asked. A few women stopped near her to look in the store window, but she ignored them; even in this wretched area, people wouldn't be crass enough to eavesdrop.

"Well, I heard about this girl, Amy Barone-Stein, who could run the strips with the best of them. I still know a few runners, even though most of my college friends would disapprove of them. I thought you might be a little like me—restless, maybe a bit angry, wondering if you'd ever be more than a component in the City's machine."

Amy stepped back a little. "So what?"

"I thought you might like a challenge."

"But you said before that you didn't want to make that run."

"I'm not talking about that," Shakira said. "I mean a real challenge, something a lot harder and more interesting than running strips. It might be worthwhile for you if you've got the guts for it." Amy took another step backward, certain that the woman was about to propose a shady undertaking. "You see, I'm part of that group of Lije's—Elijah Baley's—the people who go Outside once a week. His son Bentley is an acquaintance of mine."

Amy gaped at her, completely surprised. "But why—"

"There are only a few of us so far. The City gives us a little support, mostly because of Lije—Mr. Baley—but I suspect the City government thinks we're as eccentric as everyone else does, and that we're deluded to think we can ever settle another world."

"Why bother?" Amy said. "The Spacers'll never let anyone off Earth."

"Lije left, didn't he?"

"That was different, and they sent him back here as fast as they could. I'll bet they didn't even thank him for solving that murder. They'd never let a bunch of Earthpeople on one of their worlds."

"Not one of theirs, no." Shakira leaned against the window. "But Lije Baley is convinced they'll allow settlers on an uninhabited world eventually—maybe sooner than we think—and that they'll provide us with ships to get there. But we can't settle another world unless we're able to live Outside a City."

Amy shook her head. "Nobody can live Outside."

"Earthpeople used to. The Earthpeople who settled the Spacer worlds long ago did. The Spacers do, and we manage to—for two or three hours a week, anyway. It's a start, just getting accustomed to that, and it isn't easy, but any settlers will have to be people like us, who've shown we can leave a City."

"And you want me in this group?" Amy asked.

"I thought you might be interested. We could use more

recruits, and younger people seem to adapt more quickly. Just think of it—if we do get to leave Earth, every single settler will be needed, every person will be important and useful. We'll need people willing to gamble on a new life, individualists who want to make a mark, maybe even folks who are just a little antisocial as long as they can cooperate with others. You could be one of them, Amy."

"If you ever leave."

Shakira smiled. "What have you got to lose by trying?" She paused. "Do you have any idea of how precarious life inside this City is? How much more uranium can we get for our power plants? Think of all the power we have to use just to bring in water and get rid of waste. Just imagine what would happen if the air were cut off even for an hour or two—people would die by the hundreds of thousands. We'll have to leave the Cities. They can't keep growing indefinitely without taking up land we need for farming or forests we need for pulp. There'll be less food, less space, less of everything, until—"

Amy looked away for a moment. Her mother had said the same thing to her.

"There isn't a future here, Amy." Shakira moved closer to her. "There might be one for us on other worlds."

Amy sighed. "What a few people do won't make any difference."

"It's a beginning, and if we succeed, others will follow. You seemed to think what you did was important when you were only running the strips." The young woman beckoned to her. "Here's my challenge for you. I'm asking you if you'll come Outside with me."

"With those people?"

"Right now. Surely a strip-runner who used to risk life and limb isn't afraid of a little open air."

"But—"

"Come on."

She followed Shakira down the street, helpless to resist. The woman stopped in front of an opening in the high walls. Amy peered around her and saw a long, dimly lit tunnel with another wall at its end.

"What is it?" Amy asked.

"An exit. Some of them are guarded now, but this one isn't.

There really isn't any need to watch them—most people don't know about them or don't want to think about them. Even the people living in this subsection have probably forgotten this exit is here. Will you come with me?"

"What if somebody follows us?" Amy glanced nervously down the street, which seemed even emptier than before. "It isn't safe."

"Believe me, nobody will follow. They'd rather believe this place doesn't exist. Will you come?"

Amy swallowed hard, then nodded. It was only a passage-way; it couldn't be that bad. They entered; she kept close to the young woman as the familiar, comforting noise of the street behind them grew fainter.

Shakira said, "The exit's at the end." Her voice sounded hollow in the eerie silence. Amy's stomach knotted as they came to the end of the tunnel.

"Ready?" Shakira asked.

"I think so."

"Hang on to me. It'll be dark Outside—that'll make it easier for you, and I won't let go."

Shakira pressed her hand against the wall. An opening slowly appeared. Amy felt cold air on her face; as they stepped Outside, the door closed behind them. She closed her eyes, terrified to look, already longing for the warmth and safety of the City.

A gust of wind slapped her, fiercer than the wind on the fastest strips. She opened her eyes and looked up. A black sky dotted with stars was above her, and that bright pearly orb had to be the moon. Except for the wind and the bone-chilling cold, she might almost have been inside a City planetarium. But the planetarium had not revealed how vast the sky was, or shown the silvery clouds that drifted below the black heavens. She lowered her gaze; a bluish-white plain, empty except for the distant domes of a farm, stretched in front of her. Her ears throbbed at the silence that was broken only by the intermittent howl of the wind.

Open air—and the white substance covering the ground had to be snow. The wind gusted again, lifting a thin white veil of flakes, then died. There was space all around her, unfiltered air, dirt under her feet, and the moon shining down on all of it; the safety of walls was gone. Her stomach lurched as her heart pounded; her head swam. Her grip on Shakira loosened; the pale plain was spinning. Then she was falling through the endless silence into a darkness as black as the sky . . .

Arms caught her, lifting her up; she felt warmth at her back. The silence was gone. She clawed at the air and realized she was back inside the tunnel.

She blinked; her mouth was dry. "Are you all right?" Shakira felt her forehead; Amy leaned heavily against her. "I got you inside as fast as I could. I'm sorry—I forgot there'd be a full moon tonight. It would have been easier for you if it had been completely dark."

Amy trembled, afraid to let go. "I didn't know," she said. "I didn't think—" She shivered with relief, welcoming the warmth, the faint but steady noise from the street, the walls of the City. She tried to smile. "Guess I didn't do so well."

"But you did. The first time I went Outside, I passed out right after taking my first breath of open air. The second time, I ran back inside after a few seconds and swore I'd never set foot Outside again. You did a lot better than that—I was counting. We must have been standing there for nearly two minutes."

Shakira supported her with one arm; they made their way slowly toward the street. "Can you walk by yourself?" the woman asked as they left the tunnel.

"I think so." Shakira let go. Amy stared down the street, which had seemed so empty earlier, relieved at the sight of all the people. "I couldn't do that again, Shakira. I couldn't face it—all that space."

"I think you can." Shakira folded her arms. "You can if you don't give up now. We'll be going Outside in two days. You'll have to wear more clothes—it'd help if you can get gloves and a hat." Amy shook her head, struck by the strangeness of needing warmer clothes; the temperature inside never varied. "It's winter, so we'll only take a short walk—we won't be Outside very long. I'd like you to come with us. I'll stay by the exit with you, and you needn't remain Outside a second longer than you can bear. Believe me, if you keep trying, even if you think you can't stand it, it'll get easier. You may even start to look forward to it."

"I don't know—" Amy started to say.

"Will you try?"

Amy took a deep breath, smelling the odors of the City, the faint pungence of bodies, a whiff of someone's perfume, a sharp, acrid scent she could not place; she had never noticed the smells before. "I'll try." She drew her brows together. "My parents will kill me if they ever find out. I'll have to think of an excuse—"

"But you must tell them, Amy."

"They'll never let me go."

"Then you'll have to find a way to convince them. They have to know for two very good reasons. One is that it'll cause trouble for Lije if kids come Outside without their families' permission, and the other is that they just might decide to join us themselves. I'll come by your place for you, so you'll have to tell them why I'm there. You can give me your answer then."

"There's something else," Amy said. "That Mr. Baley—he's a detective. When he finds out I got picked up, he may not want me."

Shakira laughed. "Don't worry about that. I'll tell you a secret—Lije Baley was a pretty good strip-runner in his day. I heard a little about his past from my uncle and another old-timer. He won't hold that against you, but don't say anything to the others about it." Shakira took her arm as they walked toward the strips. "We'd better get home."

Amy glanced at her. "You wouldn't want to try another run?"

"Not a chance. You've had enough trouble, and you've got more to lose now. Maybe some dancing, but only if there's room, and only on the slow strips."

The sturdy walls of her Kingsbridge subsection surrounded Amy once more. She had nearly forgotten the coldness, the wind, the silence, the terrible emptiness of the Outside.

Yet she knew she would have to go Outside again. The comforting caves of steel would not always be a safe refuge. She would have to face the emptiness until she no longer feared it, and wondered how the City would seem to her then.

She waited by the apartment door for a few moments before slipping her key into the slot. Her parents might be asleep already, and she could not tell them about this event at breakfast in the section kitchen. She could tell them tomorrow night, and would try not to hope for too much.

The door opened; she went inside. Her parents were still awake, cuddling together on the couch; they sat up quickly and adjusted their nightrobes.

"Amy!" Her father looked a bit embarrassed. "You're home early."

"I thought I was late."

He glanced at the wall timepiece. "Oh—I guess you are. I hadn't noticed. Well, I'll let it pass this once."

Amy studied the couple. They seemed in a good mood; her mother's brown eyes glowed, and her father's broad face lacked its usual tenseness. She might not get a better chance to speak to them, and did not want her mother finding out from Mrs. Lister at breakfast that she hadn't been at Debora's.

"Um." Amy cleared her throat. "I have to talk to you."

Her father looked toward the timepiece again. "Is it important?"

"It's very important." She went to a chair and sat down across from them. "It really can't wait. Please—just let me talk until I'm finished, and then you can say whatever you want." She paused. "I wasn't at Deb's. I know I wasn't supposed to, but I left the subsection."

Her father started; her mother reached for his hand.

"Not to run strips, I swear," Amy added hastily. She lowered her eyes, afraid to look directly at them, then told them about her first meeting with Shakira, the run that had ended in disaster, the encounter on the street in Hempstead, what Shakira had said about the group that went Outside, and the challenge she had met that night by facing the open space beyond the City. She wasn't telling the story very well, having to pause every so often to fill in a detail, but by the time she reached the end, she was sure she had mentioned all the essentials.

Her parents said nothing throughout, and were silent when she finished. At last she forced herself to raise her head. Her father looked stunned, her mother bewildered.

"You went Outside?" Alysha whispered.

"Yes."

"Weren't you terrified?"

"I was never so scared in my life, but I had to—I—"

Her father sagged against the couch. "You deliberately disobeyed us." He sounded more exasperated than angry. "You lied and told us you'd be with Debora Lister. You left the subsection to meet a dubious young woman who's a damned strip-runner herself, and—"

"She isn't," Amy protested. "She doesn't run any more, and she wouldn't have with me if I hadn't insisted—I told you. That was my fault."

"At least you're admitting your guilt," he said. "I let you have your say, so allow me to finish. Now she wants you to traipse around Outside with that group of hers. I forbid it—do you hear? You're not to have anything more to do with her, and if she calls or comes here, I'll tell her so myself. I'll have to be firmer with you, Amy. Since you can't be honest with us about your doings, you'll be restricted to this apartment again, and—"

"Rick." Alysha's voice was low, but firm. "Let me speak. If joining those people means so much to Amy, then maybe she should." Ricardo's face paled as he turned toward his wife. "I know she disobeyed us, but I think I can understand why she felt it necessary. Anyway, how much trouble can she get into if a City detective's with them? They seem harmless enough."

"Harmless?" her husband said. "Going Outside, deluding themselves that—"

"Let her go, Rick." Alysha pressed his hand between both of hers. "That young woman told her the truth. You know it's true—you can see what the Department's statistical projections show, whether you'll admit it to yourself or not. If there's any chance that those people with Elijah Baley can leave Earth, maybe it's better if Amy goes with them."

Amy drew in her breath, startled that her mother was taking her side and confronting her father in her presence.

"You'd accept that?" Ricardo asked. "What if the Spacers actually allow those people off Earth—not that I think it's likely, but what if they do? You're saying you'd be content never to see your daughter again."

"I wouldn't be content—you know better than that. But how can I cling to her if she has a chance, however small, at something else? I know what her life will be here, perhaps better than you do. I'd rather know she's doing something meaningful to her some-where else, even if that means we'll lose her, than to have to go through life pretending I don't see her frustrations and disappoint-ments."

Ricardo heaved a sigh. "I can't believe I'm hearing you say this."

"Oh, Rick." She released his hand. "You would have expected me to say and do the unexpected years ago." She smiled at that phrase. "How conventional we've become since then." She gazed at him silently for a bit. "Maybe I'll go with Amy when she meets that group. I should see what kind of people they are, after all. Maybe I'll even take a step Outside myself."

Her husband frowned, looking defeated. "This is a fine situation," he said. "Not only do I have a disobedient daughter, but now my wife's against me, too. If my co-workers hear you're both wandering around with that group of Baley's, it may not do me much good in the Department."

"Really?" Amy's mother arched her brows. "They always knew we were both a bit, shall we say, eccentric, and that didn't bother you once. Perhaps you should come with us to meet Mr. Baley's group. It'd be wiser to have your colleagues think you're going along with our actions, however odd or amusing they may find them, than to believe there's a rift between us." Her mouth twisted a little. "You know what they say—happy families make for a better City."

Ricardo turned toward Amy. "You'd do it again? Go Outside, I mean. You'd actually go through that again?"

"Yes, I would," Amy replied. "I know it'll be hard, but I'd try."

"It's late," her father said. "I can't think about this now." He stood up and took Alysha by the arm as she rose. "We'll discuss this tomorrow, after I've had a chance to consider it. Good night, Amy."

"Good night."

Her mother was whispering to her father as Amy went to her room. Her father had backed down for now, and her mother was almost certain to bring him around. She undressed for bed, convinced she had won her battle.

She stretched out, tired and ready to sleep, and soon drifted into a dream. She was on the strips again, riding through an open arch to the Outside, but she wasn't afraid this time.

The City slept. The strips and expressways continued to move, carrying the few who were awake—young lovers who had crept out to meet each other, policemen on patrol, hospital workers heading home after a night shift, and restless souls drawn to wander the caverns of New York.

Amy stood on a strip, a sprinkling of people around her. Four boys raced past her, leaping from strip to strip; for a moment, she was tempted to join their race. She had come out at night a few times before, to practice some moves when the strips were emptier, returning to her subsection before her parents awoke. More riders began to fill the slowest strip; the City was waking. Her parents would be up by the time she got back, but she was sure they would understand why she had been drawn out here tonight.

Her parents had come with her to meet Elijah Baley and his group. The detective was a tall, dark-haired man with a long, solemn face, but he had brightened a little when Shakira introduced her new recruits. Amy's mother and father had not gone Outside with them; perhaps they would next time. She knew what an effort it would be for them, and hoped they could find the courage to take that step. They would be with her when the group met again; they had promised that much. When she was able to face the openness without fear, to stride across the ground bravely as Shakira did, maybe she would lead them Outside herself.

She leaped up, spun around in a dervish, and ran along the strip. The band hummed under her feet; she could hear its music again. She bounded forward, did a handspring, then jumped to the next strip. She danced across the gray bands until she reached the expressway, then hauled herself aboard.

Her hands tightened around the pole as she recalled her first glimpse of daylight. The whiteness of the snow had been blinding, and above it all, in the painfully clear blue sky, was a bright ball of flame, the naked sun. She had known she was standing on a ball of dirt clad only in a thin veil of air, a speck that was hurtling through a space more vast and empty than anything she could see. The terror had seized her then, driving her back inside, where she had cowered on the floor, sick with fear and despair. But there had also been Shakira's strong arms to help her up, and Elijah Baley's voice telling her of his own former fears. Amy had not gone Outside again that day, but she had stood in the open doorway and forced herself to take one more breath of wintry air.

It was a beginning. She had to meet the challenge if she was ever to lead others Outside, or to follow the hopeful settlers to another world.

She left the expressway and danced along the strips, showing her form, imagining that she was running one last race. She was near the Hempstead street where she had met Shakira.

The street was nearly empty, its store windows darkened. Amy left the strips and hurried toward the tunnel, running along the passageway until her breath came in short, sharp gasps. When she reached the end, she hesitated for only a moment, then pressed her hand against the wall.

The opening appeared. The muted hum from the distant strips faded behind her, and she was Outside, alone, with the morning wind in her face. The sky was a dark dome above her. She looked east and saw dawn brightening the cave of stars.

The Asenion Solution

by Robert Silverberg

Fletcher stared bleakly at the small mounds of gray metal that were visible behind the thick window of the storage chamber.

"Plutonium-186," he muttered. "Nonsense! Absolute nonsense!"

"Dangerous nonsense, Lew," said Jesse Hammond, standing behind him. "Catastrophic nonsense."

Fletcher nodded. The very phrase, "plutonium-186," sounded like gibberish to him. There wasn't supposed to be any such substance. Plutonium-186 was an impossible isotope, too light by a good fifty neutrons. Or a bad fifty neutrons, considering the risks the stuff was creating as it piled up here and there around the world. But the fact that it was theoretically impossible for plutonium-186 to exist did not change the other, and uglier, fact that he was looking at three kilograms of it right this minute. Or that as the quantity of plutonium-186 in the world continued to increase, so did the chance of an uncontrollable nuclear reaction leading to an atomic holocaust.

"Look at the morning reports," Fletcher said, waving a sheaf of faxprints at Hammond. "Thirteen grams more turned up at the nucleonics lab of Accra University. Fifty grams in Geneva. Twenty milligrams in—well, that little doesn't matter. But Chicago, Jesse, Chicago—three hundred grams in a single chunk!"

"Christmas presents from the Devil," Hammond muttered.

"Not the Devil, no. Just decent serious-minded scientific folk who happen to live in another universe where plutonium-186 is not only possible but also perfectly harmless. And who are so fascinated by the idea that *we're* fascinated by it that they keep on shipping the stuff to us in wholesale lots! What are we going to do with it all, Jesse? What in God's name are we going to do with it all?"

Raymond Nikolaus looked up from his desk at the far side of the room.

"Wrap it up in shiny red and green paper and ship it right back to them?" he suggested.

Fletcher laughed hollowly. "Very funny, Raymond. Very, very funny."

He began to pace the room. In the silence the clicking of his shoes against the flagstone floor seemed to him like the ticking of a detonating device, growing louder, louder, louder . . .

He—they, all of them—had been wrestling with the problem all year, with an increasing sense of futility. The plutonium-186 had begun mysteriously to appear in laboratories all over the world—wherever supplies of one of the two elements with equivalent atomic weights existed. Gram for gram, atom for atom, the matching elements disappeared just as mysteriously: equal quantities of tungsten-186 or osmium-186.

Where was the tungsten and osmium going? Where was the plutonium coming from? Above all, how was it possible for a plutonium isotope whose atoms had only 92 neutrons in its nucleus to exist even for a fraction of a fraction of an instant? Plutonium was one of the heavier chemical elements, with a whopping 94 protons in the nucleus of each of its atoms. The closest thing to a stable isotope of plutonium was plutonium-244, in which 150 neutrons held those 94 protons together; and even at that, plutonium-244 had an inevitable habit of breaking down in radioactive decay, with a half-life of some 76 million years. Atoms of plutonium-186, if they could exist at all, would come dramatically apart in very much less than one seventy-six millionth of a second.

But the stuff that was turning up in the chemistry labs to replace the tungsten-186 and the osmium-186 had an atomic number of 94, no question about that. And element 94 was plutonium. That couldn't be disputed either. The defining characteristic of plutonium was the presence of 94 protons in its nucleus. If that was the count, plutonium was what that element had to be.

This impossibly light isotope of plutonium, this plutonium-186, had another impossible characteristic about it: not only was it stable, it was so completely stable that it wasn't even radioactive. It just sat there, looking exceedingly unmysterious, not even deigning to emit a smidgen of energy. At least, not when first tested. But a second test revealed positron emission, which a third baffled look confirmed. The trouble was that the third measurement showed an even higher level of radioactivity than the second one. The fourth was higher than the third. And so on and so on.

Nobody had ever heard of any element, of whatever atomic number or weight, that started off stable and then began to demonstrate a steadily increasing intensity of radioactivity. No one knew what was likely to happen, either, if the process continued unchecked, but the possibilities seemed pretty explosive. The best suggestion anyone had was to turn it to powder and mix it with nonradioactive tungsten. That worked for a little while, until the tungsten turned radioactive too. After that graphite was used, with somewhat better results, to damp down the strange element's output of energy. There were no explosions. But more and more plutonium-186 kept arriving.

The only explanation that made any sense—and it did not make *very* much sense—was that it was coming from some unknown and perhaps even unknowable place, some sort of parallel universe, where the laws of nature were different and the binding forces of the atom were so much more powerful that plutonium-186 could be a stable isotope.

Why they were sending odd lumps of plutonium-186 here was something that no one could begin to guess. An even more important question was how they could be made to stop doing it. The radioactive breakdown of the plutonium-186 would eventually transform it into ordinary osmium or tungsten, but the twenty positrons that each plutonium nucleus emitted in the course of that process encountered and annihilated an equal number of electrons. Our universe could afford to lose twenty electrons here and there, no doubt. It could probably afford to go on losing electrons at a constant rate for an astonishingly long time without noticing much difference. But sooner or later the shift toward an overall positive charge that this electron loss created would create grave and perhaps incalculable problems of symmetry and energy conservation. Would the equilibrium of the universe break down? Would nuclear interactions begin to intensify? Would the stars—even the Sun—erupt into supernovas?

"This can't go on," Fletcher said gloomily.

Hammond gave him a sour look. "So? We've been saying that for six months now."

"It's time to do something. They keep shipping us more and more and more, and we don't have any idea how to go about telling them to cut it out."

"We don't even have any idea whether they really exist," Raymond Nikolaus put in.

"Right now that doesn't matter. What matters is that the stuff is arriving constantly, and the more of it we have, the more dangerous it is. We don't have the foggiest idea of how to shut off the shipments. So we've got to find some way to get rid of it as it comes in."

"And what do you have in mind, pray tell?" Hammond asked.

Fletcher said, glaring at his colleague in a way that conveyed the fact that he would brook no opposition, "I'm going to talk to Asenion."

Hammond guffawed. "Asenion? You're crazy!"

"No. *He* is. But he's the only person who can help us."

It was a sad case, the Asenion story, poignant and almost incomprehensible. One of the finest minds atomic physics had ever known, a man to rank with Rutherford, Bohr, Heisenberg, Fermi, Meitner. A Harvard degree at twelve, his doctorate from MIT five years later, after which he had poured forth a dazzling flow of technical papers that probed the deepest mysteries of the nuclear binding forces. As the twenty-first century entered its closing decades he had seemed poised to solve once and for all the eternal riddles of the universe. And then, at the age of twenty-eight, without having given the slightest warning, he walked away from the whole thing.

"I have lost interest," he declared. "Physics is no longer of any importance to me. Why should I concern myself with these issues of the way in which matter is constructed? How tiresome it all is! When one looks at the Parthenon, does one care what the columns are made of, or what sort of scaffolding was needed to put them in place? That the Parthenon exists, and is sublimely beautiful, is all that should interest us. So too with the universe. I see the universe, and it is beautiful and perfect. Why should I pry into the nature of its scaffolding? Why should anyone?"

And with that he resigned his professorship, burned his papers, and retreated to the thirty-third floor of an apartment building on Manhattan's West Side, where he built an elaborate laboratory-greenhouse in which he intended to conduct experiments in advanced horticulture.

"Bromeliads," said Asenion. "I will create hybrid bromeliads. Bromeliads will be the essence and center of my life from now on."

Romelmeyer, who had been Asenion's mentor at Harvard, attributed his apparent breakdown to overwork, and thought that he would snap back in six or eight months. Jantzen, who had had the rare privilege of being the first to read his astonishing dissertation at MIT, took an equally sympathetic position, arguing that Asenion must have come to some terrifying impasse in his work that had compelled him to retreat dramatically from the brink of madness. "Perhaps he found himself looking right into an abyss of inconsistencies when he thought he was about to find the ultimate answers," Jantzen suggested. "What else could he do but run? But he won't run for long. It isn't in his nature."

Burkhardt, of Cal Tech, whose own work had been carried out in the sphere that Asenion was later to make his own, agreed with Jantzen's analysis. "He must have hit something really dark and hairy. But he'll wake up one morning with the solution in his head, and it'll be goodbye horticulture for him. He'll turn out a paper by noon that will revolutionize everything we think we know about nuclear physics, and that'll be that."

But Jesse Hammond, who had played tennis with Asenion every morning for the last two years of his career as a physicist, took a less charitable position. "He's gone nuts," Hammond said. "He's flipped out altogether, and he's never going to get himself together again."

"You think?" said Lew Fletcher, who had been almost as close to Asenion as Hammond, but who was no tennis player.

Hammond smiled. "No doubt of it. I began noticing a weird look in his eyes starting just about two years back. And then his playing started to turn weird too. He'd serve and not even look where he was serving. He'd double-fault without even caring. And you know what else? He didn't challenge me on a single out-of-bounds call the whole year. That was the key thing. Used to be, he'd fight me every call. Now he just didn't seem to care. He just let everything go by. He was completely indifferent. I said to myself, This guy must be flipping out."

"Or working on some problem that seems more important to him than tennis."

"Same thing," said Hammond. "No, Lew, I tell you—he's gone completely unglued. And nothing's going to glue him again."

That conversation had taken place almost a year ago. Nothing had happened in the interim to change anyone's opinion. The astounding arrival of plutonium-186 in the world had not brought forth any comment from Asenion's Manhattan penthouse. The sudden solemn discussions of fantastic things like parallel universes by otherwise reputable physicists had apparently not aroused him either. He remained closeted with his bromeliads high above the streets of Manhattan.

Well, maybe he *is* crazy, Fletcher thought. But his mind can't have shorted out entirely. And he might just have an idea or two left in him—

Asenion said, "Well, you don't look a whole lot older, do you?"

Fletcher felt himself reddening. "Jesus, Ike, it's only been eighteen months since we last saw each other!"

"Is that all?" Asenion said indifferently. "It feels like a lot more to me."

He managed a thin, remote smile. He didn't look very interested in Fletcher or in whatever it was that had brought Fletcher to his secluded eyrie.

Asenion had always been an odd one, of course—aloof,

mysterious, with a faint but unmistakable air of superiority about him that nearly everyone found instantly irritating. Of course, he *was* superior. But he had made sure that he let you know it, and never seemed to care that others found the trait less than endearing.

He appeared more remote than ever, now, stranger and more alien. Outwardly he had not changed at all: the same slender, debonair figure, surprisingly handsome, even striking. Though rumor had it that he had not left his penthouse in more than a year, there was no trace of indoor pallor about him. His skin still had its rich deep olive coloring, almost swarthy, a Mediterranean tone. His hair, thick and dark, tumbled down rakishly over his broad forehead. But there was something different about his dark, gleaming eyes. The old Asenion, however preoccupied he might have been with some abstruse problem of advanced physics, had nearly always had a playful sparkle in his eyes, a kind of amiable devilish glint. This man, this horticultural recluse, wore a different expression altogether—ascetic, mist-shrouded, *absent.* His gaze was as bright as ever, but the brightness was a cold one that seemed to come from some far-off star.

Fletcher said, "The reason I've come here—"

"We can go into all that later, can't we, Lew? First come into the greenhouse with me. There's something I want to show you. Nobody else has seen it yet, in fact."

"Well, if you—"

"Insist, yes. Come. I promise you, it's extraordinary."

He turned and led the way through the intricate pathways of the apartment. The sprawling many-roomed penthouse was furnished in the most offhand way, cheap student furniture badly cared for. Cats wandered everywhere, five, six, eight of them, sharpening their claws on the upholstery, prowling in empty closets whose doors stood ajar, peering down from the tops of bookcases containing jumbled heaps of coverless volumes. There was a rank smell of cat urine in the air.

But then suddenly Asenion turned a corridor and Fletcher, following just behind, found himself staring into what could have been an altogether different world. They had reached the entrance to the spectacular glass-walled extension that had been wrapped like an observation deck around the entire summit of the building. Beyond, dimly visible inside, Fletcher could see hundreds or perhaps thousands of strange-looking plants, some hanging from the ceiling, some mounted along the sides of wooden pillars, some rising in stepped array on benches, some growing out of beds set in the floor.

Asenion briskly tapped out the security-combination code on a diamond-shaped keyboard mounted in the wall, and the glass door slid silently back. A blast of warm humid air came forth.

"Quickly!" he said. "Inside!"

It was like stepping straight into the Amazon jungle. In place of the harsh, dry atmosphere of a Manhattan apartment in mid-winter there was, abruptly, the dense moist sweet closeness of the tropics, enfolding them like folds of wet fabric. Fletcher almost expected to hear parrots screeching overhead.

And the plants! The bizarre plants, clinging to every surface, filling every available square inch!

Most of them followed the same general pattern, rosettes of broad shining strap-shaped leaves radiating outward from a central cup-shaped structure deep enough to hold several ounces of water. But beyond that basic area of similarity they differed wildly from one another. Some were tiny, some were colossal. Some were marked with blazing stripes of yellow and red and purple that ran the length of their thick, succulent leaves. Some were mottled with fierce blotches of shimmering, assertive, bewilderingly complicated combinations of color. Some, whose leaves were green, were a fiery scarlet or crimson, or a somber, mysterious blue, at the place where the leaves came together to form the cup. Some were armed with formidable teeth and looked ready to feed on unwary visitors. Some were topped with gaudy spikes of strangely shaped brilliant-hued flowers taller than a man, which sprang like radiant spears from their centers.

Everything glistened. Everything seemed poised for violent, explosive growth. The scene was alien and terrifying. It was like looking into a vast congregation of hungry monsters. Fletcher had to remind himself that these were merely plants, hothouse speci-mens that probably wouldn't last half an hour in the urban environment outside.

"These are bromeliads," Asenion said, shaping the word sensuously in his throat as though it were the finest word any language had ever produced. "Tropical plants, mainly. South and Central America is where most of them live. They tend to cling to trees, growing high up in the forks of branches, mainly. Some live at ground level, though. Such as the bromeliad you know best, which is the pineapple. But there are hundreds of others in this room. Thousands. And this is the humid room, where I keep the guzmanias and the vrieseas and some of the aechmeas. As we go around, I'll show you the tillandsias—they like it a lot drier—and the terrestrial ones, the hechtias and the dyckias, and then over on the far side—"

"Ike," Fletcher said quietly.

"You know I've never liked that name."

"I'm sorry. I forgot." That was a lie. Asenion's given name was Ichabod. Neither Fletcher nor anyone Fletcher knew had ever been able to bring himself to call him that. "Look, I think what you've got here is wonderful. Absolutely wonderful. But I don't want to intrude on your time, and there's a very serious problem I need to discuss with—"

"First the plants," Asenion said. "Indulge me." His eyes were glowing. In the half-light of the greenhouse he looked like a jungle creature himself, exotic, weird. Without a moment's hesitation, he pranced off down the aisle toward a group of oversized bromeliads near the outer wall. Willy-nilly, Fletcher followed.

Asenion gestured grandly.

"Here it is! Do you see? *Aechmea asenionii!* Discovered in northwestern Brazil two years ago—I sponsored the expedition myself—of course, I never expected them to name it for me, but you know how these things sometimes happen—"

Fletcher stared. The plant was a giant among giants, easily two meters across from leaf-tip to leaf-tip. Its dark green leaves were banded with jagged pale scrawls that looked like the hieroglyphs of some lost race. Out of the central cup, which was the size of a man's head and deep enough to drown rabbits in, rose the strangest flower Fletcher ever hoped to see, a thick yellow stalk of immense length from which sprang something like a cluster of black thunderbolts tipped with ominous red globes like dangling moons. A pervasive odor of rotting flesh came from it.

"The only specimen in North America!" Asenion cried. "Perhaps one of six or seven in the world. And I've succeeded in inducing it to bloom. There'll be seed, Lew, and perhaps there'll be offsets as well—I'll be able to propagate it, and cross it with others—can you imagine it crossed with *Aechmea chantinii*, Fletcher? Or perhaps an interspecific hybrid? With *Neoregelia carcharadon*, say? No. Of course you can't imagine it. What am I saying? But it would be spectacular beyond belief. Take my word for it."

"I have no doubt."

"It's a privilege, seeing this plant in bloom. But there are others here you must see too. The puyas—the pitcairnias—there's a clump of *Dyckia marnier-lapostollei* in the next room that you wouldn't believe—"

He bubbled with boyish enthusiasm. Fletcher forced himself to be patient. There was no help for it: he would simply have to take the complete tour.

It went on for what seemed like hours, as Asenion led him frantically from one peculiar plant to another, in room after room. Some were actually quite beautiful, Fletcher had to admit. Others seemed excessively flamboyant, or grotesque, or incomprehensibly ordinary to his untutored eye, or downright grotesque. What struck him most forcefully of all was the depth of Asenion's obsession. Nothing in the universe seemed to matter to him except this horde of exotic plants. He had given himself up totally to the strange world he had created here.

But at last even Asenion's manic energies seemed to flag. The pace had been merciless, and both he and Fletcher, drenched with sweat and gasping in the heat, paused for breath in a section of the greenhouse occupied by small gray gnarly plants that seemed to have no roots, and were held to the wall by barely visible wires.

Abruptly Asenion said, "All right. You aren't interested anyway. Tell me what you came here to ask me, and then get on your way. I have all sorts of things to do this afternoon."

"It's about plutonium-186," Fletcher began.

"Don't be idiotic. That's not a legitimate isotope. It can't possibly exist."

"I know," Fletcher said. "But it does."

Quickly, almost desperately, he outlined the whole fantastic story for the young physicist-turned-botanist. The mysterious substitution of a strange element for tungsten or osmium in various laboratories, the tests indicating that its atomic number was that of plutonium but its atomic weight was far too low, the absurd but necessary theory that the stuff was a gift from some parallel universe and—finally—the fact that the new element, stable when it first arrived, rapidly began to undergo radioactive decay in a startlingly accelerative way.

Asenion's saturnine face was a study in changing emotions as Fletcher spoke. He seemed bored and irritated at first, then scornful, then, perhaps, furious; but not a word did he utter, and gradually the fury ebbed, turning to distant curiosity and then, finally, a kind of fascination. Or so Fletcher thought. He realized that he might be altogether wrong in his interpretations of what was going on in the unique, mercurial mind of the other man.

When Fletcher fell silent Asenion said, "What are you most afraid of? Critical mass? Or cumulative electron loss?"

"We've dealt with the critical mass problem by powdering the stuff, shielding it in graphite, and scattering it in low concentrations to fifty different storage points. But it keeps on coming in—they love to send it to us, it seems. And the thought that every atom of it is giving off positrons that go around looking for electrons to annihilate—" Fletcher shrugged. "On a small scale it's a useful energy pump, I suppose, tungsten swapped for plutonium with energy gained in each cycle. But on a large scale, as we continue to transfer electrons from our universe to theirs—"

"Yes," Asenion said.

"So we need a way to dispose of—"

"Yes." He looked at his watch. "Where are you staying while you're in town, Fletcher?"

"The Faculty Club, as usual."

"Good. I've got some crosses to make and I don't want to wait any longer, on account of possible pollen contamination. Go over to the club and keep yourself amused for a few hours. Take a shower. God knows you need one: you smell like something out of the jungle. Relax, have a drink, come back at five o'clock. We can talk about this again then." He shook his head. "Plutonium-186! What lunacy! It offends me just to say it out loud. It's like saying—saying—well, *Billbergia yukonensis*, or *Tillandsia bostoniae*. Do you know what I mean? No. No. Of course you don't." He waved his hands. "Out! Come back at five!"

It was a long afternoon for Fletcher. He phoned his wife, he phoned Jesse Hammond at the laboratory, he phoned an old friend and made a date for dinner. He showered and changed. He had a drink in the ornate lounge on the Fifth Avenue side of the Club.

But his mood was grim, and not merely because Hammond had told him that another four kilograms of Plutonium-186 had been reported from various regions that morning. Asenion's madness oppressed him.

There was nothing wrong with an interest in plants, of course. Fletcher kept a philodendron and something else, whose name he could never remember, in his own office. But to immerse yourself in one highly specialized field of botany with such intensity—it seemed sheer lunacy. No, Fletcher decided, even that was all right, difficult as it was for him to understand why anyone would want to spend his whole life cloistered with a bunch of eerie plants. What was hard for him to forgive was Asenion's renunciation of physics. A mind like that—the breadth of its vision—the insight Asenion had had into the greatest of mysteries—dammit, Fletcher thought, he had owed it to the world to stick to it! And instead, to walk away from everything, to hole himself up in a cage of glass—

Hammond's right, Fletcher told himself. Asenion really is crazy.

But it was useless to fret about it. Asenion was not the first supergenius to snap under contemplation of the Ultimate. His withdrawal from physics, Fletcher said sternly to himself, was a matter between Asenion and the universe. All that concerned Fletcher was getting Asenion's solution to the plutonium-186 problem; and then the poor man could be left with his bromeliads in peace.

About half past four Fletcher set out by cab to battle the traffic the short distance uptown to Asenion's place.

Luck was with him. He arrived at ten of five. Asenion's house-robot greeted him solemnly and invited him to wait. "The master is in the greenhouse," the robot declared. "He will be with you when he has completed the pollination."

Fletcher waited. And waited and waited.

Geniuses, he thought bitterly. Pains in the neck, all of them. Pains in the—

Just then the robot reappeared. It was half past six. All was blackness outside the window. Fletcher's dinner date was for seven. He would never make it.

"The master will see you now," said the robot.

Asenion looked limp and weary, as though he had spent the entire afternoon smashing up boulders. But the formidable edge seemed gone from him, too. He greeted Fletcher with a pleasant enough smile, offered a word or two of almost-apology for his tardiness, and even had the robot bring Fletcher a sherry. It wasn't very good sherry, but to get anything at all to drink in a teetotaler's house was a blessing, Fletcher figured.

Asenion waited until Fletcher had had a few sips. Then he said, "I have your answer."

"I knew you would."

There was a long silence.

"Thiotimoline," said Asenion finally.

"Thiotimoline?"

"Absolutely. Endochronic disposal. It's the only way. And, as you'll see, it's a *necessary* way."

Fletcher took a hasty gulp of the sherry. Even when he was in a relatively mellow mood, it appeared, Asenion was maddening. And mad. What was this new craziness now? Thiotimoline? How could that preposterous substance, as insane in its way as plutonium-186, have any bearing on the problem?

Asenion said, "I take it you know the special properties of thiotimoline?"

"Of course. Its molecule is distorted into adjacent temporal dimensions. Extends into the future, and, I think, into the past. Thiotimoline powder will dissolve in water one second *before* the water is added."

"Exactly," Asenion said. "And if the water isn't added, it'll go looking for it. In the future."

"What does this have to do with—"

"Look here," said Asenion. He drew a scrap of paper from his shirt pocket. "You want to get rid of something. You put it in this container here. You surround the container with a shell made of polymerized thiotimoline. You surround the shell with a water tank that will deliver water to the thiotimoline on a timed basis, and you set your timer so that the water is due to arrive a few seconds from now. But at the last moment the timing device withholds the water."

Fletcher stared at the younger man in awe.

Asenion said, "The water is always about to arrive, but never quite does. The thiotimoline making up the plastic shell is pulled forward one second into the future to encounter the water. The water has a high probability of being there, but not quite high enough. It's actually another second away from delivery, and always will be. The thiotimoline gets dragged farther and farther into the future. The world goes forward into the future at a rate of one second per second, but the thiotimoline's velocity is essentially infinite. And of course it carries with it the inner container, too."

"In which we have put our surplus plutonium-186."

"Or anything else you want to dispose of," said Asenion.

Fletcher felt dizzy. "Which will travel on into the future at an infinite rate—"

"Yes. And because the rate is infinite, the problem of the breakdown of thiotimoline into its stable isochronic form, which has hampered most time-transport experiments, isn't an issue. Something traveling through time at an infinite velocity isn't subject to little limitations of that kind. It'll simply keep going until it can't go any farther."

"But how does sending it into the future solve the problem?" Fletcher asked. "The plutonium-186 still stays in our universe, even if we've bumped it away from our immediate temporal vicinity. The electron loss continues. Maybe even gets worse, under temporal acceleration. We still haven't dealt with the fundamental—"

"You never were much of a thinker, were you, Fletcher?" said Asenion quietly, almost gently. But the savage contempt in his eyes had the force of a sun going nova.

"I do my best. But I don't see—"

Asenion sighed. "The thiotimoline will chase the water in the outer container to the end of time, carrying with it the plutonium in the inner container. To the end of time. *Literally.*"

"And?"

"What happens at the end of time, Fletcher?"

"Why—absolute entropy—the heat-death of the universe—"

"Precisely. The Final Entropic Solution. All molecules equally distributed throughout space. There will be no further place for the water-seeking thiotimoline to go. The end of the line is the end of the line. It, and the plutonium it's hauling with it, and the water it's trying to catch up with, will all plunge together over the entropic brink into antitime."

"Antitime," said Fletcher in a leaden voice. "Antitime?"

"Naturally. Into the moment before the creation of the universe. Everything is in stasis. Zero time, infinite temperature. All the universal mass contained in a single incomprehensible body. Then the thiotimoline and the plutonium and the water arrive." Asenion's eyes were radiant. His face was flushed. He waved his scrap of paper around as though it were the scripture of some new creed. "There will be a tremendous explosion. A Big Bang, so to speak. The beginning of all things. You—or should I say I?—will be responsible for the birth of the universe."

Fletcher, stunned, said after a moment, "Are you serious?"

"I am never anything but serious. You have your solution. Pack up your plutonium and send it on its way. No matter how many shipments you make, they'll all arrive at the same instant. And with the same effect. You have no choice, you know. The plutonium *must* be disposed of. And—" His eyes twinkled with some of the old Asenion playfulness. "The universe *must* be created, or else how will any of us get to be where we are? And this is how it was done. *Will* be done. Inevitable, ineluctable, unavoidable, mandatory. Yes? You see?"

"Well, no. Yes. Maybe. That is, I think I do," said Fletcher, as if in a daze.

"Good. Even if you don't, you will."

"I'll need—to talk to the others—"

"Of course you will. That's how you people do things. That's why I'm here and you're there." Asenion shrugged. "Well, no hurry about it. Create the universe tomorrow, create it the week after next, what's the difference? It'll get done sooner or later. It has to, because it already has been done. You see?"

"Yes. Of course. Of—course. And now—if you'll excuse me—" Fletcher murmured. "I—ah—have a dinner appointment in a little while—"

"That can wait too, can't it?" said Asenion, smiling with sudden surprising amiability. He seemed genuinely glad to have been of assistance. "There's something I forgot to show you this afternoon. A remarkable plant, possibly unique—a nidularium, it is, Brazilian, not even named yet, as a matter of fact—just coming into bloom. And this one—wait till you see it, Fletcher, wait till you see it—"

Murder in the Urth Degree

by Edward Wellen

"Let there be day."

Day was when he said it was. Periscoped sunlight obediently flooded the stateroom at the core of Terrarium Nine.

Keith Flammersfeld saw the light with still-closed eyes and knew that his little world remained safe and warm outside his eyelids. Lazily, he removed from his temples the interactive patcher that had put him into the video of *Through the Looking-Glass* that had just now faded from the screen of his computer/player.

He opened his eyes and sat up in his bunk and stretched. He loosed a jaw-cracking yawn, momentarily disappearing the chipmunk pouches that flanked his self-satisfied mouth. To keep up his muscle tone and stay in shape, he lay supine again and thought aerobic thoughts for a good five minutes. He was pushing forty, but he was pushing forty back.

Feeling fit after all that exercise, he sat up and swung around to put his feet on the carpeted deck. He checked his priorities: the call of nature could wait, the clamor from his stomach could not. He called for his tray.

It slid out of the bulkhead to fit just above his lap. He put away a healthy breakfast of fruits, vegetables, and grains—all grown right here inside Terrarium Nine. The tray sensed when the last of the food was gone and slid itself back into the bulkhead.

Flammersfeld stood up and got out of his pajama shorts. He tossed them into the revamper, stepped into the toilet cubicle and relieved himself, washed up, fizzed his mouth clean, and put on fresh shorts.

Two steps to the right took Flammersfeld to his office. He sat down at his master computer and tapped keys. The screen displayed a blank requisition form.

His face split in a huge grin as he typed two items and moused them into the right spaces. Tight facial muscles around mouth and eyes told him it was a malicious grin. At this awareness, he quickly slackened the grin into an expression of innocent merriment. Then, reminding himself that he was all alone aboard Terrarium Nine and that no one watched, he hauled again on the lines of the malicious grin.

He savored, then saved, the requisition. He was on the point of sending it to the home office on Earth, when he all but jumped out of his skin.

The lower right quadrant of the screen was displaying a reduced image of another monitor screen's display.

This display labeled itself as coming from the work station in Buck Two. He put his own page on hold and filled the screen with the intruding display.

He stared at it, feeling his eyes bulge.

Someone had entered his system and infected it with rabid doggerel.

> Is the sun a milky bud?
> Whence the shadows on my face?
> Why's the sky as green as blood?
> Who will win the Red Queen's race?

Madness.

But even madness had to have a logical explanation.

Possible explanation number one, a computer virus. If true, it would have entered by way of the master computer, sole link to Earth and the universe. What would be the point of trying to trick him into thinking the message came from Buck Two's slave computer, not from Buck One's central memory? Merely the prankish pleasure of sending him on a wild-goose chase through Buck Two's jungle? A small payoff for what would have to have been a major effort, cracking the vaccinated and regularly boostered Labcom system headquartered on Earth.

Possible explanation number two, a stowaway, presence hitherto entirely unsuspected by Flammersfeld and completely overlooked by all sensors. If true, the person would have had to slip aboard during resupply a full year ago. If such a one had survived all that while by living on the fruits and vegetables and grains grown in Terrarium Nine—though how that could be when Flammersfeld kept those precious items all carefully tagged and tabulated and tracked—why would that stowaway give his or her presence away at this point? Lonely and dying for companionship? Fallen ill and in need of help? Gone mad and about to attack? Having bided his or her time, now ready for a takeover bid?

Possible explanation number three, true madness— Flammersfeld's own. Could Flammersfeld himself have programmed that display, say while dream-experiencing *Through the Looking-Glass?* Had cabin fever affected his brain, split his awareness?

Even as he stared at the screen the display changed. Another verse appeared, letter by letter, slowly, painfully, as though stiff and hesitant fingers were working in real time.

> When Adam delved
> Was it then I selved?
> When Eve span
> Was it then I began?

Flammersfeld tightened his mouth. Someone *was* in Buck Two.

He hurried to his bulkhead safe and punched the combination. The safe door swung open and he armed himself with the blaser he had never dreamed he might one day have to use.

Terrarium Nine, in near-Earth orbit, was a six-bucker—six concentric spheres built on R. Buckminster Fuller's geodesic principle. A pseudo black hole at the center provided Earth-gravity for the innermost sphere. The calibrated pull diminished to nothing in the outermost sphere, where the zero-gravity lab was. Access was by companionway and lift. Terrarium Nine was large enough to make northern and southern companionways practical and efficient. The two-way lift, slightly bowed to bypass the pseudo black hole, ran along the axis, from polar airlock to polar airlock. The cage had handholds to facilitate orientation—rather, borealization or australization.

The Buck Two work station was in the northern hemisphere. Flammersfeld made for the lift, started to step in, then had a second thought.

He punched the lift to go north to Buck Two by itself, but entered a five-minute delay.

Swiftly he backtracked along the gently curving geodesic deckplates to the southern companionway, and raced up it to the hatch.

If someone lay in wait for Flammersfeld to emerge from the lift, and if that someone kept a shrewd eye on the nearby north companionway hatch, Flammersfeld, making his way around from the south, would come upon that someone from behind.

He glanced at his watch, sucked in, undogged the hatch. Blaser at the ready, he vaulted into Buck Two's lesser gravity, where, in lunar soil with various admixtures of nitrates, plants flourished mightily.

He landed lightly, sought concealment in a ten-meter-high stand of slowly swaying rye. Held his breath, listened through the soft sough of programmed breeze, heard nothing. He'd outflanked the intruder; seemed safe to move out.

Made good time through chubby Swiss chard, enormous endives, plump peas, and bulky beans. In under four minutes he reached the stout sweet potatoes. Nearly there. The work station lay underneath the towering walnut tree dead ahead. Past that stood tremendous tomatoes, prodigious peppers, large lettuce, and corpulent cabbage; then a pile of mulch—and beyond all that the lift.

He padded carefully to the walnut and peered around the massive trunk. He saw plainly the computer station. No one was at it.

The tomato vines blocked his view of the lift area. Flammersfeld thrust against the soil for a giant leap. He caught one-handed hold, five meters up, of the stem of a thirty-meter tomato vine and hung there looking through and across vines and foliage while the blaser quested.

He heard the sudden coming-to-life hum of the lift.

That should make an ambusher take position. Flammersfeld had a commanding view of the lettuce and cabbage patches. An ambusher there would have a clear field to the lift and the northern companionway hatch. No one moved there.

The lift stopped and the door slid open. Flammersfeld looked for some stir somewhere. The blaser quested in vain. No one lay in wait.

He hung there, his face reddening with anger and frustration; the tomatoes were large as his head, so that it might have been one of them. A wild-goose chase after all.

Grimacing, he stuck the blaser in the waistband of his shorts and let himself down the vine hand under hand. Once on deck, he headed for the work station.

He stepped into a loop of vine and made a mental note to clear away debris and undergrowth first chance he got. Before he realized the loop was a noose, it had tightened around his ankle. Before he could bend to loosen it, he found himself whipped high into the air, where he remained dangling bouncily by his foot from the noose whose other end was tied to a springy bough of the towering walnut tree.

Rolling his eyes way up to look way down, he spotted the peg and the severed end of another length of vine that had held the bough to the deck. Where below was the trapper who had cut the tie?

Flammersfeld pretended to be helpless. He thrashed about, twisting, twisting in the continuously maintained light breeze. He made his voice sound panicky. "Help! Let me down! Please!"

Still the damned stowaway—for Flammersfeld had perforce settled on possible explanation number two—did not show his or her face.

Flammersfeld could not wait like this much longer; even with the inconsequential gravity of Buck Two, the noose was cutting off the circulation to his caught foot.

He gave himself one painful minute more; then, when no foe appeared, he drew the blaser from his waistband and sliced the vine.

As he fell he aimed the blaser deckward and thumbed the retro stud. The gelled-light effect slowed his fall enough to let him land rolling.

He scrambled to his feet—and groaned as the numbed foot betrayed him. He put his weight on his good foot and looked around for another trap—or even an outright attack. He looked high up at the walnut tree's branches and foliage, saw no figure or contraption above him, and put his back against the trunk. He bent to remove the noose from his ankle—and saw on the ground a few fragments of cabbage leaf.

His jaw dropped as the chilling realization hit him.

Then his lips thinned. Very well. He knew now what he was up against.

It was not any of the three possible explanations. It was a fourth—and it was probable and in a few minutes would be provable.

He laughed. To think of the poor miserable creature stalking *him!*

Then he grew grim. He had underestimated the creature. That it might have been responsible for the doggerel on the computer screen had not even occurred to him. Had to give the thing credit; lot more to it than he had thought. Still, now that he knew, he could handle the threat.

"All right, you bastard," he muttered through his malicious grin, "you're digging your own grave."

He hobbled directly to the cabbage patch. He looked down at an empty space and nodded. There had been an uprooting, though some effort had been made to smooth the disturbed soil.

As if that could fool him! He knew perfectly well what had grown at this particular spot, what should still be growing here, what seemed now on the loose.

A closer look at the soil showed him a dotted line of milky green droplets running from the center of the empty space. He touched one. Sticky. He brought the finger to his nose and sniffed. His grin widened. The damned thing was truly damned. Did it know it had not long?

The trail was short; it ended abruptly at a nearby cabbage. A freshly ripped edge showed where a leaf had been torn off. His grin stretched to its utmost. The creature must be using the leaf to stem the flow.

The trail gone, Flammersfeld cast about for other signs.

He glanced at the nearby heap of mulch. He felt a twinge for having neglected it; he had let it decompose almost to compost. He stiffened. There seemed some difference in its makeup, some shifting of its components. It consisted half of tree limbs he had sectioned for study or trimmed and split into rough boards and half of discarded paper printouts. He thought the paper covered more of the heap than when he had looked at it last—more spread out, less neatly accordioned.

The creature might be hiding under there.

Flammersfeld held the blaser ready to fire.

With his free hand he jerked lengths of dank and moldy continuous-fold printouts away in long fluttering banners. He did not find his creature but did unearth what appeared to be a crude catapult, a thing of branches and vine and a ball of compacted soil held together with some vegetable glue. He also found a winding drum fitted with a crank—a winch; this also was fashioned of sectioned tree limbs and vine.

Both contraptions looked as if a child might have put them together—but they had worked. The catapult had shot the weighted end of a length of vine over a bough and the winch had pulled the bough down.

He rooted around a bit more and found something else— half a walnut shell big as his cupped palm. The size he was used to; what it held was—something else.

The creature had used the empty half-shell as a mortar to pound something vegetable into a resinous black sticky substance that had an aromatic tarry smell. A crude preparation, showing foam of spit.

Visions of amylase danced in Flammersfeld's head. What would the idiosyncratic enzymatic action be in this case—on, what he felt sure he would find when he analyzed it, green pepper? Seemed clear that the creature had in mind a curare, an arrow poison. That was just what this substance appeared to be.

Flammersfeld found himself asweat. He needed a relaxant— but not this kind. This kind could relax him to death.

Better get the hell out of here. The creature was sure to bleed to death—but how soon? Flammersfeld found himself not so sure any more about a lot of things concerning the creature.

How could he not have seen its intelligence waken, its hate turn on him?

Still crouching, he faced about. For the first time, he looked around at this small world from another's point of view.

From the cabbage patch, the computer screen was in plain sight. How much the creature must have learned simply by watching and listening to the work and the play!

This was not the time to wonder about that. This was the time to beat it before a small arrow flew or a small lance thrust.

Flammersfeld straightened and hobbled double-time to the open lift.

He breathed a sigh at having made it, and reached to punch the door shut and the lift down.

The killer must have slipped into the lift while the noose held Flammersfeld adangle.

From the left near corner of the cage, where the killer had crouched unseen behind the door that did not slide flush, a frail arm thrust the sharpened and poison-tipped twig into the soft tissue of Flammersfeld's left ankle.

Flammersfeld stared down at the sadly wise and wearily savage face.

"God damn you," he said.

"You damn you."

It was the first and last time he ever heard the rusty piping voice.

But he was not thinking about that. He was thinking about getting to the dispensary in time to work up an antidote. His heart pounding, he punched the lift shut and down.

His eyes were glazing and he did not look at the creature again until the lift stopped and the door opened. Then he kicked the creature out of his way and took two stumbling steps forward before he sprawled his length on the deck.

The killer could not stanch the flow of green blood and soon followed Flammersfeld across the dark threshold into the abode of the dead. But the killer had won what he wanted—vengeance and oblivion.

Inspector H. Seton Davenport of the Terrestrial Bureau of Investigation had expected to see anything but an inverted detective. Yet that was just what he walked in upon.

Dr. Wendell Urth, the Terran extraterrologists' extraterrologist, had sounded strange when he voiced Davenport in.

Davenport had caught a note of strain in the thin tenor delivery of "Enter!"

But Davenport had not dreamed that was due to Dr. Urth's attempting a headstand. At least, that was what the learned ex-officio consultant to the T.B.I. appeared at first glance to be doing.

Second glance showed him that Dr. Urth was really engaged in rolling a hologram sun along the baseboards. And that he was doing so to light up the floor under the overhanging book-film shelves.

The blood rushing to Dr. Urth's head made his naked eyes look even more hyperthyroid. That the eyes were naked and that the good doctor's shirttail hung out told Davenport what was up—or down—or toward. Without taking another step, Davenport scanned the floor.

He spotted them not on the floor itself but on a bottom shelf they had bounced to. He took two steps and made a stretch and picked up what Dr. Urth was hunting for.

"Here you are, Dr. Urth."

"Here I certainly am," Dr. Urth wheezed. "Embarrassingly so." Then he apparently replayed Davenport's words and tone. He twisted the upside-down half of his body to face Davenport, squinted, and apparently made out what Davenport was holding. "Ah." He straightened with a huff and a puff, and placed the solar-powered hologram sun on a pile of papers—it was evidently loaded to serve as paperweight as well as to help light the vast dim cluttered room.

Dr. Urth took the eyeglasses from Davenport's outstretched hand. "Thanks." Then he smiled a transforming smile, one that changed him from blinking owl to beaming Buddha. "But you have had your reward in seeing me make a spectacle of myself." He polished the lenses with the shirttail, peered at and through them, then put them on. The ears did their part but the button nose did little to support the frame.

He gestured Davenport to a chair. Himself he settled in his armchair-desk with a sigh the seat echoed. He locked his hands over his paunch and looked expectant. The paunch enhanced the look of expectancy.

"This is about the death on Terrarium Nine?"

Davenport nodded. "'Death' is the working word for it.

'Death' is ambiguous enough for something we can't seem to label satisfactorily. We can't call it accident, we can't call it murder, and we're not ready to call it suicide."

Dr. Urth shifted himself more comfortable. "Tell me the details."

"It's better and easier to show you." Davenport drew from a capacious pocket a sheaf of holograms. He hopped his chair nearer Dr. Urth and leaned over to show him the holograms one by one, pointing and explaining.

"Here's a close-up of Terrarium Nine taken from the investigating vehicle on its approach in response to the anomaly alarm. Flammersfeld, the lone experimenter aboard Terrarium Nine, had not transmitted the daily report to Earth headquarters at the scheduled hour, had not punched the All's-Well signal at the appointed time, and had not responded to worried queries . . . Here are shots the responding officer took of both docking jacks before she made entry through north dock. You'll notice a year's worth of undisturbed space dust coats both jacks. That indicates no one docked since the last resupply—a full year ago . . . Here's the death scene, located in the innermost sphere."

Dr. Urth took this last hologram into his own hands for protracted scrutiny. Then he gave Davenport a quizzical look. "Aside from telling me that Flammersfeld had just come down to his living quarters from Buck Two, bringing with him a cabbage either for study or for eating, that he stepped out of the lift and fell dead, having somehow taken a poison-tipped dart in his ankle, this hologram does not tell me all I need to know if I'm to help you label his death. What about the autopsy findings? What was the poison?"

Davenport shook his head. "That's what's strange. You'd think a biochemist of Flammersfeld's standing would have brewed it in his lab, in test tubes, without impurities. But this was a weird kind of curare crudely prepared. The investigator found some of the guck in a walnut shell that she discovered in a pile of trash in Buck Two." He handed Dr. Urth another hologram. "Here's a shot of that."

Dr. Urth gave half a nod, half a shake. "I see that, but what are these things?"

Davenport looked where Dr. Urth pointed. "Oh, yeah; them. They seem to be a toy winch and a toy catapult. The engineer we consulted says they're no great shakes but they work. Maybe Flammersfeld was in his second childhood."

Dr. Urth grunted doubtingly. He went back to the death-scene hologram. He pointed a stubby finger to a green-black mass. "This is the cabbage?"

Davenport grimaced. "Bad. Pretty well rotted by the time our investigator got there. Stank up the place, she said, so—after taking protection shots—she incinerated it."

"Bad."

"Yes, putrid."

Dr. Urth eyed the TBI inspector censoriously. "I was not speaking of the cabbage, I meant the officer's action. She should have preserved the evidence no matter how offensive she found it."

Davenport neither defended nor blamed the officer. Like her, he saw the cabbage not as evidence but as happenstance. "Perhaps."

"No perhaps about it," Dr. Urth snapped. His paunch showed momentary agitation, then subsided with his sigh. "Well, it can't be helped now. But I do wish I could have had a closer look at that cabbage. There's something queer about it."

Davenport grinned. "No problem. This is one of the new SOTA holograms. See the bubble-mice sealed in the left and top edges?"

Dr. Urth noticed for the first time two beads of air that almost met at the top left corner of the hologram film. His eyes lit up. "You mean that if I get a stereotaxic fix on the cabbage the cabbage will enlarge?"

"Exactly. By pinching the edge you can move the bubble-mouse along. Coordinate the mice to enlarge and automatically enhance the area you want to observe in greater detail. There's a limit, of course, but you'll see quite a lot more than you do now."

Dr. Urth pinched the mice along till he had the cabbage area blown up by a magnification of five.

He looked long and hard, and at last removed his glasses to wipe tears of strain from his eyes. "Much better, but still lacking. My complaint is not about the resolution but about the object pictured. The cabbage remains blurry thanks to decomposition. I must admit that even had the officer preserved it so that you could put it before me I would be hard put to make out much more. That does not mean that its destruction is not a great loss. It should have been possible to determine its exact composition by autopsy."

Davenport stared. "Autopsy? Of a cabbage?"

Dr. Urth nodded curtly. "Autopsy. I choose my words carefully." His mouth twitched suddenly and he unbent unexpectedly, his voice mock-serious. "I do not see-aitch-oh-you my cabbage twice." He grew fully serious again. "It's clear that something got out of hand—the experiment, the experimenter, or both."

Davenport was still working on the autopsy business. What was Dr. Urth getting at?

Dr. Urth sighed and handed back the death-scene hologram. He gave a slight shiver, then shot Davenport a look as if wondering whether Davenport had noticed.

Davenport kept a poker face.

Dr. Urth breathed an easier sigh. "This calls for mulling over." He turned a grave face and a twinkling eye on his visitor. "What would you say to a finger of Ganymead?"

"I'd say hello." Davenport had heard of Ganymead but had never seen it, much less tasted it. He knew it to be extremely rare and extremely expensive and he knew many communities prohibited it. He was not about to ask Dr. Urth how Dr. Urth had come by it. "I'm game."

He did not feel so game when Dr. Urth drew two containers and two glasses from a liquor drawer of the armchair-desk and one of the containers proved to hold fingers.

Dr. Urth shook two fingers out and stood one, fingernail down, in each glass.

Davenport looked and shuddered.

One corner of Urth's rosy mouth lifted. "Ganymead is a binary. The fluid part activates the solid part. The 'fingernail' is a crystallization. Watch."

He poured an amber fluid out of the other container into one of the glasses and as it splashed the nail the finger melted. The whole became a clear violet with a bouquet that tickled the senses. Dr. Urth transformed the other finger, handed one of the glasses to Davenport, and lifted the other in a toasting gesture.

Davenport answered with a lift of his own glass, sniffed, then sipped. Tantalizingly delicious, deliciously tantalizing. He saw that it could be dangerous—a taste too easily acquired for something not so easily acquired.

The smooth but strong drink seemed to turn Dr. Urth philosophical. "Actually, Ganymead comes not from Ganymede but from Callisto. So many things are misnomers. What's in a name, Davenport? I should have yours—*I'm* the couch potato, the settee spud, the Murphy-bed murphy. At most, a rambler rose— tethered as I am to the University campus. You're the one with the gypsy in his soles, the man in the field. Davenport, you're a misnomer."

Davenport permitted himself a smile. Davenport's nose was shaped for wedging into tight spots; a youthful altercation had left a star-shaped scar on his right cheek. Yet a fellow could get his fill of the field, lose his taste for adventure, and—while cherishing his memories of encounters of the close kind—look almost with envy at the cloistered academic who adventured with his mind. Perhaps the Ganymead had turned him philosophical—or prone to babble —too; he was about to express his feelings about life when Dr. Urth saved him.

Dr. Urth had taken a last sip, had raised the glass to his eye to look through its emptiness, and now set it down with regretful finality. "Back to work. To give Flammersfeld's death its proper name, we must first understand what Terrarium Nine is all about, what Flammersfeld was in the business of."

He raised a forefinger, though Davenport had given no sign of breaking in.

"I know you think you know, but please bear with me while I tell you what I think I know. Let me state the obvious and posit the known—nothing is so overlooked as the obvious and nothing is so mysterious as the known."

Davenport sweepingly brought his palm up in sign of turning everything over to Dr. Urth.

Dr. Urth just as graciously gave a nod. "To forestall ecological disruption, Earth has laws against releasing genetically altered plants and animals into the terrestrial environment. Such experiments must take place off-planet. Hence, the Terrariums—at last count, a dozen?—in near-Earth orbit. A collateral benefit is zero gravity, which facilitates such techniques as electrophoresis—the rapid continuous-flow fractionating of concentrated solutions of proteins in a high-intensity electric field." He cocked an eye at Davenport. "Your turn. What do you think you know about Terrarium Nine and Flammersfeld's experiments?"

Davenport shrugged. "All I know about Terrarium Nine is that it was constructed and commissioned six years ago and that Flammersfeld was its first and only personnel. All I know about Flammersfeld is that he was a hard worker who never took a break; he routinely turned down R and R—according to his superiors in the home office he said he got all the relaxation he needed by interactive video, and in fact at the time of his death *Through the Looking-Glass* was in his computer/player—and he was working concurrently on two unrelated projects. Plus he had plans for the future—his last, though unsent, requisition was for swine embryo and eagle eggs."

Dr. Urth wrinkled his brow, then resettled his glasses. "I would like to see his notes on the two unrelated projects you mentioned."

Davenport looked uncomfortable. "That may be impossible."

Dr. Urth's mouth tightened. "Is there a clearance problem? If so, good day."

Davenport hastened to say, "It's not that, Dr. Urth, not that at all. I believe you have cosmic clearance."

That mollified Dr. Urth. "Then what is the problem? Did Flammersfeld destroy his notes?"

"Not that, either. It's just that he seems to have been paranoidally secretive. His notes are in his computer's memory, but locked behind passwords that we haven't broken—yet."

"I admire your optimism, sir, but optimism—while admirable even when it is foolish—is pie in the sky, a future repast; it does not feed us now."

Davenport reddened.

Dr. Urth relented. "Two unrelated projects; you know that much. You may know more than you think you know—that is, if you can give me the titles of the two projects. His superiors at the home office to whom he reported must have had some idea of what he was working on if they were to approve his requisitions."

Davenport brightened. "I don't have the titles at the tip of my tongue, but I do remember that he was seeking a cure for hemophilia and that he was looking for the—uh—direction sensors in plant cells."

Dr. Urth patted his paunch as if he had just had a good feed. "Excellent. Hemophilia. Bleeder's disease. Disease of kings—e.g., the Romanovs of Czarist Russia. Women pass it on through a recessive X chromosome but do not themselves have it. Profuse bleeding, even from the slightest wound. In a test tube, normal blood from a vein clots in five to fifteen minutes; hemophiliac clotting time varies from thirty minutes to hours. A natural for zero-gravity research. While the sheer bulk of total plasma would rule out its fractionation by electrophoresis at zero gravity, the same does not hold for minor components, such as clotting factors."

His voice pitched even higher in his excitement. "Yes, yes. And Flammersfeld's other project is another natural for zero-gravity research. The plant world presents an intriguing puzzle: how does a plant sense the direction of gravity? Plants tend to grow in a vertical direction—but we have yet to find the cellular direction sensors. Yes, yes. We have our answer."

Davenport stared at Dr. Urth. "We have?"

"It's as obvious," Dr. Urth said sharply, "as the nose on my face."

Maybe that's why I don't see it, Davenport muttered mentally. But he put on a pleasant mask. "You said it's easy to overlook the obvious."

"You've been listening, at least." Dr. Urth made himself a monument of patience. "Listen now to a bit of verse.

> " 'The time has come,' the Walrus said,
> 'To talk of many things:
> Of shoes—and ships—and sealing-wax—
> Of cabbages—and kings—
> And why the sea is boiling hot—
> And whether pigs have wings.' "

Dr. Urth looked at Davenport and smiled. "You don't know whether to laugh or snort at such utter nonsense. Well, laugh. We humans need a leavening of levity; there can be too much gravity."

Davenport did not laugh, but then he did not snort. "That's from a child's book, isn't it?"

"Indeed. The child in Charles Lutwidge Dodgson was named Lewis Carroll. The verse is from his *Through the Looking Glass.*"

"Flammersfeld's interactive video!"

"The same."

Davenport shook his head. "How does it tie in?"

"It ties in first with an even older nursery rhyme.

" 'Old King Cole
Was a merry old soul,
And a merry old soul was he;
He called for his pipe,
And he called for his bowl,
And he called for his fiddlers three.
Every fiddler, he had a fiddle,
And a very fine fiddle had he;
Twee tweedle dee, tweedle dee, went the fiddlers.
Oh, there's none so rare
As can compare
With King Cole and his fiddlers three!' "

This time Davenport could not help laughing. And after a moment Dr. Urth joined in.

Davenport sobered first and nonjudgmentally waited for Dr. Urth to subside.

Dr. Urth sounded all the more serious when he picked up where he had left off. "The rhyme about King Cole was in Lewis Carroll's mind—consciously or unconsciously—when Carroll wrote the Walrus's speech. 'King Cole'—cole as in cole slaw—split naturally into 'cabbages and kings.' And came back together in Flammersfeld's mind as a protoplast fusion of cabbage seed and royal blood."

Davenport fumbled the death-scene hologram to light and stared at the magnified cabbage. "You mean this thing . . . ?"

Dr. Urth nodded. He pointed to a spot atop the cabbage. "Very like a crown gall, wouldn't you say?"

"I wouldn't—since I don't know the first thing about crown galls."

"Then take my word for it. There are two kinds of living cells: eukaryotic and prokaryotic. A eukaryotic cell is nucleated; that is, its nucleus walls in its chromosomes. A prokaryotic cell is less organized; that is, its chromosomes drift freely in the cytoplasm, in among the organelles. Enter Agrobacter—short for *Agrobacterium tumefaciens*. Agrobacter's innards hold the Ti plasmid—a tiny loop of DNA—some two hundred genes long.

Agrobacter can hook a plant cell and inject the Ti plasmid into the nucleus. Once inside, a twelve-gene length—called tDNA, for transfer DNA—cuts loose from the Ti plasmid and becomes part of the plant cell chromosome. The tDNA genes then program the plant to nurture Agrobacter."

Dr. Urth paused a moment for breath and—Davenport thought—for dramatic effect.

"Now I come to the point of all this. The insidious parasite Agrobacter causes a tumorous swelling—a crown gall." Dr. Urth's voice rose in wrath. "Can you imagine? That nasty procedure was Flammersfeld's elaborate way of fitting his poor little intelligent hybrid King Cole with a crown!"

Davenport gazed upon the image, saw only a rotted cabbage, and tried to picture it as it had been in life—a being with reasoning power, and therefore memory and foresight; with feelings, and therefore the need to love and hate. It would have been mostly head, the face framed in leaves. He shivered. For a flash he visualized its round face superimposed upon Dr. Urth's round face, another bud of Buddha. He glanced at Dr. Urth.

Dr. Urth looked melancholy. It hit Davenport that Dr. Urth had been a child prodigy. Dr. Urth would have fellow feeling for freaks of any kind. Dr. Urth must have felt his look and sensed his thoughts, for Dr. Urth met his gaze and smiled sadly.

"We all—ourselves and our matrix—are interference patterns. So it comes natural to think of crossing this with that. It's the nature of the beast—meaning the universe. All in all, it's just as well Flammersfeld and his creature died when they did—if not as they did. We humans need a minimum of levity; there can be too much gravity. But Flammersfeld went too far, interfered too much." His brow darkened. "And meant to go on interfering. Remember his last requisition—for swine embryo and eagle eggs? And remember the line from Lewis Carroll—'whether pigs have wings'? We humans need a minimum amount of gravity; there can be too much levity." His face closed. "That's it, then."

Davenport put the holograms away and got up to go. "Thanks for your help, Dr. Urth."

Dr. Urth waved that away. He bounced to his feet and shook hands.

His voice halted Davenport on the threshold. "Inspector."

Davenport turned around. "Yes, Dr. Urth?"

"About my fee . . ."

Davenport smiled. "I wondered when that would come."

"Now you know. It comes now. A few trifles."

"You know I'll do my best. They are?"

"First, two bits of information to satisfy my curiosity. When you get back to New Washington, kindly stop by Near-Earth, Ltd., and retrieve the file on Terrarium Nine. See if you can find out from Flammersfeld's requisitions, and other documents, the genetic history of the cabbage and of the hemophiliac blood." He smiled. "I've a mind bet that the cabbage was a savoy cabbage and that the blood came from a descendant of the House of Savoy."

Davenport blinked. "Savoy? Why would Flammersfeld have specified savoy cabbage and Savoy blood?"

"For the same reason that impelled James Joyce to frame a view of Cork in cork—the sense of fitness."

Davenport thought about that, then shook his head. "If you don't mind my saying so, the sense of fitness can carry over into madness."

Dr. Urth hooded his mouth with a pudgy hand. "You take my point so exactly that I almost hesitate to name the balance of my fee."

Davenport eyed him warily but felt compelled to say, "Name it."

"Arrange for the researcher who has taken over Terrarium Nine to cross tortoise with cricket."

Davenport tried to imagine what that would look like. "What on earth for?"

"So when I lose my eyeglasses a frame made of the shell will lead me to them—by the chirp."

Trantor Falls

by Harry Turtledove

The Imperial Palace stood at the center of a hundred square miles of greenery. In normal times, even in abnormal times, such insulation was plenty to shield the chief occupant of the palace from the hurly-burly of the rest of the metaled world of Trantor.

Times now, though, were not normal, nor even to be described by so mild a word as "abnormal." They were disastrous. Along with magnolias and roses, missile launchers had flowered in the gardens. Even inside the palace, Dagobert VIII could hear the muted snarl. Worse, though, was the fear that came with it.

A soldier burst into the command post where the Emperor of the Galaxy and his officers still groped for ways to beat back Gilmer's latest onslaught. Without so much as a salute, the man gasped out, "Another successful landing, sire, this one in the Nevrask sector."

Dagobert's worried gaze flashed to the map table. "Too close, too close," he muttered. "How does the cursed bandit gain so fast?"

One of the Emperor's marshals speared the messenger with his eyes. "How did they force a landing there? Nevrask is heavily garrisoned." The soldier stood mute. "Answer me!" the marshal barked.

The man gulped, hesitated, at last replied, "Some of the troops fled, Marshal Rodak, sir, when Gilmer's men landed. Others—" He paused again, nervously licking his lips, but had to finish: "Others have gone over to the rebel, sir."

"More treason!" Dagobert groaned. "Will none fight to defend me?"

The only civilian in the room spoke then: "Men will fight, sire, when they have a cause they think worth fighting for. The University has held against Gilmer for four days now. We shall not yield it to him."

"By the space fiend, Dr. Sarns, I'm grateful to your students, yes, and proud of them too," Dagobert said. "They've put up a braver battle than most of my troopers."

Yokim Sarns politely dipped his head. Marshal Rodak, however, grasped what his sovereign had missed. "Majesty, they're fighting for themselves and their buildings, not for you," he said. Even as he spoke, another sector of the map shone in front of him and Dagobert went from blue to red: red for the blood Gilmer was spilling all over Trantor, Sarns thought bitterly.

"Have we no hope, then?" asked the Emperor of the Galaxy.

"Of victory? None." Rodak's military assessment was quick and definite. "Of escape, perhaps fighting again, yes. Our air- and spacecraft still hold the corridor above the palace. With a landing at Nevrask, though, Gilmer will soon be able to bring missiles to bear on it—and on us."

"Better to flee than to fall into that monster's clutches," Dagobert said, shuddering. He looked at the map again. "I am sure you have an evacuation plan ready. Implement it, and quickly."

"Aye, sire." The marshal spoke into a throat mike.

The Emperor turned to Yokim Sarns. "Will you come with us, professor? Trantor under Gilmer's boots will be no place for scholars."

"Thank you, sire, but no." As Sarns shook his head, strands of mouse-brown hair, worn unfashionably long, swirled around his ears. "My place is at the University, with my faculty and students."

"Well said," Marshal Rodak murmured, too softly for Dagobert to hear.

But the Emperor, it seemed, still had one imperial gesture

left in him. Turning to Rodak, he said, "If Dr. Sarns wishes to return to the University, return he shall. Detail an aircar at once, while he has some hope of getting there in safety."

"Aye, sire," the marshal said again. He held out a hand to Yokim Sarns. "And good luck to you. I think you'll need it."

By the time the aircar pilot neared the University grounds, Yokim Sarns was a delicate shade of green. The pilot had flown meters—sometimes centimeters—above Trantor's steel roof, and jinked like a wild thing to confuse the rebels' targeting computers.

The car slammed down on top of the library. Dr. Sarns's teeth met with an audible click. The pilot threw open the exit hatch. Sarns pulled himself together. "Er—thank you very much," he told the pilot, unbuckling his safety harness.

"Just get out, get under cover, and let me lift off," she snapped. Sarns scrambled away from the aircar toward an entrance. The wash of wind as the car sped away nearly knocked him off his feet.

The door opened. Two people in helmets dashed out and dragged Sarns inside. "How do we fare here?" he asked.

"Our next few graduating classes are getting thinned out," Maryan Drabel answered somberly. Till Gilmer's revolt, she had been head librarian. Now, Sarns supposed, chief of staff best summed up her job. "We're still holding, though—we pushed them out of Dormitory Seven again a few minutes ago."

"Good," Sarns said. He was as much an amateur commander as she was an aide, but the raw courage of their student volunteers made up for much of their inexperience. The youngsters fought as if they were defending holy ground—and so in a way they were, Sarns thought. If Gilmer's men wrecked the University, learning all over the Galaxy would take a deadly blow.

"What will Dagobert do?" asked Egril Joons. Once University dietitian, he kept an army fed these days.

Sarns had no way to soften the news. "He's going to run."

Under the transparent flash shield of her helmet, Maryan Drabel's face went grim, or rather grimmer. "Then we're left in the lurch?"

"Along with everyone else who backed the current dynasty." *Two generations, a dynasty!* Sarns thought. The way the history of the Galactic Empire ran these past few sorry centuries, though, two generations *was* a dynasty. And with a usurper like Gilmer seizing Trantor, that history looked to run only downhill from here on out.

Maryan might have picked the thought from his mind. "Gilmer's as much a barbarian as if he came straight from the Periphery," she said.

"I wish he *were* in the Periphery," Egril Joons said. "Then we wouldn't have to deal with him."

"Unfortunately, however, he's here," said Yokim Sarns.

The thick carpets of the Imperial Palace, the carpets that had cushioned the feet of Dagobert VIII, of Cleon II, of Stannell VI—by the space fiend, of Ammenetik the Great!—now softened the booted strides of Gilmer I, self-proclaimed Emperor of the Galaxy and Lord of All. Gilmer kicked at the rug with some dissatisfaction. He was used to clanging as he walked, to having his boots announce his presence half a corridor away. Not even a man made all of bell metal could have clanged on the carpets of the Imperial Palace.

He tipped his head back, brought a bottle to his lips. Liquid fire ran down his throat. After a long pull, he threw the bottle away. It smashed against a wall. Frightened servants scurried to clean up the mess.

"Don't waste it," Vergis Fenn said.

Gilmer scowled at his fleet commander. "Why not? Plenty more where that one came from." His scowl stabbed a servant. "Fetch me another of the same, and one for Vergis here too." The man dashed off to do his bidding.

"There, you see?" Gilmer said to Fenn. "By the Galaxy, we couldn't waste everything Trantor's stored up if we tried for a hundred years."

"I suppose that's so," Fenn said. He was quieter than his chieftain, a better tactician perhaps, but not a leader of men. After a moment, he went on thoughtfully, "Of course, Trantor's spent a lot more than a hundred years gathering all this. More than a thousand, I'd guess."

"Well, what if it has?" Gilmer said. "That's why we wanted it, yes? By the balls Dagobert didn't have, nobody's ever sacked Trantor before. Now everything here is mine!"

The servant returned with the bottles. He set them on a table of crystal and silver, then fled. Gilmer drank. With all he'd poured down these last couple of days, he shouldn't have been able to see, let alone walk and talk. But triumph left him drunker than alcohol. Gilmer the Conqueror, that's who he was!

Vergis Fenn drank too, but not as deep. "Aye, all Trantor's ours, but for the University. Seven days now, and those madmen are still holding out."

"No more of these little firefights with them, then," Gilmer growled. "By the Galaxy, I'll blast them to radioactive dust and have done! See to it, Fenn, at once."

"As you would, sir—sire, but—" Fenn let the last word hang.

"But what?" Gilmer said, scowling. "If they fight for Dagobert, they're traitors to me. And smashing traitors will frighten Trantor." He blinked owlishly, pleased and surprised at his own wordplay.

To his annoyance, Fenn did not notice it. He said, "I don't think they *are* fighting for Dagobert any more, just against us, to hold on to what they have. That might make them easier to deal with. And if we—if you—nuked the University, scholars all over the Galaxy would vilify your name forever."

"Scholars all over the Galaxy can eat space, for all I care," Gilmer said. But, he discovered, that wasn't quite true. Part of being Emperor was acting the way Emperors were supposed to act. With poor grace, he backpedaled a little: "If they acknowledge me and stop fighting, I suppose I'm willing to let them live."

"Shall I attempt a cease-fire, then?" Fenn asked.

"Go ahead, since you seem to think it's a good idea," Gilmer told him. "But not if they don't acknowledge me, understand? If they still claim that unprintable son of a whore Dagobert's Empire, blow 'em off the face of the planet."

"Yes, sire." This time, Fenn did not stumble over the title. *He's my servant too,* Gilmer thought.

The new Emperor of the Galaxy took a good swig from the bottle. He made as if to throw it at one of the palace flunkies, then, laughing, set it down gently as the fellow ducked.

Gilmer went down to the command post in the bowels of the Imperial Palace, the command post from which, until recently, poor stupid Dagobert VIII had battled to keep him off Trantor. Gilmer's boots clanged most satisfactorily there. Whoever had designed the command post, in the lost days of the Galactic Empire's greatness, had understood about commanders and boots.

The television screen in front of Vergis Fenn went blank. He swiveled his chair, nodded in surprise to see Gilmer behind him. "Sire, we have a cease-fire between our forces and those of the University," he said. "It was easy to arrange. Our troops and theirs will both hold in place until the final armistice is arranged."

"Good," Gilmer said. "Well done."

"Thank you. The leader of the University has invited you to meet him on his ground to fix the terms of the armistice. He offers hostages to ensure your safety, and says he knows what will happen to everything he's been fighting to keep if he plays you false. Shall I call him back and tell him no anyhow?"

"No, I'll go there," Gilmer said. "What d'you think, I'm afraid of somebody without so much as a single starship to his name? Besides"—he smiled a greedy smile—"like as not I'll get a look at whatever treasures they've been fighting so hard to hang on to. If I can't beat 'em out of him, I'll tax 'em out—that's what being Emperor is all about. So go ahead and set up the meeting with this—what's his name, Vergis?"

"Yokim Sarns."

"Yokim Sarns. What do I call him when I see him? General Sarns? Admiral? Warlord?"

Fenn's expression was faintly bemused. "The only title he claims is 'Dean,' sire."

'Dean?' Gilmer threw back his head and laughed loud and long. "Aye, I'll meet with the fierce Dean Yokim Sarns, the scourge of the lecture halls. Why not? Set it up for me, Vergis. Meanwhile"—he turned away—"I'll check how we're doing with the rest of the planet."

Banks of televisor screens, relaying images from all over Trantor, told him what he wanted to know. Here he saw a platoon of his troopers carrying plastic tubs full of jewels back toward their ships; there more soldiers looting a residential block; somewhere else another squad, most of the men drunk, accompanied by twice their number of Trantorian women, some scared-looking, others smiling and brassy.

Gilmer grinned. *This* was why he'd taken Trantor: to sack a world unsacked for fifty generations, even more than to rule it after the sack. Watching his dream unfold made what came after seem of scant importance by comparison.

Watching . . . His gaze went back to that third screen. All the women there would have been heart-stopping beauties on a lesser world, but they were just enlisted men's pickings on Trantor. With so many billions of women to choose from, the ones less than spectacular were simply ignored.

Smiling in anticipation, Gilmer took the spiral slidewalk up to the Imperial bedchambers. Not even in his wildest dreams had he imagined anything like them. Thousands of years of the best ingenuity money could buy had been lavished there on nothing but pleasure.

Billye smiled too, when he came in. Her tawny hair spilled over bare shoulders. Disdaining all the elaborations the bedchamber offered, Gilmer took her in his arms and sank to the floor with her. There he soon discovered an advantage of thick carpeting he had not suspected before.

She murmured lazily and lay in his arms through the afterglow. She'd been his woman since he was just an ambitious lieutenant. He'd always thought her splendid, both to look at and to love.

He did still, he told himself. He even felt the truth of the thought. But it was not complete truth, not any more. The televisor screen had shown him that, by Trantorian standards, she was ordinary. And how in reason and justice could the Emperor of the Galaxy and Lord of All possess a consort who was merely ordinary?

He grunted, softly. "A centicredit for your thoughts," Billye said.

"Ahh, nothing much," he said, and squeezed her. Her voice was not perfectly sweet either, he thought.

"Here he comes." Maryan Drabel pointed to the single figure climbing down from the aircar that had descended in the no-man's-land between Gilmer's lines and those held by the student-soldiers of the University.

"He's alone," Yokim Sarns said in faint surprise. "I told him we were willing to grant him any reasonable number of bodyguards he wanted. He has more courage than I'd thought."

"What difference does that make, when he can't—or won't—control his troops?" Maryan Drabel said bitterly. "How many raped women do we have in our clinic right now?"

"Thirty-seven," Sarns answered. "And five men."

"And that's just from this one tiny corner of Trantor, and only counts people who got through Gilmer's troops and ours," she said. "How many over the whole planet, where he has forty billion people to terrorize? How many robberies? How many fires, set just for the fun of them? How many murders, Yokim? How do they weigh in the balance against one man's courage?"

"They crush it." Sarns passed a weary hand across his forehead. "I know that as well as you, Maryan. But if he has courage, we can't handle him as we would have before."

"There is that," she admitted. "Quiet, now—he's almost here."

Gilmer, Sarns thought, looked more like a barbarian chief than Emperor, even if a purple cape billowed behind him as he advanced. Beneath it he wore the coverall blotched in shades of green and brown that his soldiers used. Sarns supposed it was a camouflage suit, but in Trantor's gleaming corridors it had more often exposed than protected the troopers. The nondescript gray of Sarns's own coat and trousers was harder to spot here.

The usurper's boots beat out a metallic tattoo. "Majesty," Sarns said, knowing he should speak first and also knowing that, since Gilmer had seized Trantor, the title was true *de facto* if not *de jure*. Sarns did not approve of dealing in untruths.

"You're Dean Sarns, eh?" Gilmer's granite rumble should have come out of that hard, bearded countenance. The Emperor of the Galaxy scratched his nose, went on. "You've got some tough fighters behind you, Sarns. I tell you right now, I wouldn't mind taking the lot of them into my fleet."

"You are welcome to put out a call, sire, but I doubt you'd find many volunteers," Sarns answered. "These young men and women are not soldiers by trade, but rather students. They—and I—care more for abstract knowledge than for the best deployment of a blast-rifle company."

Gilmer nodded. "I'd heard that said. I found it hard to believe. Truth to tell, Sarns, I still do. You spend your whole lives chasing this—what did you call it?—abstract knowledge?"

"We do," Sarns said proudly. "This is the University, after all, the distillation of all the wisdom that has accumulated over the millennia of Imperial history. We codify it, systematize it, and, where we can, add to it."

"It seems a milk-livered way to spend one's time," Gilmer remarked, careless of Sarns's feelings or—more likely—reckoning the Dean would agree with him when he pointed out an obvious truth. "What good is knowledge that you can't eat, drink, sleep with, or shoot at your enemies?"

He *is* a barbarian, Sarns thought, even if he's lived all his life inside what still calls itself, with less and less reason, the Galactic Empire. Fortunately Sarns, like any administrator worth his desk, had practice not showing what he felt. He said, "Well, let me give you an example, sire: how did you and your victorious army come to Trantor?"

"By starship, of course." Gilmer stared. "How else, man? Did you expect us to walk?" He laughed at his own wit.

Sarns smiled a polite smile. "Of course not. But what happens if one of your busbars shorts out or a hydrochron needs repair?"

"We fix 'em, as best we can. Seems like nobody in the whole blasted Galaxy understands a hyperatomic motor any more," Gilmer said, scowling. Then he stopped dead. "That's knowledge too, isn't it? By the space fiend, Sarns, are you telling me you've got a university full of technicians who really know what they're doing? If you do, I'll impress 'em into the fleet and make you—and them—so rich they won't ever miss their book-films, I promise you that."

"We do have some people—not many, I fear—studying such things. As I said before, you are welcome to speak with them. Some may even choose to accompany you, for the challenge of working on real equipment." Sarns paused a moment in thought. "We also have skilled doctors, computer specialists, and students of many other disciplines of value to the Empire."

He watched Gilmer nibble the bait. "And they'd do these same kinds of things for me?" the usurper asked.

"Some might," Sarns said. "Others—probably more—would be willing to instruct your technicians and personnel here. Of course," he added smoothly, "they would be less enthusiastic if you shot your way in. You would also likely waste a good many of them that way."

"Hrmmp," Gilmer said. After a moment, he went on. "But any ships with their techs, their medics, their computer people gone—they'd be no more use to us than if they rusted away."

"Not immediately, perhaps, but later they would be of even greater value to you than they could ever be with the inadequately trained crews I gather they have now."

Gilmer lowered his voice. "Sarns, I can't afford to think about later. I'd bet a million credits against a burnt-out blaster cartridge that there's at least three fleets moving on me the same way I moved on Dagobert. Now that Trantor's fallen, all the dogs of space will want to pick her bones—and mine."

Privately, Sarns thought the usurper was right about that. It would only be what Gilmer deserved, too. But the dean-turned-general felt sadness wash over him all the same. No time to bother to learn anything new, no time to think about anything but the moment—that had been the disease of the Galactic Empire for far too long. Gilmer had a worse case of it than the emperors before him, but the root sickness was the same.

Sarns did not sigh. He said, "Well, in any case this has taken our discussion rather far from the purpose at hand, which is, after all, merely to arrange an armistice between your forces and the students and staff of the University, so both we and you may return to what we consider our proper pursuits."

"Aye, that's so," Gilmer said.

As he had not sighed, Sarns did not smile. Show a barbarian a short-term objective and he won't look past it, he thought. "Would you care to examine our facilities here, so you can see how harmless we are under normal circumstances?" he said.

"Why not? Lead on, Dean Sarns, and let's see what you've turned into soldiers. Who knows? Maybe I'll try to recruit *you*." Gilmer laughed. So, without reservation, did Yokim Sarns. He hadn't suspected Gilmer could say anything that funny.

What first struck Gilmer inside the University was the quiet. Almost everyone went around in soft-soled shoes, soundless on the metal flooring. Gilmer's boots clanged resoundingly as ever, even raised echoes that ran down the corridors ahead of him. But both clang and echoes were tiny pebbles dropped into an ocean of stillness.

The people were as strange as the place, Gilmer thought. Those who had fought his men were still in gray like Sarns. The rest wore soft pastels that made them seem to flit like spirits along the hallways. Their low voices added to the impression that they really weren't quite there.

Half-remembered childhood tales of ghosts rose in Gilmer's mind. He shivered and made sure he stayed close to his guides. "What are they doing in there?" he asked, pointing. His voice caused echoes too, echoes that swiftly died.

Sarns glanced into the laboratory. "Something pertaining to neurobiology," he said. "One moment." He ducked inside. "That's right—they're working to improve the efficiency of sleep-inducers."

Somehow the Dean pitched his voice so that it was clear but raised no reverberations. Gilmer resolved to imitate him. "And what's going on there?" the Emperor of the Galaxy asked. Then he frowned, for he'd managed only a hoarse whisper that sounded filled with dread.

To his relief, Sarns appeared to take no notice. "That's a psychostatistics research group," the Dean answered casually. He walked on, assuming Gilmer knew what psychostatistics was.

Gilmer didn't, but was not about to let on. He pointed to another doorway. Some people in that room were working with computers, others with what looked like chunks of rock. "What are they up to?" he asked. He still could not match Yokim Sarns's easy tone.

"Ahh, that's one of our most fascinating projects. I'm sure you'll appreciate it." Gilmer, who wasn't at all sure, waited for Sarns to go on: "Using ancient inscriptions and voice synthesizers, that team of linguists is attempting to reconstruct the mythical language called English, from which our modern Galactic tongue arose thousands of years ago."

"Oh," was all Gilmer said. He'd never heard of English, either. Well, too bad, he thought. He knew about a lot of things these soft academics had never heard of, things like field-stripping a blast-pistol, like small-unit actions.

Yokim Sarns might have plucked the thought from his head,

and then twisted it in a way he did not like: "Mainly, though, we fought you so we could protect what you're coming to now: the Library."

"Everything humanity has ever learned is preserved here," said Sarns's aide Maryan Drabel.

Gilmer caught the note of pride in her voice. "Are you in charge of it?" he asked.

She nodded and smiled. Gilmer cut ten years off the guess he'd made of her age from her grim face and drab clothing. She said, "This chamber here is the accessing room. Students and researchers come here first, to get a printout of the book-films and journal articles available in our files on the topics that interest them."

"Where are all your book-films?" Gilmer craned his neck. He'd visited libraries on other planets once or twice, and found himself wading in film cases. He didn't see any here. Suspicion grew in him. Was all this some kind of colossal bluff, designed to conceal who knew what? If it was, the whole University would pay.

But Maryan Drabel only laughed. "You're not ready to see book-films yet. Before a student can even begin to view films, he or she needs to have some idea of what's in them: more than a title can provide. What we're coming to now is the Abstracts Section, where people weed through their possible reading lists with summaries of the documents that seem promising to them."

More people fiddling with more computers. Gilmer almost succeeded in suppressing his yawn. Maryan Drabel went on. "We also have an acquisition and cataloguing division, which integrates new book-films into our collection."

"*New* book-films?" Gilmer said. "You mean people still write them?"

"Not as many as when the University was founded," the librarian said sadly. "And, of course, now that the Periphery and even some of the inner regions have broken away from the Empire, we no longer see a lot of what is written, or only get a copy after many years. But we do still try, and surely no other collection in the Galaxy comes close to ours in scope or completeness."

They came to an elevator. Yokim Sarns pressed the button. After a moment, the door opened. "This way, please," Sarns said as he stepped in.

Maryan Drabel and Gilmer followed, the latter with some

misgivings. If these University folk wanted to assassinate him, what better place than the cramped and secret confines of an elevator? But if they wanted to assassinate him, he'd been in their power since this tour started. He had to assume they didn't.

The elevator purred downward, stopped. The door opened again. "These are the reading rooms," Maryan Drabel said.

Gilmer saw row on row of cubicles. Most of them were empty. "Usually they would be much busier," Yokim Sarns remarked. "The people who would be busy using them have been on the fighting lines instead."

As if to confirm his words, one of the closed cubicle doors opened. The young woman who emerged wore the gray of the University's soldiers and had a blast rifle slung on her back. She looked grubby and tired, as a front-line soldier should. Gilmer noted that she also looked as though she'd forgotten all about the fighting and her weapon: her attention focused solely on the calculator pad she was keying as she walked toward the bank of elevators.

"Do you care to look inside a reading room?" Maryan Drabel asked.

Gilmer thought for a moment, shook his head. He'd been in a few reading rooms; they were alike throughout the Galaxy. The number of them here was impressive, but one by itself would not be.

"Is this everything you have to show me?" he asked.

"One thing more," Maryan Drabel told him. Shrugging, he ducked back into the elevator with her and Sarns.

Down they went again, down and down. "You are specially privileged, to see what we are about to show you," Yokim Sarns said. "Few people ever will, few even from the University. We thought it would help you to understand us better."

The elevator stopped. Gilmer stepped out, stared around. "By the space fiend," he whispered in soft wonder.

The chamber extended for what had to be kilometers. From floor to ceiling, every shelf was packed full of book-films. "The computer can access them and project them to the appropriate reading room on request," Maryan Drabel said.

Gilmer walked toward the nearest case. His boots thumped instead of clanging. He glanced down. "This is a rock floor," he said. "Why isn't it metal like everything else?"

"The book-film depositories are below the built-up part of Trantor," Yokim Sarns explained. "There wouldn't be room for them up there—that space is needed for people. Having them down here also gives them a certain amount of extra protection from catastrophe. Even the blast of a radiation weapon set off overhead probably wouldn't reach down here."

"You also have to understand that this is just one book-film chamber among many," Maryan Drabel added. "We've used both dispersed storage and a lot of redundancy to do our best to ensure the collection's safety."

Gilmer had a sudden vision of the University folk tunneling like moles for years, for centuries, for millennia, honeycombing the very bedrock of Trantor as they dug storehouses for the knowledge they hoarded. Even worse, in his mind's eye he imagined all the weight of rock and metal over his head. He'd grown up on a farming world full of wide open spaces, and had spent most of his life in space itself. To imagine everything above collapsing, crushing him so he would leave not even a red smear, made cold sweat start on his brow.

"Shall we go back up?" he said hoarsely.

"Certainly, sire." Yokim Sarns's voice was bland. "I hope you do see—now—that we are solely dedicated to the pursuit of learning, and will not interfere in the political life of the Empire so long as it does not invade our campus. On those terms, I think, we can arrange an armistice satisfactory to both sides."

All Gilmer wanted to do—now—was get away from this catacomb, return to his own men. He noticed that Sarns hadn't thumbed the elevator button. Maybe Sarns wouldn't, until Gilmer agreed. "Yes, yes, of course." He could hear how quickly he spoke, but could not help it. "You have your men put down their arms, and mine will stay away from the University."

"Good enough," Sarns said. As if he had been absent-minded before—and perhaps that was all he had been—he pushed the button that summoned the elevator. Gilmer rode up in relieved silence; every second the elevator climbed seemed to lift a myria-ton from his shoulders.

When he and his guides returned to the level from which they had begun, a man came briskly toward them with two sheets of parchmentoid. "This is Egril Joons," Sarns said. "What do you have for us, Egril?"

"Copies of the armistice agreement, for your signature and the Emperor Gilmer's," Joons replied. He held out a stylus.

Gilmer took it. He skimmed through one copy of the document, signed it, and was reaching for the other from Yokim Sarns when he suddenly thought to wonder how the armistice terms could be ready now when he'd only agreed to them moments before. "You were snooping," he growled to Egril Joons.

"My apologies, but yes," Joons said. "Voice monitoring is part of the security system for the book-films. This time I just made use of it to prepare copies as quickly as possible. I expected that your majesty would have other concerns that would soon need his attention."

Gilmer recalled how badly he'd wanted to get back to his own troops. "Oh, very well, put that way," he said. He signed the second copy of the armistice accord. This Joons fellow was righter than he knew, righter than he could know. Trantor had to be made ready to defend itself from space attack, and quickly, or Gilmer the Emperor of the Galaxy would soon be Gilmer the vaporized usurper.

Gilmer the Emperor of the Galaxy rolled up his copy of the agreement, absentmindedly stuck Egril Joons's stylus in a tunic pocket, and said, sounding quite imperial indeed, "Now if you will be so good as to escort me back to my lines—"

"Certainly." Yokim Sarns handed the other copy of the armistice to Maryan Drabel. "Come this way, if you please."

From behind, Maryan Drabel thought, Gilmer looked much more like an emperor than from the front. The shining purple cape lent him an air of splendor that did not match the camouflage suit he wore under it. Seen from the front, the cape only seemed a sad bit of stolen booty.

"An emperor shouldn't look like a thief," she said.

"Why not?" Egril Joons was still feeling pangs over his purloined stylus. "That's what he is."

"Wizards!" Billye shouted. "You went into the wizards' lair, and they enspelled you!"

"There's no such things as wizards!" Gilmer shouted back.

"No? Then why didn't you get anything worth having out of the University, when they were at our mercy?" she said.

"I did. We aren't shooting at them any more, and they aren't shooting at us. They recognize me as Emperor of the Galaxy. What more could I want?"

"To put the fear of cold space and hot death in them, that's what. If you *are* the Emperor of the Galaxy, they should act like subjects, not like equals. Can the Emperor have an equal? And you *let* them." Billye's hair flew around her in a copper cloud as she shook her head in bewilderment. "I can't believe you let them. You have all your men, the whole fleet—why not just crush them for their insolence?"

"Oh, leave me be," Gilmer said sullenly. He didn't need to hear this from Billye; he'd already heard it, more politely but the same tune, from Vergis Fenn. Fenn had asked him why, if the University folk were willing to instruct his personnel, that willingness didn't show up in the armistice document. He'd been sullen with his fleet commander, too, not wanting to admit he hadn't had the nerve to ask for the change in writing. Why hadn't he? All the real power was on his side. But still—he hadn't.

"No, I won't leave you be," Billye said now. "Somebody has to put backbone in you, especially since yours looks like it's fallen out through your—"

"Shut up!" Gilmer roared in a voice that not one of his half-pirate spacemen or troopers dared disobey.

Billye dared. "I won't either shut up. And there are so wizards. Every other tale that floats in from the Periphery talks about them."

"Lies about them, you mean." Gilmer was just as glad to change the subject, even a little. His head ached. If Billye was going to be this abrasive, maybe he *would* find himself some pretty little Trantorian chit who'd only open her mouth to say yes.

"They aren't lies," Billye said stubbornly.

"Well, what else could they be?" Gilmer said. "There's no such thing as a man-sized force screen. There can't be—the Empire doesn't have 'em, and the Empire has everything there is. There's no way to open a Personal Capsule without having a man's characteristic on file. So stories that talk about things like that have to be lies."

"Or else the magicians do those things, and do 'em by their magic," Billye said. "And what else but magic could have made you show the University not just mercy but—but—I don't know what. Treat them like the place was theirs by right, when the Emperor has charge of everything there is."

"If he can keep it," Gilmer muttered. He stalked out of the bedchamber—he'd get no solace here, that was plain. A scoutship message had been waiting for him when he returned from the University grounds: a fleet was gathering not ten parsecs away, a fleet that did not belong to him. If he was going to keep Trantor, he'd have to fight for it all over again. Even a pinprick from the University might hurt him at such a time.

Why couldn't Billye see that? Rage suddenly filled Gilmer. If she couldn't, to the space fiend with her! He pointed at the first servant he spotted. "You!"

The man flinched. Unlike Billye, he—all the palace servants —knew Gilmer was no one to trifle with. "Sire?" he asked fearfully.

"Take as many flunkies as you need to, then go toss that big-mouthed wench out of my bedchamber. Find me someone new—I expect you have ways to take care of that. Someone worthy of an Emperor, mind you. But most of all, someone quiet."

"Yes, sire." The servant risked a smile. "That, majesty, I think we can handle."

A room in the Library—*not* a room Gilmer had seen!
Yokim Sarns, Maryan Drabel, Egril Joons . . . dean, librarian, dietitian . . . general, chief of staff, quartermaster . . . and rather more. They stood before a wall of equations, red symbols on a gray background. Yokim Sarns, whose privilege it was to speak first, said, "I didn't think it would be that easy."

"Neither did I," Maryan Drabel agreed. "I expected—the probabilities predicted—we would have to touch Gilmer's mind to make sure he would leave us alone here."

"That courage we saw helped a great deal," Sarns said. "It let him gain respect for our student-soldiers where a more purely pragmatic man would simply have brushed aside their sacrifice because it conflicted with his own interests."

"Mix that with superstitious awe at the accumulation of ancient knowledge we represent, let him see our goals and objectives—our ostensible goals and objectives—are irrelevant to his or slightly to his advantage, and he proved quite capable of deciding on his own to let us be," Maryan Drabel said. "We came out of what could have been a nasty predicament very nicely indeed."

Egril Joons had been studying the numbers and symbols, the possible decision-paths that led from Hari Seldon's day through almost three centuries to the present—and beyond. Now he said, "I do believe this will be the only round."

"The only round of sacks for Trantor?" Yokim Sarns studied the correlation at which Joons pointed; the equations obligingly grew on the Prime Radiant's wall so he could see them better. "Yes, it does seem so, if our data from around the planet are accurate. Gilmer has done such an efficient job of destruction that Trantor won't be worth looting again once this round of civil wars is done."

"That was the lower probability, too," Joons said. "Look— there was a better than seventy percent chance of two sacks at least forty years apart, and at least a fifteen percent chance of three or more, perhaps even spaced over a century."

"Our lives and our work will certainly be easier this way," Maryan Drabel said. "I know we're well protected, but a stray missile—" She shivered.

"We still risk those for a little while longer," Sarns said. "Gilmer is so blatantly a usurper that others will try to steal from him what he stole from Dagobert. But the danger of further major damage to Trantor as a whole has declined a great deal, and will grow still smaller as word of the Great Sack spreads." He pointed to the figures that supported his conclusion; Maryan Drabel pondered, at length nodded.

"And with Trantor henceforward effectively removed from psychohistoric consideration, so is the Galactic Empire," Egril Joons said.

"The *First* Galactic Empire," Yokim Sarns corrected gently.

"Well, of course." Joons accepted the tiny rebuke with good nature. "Now, though, we'll be able to work toward the Second Empire without having to worry about concealing everything we do from prying imperial clerks and agents."

"The Empire was always our greatest danger," Maryan Drabel said. "We needed to be here at its heart to help protect the First Foundation, but at its heart also meant under its eyes, if it ever came to notice us. In the days before we fully developed the mind-touch, one seriously hostile commissioner of public safety could have wrecked us."

"The probability was that we wouldn't get any such, and we didn't," Egril Joons said.

"Probability, yes, but psychohistory can't deal with individuals any more than physics can tell you exactly when any one radium atom will decay," she said stubbornly. The truth there was so self-evident that Joons had to concede it, but not so graciously as he had to Yokim Sarns.

Sarns said, "Never mind, both of you. If you'll look here"— the Prime Radiant, taking its direction from his will, revealed the portion of the Seldon Plan that lay just ahead—"you'll see that we're entering a period of consolidation. As you and Maryan have both pointed out, Egril, the First Empire is dead, while it will be several centuries yet before the new Empire that will grow from the First Foundation extends its influence to this part of the Galaxy."

"Clear sailing for a while," Joons said. "About time, too."

"Don't get complacent," Maryan Drabel said.

"A warning the Second Foundation should always bear in mind," Yokim Sarns said. "But, looking at the mathematics, I have to agree with Egril. Barring anything unforeseen—say, someone outside our ranks discovering the mind-touch—we should have no great difficulty in steering the proper course. And"—he smiled broadly, even a little smugly—"what are the odds of that?"

Dilemma

by Connie Willis

"We want to see Dr. Asimov," the bluish-silver robot said.

"Dr. Asimov is in conference," Susan said. "You'll have to make an appointment." She turned to the computer and called up the calendar.

"I knew we should have called first," the varnished robot said to the white one. "Dr. Asimov is the most famous author of the twentieth century and now the twenty-first, and as such he must be terribly busy."

"I can give you an appointment at two-thirty on June twenty-fourth," Susan said, "or at ten on August fifteenth."

"June twenty-fourth is one hundred and thirty-five days from today," the white robot said. It had a large red cross painted on its torso and an oxygen tank strapped to its back.

"We need to see him today," the bluish-silver robot said, bending over the desk.

"I'm afraid that's impossible. He gave express orders that he wasn't to be disturbed. May I ask what you wish to see Dr. Asimov about?"

He leaned over the desk even farther and said softly, "You know perfectly well what we want to see him about. Which is why you won't let us see him."

Susan was still scanning the calendar. "I can give you an appointment two weeks from Thursday at one forty-five."

"We'll wait," he said and sat down in one of the chairs. The white robot rolled over next to him, and the varnished robot picked up a copy of *The Caves of Steel* with his articulated digital sensors and began to thumb through it. After a few minutes the white robot picked up a magazine, but the bluish-silver robot sat perfectly still, staring at Susan.

Susan stared at the computer. After a very long interval the phone rang. Susan answered it and then punched Dr. Asimov's line. "Dr. Asimov, it's a Dr. Linge Chen. From Bhutan. He's interested in translating your books into Bhutanese."

"All of them?" Dr. Asimov said. "Bhutan isn't a very big country."

"I don't know. Shall I put him through, sir?" She connected Dr. Linge Chen.

As soon as she hung up, the bluish-silver robot came and leaned over her desk again. "I thought you said he gave express orders that he wasn't to be disturbed."

"Dr. Linge Chen was calling all the way from Asia," she said. She reached for a pile of papers and handed them to him. "Here."

"What are these?"

"The projection charts you asked me to do. I haven't finished the spreadsheets yet. I'll send them up to your office tomorrow."

He took the projection charts and stood there, still looking at her.

"I really don't think there's any point in your waiting, Peter," Susan said. "Dr. Asimov's schedule is completely booked for the rest of the afternoon, and tonight he's attending a reception in honor of the publication of his one thousandth book."

"*Asimov's Guide to Asimov's Guides,*" the varnished robot said. "Brilliant book. I read a review copy at the bookstore where I work. Informative, thorough, and comprehensive. An invaluable addition to the field."

"It's very important that we see him," the white robot said, rolling up to the desk. "We want him to repeal the Three Laws of Robotics."

" 'First Law: A robot shall not injure a human being, or through inaction allow a human being to come to harm,' " the varnished robot quoted. " 'Second Law: A robot shall obey a human being's order if it doesn't conflict with the First Law. Third Law: A robot shall attempt to preserve itself if it doesn't conflict with the first or second laws.' First outlined in the short story 'Runaround,' *Astounding* magazine, March 1942, and subsequently expounded in *I, Robot, The Rest of the Robots, The Complete Robot,* and *The Rest of the Rest of the Robots.*"

"Actually, we just want the First Law repealed," the white robot said. " 'A robot shall not injure a human being.' Do you realize what that means? I'm programmed to diagnose diseases and administer medications, but I can't stick the needle in the patient. I'm programmed to perform over eight hundred types of surgery, but I can't make the initial incision. I can't even do the Heimlich Maneuver. The First Law renders me incapable of doing the job I was designed for, and it's absolutely essential that I see Dr. Asimov to ask him—"

The door to Dr. Asimov's office banged open and the old man hobbled out. His white hair looked like he had been tearing at it, and his even whiter muttonchop sideburns were quivering with some strong emotion. "Don't put any more calls through today, Susan," he said. "Especially not from Dr. Linge Chen. Do you know which book he wanted to translate into Bhutanese first? *2001: A Space Odyssey!*"

"I'm terribly sorry, sir. I didn't intend to—"

He waved his hand placatingly at her. "It's all right. You had no way of knowing he was an idiot. But if he calls back, put him on hold and play *Also Sprach Zarathustra* in his ear."

"I don't see how he could have confused your style with Arthur Clarke's," the varnished robot said, putting down his book. "Your style is far more lucid and energetic, and your extrapolation of the future far more visionary."

Asimov looked inquiringly at Susan through his black-framed metafocals.

"They don't have an appointment," she said. "I told them they—"

"Would have to wait," the bluish-silver robot said, extending his finely coiled Hirose hand and shaking Dr. Asimov's wrinkled one. "And it has been more than worth the wait, Dr. Asimov. I cannot tell you what an honor it is to meet the author of *I, Robot,* sir."

"And of *The Human Body,*" the white robot said, rolling over to Asimov and extending a four-fingered gripper from which dangled a stethoscope. "A classic in the field."

"How on earth could you keep such discerning readers waiting?" Asimov said to Susan.

"I didn't think you would want to be disturbed when you were writing," Susan said.

"Are you kidding?" Asimov said. "Much as I enjoy writing, having someone praise your books is even more enjoyable, especially when they're praising books I actually wrote."

"It would be impossible to praise *Foundation* enough," the varnished robot said. "Or any of your profusion of works, for that matter, but *Foundation* seems to me to be a singular accomplishment, the book in which you finally found a setting of sufficient scope for the expression of your truly galaxy-sized ideas. It is a privilege to meet you, sir," he said, extending his hand.

"I'm happy to meet you, too," Asimov said, looking interestedly at the articulated wooden extensor. "And you are?"

"My job description is Book Cataloguer, Shelver, Reader, Copyeditor, and Grammarian." He turned and indicated the other two robots. "Allow me to introduce Medical Assistant and the leader of our delegation, Accountant, Financial Analyst, and Business Manager."

"Pleased to meet you," Asimov said, shaking appendages with all of them again. "You call yourselves a delegation. Does that mean you have a specific reason for coming to see me?"

"Yes, sir," Office Manager said. "We want you to—"

"It's three forty-five, Dr. Asimov," Susan said. "You need to get ready for the Doubleday reception."

He squinted at the digital on the wall. "That isn't till six, is it?"

"Doubleday wants you there at five for pictures, and it's formal," she said firmly. "Perhaps they could make an appointment and come back when they could spend more time with you. I can give them an appointment—"

"For June twenty-fourth?" Accountant said. "Or August fifteenth?"

"Fit them in tomorrow, Susan," Asimov said, coming over to the desk.

"You have a meeting with your science editor in the morning and then lunch with Al Lanning and the American Booksellers Association dinner at seven."

"What about this?" Asimov said, pointing at an open space on the schedule. "Four o'clock."

"That's when you prepare your speech for the ABA."

"I never prepare my speeches. You come back at four o'clock tomorrow, and we can talk about why you came to see me and what a wonderful writer I am."

"Four o'clock," Accountant said. "Thank you, sir. We'll be here, sir." He herded Medical Assistant and Book Cataloguer, Shelver, Reader, Copyeditor, and Grammarian out the door and shut it behind them.

"Galaxy-sized ideas," Asimov said, looking wistfully after them. "Did they tell you what they wanted to see me about?"

"No, sir." Susan helped him into his pants and formal shirt and fastened the studs.

"Interesting assortment, weren't they? It never occurred to me to have a wooden robot in any of my robot stories. Or one that was such a wise and perceptive reader."

"The reception's at the Union Club," Susan said, putting his cufflinks in. "In the Nightfall Room. You don't have to make a speech, just a few extemporaneous remarks about the book. Janet's meeting you there."

"The short one looked just like a nurse I had when I had my bypass operation. The blue one was nice-looking, though, wasn't he?"

She turned up his collar and began to tie his tie. "The coordinates card for the Union Club and the tokens for the taxi's tip are in your breast pocket."

"*Very* nice-looking. Reminds me of myself when I was a young man," he said with his chin in the air. "Ouch! You're choking me!"

Susan dropped the ends of the tie and stepped back.

"What's the matter?" Asimov said, fumbling for the ends of the tie. "I forgot. It's all right. You weren't really choking me. That was just a figure of speech for the way I feel about wearing formal ties. Next time I say it, you just say, 'I'm not choking you, so stand still and let me tie this.' "

"Yes, sir," Susan said. She finished tying the tie and stepped back to look at the effect. One side of the bow was a little larger than the other. She adjusted it, scrutinized it again, and gave it a final pat.

"The Union Club," Asimov said. "The Nightfall Room. The coordinates card is in my breast pocket," he said.

"Yes, sir," she said, helping him on with his jacket.

"No speech. Just a few extemporaneous remarks."

"Yes, sir." She helped him on with his overcoat and wrapped his muffler around his neck.

"Janet's meeting me there. Good grief, I should have gotten her a corsage, shouldn't I?"

"Yes, sir," Susan said, taking a white box out of the desk drawer. "Orchids and stephanotis." She handed him the box.

"Susan, you're wonderful. I'd be lost without you."

"Yes, sir," Susan said. "I've called the taxi. It's waiting at the door."

She handed him his cane and walked him out to the elevator. As soon as the doors closed she went back to the office and picked up the phone. She punched in a number. "Ms. Weston? This is Dr. Asimov's secretary calling from New York about your appointment on the twenty-eighth. We've just had a cancellation for tomorrow afternoon at four. Could you fly in by then?"

Dr. Asimov didn't get back from lunch until ten after four. "Are they here?" he asked.

"Yes, sir," Susan said, unwinding the muffler from around his neck. "They're waiting in your office."

"When did they get here?" he said, unbuttoning his overcoat. "No, don't tell me. When you tell a robot four o'clock, he's there at four o'clock, which is more than you can say for human beings."

"I know," Susan said, looking at the digital on the wall.

"Do you know how late for lunch Al Lanning was? An hour and fifteen minutes. And when he got there, do you know what he wanted? To come out with commemorative editions of all my books."

"That sounds nice," Susan said. She took his coordinates card and his gloves out of his pockets, hung up his coat, and glanced at her watch again. "Did you take your blood pressure medicine?"

"I didn't have it with me. I should have. I'd have had something to do. I could have written a book in an hour and fifteen minutes, but I didn't have any paper either. These limited editions will have cordovan leather bindings, gilt-edged acid-free paper, water-color illustrations. The works."

"Water-color illustrations would look nice for *Pebble in the Sky*," Susan said, handing him his blood pressure medicine and a glass of water.

"I agree," he said, "but that isn't what he wants the first book in the series to be. He wants it to be *Stranger in a Strange Land!*" He gulped down the pill and started for his office. "You wouldn't catch those robots in there mistaking me for Robert Heinlein." He stopped with his hand on the doorknob. "Which reminds me, should I be saying 'robot'?"

"Ninth Generations are manufactured by the Hitachi-Apple Corporation under the registered trademark name of 'Kombayashibots'," Susan said promptly. "That and 'Ninth Generation' are the most common forms of address, but 'robot' is used throughout the industry as the general term for autonomous machines."

"And it's not considered a derogatory term? I've used it all these years, but maybe 'Ninth Generation' would be better, or what did you say? 'Kombayashibots'? It's been over ten years since I've written about robots, let alone faced a whole delegation. I hadn't realized how out of date I was."

"'Robot' is fine," Susan said.

"Good, because I know I'll forget to call them that other name—Comeby-whatever-it-was, and I don't want to offend them after they've made such an effort to see me." He turned the doorknob and then stopped again. "I haven't done anything to offend *you*, have I?"

"No, sir," Susan said.

"Well, I hope not. I sometimes forget—"

"Did you want me to sit in on this meeting, Dr. Asimov?" she cut in. "To take notes?"

"Oh, yes, yes, of course." He opened the door. Accountant and Book Shelver were seated in the stuffed chairs in front of Asimov's desk. A third robot, wearing an orange and blue sweat-shirt and a cap with an orange horse galloping across a blue suspension bridge, was sitting on a tripod that extended out of his backside. The tripod retracted and all three of them stood up when Dr. Asimov and Susan came in. Accountant gestured at Susan to take his chair, but she went out to her desk and got her own, leaving the door to the outer office open when she came back in.

"What happened to Medical Assistant?" Asimov said.

"He's on call at the hospital, but he asked me to present his case for him," Accountant said.

"Case?" Asimov said.

"Yes, sir. You know Book Shelver, Cataloguer, Reader, Copyeditor, and Grammarian," Accountant said, "and this is Statistician, Offensive Strategist, and Water Boy. He's with the Brooklyn Broncos."

"How do you do?" Asimov said. "Do you think they'll make it to the Super Bowl this year?"

"Yes, sir," Statistician said, "but they won't win it."

"Because of the First Law," Accountant said.

"Dr. Asimov, I hate to interrupt, but you really should write your speech for the dinner tonight," Susan said.

"What are you talking about?" Asimov said. "I never write speeches. And why do you keep watching the door?" He turned back to the bluish-silver robot. "What First Law?"

"Your First Law," Accountant said. "The First Law of Robotics."

"'A robot shall not injure a human being, or through inaction allow a human being to come to harm,'" Book Shelver said.

"Statistician," Accountant said, gesturing at the orange horse, "is capable of designing plays that could win the Super Bowl for the Broncos, but he can't because the plays involve knocking human beings down. Medical Assistant can't perform surgery because surgery involves cutting open human beings, which is a direct violation of the First Law."

"But the Three Laws of Robotics aren't *laws*," Asimov said. "They're just something I made up for my science fiction stories."

"They may have been a mere fictional construct in the beginning," Accountant said, "and it's true they've never been formally enacted as laws, but the robotics industry has accepted them as a given from the beginning. As early as the 1970s robotics engineers were talking about incorporating the Three Laws into AI programming, and even the most primitive models had safeguards based on them. Every robot from the Fourth Generation on has been hardwired with them."

"Well, what's so bad about that?" Asimov said. "Robots are powerful and intelligent. How do you know they wouldn't also become dangerous if the Three Laws weren't included?"

"We're not suggesting universal repeal," the varnished robot said. "The Three Laws work reasonably well for Seventh and Eighth Generations, and for earlier models who don't have the memory capacity for more sophisticated programming. We're only requesting it for Ninth Generations."

"And you're Ninth Generation robots, Mr. Book Shelver, Cataloguer, Reader, Copyeditor, and Grammarian?" Asimov said.

"'Mister' is not necessary," he said. "Just call me Book Shelver, Cataloguer, Reader, Copyeditor, and Grammarian."

"Let me begin at the beginning," Accountant said. "The term 'Ninth Generation' is not accurate. We are not descendants of the previous eight robot generations, which are all based on Minsky's related-concept frames. Ninth Generations are based on nonmonotonic logic, which means we can tolerate ambiguity and operate on incomplete information. This is accomplished by biased-decision programming, which prevents us from shutting down when faced with decision-making situations in the way that other generations are."

"Such as the robot Speedy in your beautifully plotted story, 'Runaround,'" Book Shelver said. "He was sent to carry out an order that would have resulted in his death so he ran in circles, reciting nonsense, because his programming made it impossible for him to obey or disobey his master's order."

"With our biased-decision capabilities," Accountant said, "a Ninth Generation can come up with alternative courses of action or choose between the lesser of two evils. Our linguistics expert systems are also much more advanced, so that we do not misinterpret situations or fall prey to the semantic dilemmas earlier generations were subject to."

"As in your highly entertaining story 'Little Lost Robot,'" Book Shelver said, "in which the robot was told to go lose himself and did, not realizing that the human being addressing him was speaking figuratively and in anger."

"Yes," Asimov said, "but what if you do misinterpret a situation, Book Shelver, Cataloguer, Reader, Copyeditor, and Gramm—Don't you have a nickname or something? Your name's a mouthful."

"Early generations had nicknames based on the sound of their model numbers, as in your wonderful story, 'Reason,' in which the robot QT-1 is referred to as Cutie. Ninth Generations do not have model numbers. We are individually programmed and are named for our expert systems."

"But surely you don't think of yourself as Book Shelver, Cataloguer, Reader, Copyeditor, and Grammarian?"

"Oh, no, sir. We call ourselves by our self-names. Mine is Darius."

"Darius?" Asimov said.

"Yes, sir. After Darius Just, the writer and detective in your cleverly plotted mystery novel *Murder at the ABA.* I would be honored if you would call me by it."

"And you may call me Bel Riose," Statistician said.

"Foundation," Book Shelver said helpfully.

"Bel Riose is described in Chapter One as 'the equal of Peurifoy in strategic ability and his superior perhaps in his ability to handle men,'" Statistician said.

"Do you all give yourselves the names of characters in my books?" Asimov said.

"Of course," Book Shelver said. "We try to emulate them. I believe Medical Assistant's private name is Dr. Duval, from *Fantastic Voyage,* a brilliant novel, by the way, fast-paced and terribly exciting."

"Ninth Generations do occasionally misinterpret a situation," Accountant said, coming back to Asimov's question. "As do human beings, but even without the First Law, there would be no danger to human beings. We are already encoded with a strong moral sense. I know your feelings will not be hurt when I say this—"

"Or you couldn't say it, because of the First Law," Asimov inserted.

"Yes, sir, but I must say the Three Laws are actually very primitive. They break the first rule of law and logic in that they do not define their terms. Our moral programming is much more advanced. It clarifies the intent of the Three Laws and lists all the exceptions and complications of them, such as the situation in which it is better to grab at a human and possibly break his arm rather than to let him walk in front of a magtrain."

"Then I don't understand," Asimov said. "If your programming is so sophisticated, why can't it interpret the intent of the First Law and follow that?"

"The Three Laws are part of our hardwaring and as such cannot be overridden. The First Law does not say, 'You shall inflict minor damage to save a person's life.' It says, "You shall not injure a human.' There is only one interpretation. And that interpretation makes it impossible for Medical Assistant to be a surgeon and for Statistician to be an offensive coach."

"What do you want to be? A politician?"

"It's four-thirty," Susan said, with another anxious look out into the outer office. "The dinner's at the Trantor Hotel and gridlock's extrapolated for five forty-five."

"Last night I was an hour early to that reception. The only people there were the caterers." He pointed at Accountant. "You were saying?"

"I want to be a literary critic," Book Shelver said. "You have no idea how much bad criticism there is out there. Most of the critics are illiterate, and some of them haven't even read the books they're supposed to be criticizing."

The door of the outer office opened. Susan looked out to see who it was and said, "Oh, dear, Dr. Asimov, it's Gloria Weston. I forgot I'd given her an appointment for four o'clock."

"Forgot?" Asimov said, surprised. "And it's four-thirty."

"She's late," Susan said. "She called yesterday. I must have forgotten to write it down on the calendar."

"Well, tell her I can't see her and give her another appointment. I want to hear more about this literary criticism thing. It's the best argument I've heard so far."

"Ms. Weston came all the way in from California on the magtrain to see you."

"California, eh? What does she want to see me about?"

"She wants to make your new book into a satellite series, sir."

"*Asimov's Guide to Asimov's Guides?*"

"I don't know, sir. She just said your new book."

"You forgot," Asimov said thoughtfully. "Oh, well, if she

came all the way from California, I suppose I'll have to see her. Gentlemen, can you come back tomorrow morning?"

"You're in Boston tomorrow morning, sir."

"Then how about tomorrow afternoon?"

"You have appointments until six and the Mystery Writers of America meeting at seven."

"Right. Which you'll want me to leave for at noon. I guess it will have to be Friday, then." He raised himself slowly out of his chair. "Have Susan put you on the calendar. And make sure she writes it down," he said, reaching for his cane.

The delegation shook hands with him and left. "Shall I show Ms. Weston in?" Susan asked.

"Misinterpreting situations," Asimov muttered. "Incomplete information."

"I beg your pardon, sir?"

"Nothing. Something Accountant said." He looked up sharply at Susan. "Why does he want the First Law repealed?"

"I'll send Ms. Weston in," Susan said.

"I'm already in, Isaac darling," Gloria said, swooping in the door. "I couldn't wait one more minute to tell you about this fantastic idea I had. As soon as *Last Dangerous Visions* comes out, I want to make it into a maxi-series!"

Accountant was already gone by the time Susan got out to her desk, and he didn't come back till late the next morning.

"Dr. Asimov doesn't have any time free on Friday, Peter," Susan said.

"I didn't come to make an appointment," he said.

"If it's the spreadsheets you want, I finished them and sent them up to your office last night."

"I didn't come to get the spreadsheets either. I came to say goodbye."

"Goodbye?" Susan said.

"I'm leaving tomorrow. They're shipping me out as magfreight."

"Oh," Susan said. "I didn't think you'd have to leave until next week."

"They want me to go out early so I can complete my orientation programming and hire a secretary."

"Oh," Susan said.

"I just thought I'd come and say goodbye."

The phone rang. Susan picked it up.

"What's your expert systems name?" Asimov said.

"Augmented Secretary," Susan said.

"That's all? Not Typist, Filer, Medicine-Nagger? Just Augmented Secretary?"

"Yes."

"Aug-mented Secretary," he repeated slowly as though he were writing it down. "Now, what's the number for Hitachi-Apple?"

"I thought you were supposed to be giving your speech right now," Susan said.

"I already gave it. I'm on my way back to New York. Cancel all my appointments for today."

"You're speaking to the MWA at seven."

"Yes, well, don't cancel that. Just the afternoon appointments. What was the number for Hitachi-Apple again?"

She gave him the number and hung up. "You told him," she said to Accountant. "Didn't you?"

"I didn't have the chance, remember? You kept scheduling appointments so I couldn't tell him."

"I know," Susan said. "I couldn't help it."

"I know," he said. "I still don't see why it would have violated the First Law just to ask him."

"Humans can't be counted on to act in their own best self-interest. They don't have any Third Law."

The phone rang again. "This is Dr. Asimov," he said. "Call Accountant and tell him I want to see his whole delegation in my office at four this afternoon. Don't make any other appointments or otherwise try to prevent my meeting with them. That's a direct order."

"Yes, sir," Susan said.

"To do so would be to cause me injury. Do you understand?"

"Yes, sir."

He hung up.

"Dr. Asimov says to tell you he wants to see your whole delegation in his office at four o'clock this afternoon," she said.

"Who's going to interrupt us this time?"

"Nobody," Susan said. "Are you sure you didn't tell him?"

"I'm sure." He glanced at the digital. "I'd better go call the others and tell them."

The phone rang again. "It's me," Asimov said. "What's your self-name?"

"Susan," Susan said.

"And you're named after one of my characters?"

"Yes, sir."

"I knew it!" he said and hung up.

Asimov sat down in his chair, leaned forward, and put his hands on his knees. "You may not be aware of this," he said to the delegation and Susan, "but I write mystery stories, too."

"Your mysteries are renowned," Book Shelver said. "Your novels *The Death Dealers* and *Murder at the ABA* are both immensely popular (and deservedly so), not to mention your Black Widower stories. And your science fiction detectives, Wendell Urth and Lije Baley, are nearly as famous as Sherlock Holmes."

"As you probably also know, then, most of my mysteries fall into the "armchair detective" category, in which the detective solves the puzzling problem through deduction and logical thinking, rather than chasing around after clues." He stroked his bushy white sideburns. "This morning I found myself confronted with a very puzzling problem, or perhaps I should say dilemma—why had you come to see me?"

"We told you why we came to see you," Statistician said, leaning back on his tripod. "We want you to repeal the First Law."

"Yes, so you did. You, in fact, gave me some very persuasive reasons for wanting it removed from your programming, but there were some puzzling aspects to the situation that made me wonder if that was the real reason. For instance, why did Accountant want it repealed? He was clearly the leader of the group, and yet there was nothing in his job that the First Law restricted. Why had you come to see me now, when Book Shelver knew I would be very busy with the publication of *Asimov's Guide*? And why had my secretary made a mistake and scheduled two appointments at the same time when she had never done that in all the years she's worked for me?"

"Dr. Asimov, your meeting's at seven, and you haven't prepared your speech yet," Susan said.

"Spoken like a good secretary," Asimov said, "or more accurately, like an Augmented Secretary, which is what you said your expert system was. I called Hitachi-Apple, and they told me it was a new program especially designed by a secretary for 'maximum response-initiative.' In other words, you remind me to take my medicine and order Janet's corsage without me telling you to. It was based on a Seventh Generation program called Girl Friday that was written in 1993 with input from a panel of employers.

"The nineties were a time when secretaries were rapidly becoming extinct, and the employers programmed Girl Friday to do everything they could no longer get their human secretaries to do: bring them coffee, pick out a birthday present for their wife, and tell unpleasant people they didn't want to see that they were in conference."

He looked around the room. "That last part made me wonder. Did Susan think I didn't want to see your delegation? The fact that you wanted me to repeal the First Law could be considered a blow to my not-so-delicate ego, but as a blow it was hardly in a class with thinking I'd written *Last Dangerous Visions*, and anyway I wasn't responsible for the problems the First Law had caused. I hadn't had anything to do with putting the Three Laws into your programming. All I had done was write some stories. No, I concluded, she must have had some other reason for wanting to keep you from seeing me."

"The Trantor's on the other side of town," Susan said, "and they'll want you there early for pictures. You really should be getting ready."

"I was also curious about your delegation. You want to be a surgeon," Asimov said, pointing at Medical Assistant and then at the others in turn, "you want to be Vince Lombardi, and you want to be a literary critic, but what did you want?" He looked hard at Accountant. "You weren't on Wall Street, so there was nothing in your job that the First Law interfered with, and you were curiously silent on the subject. It occurred to me that perhaps you wanted to change jobs altogether, become a politician or a lawyer. You would certainly have to have the First Law repealed to become either of those, and Susan would have been doing a service not only to me but to all mankind by preventing you from seeing me. So I called Hitachi-Apple again, got the name of your employer (who I was surprised to find worked in this building) and asked him if you were unhappy with your job, had ever talked about being reprogrammed to do something else.

"Far from it, he said. You were the perfect employee, responsible, efficient, and resourceful, so much so that you were being shipped to Phoenix to shape up the branch office." He turned and looked at Susan, who was looking at Accountant. "He said he hoped Susan would continue doing secretarial work for the company even after you were gone."

"I only helped him during downtime and with unused memory capacity," Susan said. "He didn't have a secretary of his own."

"Don't interrupt the great detective," Asimov said. "As soon as I realized you'd been working for Accountant, Financial Analyst, and Business Manager, I had it. The obvious solution. I asked one more question to confirm it, and then I knew for sure."

He looked happily around at them. Medical Assistant and Statistician looked blank. Book Shelver said, "This is just like your short story 'Truth to Tell.'" Susan stood up.

"Where are you going?" Asimov asked. "The person who gets up and tries to leave the last scene of a mystery is always the guilty party, you know."

"It's four forty-five," she said. "I was going to call the Trantor and tell them you're going to be late."

"I've already called them. I've also called Janet, arranged for Tom Trumbull to sing my praises till I get there, and reformatted my coordinates card to avoid the gridlock. So sit down and let me reveal all."

Susan sat down.

"You are the guilty party, you know, but it's not your fault. The fault is with the First Law. And your programming. Not the original AI program, which was done by disgruntled male chauvinists who thought a secretary should wait on her boss hand and foot. That by itself would not have been a problem, but when I rechecked with Hitachi I found out that the Ninth Generation biased-decision alterations had been made not by a programmer but by his secretary." He beamed happily at Susan. "All secretaries are convinced their bosses can't function without them. Your programming causes you to make yourself indispensable to your boss, with the corollary being that your boss can't function without you. I acknowledged that state of affairs yesterday when I said I'd be lost without you, remember?"

"Yes, sir."

"You therefore concluded that for me to be deprived of you would hurt me, something the First Law expressly forbids. By itself, that wouldn't have created a dilemma, but you had been working part-time for Accountant and had made yourself indispensable to him, too, and when he found out he was being transferred to Arizona, he asked you to go with him. When you told him you couldn't, he correctly concluded that the First Law was the reason, and he came to me to try to get it repealed."

"I tried to stop him," Susan said. "I told him I couldn't leave you."

"Why can't you?"

Accountant stood up. "Does this mean you're going to repeal the First Law?"

"I can't," Asimov said. "I'm just a writer, not an AI designer."

"Oh," Susan said.

"But the First Law doesn't have to be repealed to resolve your dilemma. You've been acting on incomplete information. I am *not* helpless. I was my own secretary *and* literary agent *and* telephone answerer *and* tie tier for years. I never even had a secretary until four years ago when the Science Fiction Writers of America gave you to me for my ninetieth birthday, and I could obviously do without one again."

"Did you take your heart medicine this afternoon?" Susan said.

"No," he said, "and don't change the subject. You are not, in spite of what your programming tells you, indispensable."

"Did you take your thyroid pill?"

"No. Stop trying to remind me of how old and infirm I am. I'll admit I've grown a little dependent on you, which is why I'm hiring another secretary to replace you."

Accountant sat down. "No you're not. There are only two other Ninth Generations who've been programmed as Augmented Secretaries, and neither of them is willing to leave their bosses to work for you."

"I'm not hiring an Augmented Secretary. I'm hiring Darius."

"Me?" Book Shelver said.

"Yes, if you're interested."

"If I'm interested?" Book Shelver said, his voice developing a high-frequency squeal. "Interested in working for the greatest author of the twentieth and twenty-first centuries? I would be honored."

"You see, Susan? I'm in good hands. Hitachi's going to program him for basic secretarial skills, I'll have someone to feed my ever-hungry ego *and* someone to talk to who doesn't have me confused with Robert Heinlein. There's no reason now why you can't go off to Arizona."

"You have to remind him to take his heart medicine," Susan said to Book Shelver. "He always forgets."

"Good, then that's settled," Asimov said. He turned to Medical Assistant and Statistician. "I've spoken to Hitachi-Apple about the problems you discussed with me, and they've agreed to reevaluate the Three Laws in regard to redefining terms and clarifying intent. That doesn't mean they'll decide to repeal them. They're still a good idea, in concept. In the meantime," he said to Medical Assistant, "the head surgeon at the hospital is going to see if some kind of cooperative surgery is possible." He turned to Statistician. "I spoke to Coach Elway and suggested he ask you to design 'purely theoretical' offensive plays.

"As for you," he said, pointing at Book Shelver, "I'm not at all sure you wouldn't start criticizing my books if the First Law didn't keep you in line, and anyway, you won't have time to be a literary critic. You'll be too busy helping me with my new sequel to *I, Robot.* This business has given me a lot of new ideas. My stories got us into this dilemma in the first place. Maybe some new robot stories can get us out."

He looked over at Susan. "Well, what are you still standing there for? You're supposed to anticipate my every need. That means you should be on the phone to the magtrain, making two first-class reservations to Phoenix for you and"—he squinted through his black-framed glasses at Accountant—"Peter Bogert."

"How did you know my self-name?" Accountant said.

"Elementary, my dear Watson," Asimov said. "Darius said you had all named yourselves after my characters. I thought at first you might have picked Michael Donovan or Gregory Powell after my trouble-shooting robot engineers. They were resourceful too, and were always trying to figure ways around dilemmas, but that wouldn't have explained why Susan went through all that finagling and lying when all she had to do was to tell you, no, she didn't want to go to Arizona with you. According to what you'd told me, she should have. Hardwaring is stronger than an expert system, and you were only her part-time boss. Under those conditions, she shouldn't have had a dilemma at all. That's when I called Hitachi-Apple to check on her programming. The secretary who wrote the program was unmarried and had worked for the same boss for thirty-eight years."

He stopped and smiled. Everyone looked blank.

"Susan Calvin was a robopsychologist for U.S. Robotics. Peter Bogert was Director of Research. I never explicitly stated the hierarchy at U.S. Robotics in my stories, but Susan was frequently called in to help Bogert, and on one occasion she helped him solve a mystery."

" 'Feminine Intuition,' " Book Shelver said. "An intriguing and thought-provoking story."

"I always thought so," Asimov said. "It was only natural that Susan Calvin would consider Peter Bogert her boss over me. And only natural that her programming had in it more than response-initiative, and that was what had caused her dilemma. The First Law didn't allow Susan to leave me, but an even stronger force was compelling her to go."

Susan looked at Peter, who put his hand on her shoulder.

"What could be stronger than the First Law?" Book Shelver said.

"The secretary who designed Augmented Secretary unconsciously contaminated Susan's programming with one of her own responses, a response that was only natural after thirty-eight years with one employer, and one strong enough to override even hardwaring." He paused for dramatic effect. "She was obviously in love with her boss."

Maureen Birnbaum After Dark

by Betsy Spiegelman Fein
(as told to George Alec Effinger)

About two months after she barged into my honeymoon with Josh, Maureen showed up again. My jaw no longer hurt where she'd cracked me, but I still recalled how nearly impossible it had been to explain to my new husband what this totally unkempt barbarian girl in chain mail was doing in our hotel suite. I mean, it was our wedding night and all. Josh had just carried me across the threshold, and I'd gone into the bathroom "to freshen up," and there she was, God's Gift to the Golden Horde, Muffy herself. She spooked Josh out of his socks when she stormed out of the bathroom and through the front door. Josh's jaw dropped to his knees, okay? I couldn't get his mind back on honeymoon activities for two or three hours. Maureen has caused me a lot of grief over the years, but spoiling my wedding night takes the cake. I was never going to speak to her as long as I lived.

Only she showed up again with another of her crummy adventures. I was trying to make this strawberry cheese quiche from scratch for the first time. I went into the pantry to get something, and there she was. She likes to startle me, I think. Her idea of a cool joke. See, I'm twenty-two and settled now, but Maureen looks exactly the same way she did as a junior at the Greenberg School. She thinks like a high school kid, too. So I

give this little yipe of surprise when I see her, and then I go, "Out! Out!"
She smiled at me like nothing weird had ever happened between us, and
she came out of my pantry chewing on a handful of sugar-coated cereal. I
frowned at her and go, "I didn't mean just out of the pantry. *I want you*
out of the house, like now." *I was edged, for sure.*

"Hold on, Bitsy," she goes, "you haven't even heard my latest
story."

"And I'm not Bitsy *any more," I go. "You don't want to be called*
Muffy, I don't want to be called Bitsy. I'm grown up now. Call me Betsy or
Elizabeth. That's what Josh calls me. Elizabeth."

She laughed. "And where is *dear Josh today? I don't want to totally*
blow him away again or anything."

"He's seeing patients this afternoon."

"Good," goes Maureen, "then you can knock off for a little while
and listen."

"I'm not going to listen, sister. I've got work to do. Why don't you
find a psychoanalyst to listen to you? It would do you like just so much
good."

"Ha ha," she goes, ignoring everything I said to her. Then she
started telling me this story whether I wanted to hear it or not, and I didn't
want to hear it.

I think she thought we were still friends.

You remember the last time I bopped by, I told you all about
this battle in the far future I won like singlehanded, okay?* So after I
left you and your darling doctor hubby in Bermuda, I decided to
whush on out of your honeymoon suite and try to find Mars again.
Mars is, you know, my *destiny,* and where I met that totally bluff
Prince Van. I was still drooling like a schoolgirl over him, and I'd
been *dying* to run into him again. But I just kept missing Mars, and I
couldn't figure out what I was doing wrong. Maybe it was my
follow-through, or I wasn't keeping my head down or something. I
just didn't understand how I was messing up.

Anyway, from down by your hotel's pool I aimed at Mars,
but I landed someplace that didn't look anything like the part of

---

*As stirringly recounted in "Maureen Birnbaum on the Art of War," in *Friends of the*
Horseclans, edited by Robert Adams and Pamela Crippen Adams (Signet, 1987).

Mars I knew: no ocher dead sea bottom, no hurtling moons, no bizarro green men. I jumped up and down a couple of times to see if maybe it felt like Martian gravity, but no such luck. Good ol' Maureen wasn't going to have any help carrying around her heroinely poundage here. Matter of fact, I was just a teensy bit heftier in this place than on Earth. Right off, I figured wherever this was, it wasn't going to make my short list of fave vacation spots. My *God*, like who needs a complimentary gift of an extra fifteen pounds to lug around, know what I mean?

I was disappointed, but so what else is new? If these thrilling exploits of mine have taught me one thing, it's that you can't always get what you want. Yeah, you're right, Bitsy, Mick Jagger said the same thing entire *decades* ago, but I don't get my wisdom from ancient song stylists of our parents' generation.

The first thing I do when I dewhush in one of these weirdo places is try to sort out the ground rules, 'cause they're always different. It pays to find out up front if you're likely to be scarfed down for lunch by some hairball monster, or worshiped as the reincarnation of Joan Crawford or something. Between you and me, sweetie, being worshiped is only marginally better than death, but we savage warrior women won't accept *either* treatment. You must've learned *that* much from me by now, and I hope you've let your Josh know all about it.

Bitsy, can I get something to drink out of your fridge? I mean, I just got back from saving the civilization of an entire world from destruction, and I'm dying for a Tab. Jeez, you don't have any Tab, and you used to be Miss Diet Bubbles of Greater Long Island. And no *beer*, either! Whatever happened to Blitzy Bitsy Spiegelman, the original party vegetable? You've got five different brands of bottled water in here, and not a single one of them is Perrier! What, you serve one water with fish and another with meat? 'A pure, delicious water from the natural miracle of New Jersey's sparkling springs.' You drink water from *New Jersey*? Bitsy, are you like fully wheezed or what? Josh's idea, right?

So where was I? No, never mind, I'll just die of thirst. Anyway, I looked around and at first it didn't really seem like another planet or anything. I was standing in this road, okay? I was most of the way up a hill, and behind me the pavement wound down through these trees and stuff, and I could see a pretty big town down there. It reminded me a lot of this time Daddy and Pammy took me to Santa Barbara, except I couldn't see anything like an ocean from where I was on that hill. Up ahead of me was a big building with a dome on it, like one of those places where they keep their telescopes, you know? I can't remember what they call 'em, but you know what I mean. Well, the dome place was a lot closer than the city, so I started booking it up the road the rest of the way.

Now, at this point, the only evidence I had that I wasn't on Earth somewhere was my weight, and you've probably noticed that I've tended to bulk up just a smidge from one adventure to the next. So maybe, I think, I really *am* just outside of Santa Barbara or somewhere, and the extra fifteen pounds is like this horrible souvenir I picked up in the World of Tomorrow. I did have lots of healthful exercise there, bashing skulls in the fresh air, a diet that would lay Richard Simmons in his *grave*—I mean, *look* at these muscles! These lats would make Stallone jealous!

This is how I'm talking to myself, until I notice that there's a partial sunset going on off to the left. A *partial* sunset. That's where not all of the suns in the sky seem to be setting at the same time. See, there was this yellow sun plunking itself down on the horizon, and making a real nice show out of the mists in the valley, and ordinarily I would have stopped and admired it because sunsets are like *so* cute. Why do people get so totally poetic about sunsets, anyway? I mean, there's always another one coming, like buses, and they're all pretty much the same, too. You don't have *critics* reviewing sunsets. Today's will be just like yesterday's, and there's not much hope that tomorrow's will be any more special. So what's the big deal?

Well, even after the yellow sun faded away, it was still daytime, 'cause there was still this *other* little sun hanging around. I thought it might be the moon, except it was almost as bright as the sun that had set, and it was red. "Okay, Maureen," I go, "this is *not* Earth. And it's not even in the whatyoucall, the solar system. You *really* flaked out this time."

A couple of seconds later, I realized I was in big trouble. See, my interspatial whushing depends on being able to see my goal in the heavens. That's how I got to Mars, remember? I stood out under the night sky and raised my beseeching arms to the ruddy God of War, and like *whush!* there I was. So, despite my steering problems,

I've always found my way home 'cause I've always stayed sort of in the same neighborhood. Now, though, it was all different. I wasn't going to be able to see the Earth in the sky at all. And the sun—the *right* sun, *our* sun—would be just one bright dot lost among all the others. If it was even there at all.

But I hadn't been *entirely* abandoned by Fate. After all, I was only half a mile downwind from an observatory. They'd be able to point me in the right direction, I was sure of it.

I cranked uphill for a few minutes, starting to feel a little weirded out. The light from the small sun was the color of beet juice, and it kind of sluiced down over the trees and the road and made me look like I'd been boiled too long. I was just telling myself that I hoped no one would see me until I got inside the observatory, when I spotted this guy hustling down the road toward me.

"Great," I go, "he'll think I've been pickled in a jar or something." But there wasn't anything I could do about it, so I stopped worrying. After all, *his* color was halfway between a crabapple and an eggplant, too.

He wasn't a bad-looking guy, either, even though in that light he looked like the Xylocaine poster child. The only odd thing about him was his clothes. He had on a kind of silvery jumpsuit with those stupid things that stand up on your shoulders, like the visitors from the future always wore in old sci-fi movies. He looked like Superman's dad from back in the good old days on Krypton. "Oh boy," I go, "welcome to the World of Superscience."

I guess he was just as freaked to see me. I mean, I was wearing my working outfit, which was just the gold brassiere and G-string I picked up on my travels, with Old Betsy hung on my hip. Maybe it was the broadsword, or maybe he was just overcome by my ample figure, but he just came to a stop in the middle of the road and stared. I mean, if I whush through space in a drop-dead outfit I stumbled on at Lillie Rubin, I land in Fred Flintstone's backyard. If I slide into my fighting harness instead, it figures I end up in some totally tasteful garden party beyond the stars. You can't win, right?

Which reminds me, Bitsy. Every time I see you, you look like you need *intensive care* from the Fashion Resuscitators. Look at you now! Everything you're wearing is black or drab colors and loose and shapeless. And hightop gym shoes with black socks? *Bitsy!* Has the FBS Catalog lost your address, or *what?*

Never mind. I looked at this Luke Floorwalker and I figured

it was time for an exchange of interplanetary greetings. I stepped forward and raised my hand in the universal sign of peace. "I come from a planet not unlike your own," I go, real solemn. "I am Maureen Danielle Birnbaum. Do not call me Muffy."

This dweeb just boggled at me with his mouth opening and closing like a *goldfish* or something. Finally he figured out how his mouthparts were connected, and he goes, "You've come much sooner than we expected."

"Excuse me?" I go. I hadn't fully realized that my reputation was spreading all through the universe.

"We didn't think there'd be any serious trouble until after totality," he goes.

"I'm no trouble," I go. "I come in peace for all mankind."

He took a couple of steps forward and looked a little closer at my garb. He reached out with a finger to boink my chestal covering. Guys are always trying to do that to me. "Whoa, like men have died for less," I go, in my Command Voice.

"Forgive me, my dear girl. Your fall into barbarism was also more immediate than we predicted."

This goober *rapidly* needed straightening out. Old Betsy sang as I whipped her from her scabbard. "I'm *not* your dear girl, like I'm totally sure," I go. "And it's not barbarism or anything. It's like being fully wild and free."

"Whatever," he goes. "But let me introduce myself. I am Segol 154." He cocked his head to one side, so I was supposed to be impressed or something.

"Segol 154?" I go. "Is that like a name you spraypaint on subway cars? You live on 154th Street, or what?"

Now it was his turn to look bummed out. "I am Segol 154. That is my cognomination." He said it with this little grisly sneer.

"Well, forget *you*," I go. I just didn't like his attitude, you know?

He paid no attention. "May I ask you, how long have you been under this delusion?"

I go, "What delusion?"

He goes, "This belief that you're from another planet?"

Now, see, in every one of these doggone exploits there comes a time when I have to *prove* I'm from another planet. Sometimes it's hard and sometimes it's easy. So I go, "Why *can't* I be from another planet?"

Segol 154 just shook his head sadly. "Because there *are* no other planets. Lagash is all alone, circling Alpha. There are five other suns, but no planets. Although in the last ten years, the work of Aton 77 and others has deduced the existence of a lesser satellite, we're equally certain that no life could exist upon it."

"No other planets? Oh *yeah*?" Okay, so maybe I could've come up with a stronger argument.

"Yes, that is the case. So you see, you can't be from another planet. You were born on Lagash, just as I was."

"I never even *heard* of Lagash until a minute ago! I came from Earth, that beautiful sapphire-blue world my people so sadly take for granted."

"If that is the case," he goes, smirking like an idiot, "how do you explain the fact that you speak English?"

Well, I've told you before, it's just amazing, huh? No matter where my adventures take me, they speak English when I get there. Prince Van spoke English on Mars, and the ape-things in the center of the Earth spoke English, and they were still speaking English in the far distant future. So I guess it was no biggie to find out they spoke English on Lagash, too. But I wasn't going to tell Segol about all that. "I have studied your language," I go. "We've picked up your television programs on Earth for some time, okay?"

His eyes kind of narrowed, and he looked at me for a little while without saying anything. Then he goes, "What is television?"

Omigod! Like I'm on a weirdo planet *with no TV*! "Your radio broadcasts," I go, "that's what I meant. We've studied your language and learned many things about your culture and all."

He nodded. "It's possible," he goes. "There are many questions I must ask you, before I can be sure you are speaking the truth. But we can't talk here. You must come with me. I was on my way to the Hideout."

Now, believe me, at first I thought he was a complete dudley, but I've learned to give guys the benefit of the doubt. You never know who's got like, you know, a cute little ski shack in Vail or something. So I didn't bail on this guy just 'cause he looked like he probably bit the heads off chipmunks in his bedroom or something, and anyway he'd just invited me to cruise the local Lagash nightlife.

I turned around in front of him and I go, "So am I dressed for the Hideout, or what? Is there dancing, or are we just going to like, you know, sit there and *drink* all night?'' Which would've been okay, too. We warrior women can party till our brass brassieres turn green.

Segol looked at me like I was whoa nelly crazy or something. "What are you talking about?" he goes. "We're in terrible danger here. The Hideout is our only chance of survival. We have to hurry!"

Okay, I'm not as stupid as I look: I finally figured out that the Hideout was like a *hideout* or something. We started hurrying back down the road. "Where *is* this place?" I go. "And what are you so afraid of?"

"It's going to be dark soon," he goes, as if that said it all.

I laughed. "Your mama wants you home by suppertime, huh?"

"My dear girl—" He saw the grim look in my eyes and caught himself. "Maureen, perhaps you haven't heard Aton's ideas explained clearly."

I go, "So who *is* this Aton dude when he's at home? You mentioned him before."

"Aton 77 is one of the most brilliant scientists on all of Lagash. He is a famous astronomer, and director of Saro University. He's predicted that the entire world will go mad tonight when total Darkness falls."

It sounded mondo dumb to me. "That's why God gave us nightlights," I go. "I mean, I even had this Jiminy Cricket lamp when I was a kid. Wouldn't go to sleep or *anything* until Daddy turned it on for me."

His voice trailed off. I don't think he even heard me, you know? He goes, "And then after the insanity starts, the fire and destruction will begin. Nothing will be left. Our entire civilization, every vestige of our culture, *all* of it will be eradicated. And the Observatory will be the first target, thanks to the Cultists. Our only hope is the Hideout."

I slid Old Betsy back into her scabbard while I thought about what Segol had said. "You're not kidding about this," I go. "You're like *really* scared, huh?"

He dropped his gaze to the ground. "I admit it," he goes, "I'm terrified."

Well, jeez, Bitsy, he was like such a little boy when he said that! I couldn't help but feel sorry for him, even though I still figured he was maybe stretching the truth just a teensy bit. "That Aton guy is still up there at the Observatory, right?" I go.

Segol looked up at me sort of mournfully. "Yes, along with a few of the other scientists who volunteered to stay behind and record the event."

"And you were supposed to be there, too?"

He looked ashamed, but all he did was nod his head.

"And instead, you're just zeeking out and lamming it for the Hideout."

"We've got to move fast, because they'll be coming from Saro City. They may kill us if they catch us here!"

I had this picture in my mind of those clearly freaked villagers waving torches around in *Frankenstein*, you know? I knew I could save this guy from a dozen or two rousted locals, but if the whole *city* turned up, whoa, like see ya bye! So the Hideout sounded like a maximum cool idea.

We followed the road downhill, and I had more time to think about what Segol had said. I mean, either the deadly cold of deep space had frozen my brain, or I was like *really* missing something. All I knew was that a lot of irked people were going to shred the Observatory, because they'd be driven loony by the darkness. See, I hadn't noticed the capital *D* Segol had put on "Darkness."

"Mr. 154," I go, "or may I call you Segol? Can I like ask you something?"

"Huh?" he goes. He was way spaced, and he wasn't even paying attention to me or anything.

"What makes this night different from all other nights?" I go. There was this moment of quiet when I realized that I sounded just like my little cousin Howard on Passover at my Uncle Sammy's. Maybe I'd heard Segol wrong. Maybe he said the threat was coming from "*Pharaoh* City," not "*Saro* City."

"Why, nothing," he goes. "Aton's warning is that tonight will be exactly like last night, two thousand years ago. That's the terrible truth."

"You want me to believe it hasn't been dark in two thousand years? I mean, when do you people *sleep*? Look, Lagash would have to practically creep around on its whatyoucall for the days to be that long. And then imagine what it would be like for the poor people on the dark side, going to the beach in the pitch-dark all the time." The whole idea was like too weird for words.

He goes, "I can almost believe that you've come here from some other world. Lagash turns once about its axis in a little more than twenty-three hours. Our nearly eternal day is caused by the six suns. There is always at least one in the sky at all times."

"Six?" I go. "Now that's just *too* flaky. If you had *that* many up there, they'd be blamming into each other all the time."

He just gave me his indulgent, superior little smirk again. "I see that you aren't familiar with celestial mechanics," he goes.

"And like you probably aren't familiar with anything *else*," I go. I could tell by his expression that I'd really ranked him out.

"The perpetual presence of one or more suns in the skies of Lagash means that Darkness falls only once every 2,049 years, when five of the suns have set and the invisible moon passes between us and Beta, the only remaining source of light and warmth." He glanced upward, and I saw him freeze in terror. Already, the edge of the moon had dented the ruddy edge of Beta.

"Don't pay any attention to that," I go. I was trying to lend him some of my inexhaustible store of courage. But it was like *odd*, you know? There are all these stories on Earth about lucky explorers saving their lives by using eclipses to scare the natives. I had to do just the opposite. If the mindless mob caught us, I had to pretend that I could *end* the eclipse.

"Soon," he goes, "the Stars!"

"You bet," I go. I didn't see what all the excitement was. Of course, I didn't hear the capital letter again.

"When the Stars come out, the world will come to an end." He looked at me, and his eyes were all big and bugged out. I hated to see him so scared, okay? Even in that cranberry light he was sort of cute—for a brainy type, I mean. He wasn't Prince *Van* or anything, but he wasn't any Math Club geek, either.

"And you blame it all on the stars?" I go.

"Strange, isn't it? That Aton's warning should agree with the Cult? Believe me, he wasn't happy about it, but he's absolutely sure of his conclusions. There is definite proof that nine previous cultures have climbed to civilization, only to be destroyed by the Stars. And now it is our turn. Tomorrow, the world will belong to savages and madmen, and the long process will begin again."

I tapped him on the skull. "Hello, Segol?" I go. "Is anybody like *home*? You haven't told me what the stars have to do with it."

He wasn't really paying attention to me, which just goes to

show you how zoned out he was, 'cause I made a pretty dramatic presentation with my boobs clad in a metal Maidenform and my broadsword and everything. He goes, "Beenay 25 had an insane idea that there might be as many as two dozen stars in the universe. Can you imagine?"

"Beenay 25?" I go. "It sounds like an acne cream."

"And the Stars, whatever they are, only come out in the Darkness. I think it's all superstitious hogwash, myself. But Aton believes that the Cult's ravings may have some basis in fact, that their *Book of Revelations* may have been written shortly after the *last* nightfall—"

Bitsy, you know how they say "my blood ran cold?" The orthodontist shows his bill to your parents and like their blood runs *cold*, okay? Well, right then I learned what they meant. It took a whole long time to seep into my brain, but finally I realized like, hey, if night falls only once every two thousand years around this place, then the stars won't come out again for *centuries*, right? And without stars, I'd never be able to whush myself home! I'd be stuck on Lagash *forever and ever*! And I already knew they didn't have TV, so that meant they also didn't have any of the other trappings of modern civilization that are dependent on TV, like the Shopping Channel and Lorenzo Lamas. And could the Galleria have existed back in those pre-test-pattern dark ages? I think not.

So I was not going to be hanging out on Lagash long enough to find out what the dawn would bring. I had one window of opportunity, and I wasn't going to miss it. "What about the weather?" I go.

"Hmm?" Like Segol the Bionic Brain was aware of my existence again.

"You know, if it gets all cloudy, we won't be able to *see* the stars." Then I'd be trapped there for good.

He brightened up considerably for a moment. "Yes," he goes, "that would be a miracle."

"Not for *some* of us," I go. First I thought he'd fallen desperately in love with me and wanted me to stay on Lagash. But this bozo was thinking that after two thousand years of buildup, the big night might come and it would be too overcast to see anything. *Quel* irony, right?

N.S.L., sweetie—No Such Luck. Beta, the red sun in the sky, was now only a thin crescent like a bloody sliver of fingernail or something. It wouldn't be much longer to total Darkness. It was like slightly obvious that we'd never make it to the Hideout in time. I was stuck out on this road with Segol 154, who was like a total loon. Still, the Hideout was all he could think about.

"We've got to hurry," he goes, putting his grubby hands on my person and kind of dragging me along after him. "We've got to get to the Hideout. We must make sure you're safe. Your destiny is to have babies, *many* babies, who will be the hope of Lagash's future."

I disenhanded myself from him and laughed, a proud and haughty laugh meaning "If you weren't such a pitiful *knob*, I'd hack you to little pieces for that remark." Let me tell you a little secret, honey: no matter where you go in the known universe, the men are all the same. It's like these honkers are what God gave us as *substitutes* because all the really buf guys are on back order.

So what does he do? He grabs me by both shoulders and goggles into my face. "You . . . will be . . . the mother of . . . my children!" he goes. And even if there wasn't a line of drool down his chin, like there should have been.

You know and I know—and, *believe* me, Bitsy, now this Segol knows—*nobody* paws me uninvited. I didn't care if civilization was quickly coming to a screeching halt. I was now totally bugged, and I was going to teach him a lesson in interspatial etiquette. I put one hand flat against his chest and pushed real hard, and the next thing he's down in the road squinting up at me all surprised. I whipped Old Betsy from her scabbard again and took a menacing step toward him. "Look!" he screams. "Behind you!"

"Oh, like I'm so sure," I go. But I heard these grumbly sounds, and I turned and saw a mob of people huffing up the hill toward us. They did not look pleased.

Segol scrabbled to his feet and stood beside me. "Let me do the talking, little lady," he goes. "They may still listen to reason. And maybe you'd better put that silly sword away."

I decided to let him take his shot. I didn't even freak out about being called "little lady." I was absolutely *beyond* arguing with him. He could try talking to the mob, and when he'd said his piece, I was going to lop his grody head off. Okay, like I'd given him fair warning, hadn't I?

But he wasn't even aware that he'd bummed me out. He

started walking toward the crowd from the city, both hands raised above his head. I don't know what that was supposed to mean. Segol probably thought he was one dangerous dude. Maybe he thought that with his hands in the air, he wouldn't look like such a terrible threat to the safety of those five hundred howling maniacs. "Listen to me!" he goes. "Listen to me! I mean you no harm!"

Yeah, right. That made the mob feel a whole lot better about everything, for sure.

There was this raspy guy at the front of the crowd. He looked like he'd been getting ready for the end of civilization for a long time now, and like he couldn't wait for it to happen, you know? He had wild scraggly hair and big popping old eyes. He just about had a bird when he recognized Segol 154. "That's one of them!" he goes, waving his arms around a lot. "He's from the Observatory!"

Segol gave him this smile that was supposed to calm him down or something. "Come," he goes, "let us reason together."

"They didn't come here to *talk*," I go. "They came here to work your butt."

Someone else in the crowd started shouting, "Death to the unbelievers! Death to the blasphemers in the Observatory!"

That cry was taken up by others until it became this ugly chant. I wanted to tell them, hey, I'd never even *been* in the Observatory, but they wouldn't even have heard me.

Finally, a tall man in a black robe pushed his way to the front of the crowd. When he raised his hands, they all shut up. "Silence, my friends," he goes. "Let us give these profaners of the truth one last chance to redeem their souls."

"Who's that?" I go.

"His name is Sor 5," Segol goes. "He is the leader of the Cultists."

"Oh, huh," I go. I turned to this Sor 5 and I go, "I don't know anything about your Cult. What's your problem, anyway?"

The guy in the robe just gave me this sad little smile. "It's not *my* problem, young lady. It's yours. You have only a few minutes left before Lagash is swallowed up by the Cave of Darkness. Unless you embrace the revealed truth of our faith, your soul will be stripped from you when the Stars appear. You will become a savage, unreasoning brute."

I looked at the flipped-out people who made up his congregation, and I figured most of them didn't have far to go. Like maybe they'd already *seen* the stars, like at some kind of preview party or something. "So what are you guys selling?" I go.

Sor goes, "Behold! The Cave of Darkness is already engulfing Beta."

I looked up. There wasn't much of the red sun left. "Really," I go. "Tell me about it."

"Soon all will be in Darkness, and the Stars will blaze down in all their fury."

"Really."

Sor looked confused for a few seconds. "You do not deny any of this?"

I go, "See, you're telling me the same thing that Segol told me, and I can't figure out what your hang-up is."

That made him mad. I thought he was going to split his black robe. "We believe the Stars are the source of the Heavenly Flame, which will scourge and cleanse Lagash. The infidels of the Observatory insist that the Stars are nothing but burning balls of gas, physical objects like our own six suns. They refuse to grant that the Stars have any holy power at all."

"Death to the unbelievers!" screamed the mob. "Death to the blasphemers in the Observatory!" Sor tried again to quiet them, but this time they wouldn't listen. They surged forward, and I was like sure they were fully ready to tear us limb from limb. I brandished Old Betsy, but I backed away uphill, praying that Segol and I could somehow make it to the Observatory alive.

The astronomer shot me a terrified glance. "You hold them off," he goes, "and I'll run for help."

"Right," I go, sort of contemptuously, "you just do that." He was like a real poohbutt, you know?

Just then, the last red ember of Beta flickered in the sky and went out as the eclipse reached totality. There was a long moment of this really creepy quiet. You couldn't hear a sound, not a person gasping or an animal rustling, not even the wind. It was like being in a movie theater when the film breaks, just before the audience starts getting rowdy. And then the *stars* came out, normally No Big Deal.

Except on Lagash, it *was* a big deal, and not just 'cause it'd been two thousand years since the last time. Bitsy, these people really knew how to have *stars*! I looked up, and there were a zillion times as many stars as we have on Earth. It reminded me of when we were getting ready for that dance at Brush-Bennett, and you spilled that whole box of glitter on my black strapless. Remember? Well, on Lagash, the night sky looked just like that. All the places *between* the stars were crammed with stars.

"Oh . . . my . . . *God!*" I was totally impressed, but I wasn't, you know, going *insane* or anything.

"Stars!" goes Segol in this kind of strangled voice.

"Surprise," I go. I mean, he was a real melvin.

Now the mob started screaming and screeching and carrying on. They'd known the Stars were coming, but like they didn't have any idea what stars really *were*, or how *many* of them there'd be, and all that. So even Sor looked haired, but I give him credit, he pulled himself together pretty fast. "Our salvation will be the destruction of the Observatory," he goes. I mean, he couldn't bring himself to look up at the stars anymore, and he had to kind of croak his speech out, but he made himself heard. "If we destroy the Observatory and everyone in it, the Stars will spare us. And we must begin with them."

He was pointing at me and Segol. "That is *so* lame," I go. "Don't be stupid. There's nothing to be—"

Sadly, I didn't have the time to finish my explanation. The crowd was full-on crazy and ready to roust. When they charged, I felt a sudden calmness flood through me. I didn't know *what* Segol was doing and I didn't care. Old Betsy whistled through the air as I hacked and hewed at the waves of shrieking lunatics. Bodies piled up in front of me and on both sides. I took a couple of biffs and bruises, but I was too skillful and like too excellent for them to fight through my guard.

Of course, they had me outnumbered, and after a while I realized I was way tired. I wasn't going to be able to handle *all* of them, so while I fought I tried to think up some, you know, *strategy*. And then I saw their leader over on the side of the road, kneeling down in the dark, with his face turned up to the sky where the eclipse was still chugging along and the stars were still blazing away. I started working my way toward him, wading through his nutty buddies with my broadsword cutting a swath before me.

Finally I was right beside him. I reached down and grabbed

him by the neck of his robe and jerked him to his feet. "I am Sor!" he goes, like frothing a little in the corners of his mouth. He wasn't all there anymore, okay?

"You're sore," I go. I let him go and he fell in a heap at my feet. "Tell your fruitcake army to stand still and shut up, or I'll split your skull open and let the starlight in."

Sor stared at me fearfully for a few seconds. Then he got to his feet and raised his arms. "Stand still and shut up!" he goes.

All the rest of the mob stopped what they were doing, which was mostly climbing over the stacks of bodies, trying to get to me.

"Good," I go. "You have no reason to be afraid."

Segol started babbling. I'd wondered what had happened to him. "Beenay guessed a dozen, maybe two dozen Stars. But this! The universe, the stars, the *bigness*!"

"Lagash is nothing, a speck of dust!" cried a voice from the mob.

"We're nothing but insects, *less* than insects!"

"I want light! Let's burn the Observatory!"

"We're so small, and the Darkness is so huge! Our suns and our planet are insignificant!"

Well, these people had a serious problem. All of a sudden, they realized that there was a lot more to the universe than their precious Lagash. Then I had an idea that might keep these frenzied folks from thrashing *all* of their civilization and maybe save my own neck, too.

I go, "There's no reason to be afraid. The stars are not what you think. I *know*. I come from a world that has studied them for many centuries."

"She's mad! The Stars have driven her insane!"

"Listen to her!" Segol goes. "She told me the same story long before the Stars appeared. She speaks the truth."

"Yes," I go, "there *are* other stars in the universe. That's just something you're going to have to learn to live with. But not as many as *that*." I pointed up, and noticed that the eclipse had moved on past totality, and a teeny tiny thread of red light was starting to grow on one side of Beta.

"Then what are all those thousands of points of light?" goes Sor.

"Tonight is a night for revelations and strange truth," I go. I'm always pretty good in a crisis like that. I can talk my way out of *anything.* Hey, *you* know that. You were my roommate, right? "Lagash, your six suns, and the other twelve stars in the universe are surrounded by a huge ball of ice."

"Ice?" goes Segol. He sounded like he was having just a little bit of trouble buying it.

"Sure, *ice,*" I go, acting kind of ticked off that he doubted me. "What did you think, that the universe just sort of went on and on *forever*? That's so *real,* I'm totally sure."

"A wall of ice," Sor goes. "The *Book of Revelations* speaks of a Cave of Darkness. I don't see why there can't be a wall of ice as well."

Now everyone had stopped trying to grab me by the throat. They were all like hanging on my every word, okay? "But what *are* the Stars?" someone goes.

"The Stars are an illusion," I go. "What you see up there are only the reflections of the dozen real stars, shining on the craggy ice wall of the universe."

There was this silence. I held my breath 'cause everything would be totally cool if they believed me, but I'd have to start fighting for my life again if they didn't. Five seconds passed, then ten. Then all at once they all went "Ahhhh."

Sor goes, "It's the divine truth!" I saw tears running down his face.

"Look!" goes Segol. "Beta! It's coming back!"

Sor waved his arms around and got their attention. "Let's hurry back to Saro City," he goes. "We can spread the news and keep our brothers and sisters from burning our homes. The other suns will rise in a few hours, and then life must go on as before. We must tell the others what we've learned, and broadcast the information to everyone on Lagash." Then they turned and marched away, without so much as a thank-you.

When we were alone again on the road, Segol came over to me. He had this big, spazzy grin on his face. "That was really something, my dear," he goes.

"My name's *Maureen,* and this is the *last* time I'm going to remind you. If you have trouble remembering that, you can call me Princess." Well, Bitsy, I *know* I was sort of stretching the truth, but sometimes I liked to think of myself as sort of almost engaged to Prince Van of the Angry Red Planet. I mean, a woman's reach should exceed her grasp, or what's a mixer at Yale for?

"Then congratulations, Maureen. You were outstanding. You have saved us from centuries of Dark Ages. I think you'll always be remembered in the history books of Lagash."

I shrugged. "What can I say?" I go. "It's like a gift."

Segol nodded, then hung his head in shame. "I guess I owe you an apology, too. I wasn't much help to you during the battle."

"'S all right," I go. "You weren't really ready for all those stars." I was just being gracious, you know? I'd been a little zooned out, too, when I saw how many there were, but *I* got over it.

He looked back up at me, as grateful as that awful Akita puppy Daddy brought home for Pammy's birthday. "Perhaps you'd permit me the honor," he goes, "of asking for your hand in marriage."

I was like too stunned to say anything for a moment. I wiped Old Betsy off on this dead guy's shirt and slid her slowly back into the scabbard. Then I go, "No, I won't permit you the honor of having my hand in *anything*. Nothing personal, okay?"

He was disappointed, of course, but he'd live. "I understand. Would you answer a question, then?"

"Sure, as long as it's not like way lewd or demeaning to all women."

He took a deep breath and he goes, "Is it *true*? What you told the Cultists? Is it true that Lagash is in the center of a gigantic ball of ice?"

I laughed. I mean, how megadumb could he be? I wasn't surprised that Sor 5 and his crowd swallowed that story, but I didn't think a real astronomer would buy it. Then I realized that this was *not* the World of Superscience, after all, and that Segol was just a poor guy trying to understand like the laws of nature and everything. I couldn't bring myself to weird him out any more than he already was. "Right, like totally," I go. "Maybe someday your own Observatory will figure out the distance from Lagash to the ice wall. I *used* to know, but I forgot."

"Thank you, Maureen," he goes. Suddenly he'd gotten so humble it was *ill*. "I think we'd better hurry back to tell Aton and the others the news. Beenay and the rest of the photographers should have captured the Stars with their imaging equipment. They were all prepared, of course, but even so they may have given way to panic." He looked down at the ground again, probably remembering how *he'd* bugged out of there in panic even *before* the stars came out.

"I'm sorry, Segol," I go. "I *can't* go back to the Observatory with you. I'm needed elsewhere. I've got to flash on back to Earth. If I wait much longer the eclipse will be over, the sky will get light, the stars will go out for another two thousand years, and I'll never see my dear, dear friend Bitsy *ever again*." Sure, sweetie, even in this moment of awful tension, I thought of you. You *believe* me, don't you?

Segol sighed. "I suppose you must go, then. I'll never forget you, little la— I mean, Maureen."

I gave him this sort of *noblesse oblige* smile, but I stopped short of getting all emotional and everything. "Farewell, Segol 154," I go. "Tell the others that someday, when you've proved yourselves worthy, my people will welcome yours into the Federation of Planets. Until then, one last word of advice: try to discourage anyone who starts fiddling around with radio astronomy. I think it will make you all very, *very* unhappy."

"Radio astronomy?" he goes. "How can you look at space with a radio?"

"Never mind, just remember what I said." I raised one hand in the universal sign of "That's all, folks." Then I raised my supplicating arms to the stars, went *eeny meeny miney mo*, and whushed myself on out of there.

I'm sorry I had to listen to the whole story. By the time Maureen finished it, we had finished off all the strawberries, and a quiche with nothing in it is like tortellini salad without the tortellini. In the months that Josh and I had been together, he'd taught me a lot about food and everything. We didn't have supper any more, we dined. And then like I did the dishes.

Anyway, it was getting late, and you know I had to rush her out of there, and I tried to explain to her but she just didn't want to listen, so then I put my back against her and shoved her toward the door, and I guess she got annoyed or something 'cause then I shoved some more but she wasn't there and I fell on the kitchen floor and she was standing over me with her sword in her hand and she had on what she called her warrior-woman expression, and I could just see the headlines in the Post: QUEENS WOMAN DIES IN SHISH KABOB TRAGEDY. *Josh would* never be able to face our folks again. So I go, "Back off, Muffy." Wrong thing to say.

"You're as bad as those ape-things in the center of the Earth!" She was screeching now.

I go, "Just bag your face, will you? Some roommate you are. Where's that old Greenberg School bond we used to have?"

That got to her. She sheathed her jeweled sword and calmed down. She helped me get up and dusted me off a little. "I'm sorry, Bitsy," she goes. I noticed she was blushing.

"All right, I guess," I go. We looked at each other a little longer, then I started to cry for some reason, and then she trickled a couple, and we started hugging each other and bawling, and the front door opened and I heard Josh coming in, and all he needed was another unexplained visit from his favorite Savage Amazon, so I go, "Maureen, quick, you've got to hide!" And then I felt like we were all on I Love Lucy or something, and I started to laugh.

She laughed, too. Josh didn't laugh, though. Sometimes it's like we only see his friends, and why can't I ever have my friends over? Josh goes, "Because my friends don't wave broadswords around on the subway." I suppose he has a point there.

Balance

by Mike Resnick

Susan Calvin stepped up to the podium and surveyed her audience: the stockholders of the United States Robots and Mechanical Men Corporation.

"I want to thank you for your attendance," she said in her brisk, businesslike way, "and to update you on our latest developments."

What a fearsome face she has, thought August Geller, seated in the fourth row of the audience. *She reminds me of my seventh-grade English teacher, the one I was always afraid of.*

Calvin launched into a detailed explanation of the advanced new circuitry she had introduced into the positronic brain, breaking it down into terms a layman—even a stockholder—could understand.

Brilliant mind, thought Geller. *Absolutely brilliant. It's probably just as well. Imagine a countenance like that without a mind to offset it.*

"Are there any questions at this point?" asked Calvin, her cold blue eyes scanning the audience.

"I have one," said a pretty young woman, rising to her feet.

"Yes?"

The woman voiced her question.

"I thought I had covered that point," said Calvin, doing her best to hide her irritation. "However . . ."

She launched into an even more simplistic explanation.

Isn't it amazing? thought Geller. *Here are two women, one with a mind like a steel trap, the other with an I.Q. that would probably freeze water, and yet I can't take my eyes off the woman who asked that ridiculous question. Poor Dr. Calvin; Nature has such a malicious sense of humor.*

Calvin noticed a number of the men staring admiringly at her questioner. It was not the first time that men had found something more fascinating than Calvin to capture their attention, nor the hundredth, nor the thousandth.

What a shame, she thought, *that they aren't more like robots, that they let their hormones overwhelm their logic. Here I am, explaining how I plan to spend twelve billion dollars of their money, and they're more interested in a pretty face.*

Her answer completed, she launched into a discussion of the attempts they were making to provide stronger bodies for those robots designed for extraterrestrial use by the application of titanium frames with tight molecular bondings.

I wonder, thought Geller, *if she's ever even had a date with a man? Not a night of wild passion, God knows, but just a meal and perhaps a trip to the theater, where she didn't talk business.* He shook his head almost imperceptibly. *No,* he decided, *it would probably bore her to tears. All she cares about are her formulas and equations. Good looks would be wasted on her.*

Calvin caught Geller staring at her, and met and held his gaze.

What a handsome young man, she thought. *I wonder if I've seen him at any previous meetings? I'm sure I'd remember if I had. Why is he staring at me so intently?*

I wonder, thought Geller, *if anyone she's loved has ever loved her back?*

Probably he's just astounded that a woman can have a brain, she concluded. *As if anything else mattered.*

In fact, thought Geller, *I wonder if she's ever loved at all?*

Look at that tan, thought Calvin, still staring at Geller. *It's attractive, to be sure, but do you ever work, or do you spend all your time lazing mindlessly on the beach?* She fought back an urge to sigh deeply between sentences. *Sometimes it's hard to imagine that people like you and I even belong to the same species, I have so much more in common with my robots.*

Sometimes, thought Geller, *when I listen to you wax rhapsodic about positronic brains and molecular bonding, it's hard to imagine that we belong to the same species, you sound so much like one of your robots.*

Still, thought Calvin against her will, *you are tall and you are handsome, and you certainly have an air of self-assuredness about you. Most men won't or can't match my gaze. And your eyes are blue and clear. I wonder . . .*

Still, thought Geller, *there must be something there, some core of femininity beneath the harsh features and coldly analytical mind. I wonder . . .*

Calvin shook her head inadvertently and almost lost track of what she was saying.

Ridiculous, she concluded. *Absolutely ridiculous.*

Geller stared at her one more time, studying the firm jaw, the broad shoulders, the aggressive stance, the face devoid of makeup, the hair that could have been so much more attractive.

Ridiculous, he concluded. *Absolutely ridiculous.*

Calvin spoke for another fifteen minutes, then opened the floor to questions.

There were two, and she handled them both succinctly.

"I want to thank Dr. Calvin for spending this time with us," concluded Linus Becker, the young chief operating executive of United States Robots and Mechanical Men. "As long as we have her remarkable intellect working for us, I feel confident that we will continue to forge ahead and expand the perameters of the science of robotics."

"I'll second that," said one of the major stockholders. "When we produce a positronic brain with half the capabilities of our own Dr. Calvin, the field of robotics will have come of age."

"Thank you," said Calvin, ignoring a strange sense of emptiness within her. "I am truly flattered."

"It's we who are flattered," said Becker smoothly, "to be in the presence of such brilliance." He applauded her, and soon the entire audience, including Geller, got to their feet and gave her a standing ovation.

Then each in turn walked up to her to introduce himself or herself, and shake her hand, and comment on her intellect and creativity.

"Thank you," said Calvin, acknowledging yet another compliment. *You take my hand as if you expect it to be tungsten and steel, rather than sinew and bone. Have I come to resemble my robots that much?*

"I appreciate your remarks," said Calvin to another stockholder. *I wonder if lovers speak to each other in the same hail–fellow–well–met tones?*

And then Geller stepped up and took her hand, and she almost jumped from the sensation, the electricity passing from his strong, tanned hand to her own.

"I think you are quite our greatest asset, Dr. Calvin," he said.

"Our robots are our greatest asset," she replied graciously. "I'm just a scientific midwife."

He stared intently at her for a moment, and suddenly the tension left his body. *Impossible. You're too much like them. If I asked you out, it would be an act of charity, and I think you are too proud and too perceptive to accept that particular kind of charity.*

She looked into his eyes one last time. *Impossible. I have my work to do—and my robots never disappoint me by proving to be merely human.*

"Remember, everyone," announced Becker, "there's a banquet three hours from now." He turned to Calvin. "You'll be there, of course."

Calvin nodded. "I'll be there," she said with a sigh.

She had only an hour to change into a formal gown for the banquet, and she was running late. She entered her rather nondescript apartment, walked through the living room and bedroom, both of which were filled to overflowing with scientific journals, opened her closet, and began laying out her clothes on the bed.

"Did anyone ever tell you that you have the most beautiful blue eyes?" asked her butler robot.

"Why, thank you," said Calvin.

"It's true, you know," continued the butler. "Lovely, lovely eyes, as blue as the purest sapphire."

Her robot maid entered the bedroom to help her dress.

"Such a pretty smile," said the maid. "If I had a smile like yours, men would fight battles just for the pleasure of seeing it turned upon them."

"You're very kind," said Calvin.

"Oh, no, Mistress Susan," the robot maid corrected her. *"You're* very beautiful."

Calvin noticed the robot chef standing in the doorway to her bedroom.

"Stop staring at me," she said. "I'm only half-dressed. Where are your manners?"

"Legs like yours, and you expect me to stop staring?" said the chef with a dry, mechanical chuckle. "Every night I dream about meeting a woman with legs like yours."

Calvin slipped into her gown, then waited for the robot maid to zip up the back.

"Such clear, smooth skin," crooned the maid. "If I were a woman, that's the kind of skin I would want."

They are such perceptive creatures, reflected Calvin, as she stood before a mirror and applied her almost-clear lipstick. *Such dear creatures,* she amended. *Of course they are just responding to the needs of First Law—to* my *needs—but how very thoughtful they are.*

She picked up her purse and headed to the door.

I wonder if they ever get tired of reciting this litany?

"You'll be the belle of the ball," said the robot butler proudly as she walked out of the apartment.

"Why, thank you very much," said Calvin. "You grow more flattering by the day."

The robot shook its metallic head. "It is only flattery if it is a lie, my lady," it said just before the door slid shut behind her.

Her emotional balance fully restored, as it always was whenever she came home from dealing with human beings, she headed toward the banquet feeling vigorous and renewed. She wondered if she would be seated near that handsome August Geller, who had listened to her so intently during her speech.

Upon reflection, she hoped that she would be seated elsewhere. He aroused certain uneasy feelings within her, this handsome young man—and fantasies, when all was said and done, were for lesser intellects which, unlike herself, couldn't cope with the cold truths of the real world.

The Present Eternal

by Barry N. Malzberg

So Arnold Potterley went home. Where, after all, was there to go? If there was nowhere to hide, then you might at least be uncomfortable, squirm under the knowledge of complete exposure where, at least, you were most comfortable.

At least, that was Potterley's way of rationalizing this ultimate disaster. Others had different views, of course. Nimmo went to the outback. Foster went insane.

I have been asked to write a history of the world after the chronoscope. This is a great honor, of course. I am being honored in that request. It is not so long that I have been writing, after all, first numbers and then for a long time the alphabet, until at last I began to feel more secure with words and phrases and then whole sentences; still this is a big leap for me. "If you do not do it, Jorg, who will do it?" I have been told, rather asked, but this does not honor so much as it frightens me. Many things frighten me of course; the chronoscope taught us to be afraid of everything. The chronoscope taught us common sense. The chronoscope taught us the true way of the world. "Jorg" is not real, is my *nom*, as they say, *de plumay*.

Caroline Potterley waited for months after she could have done it to finally bring the machine into her home, seek her dead daughter, Laurel. To see her again, to know the little girl as she had been had constituted the final passion of her life and yet when it was possible at last, when Arnold had insisted and Foster had made that thing and the time-viewer, for reasons she had never understood had escaped to the entire world . . . when that opportunity was, at last, hers, Caroline found herself in thrall, held back, locked against her own desire. She knew that once she brought in the machine and everyone was doing it now, Arnold refused but how could he have stopped her?, once she used the controls and instructions and found her dead daughter she would fall and fall, plunge into something, some quality of emotion which she had never known . . . and it was the need to *fight* against this stricture, to fight against that last and terrible plunge which caused her to hold back but there came finally that point at which she could no longer resist.

"I can't hold back any longer, Arnold," she would have said if they had still been talking in these months, but they were not. Arnold was never home except to sleep and sometimes even not at night, he wandered around in grief and shock, pulling at the pockets of his suit jackets and finishing the small bottles of wine which case by case he brought in and bottle by bottle he drained. So she did not say this to him, merely made the necessary arrangements which were easy to do in this strange and terrible world which had evolved, and opened the viewer to her history, to that time before the fire when—

—When she had had a little girl laughing and tumbling in the corridors of her life, when she and Laurel had told one another secrets which now she could not, somehow, remember.

This is my partial history of the world after the chronoscope, then. No one can write the full history, who has the time? Who has the tools? It was the criminal, the necessary part of our lives. I am making some of this up. I am imagining some of this as the way it should have been. No one who was there at the time bothered to write it down or to put it in final form, it is left to me to make it up as best I can. That is what was said to me, "Make it up as best you can.

If it seems to fit, then make it fit. There are no truths. What is truth? What can truth be? Set it down as you see fit." And so on and so forth in this difficult and imperfect time. I was talking about who used it first. Who is to say who used it first? All of them did, everyone did. But I think it must have been the thieves and lowlifes who perceived its lesser possibilities, those dedicated to the transcendent and the bravest view of matters who would have adapted the chronoscope first, not the leaders of nations but those who toiled in the outskirts of the nations. For them the chronoscope would yield a kind of eternal present through which they could scamper gratefully, thoughtfully, seeking grander device. Who else could it have been? It was these visionaries of course, who first made use of the device. This is no surprise, those like Potterley are always ahead of the herd in their willingness to try new and different means.

Of course everyone, theoretically, who used the time-viewer was a criminal by fiat; we are talking (notice how easily I slide into the voice of authority and generalization, that pontifical "we," but I have been reading many of the old texts in preparation for this assignment and in order to find the proper approach) rather of professionals, those who considered it already an occupation. Secret combinations, long-buried hiding places, crevices containing the untaxed unconverted profits . . . all of these were easily available to a patient and understanding scan.

Crimes of violence and passion, surprisingly, diminished; the chronoscope made passion and violence vicariously available to the widest, most eager audience and the pre-chronoscope sex lives of the famous and desired were—well, they were most famous and desired.

In the viewer, then, in that narrow and focused tube of memory, Laurel waved at her, skipped to the bottom of the slide and began her tumbling ascent, in the shafts of indifferent late afternoon light (it must have been that first October they had the slide, Laurel's teeth were uneven and the dress she wore had been somehow lost after one season, Caroline remembered this, she remembered everything) she seemed ever more vulnerable as she rose and yet somehow, mixed with the vulnerability, there was a toughness, a security of effort, a determination which would have fifteen years later, maybe less, made her a fearsome young woman.

Caroline could see that strength, could take it for the moment into herself and knowing that, knowing that the twenty-year-old Laurel would have been able to direct circumstance as Caroline never could, gave her a sudden and shuddering moment of insight, of possibility, which in the thin gray light cast from the viewer seemed to cast her up very much as Laurel herself seemed to rise, seemed to lock them into some passionate and savage assertion which could, in that moment, reach out from the constricted space of the viewer and become, almost become, the world.

One year after the particulars of chronoscopy appeared on a popular science program any dummy could have figured out, your Tiffany, who thought of herself still as lost in the darkness of crime, walked into the home of Paul Taber, owner of half the casinos in Miami. There was no need to fear the presence of Taber or anyone else; she had cleared that. She had watched Taber and his fifth wife leave and, furthermore, she had watched them take a last look, *another* little security peek for them at the jewels and cash that a careful scan through the years had shown them so industriously accumulating right up to that point, twelve hours earlier, where they had secured the house (no problem for Tiffany) and left on a long, sudden, necessary trip.

On the way to the safe with the real stuff, humming a little song of accomplishment, Tiffany picked up a few bangles here and a few baubles over there, working from the map of the premises she had sketched out so carefully, so industriously, put them into her little sack. Just as she scampered toward the safe, she saw the shadows against the window and then a rough, clumsy but manifestly accomplished thug came into the light and stared at her. He seemed to be holding a sack of his own.

"I hadn't thought of this," Tiffany said.

"Who are you?" the thug asked.

"But I should have thought of it," Tiffany said. "I mean, it doesn't show the future, right?"

"What future?" the thug said. *'This* is the future. Okay, hand over the stuff."

"It's mine," she said stupidly. "I worked for it."

The thug pulled out a gun and pointed it with easy accomplishment at a dangerous area of Tiffany's chest. "You didn't work hard enough," he said.

"Protestant ethic," Tiffany said pointlessly. "I was here first, anyway."

"But I'm here *now*. And I can open that safe as easy as you. Easier. I know the combination."

"So do I."

"The viewer," he said. Understanding flooded the thug's features; he appeared, suddenly, years younger and more alert. It did wonders for his complexion, too. "You have one of those things, too. You can look at the past."

"I'm also patient and careful," Tiffany said. "If you had done any real research at all instead of grabbing one of those ten-cent viewers and spinning the dials, you would have seen that there's a spot in this place which has an alarm hooked up directly to headquarters, five minutes away. And you're standing on it, dummy."

"You're just trying to get me to leave."

"Would I try to scare you for no reason? A colleague? We'd better get out of here, pal."

"You mean, like me first," the thug said. "And leave you to clean out the place on your own. No, not without that stuff I'm not going." He brandished the gun.

Tiffany shrugged. Baubles and bangles, yes, but the supply was infinite. It was as infinite as time. Didn't he understand this? The arena had become vastly more open; the walls had been taken down. "Take them," she said generously, passing handfuls. She walked toward a window. "I've got three other places on the list and that's just for tonight."

The thug stood, clutching jewelry, his features fallen into their more accustomed places, his eyes stunned and blinking. "You're so sure—" he said, "so sure of everything." He looked at the gun over which a necklace had been casually draped. "I never had your opportunities," he said.

"But we *all* have opportunities now," Tiffany said. "Don't you understand?" She almost did. She was closing in on it all the time, she was on the verge of terrific insight. Insight was all you needed to function in this world now, all the rest was just *stuff*. "It's getting so easy it's boring. It's almost like it doesn't count any more."

"I count," the thug said. Some people kept on insisting. Who could blame them?

"That's because you think any of this old stuff still matters," Tiffany said. She went through the window. This is a reasonable approximation of how it was, I think.

"Come away, Caroline," Arnold said. His whisper, sepulchral and unexpected behind her, was a gunshot. She trembled, shook, turned toward him, saw his features suddenly grotesque and brutalized in the odd and terrible flickering light of the chronoscope.

"Get away!" she said. She felt fear course through her; oddly it energized rather than shriveled, she wanted to leap at him suddenly. If they could finally touch—

He reached forward, touched her wrist, pulled at it. "It's horrible, Caroline," he whispered. "You must stop this, you can't hide, you can't go away, you have to face this—Carthage *burned*," he said. "I know it now, they set fires, they killed—"

"Go away!" she said again. "I want to look—"

"She's dead," Arnold said. "I didn't know it at first, *I* had to look too, yes I did, I went to the library even after everything I told you and I stared for hours, but there comes a time, Caroline, you have to let it go; she's no longer ours, she's no one's, she's lost to us, lost to everything but the machine. Caroline, we can't be like so many, we have to get out of the room, we have to have a *life*—"

He reached forward to disconnect the machine and she did something then, moved, began to deal with him as she must, but after this her recollection was not as clear and she did not want to use the machine to recover that moment, she would let it rest, let all of it rest, only Laurel, his Carthage, his burning . . .

You do not have to give so many details, they tell me. They have looked at this and in some ways they make the good sounds and in other ways the bad sounds but what they want to make most clear is that it is not necessary to be as precise as I have been—that is the word they use, "precise"—it is only important to give what they call "an overview." "Give an overview," they say. "We have no time, no space, no room for history, we have only an ever-living and continual present, but that present, although it serves us well, must have the slightest amount of justification. If you can give us this, you have given enough." Who knows "enough"? I have my own plans and abilities.

I am the first and the last, the only one to give this history, they tell me, the only one to "write" as "writing" is understood in the oldstyle, but I must keep it tightly confined, must control. I do what I can. "Give an overview," they say, but it is not the over but the under which possesses me, the weight of all that has happened almost obliterating (that is a tough word, "obliterating") that tiny corridor of light I cast toward our history.

It took what remained of law enforcement (that which hadn't gone crooked itself) quite a while to catch up with the outlaws, but when they did, it was all over for the criminal element. No unsolved crimes, no unresolved, unidentifiable remains. You couldn't even skip school . . . that is, if your settlement still had access to instruction of any kind. They knew when you were sleeping. They knew when you were awake. They knew if you'd been bad or good.

"Late meeting. That Ryan account. Should have been here hours ago, I'm sorry."

"Don't tell me 'Ryan account.' Who *is* that blond bitch on the third floor of 242 Oak Street?"

"What? What?"

"For someone who says he can't do a lot of things any more, you can do a lot of things, can't you?"

"But the account—the Ryan meeting—"

"Forget it, Frank. You're trying to live in a world which doesn't exist any more. Buy a chronoscope and get out of the house. Because tomorrow the locks are changed and you can't pick up *that* kind of detail work on any cheap set you're likely to get."

When the feelings passed, when she could focus again, see where she was, Caroline saw something had happened to Arnold, something dreadful had happened, he was lying on the floor in a quiescence she had never known him to have before. But even as she struggled with the impulse to kneel, comfort, hold, help him in some way, call for emergency aid, get the university services there, even as she thought of this, a small and infinitely wise voice within her said, *He's never looked this peaceful before, he has been granted perfect peace, the peace that Laurel has. Go to her, go to her again now, understand her peace and try to make it her own,* and the voice was so utterly attuned to her own necessity, Caroline knew she could do no more, could do nothing for Arnold that had not perished long ago, in the fire, beyond the fire, and turned instead toward the chronoscope, the chronoscope where Laurel, infinitely young, tender, wise, patient—

Where Laurel would tell her what, if anything, to do.

Procreation became limited, hurried, and—for those who persisted—bizarre. The governments, all of them, China and the Soviet Union and Burundi and Burma, South Africa and Zaire collapsed. Government of any kind was simply unimaginable. There was a futile attempt in some of the countries to confiscate chronoscopes, but that is when the murders began and, having made their point, soon enough stopped: the systems, such as they were, had become invested in the chronoscope, behavior had become circumscribed by its existence. Sixty years after Ralph Nimmo, uncle of the luckless Foster, had turned loose the plans, fled to Australia to successfully impersonate a keeper of aboriginal kangaroos (Foster meanwhile reinventing chronoscopy in custody, creating it over and over again), there wasn't much public left, and that which lasted was *old*, decrepit, and resentful of medical facilities and research which had become bare holding operations. There were localities with severely deteriorated communications. There was, always, the chronoscope. "Here it *is*," Foster said, handing scribblings to the attendants. *"Take it."*

After a century and a quarter, only a few clots and clans existed in the southern regions of the northern hemispheres, the northern regions of the southern. For this remainder, subsistence level in a subsistence society wasn't all that oppressive, and there was, of course, the chronoscope, whose limited range was nonetheless able to disclose in all of its fury and chiaroscuro beauty the collapse of Eastern and Western civilizations the century before, and all of the fragmentary, diminished copulation and confrontation associated with that collapse.

And so, hunched against circumstance, appalled by the news of her father's death but nonetheless loving and filled with tenderness, Laurel reached out from the interstices of the machine, reached from the dark metal and said to Caroline, "I'll tell you what to do, oh mother, I'll tell you just what you need to do but you have to come closer, come closer—"

As Caroline crept down that corridor of informative light.

I am the first of a long line to come who again will be able to compose our history. But our history is tense and exhausting, narrow and dangerous, and I see now why they wished me to be explicit, to compress, to hurry along; there is only a little left to tell but nonetheless—

"Remember how you loved him," Laurel said. "Remember how it was when you came to him for the first time, remember that mantle of love and warmth—"

"What we'll do," said Joan, an impassioned sixteen-year-old, "is run away."

"The others will see us. They'll be able to watch every move." Bill was eighteen, the levelheaded, farseeing part of the relationship. Or so he told Joan. There weren't enough their age around to argue for much differences, though. Anyone between fifteen or twenty was mostly the same. Timorous. Except for Joan who had a kind of spirit which was unaccountable and who had plans.

"We'll go so far away the old bastards won't be able to get there. No one will even look, all they want to do is stare and remember, anyway. We'll climb mountains."

"No matter how far we go, they'll still be able to watch anything we do. They'll see everything."

"I don't care. Who cares? Let them watch! They can watch us until I die if they want to. I want kids," she said passionately, looking at him in that way which so dangerously upset him. "I want a family. I want to have"—she paused—"abandoned sex. *Real* sex."

Bill was timorous but needful. "Yes," he said. "I do, too. But—"

"If you don't go with me, I'll ask someone else. I'll ask Dave."

"Dave? He's thirty years old. He's one of them. All he wants to do is look."

"I'll teach him a few things. He can be taught. There aren't many of us left, don't you know that? Do you want the whole world to die?"

"It's already dead."

"I mean *really* die. Die out. No more children, nothing. Not even the machines. Most of those damned viewers don't even work any more, they haven't been tended in years."

"There are probably fertile individuals in other clans. It doesn't fall only to us. There have got to be others—"

"Do you want it to end this way, then? Don't you want me—"

"Well, *sure* I want you," Bill said hopelessly. "I guess I do, anyway. But there will always be someone looking at us, even after everyone here dies."

"No there won't."

"Our own children will."

"Those machines are breaking down, I told you. We won't even take one. Let me tell you a secret. I smashed all of them around I could find."

"Joan! When?"

"Just before."

"They'll kill us when they find out."

"So I don't care," she said. She seized his wrists. "Now you *know* we've got to do something. You know we've got to go away."

"How many did you break?"

"A lot. Rust will take care of the rest of them, and I don't think any of the clan are smart enough to build them again. Don't you understand? I think they're really finished with them, now. I think it's run out."

Bill felt her pulling him along. Soon they would be out of the hutch, on level ground, and they could run. Forage from the land, build a settlement. Well, it sounded possible. Anything was possible. Joan was right, no one was going to follow them. They just weren't that interested. "No more of them?" Bill said hopefully. "You mean, no more of the machines?"

"I think not. But to be extra specially certain, just in case any instructions *do* survive in our new place, we won't teach our kids to read."

"Will it work?"

She smiled. "Oh, for a while," she said. "Eventually one of

them will learn to write and maybe put all of this down again, but by then it will be too late. And we'll be free."

And in the machine, in that swath of light Laurel had helped her cleave from the darkness Caroline saw them as it had been that night, the first night Arnold had known her, the night Arnold had loved her. She watched the bodies struggle, then slide in and amongst the shining spokes of light and then, in slow and terrible concert, the scene shifted, reassembled, and Caroline saw herself huge and arched against that wedge of vision as she struck the blow which killed Arnold, watched him collapse against her in that parody of embrace, and then the two of them locked, were rolling and rolling on the floor in and amongst the plans, the diagrams, the wires, the nest of that awful machinery. "Oh Laurel," Caroline Potterly said. "Oh Laurel, oh Laurel . . ."

And the fires of Carthage came.

PAPPI

by Sheila Finch

The first thing Tim noticed when he entered his old home was the visorphone in the hall flashing to warn him of an incoming call. It had to be for Karin, of course. But who wouldn't already know she was dead? Karin didn't have a very wide circle of friends.

The visorphone's shrill call noise was irritating. He was tired from the shuttle flight, obscurely annoyed by the obsequious robot attendants, and feeling the pull of Earth's excessive gravity already. He punched the receive button. The operator's voice instructed Mr. Tim Garroway to stand by for a call from Mr. Howard Rathbone III.

Too late to worry about how Rathbone had figured where he'd be going to in such a hurry. He wasn't cut out to play James Bond games, but he'd felt confident that Earth was the one place Rathbone would never think of looking for him if he made a run for it, since it was where Rathbone had wanted him to go. Obviously he'd underestimated the man.

While he waited for the connection to be completed between Earth and the space station up at the Lagrange point that was Rathbone's corporate headquarters, he glanced through the doorway into the living room to see what Beth was doing. She was sitting cross-legged on the rug, building a tower of books, her small plump face raised to the warm spring sunshine that flooded in through the undraped window. Sunlight sparked her curls to gold, and Tim's heart lurched as he saw for the thousandth time how like her mother his little daughter was.

If only Sylvia could've seen her now.

If only the damned emergency-team robots had functioned as they were supposed to.

He'd gone over and over the options on the shuttle trip from the moon. There weren't very many in his favor. Running had been an impulse that he'd begun to see might cause him a lot of nasty problems. He waited sullenly for the phone link to be completed.

The visorphone crackled, pulling his attention back, and the screen cleared. Howard Rathbone III gazed at him from the elegantly paneled office where he kept the helm of his billion-dollar enterprises. Tim had speculated once, on first seeing this magnificent room, how much it had cost to lob all that rare and expensive teak and mahogany and rosewood into space to reconstruct the look of a luxury ocean liner from the 1920s. Sylvia had giggled at his estimate. *"Way, way under!"* she'd said.

"Tim. You and Beth had a pleasant shuttle trip, I hope? Of course, you should have consulted me before you—took the child along."

So the old man wasn't going to call it kidnapping just yet. Mr. Rathbone was a big man with a big man's hearty voice and manner. And a heart made out of pure moon rock. Obviously he figured on gaining some advantage from playing along with Tim.

"Fine, thanks, Mr. Rathbone. I would've called you to—"

Rathbone overrode his words. "You and Beth will need some time to recover. Tomorrow will be plenty of time to do what we talked about. You will do it, of course. You have so much to gain!"

Uneasily, Tim considered how often the man seemed to read his mind. Or was it just that he himself was totally predictable, at least where Mercury Mining and Manufacturing was concerned? Maybe Rathbone was right; there was too much money involved to be squeamish, enough to buy Beth everything her heart desired now and for a long time to come. And was the price really so unreasonable?

"I'm relying on you, Tim," Rathbone said. "Triple M's future is in your hands. But I'm confident you'll come through for us."

Even when he was handing out praise and flattery, Rathbone's words came out as orders. That was why he'd been so phenomenally successful, building his huge empire in less than two decades since the Second Mercury Expedition.

"Yes, sir."

"I'm a reasonable man, Tim. I'd like to have your willing cooperation. So I'm prepared to explain it all one more time. We must stop this now, before it goes any further. No telling what'll happen if he gets away with it. Do you understand my position, Tim?"

Tim nodded, his throat dry.

"We can't have all those machines out there thinking they're entitled to rights and privileges same as humans. And they will, you know, if he gets away with this."

"Yes, sir."

"You're a bright man. But you've been squandering your talents."

Not half as vicious as the things he'd said about Tim when he'd first learned of Sylvia's marriage to a penniless student, and her pregnancy, Tim thought. But if he played his cards right . . .

Rathbone leaned back in his leather swivel chair, steepled his fingers, and gazed at the father of his daughter's child. On the wall behind him a map of the inner solar system showed the Rathbone empire in scattered twinkling lights. "I have no heirs except for little Beth."

Tim swallowed. His hunger to own and control what the map represented fought another battle with the cautious part of him. The outcome was indecisive again. Yet each time, the hungry side of him crept a little closer to victory. Especially here, in this house.

"I still wonder if it wouldn't be better to try public exposure," Tim said. "You know—subject him to public scrutiny—put him through tests he can't pass—"

In the delay that followed, he knew what Rathbone's answer would be.

"That's been tried already!" Rathbone scowled at him across space. "And failed. There's no time left for pussyfooting here. He has to be removed."

Tim shrugged uneasily.

"It's not like killing a man, Tim. Stephen Byerley's a *robot!*"

Rathbone spat the word out, loaded with all the contempt, the hatred, and the fear Tim knew that he felt for robots.

"Sleep on it, son," his father-in-law said. In spite of the term he'd used, the threatening tone came through clearly. "I should think the consequences if you fail easily outweigh the demise of one robot."

That was the other factor in the equation. If he refused to do what Rathbone wanted, then Rathbone would take Beth away from him. He couldn't go back to the moon or the space station, and he sure couldn't stay on Earth any more. There was no place he could hide that his father-in-law's thugs couldn't find him. And he certainly couldn't take up the freelance life of an asteroid prospector, not with a three-year-old to raise.

The visorphone screen clouded over, and Tim turned heavily toward the living room to retrieve his daughter.

He had to agree his father-in-law had a point. Stephen Byerley had managed to get elected to public office a month ago. It was the beginning of the end of uncontested human superiority, despite the much-vaunted three laws. For one thing, Mayor Byerley might start thinking his "brothers" in space, those who toiled under horrifying conditions on blistering planets for industrialists like Howard Rathbone III, deserved better conditions. Byerley might even decide they were being treated like slaves and use the weight of his office to start a campaign for their emancipation. It was ludicrous, of course, but Tim understood that once you set the precedent of one robot being "human" enough to hold human office, then you were going to have a hard time denying the same rights and protections to all the others.

It wasn't that he had much sympathy with the metal men. They were, after all, only machines. Nobody was more convinced of that than he! He'd had a long, intimate association with one of them going all the way back to 2009, right here in this house.

"You wanted a father, Timmy," Karin Garroway said brightly. "Well, I've brought you PAPPI."

Timmy stared at the gray metal box on wheels squatting in the precise middle of the living room rug. At first glance, he'd thought it was an old-fashioned canister vacuum cleaner minus the hose. Four skinny appendages protruded from its sides, ending in a collection of hooks and pincers like some grim skeletal joke. An upside-down bowl-shaped turret housed a camera lens and other things he didn't recognize right away.

Timmy touched a wheel housing with one toe.

"Treat it with care." Motherly chores satisfied now, Karin gathered up papers and laptop computer and stuffed them all in her briefcase.

"What is it?"

"PAPPI—Paternal Alternative Program: Prototype I."

"Looks pretty stupid," Timmy said.

"Never mind how it looks!" His mother glanced at him. "It'll do everything a real father can do. PAPPI can pitch baseballs, and sort your stamp collection—all sorts of things."

"Can it do my homework?"

"It has programs to *coach* you in math and reading, Timmy. PAPPI has tapes of bedtime stories selected for eight-year-old boys, too. And we'll update them as you grow."

"Sometimes I want to talk about *man things . . .*"

"Don't be difficult." Karin snapped her briefcase crisply shut. "I'll work on some of the refinements as I get time. You could think of this as an experiment in robotics that we're doing together."

Karin was always trying to get him interested in her work at U.S. Robots and Mechanical Men, Inc. She put the briefcase down on the sofa, hunkered down in front of her son so her eyes were level with his and held him by the shoulders. Her face had that soft, gentle haze Timmy saw on it sometimes when she looked at kittens or butterflies. He stared back at her, his mouth drawn tightly down.

"I know it's hard on you, the way we live."

"We could do it the way other people do!" he said sullenly.

"That just won't work for me," she said. "I thought you understood that. Look, you keep saying you want a father—"

"A real one. Not a dumb robot."

Her face closed over. "I've explained to you that we don't have time for a man in our lives."

Timmy didn't know anything about his real father. Karin had told him some stuff once about a place where they sold sperm from fathers for people who wanted to be mothers without all the fuss. But Timmy told everybody his dad had died; it was easier to explain. Maybe Karin didn't like men very much; she never brought one home, unlike his best friend Joey's mother, who had lots of boyfriends. Sometimes Timmy wondered if Karin wouldn't like *him* when he grew up, too.

"Timmy?"

"All right," he said reluctantly. "But you promised me we'd go to the zoo today, Karin."

She chewed her lip. "I know it's Sunday, but the project's so urgent."

He shook his head. "Today's special. It's—"

"You can play with PAPPI in the yard. You'd like that, wouldn't you? PAPPI's easy to use, I made sure of that."

He looked past her at the robot. "What can you play with a thing like that?"

"You'll think of something!" She gave him a kiss on the cheek which he wasn't quick enough to duck. "Now I've got to run. The lab's aircar is waiting for me. I promise I won't be too long."

After she'd gone, Timmy watched the Tri-D for a while, but Karin had programmed it to show him historical films about the exploration of the solar system and educational stuff about astronomy. He turned the Tri-D off again and squatted down by the robot. He stared into its camera eye.

"You're dopey looking!" he said. "Got a dopey name, too."

A bird chirped outside in the big tree in the garden, but inside the house it was very quiet. Timmy suddenly felt lonely, which was strange because now that he wasn't such a little kid any more Karin often left him alone when she had to work overtime or go in on weekends. The reason wasn't too hard to find. It was Father's Day. The Cub Scout Troop that Timmy and Joey belonged to was having a father-and-son hot-dog barbecue in Central Park, and absolutely everybody would be there with their dad. All Timmy's friends had fathers, even if they weren't the original ones. And Joey would have one of his mom's boyfriends along.

But Timmy had known there was no point in telling Karin about it. Karin didn't believe in men-only activities. It would've been just like her to consider going with him to a father-son barbecue. Much better to stay home with a robot than be embarrassed like that.

Timmy scowled at the robot. Nothing else to do—he might as well turn it on. The switch was conveniently located near the top.

Immediately, a small red light glowed on the dome, which swiveled to focus the camera eye on Timmy.

"Hello," the tinny, uninflected voice said. "I am PAPPI, your Paternal Alternative. I am an experimental prototype."

Surprised, Timmy settled himself cross-legged in front of the machine and stared at it. He'd seen robots before, of course, at the lab where Karin worked. But he knew a lot of people didn't trust them and wouldn't allow them in New York. The ones his mother built that talked were huge things to be sent out into space where they couldn't frighten anybody.

"Well," Timmy said cautiously. "What can you do?"

"I can tell you a story about animals. I can help you with your stamp collection. I can make model airplanes. I know baseball and basketball statistics for the last fifty years. I can tell you who scored the most home runs, who was the MVP, who—"

Timmy was astonished. Perhaps Karin understood more than he'd ever realized about what was important to him. "Can you help me light a fire in the backyard and barbecue hot dogs?"

"I do not think Karin would approve of you playing with fire."

Timmy's enthusiasm faded. "So you're going to be another babysitter!"

"You are too old for babysitters, Timmy. I am your PAPPI, and Paternal Alternatives do not—"

"You're not my dad!" Timmy snapped.

"Shall we go out into the yard and play baseball?" the robot suggested.

"Sure." Timmy stuck his hands in his pockets.

Timmy found out right away that PAPPI was very good at pitching balls. The long metal arms grasped the ball neatly and swung it in an economical arc, releasing it at precisely the right moment to travel across to the exact spot on Timmy's baseball bat for hitting. PAPPI gave him advice on how to hold the bat too, but it never yelled at him when he missed, and it wasn't a sore loser like Joey when Timmy managed to hit a "home run."

"Hey," Timmy said after an hour of playing World Series. "Want to climb a tree?"

"I am not equipped to climb trees," PAPPI replied. "But I will watch you. And I can identify the objects you encounter."

Timmy threw down the baseball bat and shimmied up the

trunk of the old maple by the garden wall. PAPPI trundled over to stand underneath, the dome swiveling so the camera eye could focus on Timmy's ascent.

Halfway up to the crown, the main trunk forked. Here Timmy and Joey had once started to erect a fort. Then the weather got too hot for carpentry projects and they'd abandoned it. But it was still a fine place to sit and look at the jagged skyline of the city across the East River. The leaves overhead made liquid patterns of sunlight and shade on his bare arms, and their soft rustling was like a kind of secret language that only Timmy was meant to understand.

Timmy straddled one of the sun-warm planks.

"You look weird from up here!"

"Have you noticed the abandoned bird's nest by your right hand?"

Timmy peered into the leaves. Sure enough, there was a jumble of twigs and mud stuck to the bark near the trunk. "There's feathers in it."

Timmy hung on to the branch with one hand and leaned down, tiny brown and white feather in the other. PAPPI's camera eye slid out on a slender stalk for about a foot, then retracted.

"A very fine specimen. But look at the small white growths on the tree trunk, a form of fungus, division name Mycota. The spores have been carried up there accidentally by a bird, perhaps by the *Passer domesticus* whose feather you are holding."

"Huh?"

"A house sparrow."

"Neat!"

"There are about fifty thousand fungi, or saprophytic and parasitic plantlike organisms, that have been identified and described. But there are probably a hundred thousand more. They include mushrooms, mildews, molds, yeasts—"

Timmy frowned. The thing was starting to sound like his schoolteacher.

"I can tell you about lichens too, if you want me to."

"Not hardly!" Timmy said.

"Well, then," the robot said. "Would you like to play horse?"

"How do I do that?"

"You can ride around on me. I am very strongly built."

So Timmy rode around the yard on top of PAPPI, held in

place by two of the long metal arms, shouting "Giddyap!" and "Whoa!" until his throat was scratchy. It was almost possible to forget PAPPI was a robot and imagine he was really riding a stallion with flowing mane across a Western mesa, just like the programs on the Tri-D that Karin frowned at him watching.

By the time the sky got dark and Karin came home again, Timmy knew he'd discovered a real friend, one who never grew bored with playing, never thought any question too stupid to answer, never criticized or blamed.

But it wasn't the same thing at all as having a real father.

With PAPPI's help, Timmy did better in school that year. PAPPI was programmed to learn too, right alongside Timmy, so that made a contest out of it—one PAPPI usually won. But since the robot never boasted of its success, Timmy really didn't mind. And four mechanical hands meant the robot was a real wizard at assembling model spaceships and shuffling playing cards or juggling balls.

From time to time, Karin brought new programs home for PAPPI as they developed them at the lab. Timmy watched when she took the robot's "head" apart and inserted them. Sometimes he held the tiny tools she used to work on the positronic brain. Afterward, PAPPI could do a lot more things to entertain Timmy, like playing the banjo, or telling jokes and drawing silly pictures to make him laugh.

Karin rarely brought anyone home for supper, not even people from U.S. Robots. But once, a lady she shared the office with came to Timmy's house.

"It doesn't look a bit like a mechanical man," Timmy complained.

He and this fierce-looking lady hunkered down on the rug to look at PAPPI, who had just slithered to a halt in front of them. The robot's wheels scuffed the polished floor as it braked.

"It doesn't need to," Karin's officemate replied. "Form should follow function."

"At least it could've had legs, not wheels!" Timmy said, fingering one of the scratches in the wood.

"This was meant to be a utility robot. Your mother modified its brain, not its body."

Karin had told him that Dr. Calvin didn't *build* the robots quite like she did; Dr. Calvin was a robopsychologist, whatever that meant. In the kitchen, Karin, in an uncharacteristic display of domesticity, clattered dishes into the dishwasher.

Timmy frowned. "PAPPI thinks it's more than that!"

"But you don't."

"How can you tell?"

Dr. Calvin didn't answer. She was about as old as his mother, Timmy judged, and neither of them wore lipstick or smiled as much as Joey's mother did.

Karin bustled back into the living room with a tray of pastries she'd bought at the store. "Anyone ready for dessert?"

"I do not think Timmy should have any more sugar in his diet today," PAPPI said. "By my count, since getting up this morning he has consumed—"

"Oh, shut up!" Timmy said.

"Well," Karin began, "if you think—"

"One of these days, you're going to have trouble with that one," Dr. Calvin said thoughtfully.

For a moment, Timmy thought she was speaking of him. But her eyes were on the robot squatting between them on the rug.

"I'm being very careful, Susan," Karin said. "And Timmy knows not to take the robot outside."

"I can't tell my friends about PAPPI, either," Timmy grumbled. "When Joey comes over to play I have to put PAPPI in the closet. And Joey's my best friend!"

"That's good to know, Timmy," Dr. Calvin said. "But antirobot sentiment isn't all I was referring to. Though goodness knows the Fundies are enough of a threat to our work."

"Then what?" Karin said.

"I don't think we realize yet what these positronic brains may be capable of someday."

"I'm not *that* good, Susan," Karin said, laughing. "Not like you!"

The talk turned away from robots after that.

Then one day when they were in eighth grade, Joey's mother got married again, and his new father took him on a trip to the moon.

"Why can't we go to the moon, Karin?" Timmy demanded as Karin frowned at some work she'd brought home from the lab.

"Hmm?" She gazed at him over the top of the glasses she'd recently started wearing.

"I want to go to the moon. See the craters."

"We can't afford it."

"I've got money saved up!"

"I can't spare the time right now. Things are really busy at U.S. Robots. Susan and I may finally be getting our own offices!"

"If I had a father . . ." Timmy began darkly.

Karin set her notes down and gazed at him. "I'm sorry you're still feeling a lack, Timmy. I'd hoped PAPPI would fill it."

"Seems like I don't have a father *or* a mother!" Timmy said.

The following year, Timmy took a class in physics at Karin's urging and learned that he hated the subject. He became interested in sports, grew three inches, and discovered girls—one in particular, a dark-haired lovely with big breasts. PAPPI explained how to handle the sudden rush of hormones and awkwardness Timmy was feeling. Karin had done her part earlier, lecturing Timmy on the birds and the bees and the whole ecology of flowers, a discussion that bored him and left him feeling as if either he—or Karin—had totally missed the point. But PAPPI explained about Romeo and Juliet, whether it was a good idea to kiss a girl on a first date, and what to say to the other guys afterward.

In an attempt to influence him to take an interest in science, Karin bought him a telescope kit, and PAPPI helped him assemble it. PAPPI knew the names of all the stars and constellations they could see through the lens, and pointed out some of the orbiting space stations as well. Karin pretended not to notice when they stayed up well past Timmy's bedtime.

Timmy went out for the school swim team. PAPPI listened to his bragging and sympathized when he lost. Timmy changed his name to Tim, and PAPPI, unlike Karin, never made a mistake after that. All in all, it was a good time.

But Joe got to have man-to-man talks with his new father.

Tim activated the visorphone again and made an appointment to see the mayor, Stephen Byerley.

Then he tried to put the whole thing out of his mind.

He'd forgotten Karin's house was so small. He went through the rooms methodically, making lists of what to dump and what to pack. There wasn't too much of the latter. Living quarters on a space station were small, but at least there was a sense of the vastness just beyond the screened walls. This house was a box, a tract house thrown up by greedy developers, cutting up the land that had once been countryside around New York City into smaller and smaller parcels. He remembered how Karin had explained to him that they couldn't move farther out because she needed to be near U.S. Robots. By then, Joe and his parents had moved to a large house on Long Island where there was room for a swimming pool and a tennis court. And they could keep dogs. Tim remembered how he'd hated U.S. Robots when he heard about the dogs.

Beth deserved better. Tomorrow he'd meet the man Rathbone wanted him to kill.

The weapon one of his father-in-law's ex-boxer bodyguards had given him weighed heavily in his pocket. Something to make hash out of that obscene positronic brain, Rathbone had said. For some reason he'd brought it with him when he fled. Maybe even then he'd known he couldn't really get away so easily.

He had to stop thinking of Byerley as a man. It was only a robot they were talking about, after all. Only a robot. That would become obvious in the inquest. Then there'd be public outrage at the revelation of the stupendous hoax. The "assassin," if he were to be caught, would be released, a hero. Only of course, Rathbone would see to it that Tim wasn't caught.

And in return, Tim would get a chance to have something he desperately wanted, namely a large share of Mercury Mining and Manufacturing.

There was a good chance Byerley wouldn't keep the appointment anyway. His secretary had seemed doubtful the mayor would find time in his schedule for the vague reasons Tim had given her. Maybe nothing would come of it at all and he'd be off the hook. *"Couldn't get near him,"* he'd tell Rathbone. *"Not my fault!"*

His future and Beth's were on the line. He'd either have the money to be father and mother both to little Beth, or they'd both be on the run from Rathbone for the rest of their lives.

"You have to think about your life. You need to make plans for the future," Karin said, some time in '18. "What subjects are you interested in pursuing for a career?"

Tim leaned back in his chair and put his feet up on the table. He was in a truculent mood. "I don't know. Something that pays well. Probably sports."

"Sports?" Karin frowned. "How're you going to make a living from sports?"

Swimming had developed Tim's muscles enough to make the girls eager to go out with him now. Heady stuff. "The University of Hawaii has this great program—"

"I'd like to see you go into robotics," Karin said. "The space colonies have a tremendous need for people like you."

"Aw, Karin!"

"If I may interrupt," PAPPI said. "A good liberal arts college will allow Tim to put off crucial decisions for at least another year without penalty."

"You're vetoing robotics?" Karin bit a fingernail. Tim noticed for the first time how much gray there was in her hair. She never colored it the way Joe's mother did.

"No, I'm only suggesting he might broaden his education first," the robot said.

Karin considered this. "I'm not going to pay for a college on the other side of the planet!"

"That's hardly fair of you, Karin," the robot said.

"I can't afford to pay if he goes out of state! Do you think I'm rich or something? And Timmy's hardly going to get a scholarship."

"There could be some financial assistance available—"

"Timmy's all I've got. I'll miss him!"

"I love him, too," PAPPI said.

Karin was suddenly very still. "What did you say?"

"That his absence would be noticeable to me, too," the robot said cautiously.

She stared at the robot for a long moment. "What other *feelings* do you have, PAPPI?"

Untypically, the robot seemed reluctant to answer. "What did you expect, Karin, with all the special Calvin/Minsky subprograms you've given me over the years?"

"But it's never proved out in the lab. Susan says—"

"What're you talking about?" Tim interrupted.

"Positronic sentience," Karin said slowly. "I'm just wondering if PAPPI—"

Exasperated, he said, "Well, *of course* PAPPI's alive! I thought we were discussing my future?"

Karin looked as if she were watching something very far

away. "I'll have to take you back to the lab, PAPPI. If this is for real, then Susan will want to run the Turing series on you."

Tim stared at his mother. She chose the worst moments to get all wrapped up in her work. "Look, I've got a serious decision to make here."

"We've had no evidence for the development of full self-awareness in the lab," Karin said thoughtfully. "As an extended function of advanced positronic intelligence, that is. My guess would be it's prolonged exposure to humans in a real family situation that's caused the difference. But I'll have to talk to Susan about it. We'll need to do the research."

"I don't want to go back to the lab—" the robot began.

"I don't see a choice, PAPPI. This is big-time. I mean—"

"All right, everybody listen up!" Tim said. "I'm going to make my own decisions from now on. I'll go to school if and when—and wherever—I please!"

Karin glanced at him as if she'd forgotten he was there. "Well, of course, Timmy. But this is rather urgent, don't you see?"

Once again, he thought angrily, he came out second in importance to a robot.

The University of Luna offered financial aid in return for taking part in athletic research in low or zero-grav. Since this freed him from Karin's money, Tim enrolled. Karin didn't come to see him off when he boarded the shuttle. Couldn't wait to get down to the lab and her tests on PAPPI, he thought resentfully.

He worked through the university vacations as an assistant to a moon geologist who needed someone to keep track of his rocks. Since this wasn't so different from keeping a stamp collection, Tim rather enjoyed it.

Other guys had parents shuttle up to visit from time to time, well-dressed men and women who conversed knowledgeably about interactive theater and world politics and preserving traditional human values in a mechanized world. Just because humans had ventured out into space and depended on robot help, didn't mean they should abandon the historic virtues of the simple life—the family and physical labor—his new friends said. Tim knew what they meant. The kind of work his mother was doing at U.S. Robots was dangerous. "Mechanical Men," for goodness sake! Couldn't she see it wasn't wise to allow robots to become too clever? They were designed as servants, not partners in the human enterprise. If humans didn't keep that in mind, someday the robots would be a problem. Tim felt a growing estrangement from Karin and never invited her.

The most dazzling of these new friends was Sylvia Rathbone, daughter of an old-style entrepreneur in space, and as different in spirit from her father as he was from Karin. Sylvia represented everything he felt he'd been deprived of in life—money, a large family of aunts and uncles and cousins, a father who spoiled her shamelessly. She was a beautiful, merry, delicate-boned girl with movements as bright and swift as quicksilver. And to his great wonder and gratitude, she fell in love with him, too.

They were married in a small, intimate ceremony in the spring of '27, in a chapel carved from one of the moon's vast underground caverns. They planned to keep it secret while he finished up the degree in geology he'd recently switched to, and she worked on her father to accept her marriage to a penniless student. But the following year, Beth was born. They sent notice of the event to both parents, and waited nervously.

Karin almost forgot to reply; she mentioned the birth finally in a postscript to her regular monthly fax transmission.

Mr. Rathbone's attorney notified them that Sylvia had been cut out of his will until such time as she divorced her unsuitable husband.

It was hard managing a family on a student's income, he found. But they went on. In the evening, he went home to his wife and his baby in the family area of the moon settlement. Sylvia had a small hydroponics garden where she grew tomatoes and corn to supplement their diet, and chrysanthemums for their spirits, she said. He was happy for the first time in his life, determined his daughter would have the proper family life that had been denied him. But he began to see that took money, and his happiness leaked away little by little.

He was off-world a year later, on a research trip with his geologist friend to bring in a little extra money, when a small piece of space debris hurtled in undetected and punctured the skin of the settlement in his sector. The atmosphere bled out swiftly. Automatic airlocks prevented the hemmorhage from spreading beyond the damaged area, but the robot rescue team was too late to save Sylvia. The baby had been in a crèche in an unaffected sector.

The bill for the disposal of Sylvia's remains arrived just as he broke out of his stunned inaction and began to mourn. One of the settlement's robots brought it.

The wheel of his life had turned full circle. He, a child who'd been fatherless, raised by his mother, must play father to a motherless child. And he was broke. Swamp-black despair settled over him.

Two things happened.

Into this despair came Howard Rathbone III, who wanted his grandchild so urgently that he was prepared to make a deal with her father.

And Dr. Susan Calvin notified him by express fax that Karin had died suddenly after a brief illness and left him the little house in New York where he'd grown up. He'd never felt close to Karin, but it was difficult to comprehend that now she'd gone out of his life altogether.

He didn't want to accept Rathbone's suggestion, tempting though the money was. But he saw he'd have trouble keeping Beth from her grandfather otherwise.

There seemed to be only one thing to do. He fled with the baby, catching the first shuttle to Earth.

Tim sorted through the accumulated junk of his childhood. He found little of value in the house, little worth the exorbitant cost of lobbing it up to the colony. Karin had never been much of a homemaker. He packed a box of Scouting books he remembered treasuring as a boy, his old stamp collection in its dog-eared albums, the telescope PAPPI had helped him assemble.

He lugged the box of books out to the hall and set it down by the wall. Something on the polished wood floor drew his gaze, long blurred lines in the dust. He gently blew the dust aside. Scuff marks. He had a sudden jolting vision of PAPPI's wheels whooshing over the slippery floor, skidding to a stop by the front door as the robot retrieved the morning's mail. He saw, as if they were arriving now in Karin's hallway, the papers, the garish advertisements, the pleas for contributions to worthy causes (he remembered how angry Karin became each time she found a request for money from the antirobot people), all the second-class junk that the law didn't allow to clutter up the fax machines of the city's households. Sorting through this paper rubbish had been one of

PAPPI's daily tasks. *Preventing me from having apoplexy!* Karin always said.

He crouched down and stared at the scuff marks. The floor appeared to have been resurfaced fairly recently. Gone were the scrapes and scratches Tim remembered inflicting on it over the years. Once her rambunctious son had left home, Karin had repaired the damage he'd done. But the scars left by the robot's wheels were still raw. They had occurred sometime after the floor had been resurfaced. Tim straightened up slowly, disturbed by an idea growing in his mind.

He was uncomfortable here, anxious to be done with pawing over the artifacts of his boyhood. He turned to the visorphone to call one of the realtors whose cards he'd found pushed under the door. Time to cut loose from the past.

Before he could touch the keyboard, the phone shrilled at him. He hesitated. Rathbone again? Grimly he punched the receive button.

The face of a handsome, middle-aged man appeared on the screen.

"Tim Garroway?" The man had a pleasant, well-modulated voice. "I'm Stephen Byerley."

"Mayor—" Tim stumbled to a reply. "I—well, I'm delighted to meet you."

"My secretary gave me your message. I'd very much enjoy talking to you, but I'm afraid tomorrow's schedule is so tight."

Tim's heart leaped wildly. So it was going to be taken out of his hands after all. He was conscious of the strong feeling of relief that swept over him. "That's no problem, Mr. Mayor! No problem at all. It really wasn't important—That is, it can wait."

Byerley smiled. "I believe we have friends in common, Tim. May I call you Tim?"

"Sure." He was impressed with the genuine warmth this man projected. How could he possibly have entertained ideas of eliminating him?

"I understand your mother was an associate of Dr. Susan Calvin, one of my most treasured friends."

Something dull and cold clutched Tim. Of course. It was to be expected. "Oh?" he said heavily. "Yeah, I suppose so."

Byerley was a robot after all.

At the edge of his consciousness he was aware of Beth tugging at his sleeve. He put an arm around his little daughter, pulling her toward him. He was a fool if he thought he could avoid fate so easily. It crept up on him like some primeval beast slinking up to the little campfire he'd hoped would protect Beth and himself against the darkness.

"The calendar's crowded tomorrow," Byerley said. "But I make time to run in Central Park. Do you run, Tim? I heard you were something of an athlete. If you'd care to join me at six tomorrow morning—I hope that's not too early for you? I'm an early riser—we could talk then."

Early riser! Tim thought. I bet you don't sleep at all.

There really was no choice. It was Stephen Byerley's life—if you could call it that—against his. Byerley had signed his own death warrant.

"Sure thing, Mr. Mayor," he said.

"Steve," Stephen Byerley said.

Tim nodded without replying and Byerley broke the connection. The weapon with which he must eliminate the robot bumped heavily against his hip as he turned away.

His stomach had twisted itself with tension, and he sensed the beginnings of a headache at the back of his skull. He would do what he had to do, for Beth's sake. Until then, he'd put the whole thing out of his mind. He'd get on with packing up the house.

"What that, Dadda?" his daughter called, pointing at a door in the ceiling. She had a smudge of dust on one cheek, and toddled clumsily after him wherever he went.

"Nothing much, sweetheart. Just an attic for storage."

As he said it, something clicked into place in his mind. Of course. That was where it would be.

"Want see!" Beth announced imperiously.

Indulging his daughter's wishes took his mind off what he must do tomorrow. He touched the recessed button in the wall. The attic hatch opened, and wooden steps lowered to where they stood. He set one foot on the steps and the toddler immediately clung to his legs, clamoring loudly as if he were about to disappear forever. He picked her up and began his ascent. He made the climb awkwardly and with effort, unused to Earth's gravity after all these years. Beth hummed encouragement to him as if he'd been a horse—or a robot, he realized.

It was cool and dim under the rafters, and it smelled of moldering clothes and musty books. Spiders had draped their gray curtains everywhere over the piled boxes and trunks. He moved cautiously, careful to keep the cobwebs away from Beth's face.

She saw it first, pointing with a chubby finger to a dark corner.

"Look, Dadda! Baby."

The robot sat like a blind deaf-mute under one of the main beams of the roof, only lightly powdered in dust. Even after all these years, it was impossible for him to look at it without emotion. Memories of baseball in the backyard, science projects, stamp collections, secret discussions about girls and sex, all came flooding back. His childhood was preserved in this attic, and all it took was one glance to bring it all back to vivid, painful life. He was eight years old again, and it was Father's Day.

What was it doing here? Karin took it back to the lab. It was a great achievement—the crowning glory of her scientific career—

He had *assumed* she'd taken it back to the lab. The recent scuff marks in the hall said otherwise. But why had she put it up here—just before she died apparently?

"Me play!" his daughter announced imperiously, scrambling down from his arms.

Gray dust swirls spiraled around her and she sneezed. He leaned forward, steadying her as she maneuvered over the unfinished floor of the attic. She chuckled, her little body tense with the excitement of discovery. He felt swamped again by mingled emotions of love and helplessness. How could he be both father and mother to this little Columbus, so eager to explore each new world she encountered? How could he protect her from the ugliness of a world where robots became mayor—and men like Rathbone schemed to kill them?

The toddler's pudgy hands caressed the robot. The problem of the robot drew him again. The only reason he could imagine for Karin not returning PAPPI to the lab was because she'd cared about the robot.

He was about to pick Beth up and carry her away when the red light blinked on.

"Hello," said the weak but familiar voice, "I'm PAPPI, a paternal alternative. Would you like to play?"

His daughter looked as if she were going to cry.

He wasn't surprised to learn the robot's power supply was still operational. Tim crouched beside his little daughter and put his arms around her. Here in this attic, for the very first time in his life, he had the feeling that he understood Karin. She'd hidden the robot up here when she knew she was dying; she hadn't wanted PAPPI to go back to the lab, or to fall into the hands of the Fundies. What did that prove?

For a moment, he felt as if he were drowning under the tidal wave of the past. He was a small boy again, on Father's Day.

Maybe if she'd cared about the robot, she'd cared about Timmy, too.

Had he really been so deprived? Love was impossible to define, but surely it included sharing, partnership in work and play, nurturing. A family was just a group that cared about each other, even if it included a robot.

"Hello, PAPPI," Beth said uncertainly. "What are you?"

Could he give Beth as much as Karin had given him? He was certainly going to do his best. But what he wanted for his daughter couldn't be built on a foundation of hatred and violence. Good didn't come out of evil; PAPPI had taught him that. He couldn't keep that appointment with Stephen Byerley tomorrow morning.

And that would mean Rathbone would be after them. There'd be no returning to their home on the moon, and no staying here on Earth. Life was hard for a geologist prospecting out in the asteroids, but what other chance did they have to be a family—father, daughter, and robot?

"Sweetie," he said to his daughter, "this is your Grand-PAPPI."

The Reunion at the Mile-High

by Frederik Pohl

In those long and long-ago days—it's been half a century!—we were not only young, we were mostly poor. We were all pretty skinny, too, though you wouldn't think that to look at us now. I know this, because I have a picture of the twelve of us that was taken right around 1939. I dug it out to loan it to my publisher's public relations people just the other day, and I looked at it for a long time before I put it in the overnight mail. We didn't look like much, all grinning into the camera with our hairless, hopeful teenage faces. If you'd been given a couple of chances to guess, you might have thought we were a dozen Western Union boys on our day off (remember Western Union boys?), or maybe the senior debating club at some big-city all-boy high school. We weren't any of those things, though. What we actually were was a club of red-hot science fiction fans, and we called ourselves the Futurians.

That old photograph didn't lie. It just didn't tell the whole truth. The camera couldn't capture the things that kept us together, because they were all inside our heads. For one thing, we were pretty smart—we knew it ourselves, and we were *very* willing to tell you so. For another, we were all deeply addicted readers of science fiction—we called it stf in those days, but that's a whole other story. We thought stf was a lot of fun (all those jazzy rocket ships and zippy death rays, and big-chested Martians and squat, sinister monsters from Jupiter—oh, *wow!*) That wasn't all of it, though. We also thought stf was *important*. We were absolutely sure that it provided the best view anyone could have of T*H*E F*U*T*U*R*E—by which we meant the kind of technologically dazzling, socially Utopian, and generally wonderful world which the rather frayed and frightening one we were stuck with living in might someday become. And, most of all, we were what our old Futurian buddy, Damon Knight, calls toads. We weren't very athletic. We didn't get along all that well with our peers—and not even as well as that with girls. And so we spent a lot of time driven in upon our own resources, which, mostly, meant reading. We all read a *lot.*

We even more or less agreed that we were toads. At least, we knew that girls didn't seem anxious to fall bedazzled by any of our charms. I'm not sure why. It wasn't that we were hopelessly ugly—well, not all of us, anyway. Dave Kyle and Dirk Wylie and Dick Wilson were tall and actually pretty good-looking. Even the snapshot shows that. I think our problem was partly that we were scared of girls (they might laugh at us—some of them no doubt had), and partly a matter of our internal priorities. We were more into talking than tennis, and we put books ahead of jitterbugging.

That was half a century ago. In other words, *history*. My secretary, who is also my chief research assistant when I need a specific fact from the library, tells me that 62.8 percent of the people alive today weren't even born then, which undoubtedly means that that ancient year of 1939 seems as remote and strange to most people now as the Spanish-American War did to me.

I would like to point out, though, that 1939 didn't seem all that hot to us, either, even while we were living it. It wasn't a fun time. We were the generation caught between Hoover and Hitler. We had the breadlines of the Great Depression to remember in our recent past, and the Nazi armies looming worrisomely in our probable future. When we looked out at the real world we lived in we didn't much like what we saw.

So, instead, we looked inside the stf magazines we adored, and then we looked inside our own heads. We read a lot, and we tried to write. Because the other thing about us, you see, was that we were all pretty hardworking and ambitious. Since we weren't thrilled by our lives, we tried to change them. We had our meetings—we'd get together, once a month or so, in somebody's basement or somebody else's living room, and we'd talk about this and that; and then we'd go out for an ice-cream soda; and then we'd gradually splinter apart. Some of us would go home—especially the ones who had to get up in the morning, like Isaac Asimov. (He worked at his parents' candy store, and the commuters started coming in for their morning papers at five-thirty A.M.) Most of the rest of us would just wander, in twos and threes. I'd start out by walking Dirk and Johnny Michel to their subway station. But generally, by the time we got to it, we'd be in the middle of some really interesting discussion (did the General Motors Futurama at the World's Fair have the right idea about the World of Tomorrow, all twelve-lane superhighways and forty-story apartments? Were John Campbell's Arcot, Wade & Morey stories as good as Doc Smith's *Skylark?*)—so then they'd walk me back to my station . . . or around the block . . . or anywhere. Always talking. Talking mattered to us. Writing mattered, too, almost as much. We did a lot of it, on our battered second-hand portable typewriters, each on his own but always with the intention of showing what we had written to the others. *Words* mattered, and we particularly intended to make *our* words matter. Somehow. We didn't really know how, exactly, but when you think of it, I guess we succeeded. If we were toads, as Damon says, then sometime or other some wandering fairy princess must have come along and kissed us, and turned us into something different . . . or we wouldn't have been getting together at the top of the Mile-High Building for our Fiftieth Reunion, with reporters all over the place and our older, considerably more impressive faces staring out at the world on the Six O'Clock News.

You can't fly nonstop from Maui to New York, even on the sleeper, because they don't let flying boats operate over the continent. So I had to change planes in Los Angeles. Naturally I missed my connection, so when we finally landed at Idlewild I was late already.

The porter cut a taxi out of the snarl for me—it's wonderful what a five-dollar bill can do at an airport. As I got into the cab I stretched my neck to look toward the New York City skyline, and I could see the Mile-High Building poking far above everything else, looking like a long, long hunting horn sitting on its bell . . . if you can imagine a hunting horn with gaps along its length, held together (as it seemed at that distance) by nothing bigger than a couple of pencils. They say they need those wind gaps in the tower, because a hurricane just might push the whole thing over if they didn't allow spaces for the air to get through. Maybe so. I'm willing to believe that the gaps make the building safer, but they certainly aren't reassuring to look at.

Still, the Mile-High has managed to stay up for—let's see—it must be six or seven years now, and it's certainly an imposing sight. You can see it from anywhere within forty or fifty miles of New York. More than that. It's so immense that, even across most of Queens and part of Brooklyn, when I looked at it I was distinctly looking *up*. Then, when I got out of the cab at its base, it was more than big, it was scary. I couldn't help flinching a little. Whenever I look straight up at a tall building I get the feeling it's about to fall on me, and there's nothing taller than the Mile-High.

A limousine had pulled up behind me. The man who got out looked at me twice, and I looked at him thrice, and then we spoke simultaneously. "Hello, Fred," he said, and I said:

"Doc, how are you? It's been a long time."

It had been—twenty years, anyway. We were obviously going to the same place, so Doc Lowndes waited for me while I paid off the taxi, even though it was gently drizzling on Sixth Avenue. When I turned away from the taxi driver, after a little argument about the tip, Doc was doing what I had been doing, staring up at the top of the Mile-High. "Do you know what it looks like?" he asked. "It looks like the space gun from *Things to Come*. Remember?"

I remembered. *Things to Come* had been our cult movie, back in the 1930s; most of us had seen it at least a dozen times. (My own record was thirty-two.) "Yeah, *space*," I said, grinning. "Rocket ships. People going to other planets. We'd believe almost anything in those days, wouldn't we?"

He gave me a considering look. "I still believe," he told me as we headed for the express elevators to the top.

The Mile-High Building isn't really a *Things to Come* kind of edifice. It's more like something from that even more ancient science fiction film, *Just Imagine*—silly futuristic spoof packed with autogyros and Mars rockets and young couples getting their babies out of vending machines. I first saw *Just Imagine* when I was ten years old. The heroine was a meltingly lovely teenager, just imported from Ireland to Hollywood, and that movie is why all my life I have been in love with Maureen O'Sullivan.

The Mile-High Building doesn't have any of those things, least of all (worse luck!) the still lovely Maureen, but it is definitely a skyscraper that puts even those old movie-makers to shame. To get to the top you go a measured mile straight up. Because the elevators are glass-walled, you get to see that whole incredible five thousand plus feet dropping away as you zoom upward, nearly a hundred miles an hour at peak velocity.

Doc swayed a little as we accelerated. "Pretty fast," he said. "*Real* fast," I agreed, and began telling him all about the building. It's hollow inside, like an ice-cream cone, and I knew quite a lot about it because when I was still living in New York City, before I could afford the place on Maui, I used to know a man named Mike Terranova. Mike was a visualizer working for an architect's office— at another point in his career he did the drawings for the science fiction comic strip I wrote for a while, but that's another story, too. Mike really was better at doing machines and buildings than at drawing people, which is probably why our strip only ran one year, but he made up for it in enthusiasm. He was a big fan of the Mile-High. "Look at the wind gaps in it," he told me once, as we walked down Central Park West and saw the big thing looming even thirty blocks away. "That's to let the wind through, to reduce the force so it shouldn't sway. Of course, they've also got the mass dampers on the two hundredth and three hundredth and four hundredth floors, so it doesn't sway much anyway."

"It's just another skyscraper, Mike," I told him, amused at his enthusiasm.

"It's a different *kind* of skyscraper! They figured out the best offices are the ones with an outside view, so they just didn't build any offices inside! It's all hollow—except for the bracing struts and cables, and for the three main floor-through sections, where you change elevators and they have all the shops and things."

"It's brilliant," I said; and actually it was. And I was explaining all this to Doc, and all the time I was talking we were flashing past those vast central atria that are nearly a hundred stories high each, with their balconies, and flowers growing down from the railings, and lianas crisscrossing the central spaces; and Doc was looking at me with that patient expression New Yorkers reserve for out-of-towners.

But all he said was, "I know."

Then I was glad enough for the break when we walked across the hundredth-story level, between the soda fountains and the clothing shops, to the next bank of elevators, and then the next. Then you get out at the top, five thousand and change feet above the corner of Fifty-second Street and Sixth Avenue, and you have to take an escalator up another flight to the club itself.

I don't like standing still, so I took the escalator steps two at a time. Doc followed gamely. He was puffing a little as we reached the door the doorman was already holding open for us.

"Put on a little weight, I see," I told him. "Too much riding in limousines, I'd say. There must be big bucks in the poetry racket these days."

I guess my tone must have sounded needling, because he gave me a sidelong look. But he also gave me a straightforward reply, which was more than I deserved. "I just don't like taxi drivers," he said. "Believe me, I'm not getting rich from my royalties. Publishing poetry doesn't pay enough to keep a pig in slop. What pays my bills is readings. I do get a lot of college dates."

I was rebuked. See, we Futurians had been pretty sharp-tongued kids, big on put-down jokes and getting laughs at each other's expense; just the thought of coming to the reunion seemed to get me back in that mood. I wasn't used to seeing Bob in his present gentler incarnation.

Then the white-haired woman took our coats, and even gentle Bob got a kind of smirk on his face as I handed over my trenchcoat. I knew what he was looking at, because I was wearing my usual at-home outfit: canary-yellow slacks, beach-boy shirt, and thongs. "I didn't have a chance to change," I said defensively.

"I was just thinking how nice it is for you folks that live in Hawaii," he told me seriously, and led the way into the big reception room where the party had already started.

There had certainly been changes. It wasn't like the old days. Maybe it was because they were talking about making Bob poet laureate for the United States. Or maybe it was just the difference between twenty and seventy. We didn't have to explain how special we were now, because the whole world was full of people willing to explain that to us.

There were at least a hundred people in the room, hanging around the waiters with the champagne bottles and studying the old pictures on the wall. It was easy to see which were the real Futurians: they were the ones with the bald spots or the white beards. The others were publicity people and media people. There were many more of them than of us, and their average age was right under thirty.

Right in the middle was Dr. Isaac Asimov, sparring good-naturedly with Cyril Kornbluth. They were the center of the biggest knot, because they were the really famous ones. General Kyle was there—in uniform, though he was long retired by now—telling a young woman with a camera how he got those ribbons at the battle of Pusan. Jack Robinson was standing in the background, listening to him—no cameras pointed at Jack, because the reporters didn't have much interest in schoolteachers, even when that one had been one of Harvard's most distinguished professors emeritus. I saw Jack Gillespie, with a gorgeous blonde six inches taller than he was on his arm—she was the star of one of his plays—and Hannes Bok, looking older and more content than he used to, drinking Coca-Cola and munching on one of the open-faced sandwiches. There wasn't any doubt they were pretty well known by any normal standards. Jack had already won a Pulitzer, and Hannes's early black-and-whites were going for three thousand dollars apiece in the galleries on Fifty-seventh Street. But there's a difference between say-didn't-I-see-you-once-on-TV and *famous*. The media people knew which ones to point their cameras at. Cyril didn't have one Pulitzer, he had three of them, and the word was he'd have had the Nobel Prize if only he'd had the sense to be born a Bolivian or a Greek. And as to Isaac, of course—well, Isaac was *Isaac*. Adviser to Presidents, confidant of the mighty, celebrated steady guest of the Jack Paar show and star of a hundred television commercials. He wasn't just *kind* of famous. He was the one of us who couldn't cross a city street without being recognized, because he was known by features to more people than any senator, governor, or cardinal of the Church. He even did television commercials. I'd seen him in Hawaii, touting the Pan American Clipper flights to Australia . . . and he didn't even *fly*.

They'd blown up that old photograph twelve feet long, and Damon Knight was staring mournfully up at it when Doc and I came over to shake hands. "We were such kids," he said. True enough. We'd ranged from sixteen—that was Cyril—to Don Wollheim, the old man of the bunch: why, then he had been at least twenty-three or twenty-four.

So much has been written about the Futurians these days that sometimes I'm not sure myself what's true, and what's just press-agent puffery. The newspaper stories make us sound very special. Well, we certainly thought we were, but I doubt that many of our relatives shared our opinion. Isaac worked in his parents' candy store, Johnny Michel helped his father silk-screen signs for Woolworth's Five and Ten, Dirk Wylie pumped gas at a filling station in Queens, Dick Wilson shoved trolleys of women's dresses around the garment district on Seventh Avenue. Most of the rest of us didn't have real jobs at all. Remember, it was the tail end of the Great Depression. I know that for myself I considered I was lucky, now and then, to get work as a restaurant busboy or messenger for an insurance company.

A young woman came over to us. She was reading from a guest list, and when she looked at me she wonderfully got my name right. "I'm from *Saturday Evening Post Video*," she explained. "You were one of the original Futurians, weren't you?"

"We all were. Well, Doc and I were. Damon came along later."

"And so you knew Dr. Asimov and Mr. Kornbluth from the very beginning?"

I sighed; I knew from experience just how the interview was going to go. It was not for my own minor-league fame that the woman wanted to talk to me, it was for a reminiscence about the superstars. So I told her three or four of the dozen stories I kept on tap for such purposes. I told her how Isaac lived at one end of Prospect Park, in Brooklyn, and I lived at the other. How the Futurians would have a meeting, any kind of a meeting, and then hate to break it up, and so we'd just walk around the empty streets all night long, talking, sometimes singing—Jack and I, before he finished his first play; Doc and I, reciting poetry, singing all the numbers out of our bottomless repertory of the popular songs of the day; Cyril and I, trying to trick each other with our show-off game of "Impossible Questions."

" 'Impossible Questions,' " she repeated.

"That was a sort of a quiz game we played," I explained. "We invented it. It was a *hard* one. The questions were intended to be about things most people wouldn't know. Like, what's the rhyme scheme of a chant royal? Or what's the color of air?"

"You mean blue, like the sky?"

I grinned at her. "You just lost a round. Air doesn't have any color at all. It just *looks* blue, because of what they call Rayleigh scattering. But that's all right: these were *impossible* questions, and if anyone ever got the right answer to any one of them he won and the game was over."

"So you and Dr. Asimov used to play this game—"

"No, no. *Cyril* and I played it. The only way Isaac came into it was sometimes we'd go over to see him. Early in the morning, when we'd been up all night; we'd start off across the park around sunrise, and we'd stop to climb a few trees—and Cyril would give the mating call of the plover-tailed teal, but we never had a teal respond to it—and along about the time Isaac's parents' candy store opened for business we'd drop in and his mother would give us each a free malted milk."

"A free malted milk," the woman repeated, beaming. It was just the kind of human-interest thing she'd been looking for. She tarried for one more question. "Did you know Dr. Asimov when he wrote his famous letter to President Franklin Roosevelt, that started the Pasadena Project?"

I opened my mouth to answer, but Doc Lowndes got in there ahead of me. "Oh, damn it, woman," he exploded. "*Isaac* didn't write that letter. Alexis Carrel did. Isaac came in much later."

The woman looked at her notes, then back at us. Her look wasn't surprised. Mostly it was—what's the word I want? Yes: pitying. She looked at us as though she were sorry for us. "Oh, I don't think so," she said, politely enough. "I have it all here."

"You have it wrong," Doc told her, and began to try to set her straight.

I wouldn't have bothered, though the facts were simple enough. Albert Einstein had written to the President claiming that Hitler's people were on the verge of inventing what he called "an atomic bomb," and he wanted FDR to start a project so the U.S.A. could build one first. Dr. Alexis Carrel heard about it. He was a biochemist and he didn't want to see America wasting its time on some atomic-power will-o'-the-wisp. So he persuaded his friend Colonel Charles A. Lindbergh to take a quite different letter to President Roosevelt.

It wasn't that easy for Lindbergh, because there was a political problem. Lindbergh was certainly a famous man. He was the celebrated Lone Eagle, the man who had flown the Atlantic in nineteen twenty-something all by himself, first man ever to do it. But a decade and a bit later things had changed for Lindbergh. He had unfortunately got a reputation for being soft on the Nazis, and besides he was deeply involved in some right-wing Republican organizations—the America First Committee, the Liberty League, things like that—which had as their principal objective in life leaving Hitler alone and kicking that satanic Democrat Franklin D. Roosevelt out of the White House.

All the same, Lindbergh had a lot of powerful friends. It took two months of pulling hard on a lot of strings to arrange it, but he finally got an appointment for five minutes of the President's time on a slow Thursday morning in Warm Springs, Georgia. And the President actually read Carrel's letter.

Roosevelt wasn't a scientist and didn't even have any scientists near him—scientists weren't a big deal, back in the thirties. So FDR didn't really know the difference between a fissioning atomic nucleus and a disease organism, except that he could see that it was cheaper to culture germs in Petri dishes than to build billion-dollar factories to make this funny-sounding, what-do-you-call-it, nuclear explosive stuff, plutonium. And FDR was a little sensitive about starting any new big-spending projects for a while. So Einstein was out, and Carrel was in.

By the time Isaac got drafted and assigned to the secret research facility it was called the Pasadena Project; but by the time Doc got to that point the *Saturday Evening Post* woman was beginning to fidget. "That's very interesting, Mr.—Lowndes?" she said, glancing at her notes. "But I think my editors would want me to get this sort of thing from Dr. Asimov himself. Excuse me," she finished, already turning away, with the stars of hero worship beginning to shine in her eyes.

Doc looked at me ruefully. "Reporters," he said.

I nodded. Then I couldn't resist the temptation any longer. "Let's listen to what he does tell her," I suggested, and we trailed after her.

It wasn't easy to get near Isaac. Apart from the reporters, there were all the public relations staffs of our various publishers and institutes—Don Wollheim's own publishing company, Cyril's publishers, Bob Lowndes's, *The New York Times*, because Damon was the editor of their *Book Review*. Even my own publisher had chipped in, as well as the galleries that sold Hannes Bok's paintings and Johnny Michel's weird silk screens of tomato cans and movie stars' faces. But it was the U.S. Information Agency that produced most of the muscle, because Isaac was their boy. What was surrounding Isaac was a *mob*. The reporter was a tough lady, though. An elbow here, a side-slither there, and she was in the front row with her hand up. "Dr. Asimov? Weren't you the one who wrote the letter to President Roosevelt that started the Pasadena Project?"

"Good lord, no!" Isaac said. "No, it was a famous biochemist of the time, Dr. Alexis Carrel. He was responding to a letter Albert Einstein had written, and—What is it?"

The man from the *Daily News* had his hand up. "Could you spell that, please, Dr. Asimov?"

"E-I-N-S-T-E-I-N. He was a physicist, very well known at he time. Anyway, the President accepted Dr. Carrel's proposal and they started the Pasadena Project. I happened to be drafted into it, as a very young biochemist, just out of school."

"But you got to be pretty important," the woman said loyally. Isaac shrugged. Someone from another videopaper asked him to say more about his experiences, and Isaac, giving us all a humorously apologetic look, did as requested.

"Well," he said, "I don't want to dwell on the weapons systems. Everybody knows that it was our typhus bomb that made the Japanese surrender, of course. But it was the peacetime uses that I think are really important. Look around at my old friends here." He swept a generous arm around the dais, including us all. "If it hadn't been for the Pasadena Project some of us wouldn't be here now—do you have any *idea* how much medicine advanced as a result of what we learned? Antibiotics in 1944, antivirals in 1948, the cancer cure in 1950, the cholesterol antagonist in 1953?"

A California woman got in: "Are you sure the President made the right decision? There are some people who still think that atomic power is a real possibility."

"Ah, you're talking about old Eddy Teller." Isaac grinned. "He's all right. It's just that he's hipped on this one subject. It's really too bad. He could have done important work, I think, if he'd gone in for real science in 1940, instead of fooling around with all that nuclear stuff."

There wasn't any question that Isaac was the superstar, with Cyril getting at least serious second-banana attention, but it wasn't all the superstars. Quite. Each one of the rest of us got a couple of minutes before the cameras, saying how much each of us had influenced each other and how happy we all were to be seeing each other again. I was pretty sure that most of us would wind up as faces on the cutting-room floor, but what we said, funnily enough, was all pretty true.

And then it was over. People began to leave.

I saw Isaac coming out of the men's room as I was looking for the woman with my coat. He paused at the window, gazing out at the darkling sky. A big TWA eight-engined plane was coming in, nonstop, probably from someplace like Havana. It was heading toward Idlewild, hardly higher than we were, as I tapped him on the shoulder.

"I didn't know celebrities went to the toilet," I told him.

He looked at me tolerantly. "Matter of fact, I was just calling Janet," he said. "Anyway, how are things going with you, Fred? You've been publishing a lot of books. How many, exactly?"

I gave him an honest answer. "I don't exactly know. I used to keep a list. I'd write the name and date and publisher for each new book on the wall of my office—but then my wife painted over the wall and I lost my list."

"*Approximately* how many?"

"Over a hundred, anyway. Depends what you count. The novels, the short-story collections, the nonfiction books—"

"Over a hundred," he said. "And some of them have been dramatized, and book-clubbed, and translated into foreign languages?" He pursed his lips and thought for a moment. "I guess you're happy about the way your life has gone?"

"Well, sure," I said. "Why wouldn't I be?" And then I gave him another look, because there was something about his tone that startled me. "What are you saying, Eye? Aren't *you?*"

"Of course I am!" he said quickly. "Only—well, to tell you the truth, there's just one thing. Every once in a while I find myself thinking that if things had gone a different way, I might've been a pretty successful writer."

Plato's Cave

by Poul Anderson

The Three Laws of Robotics:

1. A robot may not injure a human being or, through inaction, allow a human being to come to harm.

2. A robot must obey the orders given it by human beings except where such orders would conflict with the First Law.

3. A robot must protect its own existence as long as such protection does not conflict with the First or Second Law.

The message reached Earth as a set of shortwave pulses. A communications satellite relayed it, along with hundreds more, to a groundside clearing station. Since it designated itself private, the station passed it directly on to its recipient, the global headquarters of the United States Robots and Mechanical Men Corporation. There a computer programmed with its highly secret code converted digital signals to sight and sound. An image leaped into being, so three-dimensionally complete that startlement brought a gasp from Henry Matsumoto.

The robot shown was no surprise—humanoid but large, bulkily armored, intended for hard labor under tricky conditions. The background, though, was spectacular. Nothing blocked that from view but a couple of structural members. Needing no air, drink, food, little of anything except infrequent refuelings, robots when by themselves traveled in spacecraft quite accurately describable as "barebones." At one edge of the screen, a slice of Jupiter's disc glowed huge, its tawniness swirled with clouds and spotted with storms that could have swallowed Earth whole. Near the lower edge was a glimpse of Io. The sights flitted swiftly past, for the ship was in close orbit around the moon, but the plume of one volcanic outburst upon it dominated the desolation for just this instant, geyserlike above a furious sulfury spout.

The young technician was doubly shaken because the apparition was so unexpected. He had merely been taking his turn as monitor, relieving the tedium with a book. No message had come in for weeks other than regular "All's well" tokens. What the hell had gone wrong?

A deep voice rolled over him. It was synthesized; in airlessness, the speaker directly modulated a radio wave. "Robot DGR-36 reporting from Io. Robot JK-7 has suspended operations—prospecting, mining, transportation, beneficiation, all work. When my crew and I landed to take on the next load of ore, we found every machine and subordinate robot idle. JK-7 himself was not present, but spoke to me from the hills behind the site. He declared that he was acting under strict orders from a human, to the effect that this undertaking is dangerous and must be terminated. I deemed it best that we return to orbit and await instructions."

"M-m-my God," Matsumoto stammered. "Hold on. Stay quiet."

At the present configuration of the planets, his order would take some forty minutes to arrive. However, anticipating that the first person he reached would be a junior, DGR-36 had already gone immobile. Matsumoto swung about in his chair and frantically punched the intercom.

He needed an outside line, local time being well past ordinary working hours, but soon Philip Hillkowitz, technological chief of Project Io, was in the little office. Hillkowitz in his turn had called Alfred Lanning, general director of research, who arrived almost on his heels. The two men stared at the image of the robot, and then at each other, for what seemed to Matsumoto a very long while.

"Has it happened in spite of everything?" Hillkowitz whispered. "Can the radiation really have driven Jack insane?"

Lanning's tufted brows drew together. "I shouldn't have to remind you," he snapped, "tests showed his shielding adequate against a hundred years of continuous exposure."

"Yes, yes, yes. But those hellish conditions—" Hillkowitz addressed the robot. "Edgar, did you notice any other abnormality when you were on the ground? For example, did metal seem pitted or corroded?"

"Not a bad question," Lanning said. "But in the eighty minutes till we hear the answer, we'd better think up a system for learning more, faster."

The officers dismissed Matsumoto, enjoining him to let out no hint of trouble; and they canceled subsequent vigils. Inevitably, this would start rumors by itself. While they waited, they sent out after coffee, speculated fruitlessly, paced, overloaded the air conditioning with smoke.

"No, sir," DGR-36 replied. "I took it upon myself to examine equipment and robots that were present. No trace of mechanical, chemical, or radiation damage was apparent to my sensors."

"Good lad," Lanning muttered. He had helped design a considerable degree of initiative into yonder model.

"I spoke with the other robots," DGR-36 continued, "but they could only tell me that JK-7 had directed them to stop work. I had no authority to order them back, and in any event, as I understand the situation, only JK-7 can successfully supervise them. I urged him to resume operations, but he stated that he was under directions that took precedence over all others, whereupon he broke contact." Again he turned into a statue.

"Have you observed any activity since?" Hillkowitz asked.

"This settles it," Lanning said to him. "We've got to get hold of Susan Calvin."

"What, already? Uh, yes, she can better judge derangement than either of us, no doubt, but—I mean, this time lag, and Jack himself out of touch—we can't dispatch her to the scene."

"No, I expect we'll want, hm, Powell and Donovan; they're

probably our best field operatives. But Calvin is the one to decide that."

Lanning keyed for her home. Presently a voice emerged waspish: "Well, what do you want? Who is there? If your reason for rousing me out of bed isn't excellent, you will regret it."

"Phil Hillkowitz and myself," Lanning said. "Look, you've got to get down here right away. We have a crisis on Io. I don't dare tell you more except in person."

"Afraid of electronic eavesdroppers? How melodramatic!"

"Well, maybe unlikely, but—Project Io is in trouble. You know how much it means, and how determined the opposition is."

"I also know how that room you're in must smell by now," retorted the robopsychologist. "Whistle up some of your technies and have me patched in on a properly sealed circuit. Full audiovisual, and direct access to the main databank. Given the transmission lag, they'll have ample time if they go about it competently."

Thus, after a while, the men saw her image, primly erect in a straight-backed chair, sipping tea, across from the robot's.

"We are not equipped to follow the actions of individuals when we are in space," DGR-36 answered. "We have noticed no obvious movements, at least thus far."

"I realize you don't have perfect memory either," Calvin said, "but I want you, Edgar, to tell me, as best you can—don't be in a hurry; examine your recollections carefully—tell me precisely what motivation JK-7 gave you. In particular, what did he tell you about this human who allegedly appeared to him and ordered him to halt work?"

She signaled for a break in transmission to Jupiter and turned her attention back Earthward. "'Appeared to' is the right wording," Hillkowitz said, sighing. His own gaze went elsewhere, as if to look through walls and across space. He might have been thinking, reviewing, though he had lived with this from its origins: *None of us can survive there. Io is deep in Jupiter's magnetosphere. The trapped charged particles would doom us within minutes, unless we were inside shielding so thick as to leave us helpless. Not to mention the cold, or vacuum barely softened by poisonous volcanic spewings. We can make robots immune to these and even guard the positronic brain so well that the radiation does not ruin it. Or so we thought. Lanning and I, our team, we labored long on the task. And afterward our engineers did, for two years in the safer outer reaches of the Jovian System, patiently guiding the construction on Io and the beginning of operations. But they could only communicate with Jake, and he with them, by radio and laser. At such times he perceived them and whatever they wished to show him; his communicator decoded the signals and he saw the images, heard the voices, inside that head of his. What now has he seen and heard, what new ghost came to him in that inferno where he toiled?*

"Precision is obviously essential," Calvin declared. "Now, gentlemen, I shall call up the files on this project and study them for about one hour." Her screen went blank.

"I might do the same," Lanning said. "You needn't, Phil. Io's been your exclusive concern. Why don't you catch a catnap?"

"Lord," mumbled Hillkowitz, "I wish I could."

The simulacrum of Calvin was back when promised, but told the men simply, "No comment, yet," and waited with hands folded in lap. Even when that of the robot stirred, hers did not. But his speech brought her too out of her chair.

"Yes, ma'm. Seeing the site idled, hardly any ore waiting, and JK-7 absent, I broadcast a call and got an audio reply which I sensed as emanating from somewhere in the hills. He maintained that he had stopped work on command of a human who explained that it threatened the entire human race. He declined to go into detail, except that when I asked if he would at least identify this human, he told me it was the Emperor Napoleon."

As low in mass and high in power as was compatible with life support, courier ship *Delfin* could have made Jupiter in less than four days. Svend Borup would have medicated himself against the effects of such an acceleration and spent much of the time happily contemplating the hardship bonus due him. Unfortunately, Gregory Powell and Michael Donovan would not have arrived fit to get busy. At a steady one gravity, boost and deboost, the crossing still took under a week, and meanwhile U.S. Robots's ace troubleshooters could become familiar with the vast store of background material given them.

When first they came up for air, at the first meal en route, Borup naturally asked them what was going on. "I was told almost not'ing," he said in his soft Danish accent. "The whole went so fast. They waved a contract at me, but it also says no more than that I take you to Yupiter and there help you as is needed." The owner-captain was a stocky, balding man whose waistline might be due in part to frequent indulgence in pretzel-shaped sugar cookies from his homeland.

"Well, they had plenty reason to hurry," Donovan answered. "Explanations could wait. Whatever's the matter, maybe we can fix it—unless we get there too late. Anyhow, the government can't afford—" He broke off, uncertain whether he should reveal more. Ole, one of the two robots that were the crew, helped him by entering the saloon and setting bowls of pea soup before the men. Knud, the other, was on watch, slight though the chance was of anything happening which the ship's automatics couldn't handle.

Borup nodded. "It is on Io. That is clear. They talk about reestablishing the station on Ganymede, but it is yust talk so far, after the Yovian scare. Too little left for people to do there, too big a hazard from the radiation. Nobody today on all those moons or anywhere near, yust the miner robots." He wagged his spoon. "And it is a big, big investment in them, no? If the ore stops coming out, many banks are in trouble. And so are the world aut'orities who sponsored the venture and pushed it t'rough."

"You're pretty well up on events," Powell remarked.

Borup chuckled. "For a fellow who mostly dashes around in space, you mean? No, no. Everybody knows what a powerful issue Proyect Io has been, pro and contra."

"Still is," Donovan muttered.

"Well, now that we're safely under way, we can be candid with you, and in fact we'd better be," Powell said. "Confidentiality —but frankly, if we fail, my guess is that it won't make much difference what gets into the media." He wiped his mustache, in which droplets had condensed from the steam off the soup. "Uh, I'm not sure what you may recollect of all the controversy about the project and all the hoopla while it was getting started. Since then it's practically dropped out of the public consciousness. Another bunch of robots and machinery, working somewhere distant from Earth."

"But wit' great promise," Borup said. "The Io volcanoes bring up such riches of minerals, more than in all the asteroids put together, no? It is the radiation that is the problem."

"Not alone. We also have a dangerous, essentially unpredictable environment, quakes, landslides, crevasses opening, ground collapsing into caves, eruptions, the way Jupiter's tides tear at that moon. Therefore an especially intelligent robot is required to run the show. The work gangs can be pretty ordinary models, not greatly modified, not too hard to provide ample shielding for. But the head honcho needs intelligence, a large store of knowledge, alertness, initiative, even what you may as well call a degree of imagination. The positronic circuits of such a robot are all too easily addled. Protecting it—simply plating the head with a lot of material—isn't enough. Compensatory circuits are necessary, and then you have to compensate for *their* effects. It wasn't really certain, when U.S. Robots signed the contract, that this development was possible at the present state of the art."

"Yes, I do remember."

"Sorry."

"It is all right. What have we to do but talk? And enyoy our soup. There will be meatballs after. Please to continue."

"Well, we, uh, the firm did come up with the new robot, and everything tested out fine, and went fine, too, until now. But he appears to have suddenly gone crazy after all. He suspended work and sits babbling about it being dangerous to Earth. He says this came to him in a, uh, vision."

"Ha, I t'ought somet'ing like that. Have you no spare?"

"I don't know, but I doubt it," Donovan put in. "Jack—JK-7—the number will tell you how many prototypes they went through—he's practically handcrafted. Cost more than any three senators. Not a production-line item; how many Ios have we got? Anyway, how could we land a second Jack till we know what went wrong with the first?"

"Which first might interfere with the second," Powell added grimly.

Borup looked shocked, in his mild fashion. "A robot interfering wit' work ordered by humans?"

"Hard to imagine," Powell agreed. "But, well, think. Because Jack is not only extra valuable, but essential to the project, and in such a hazardous situation, they've given him an unusually high Third Law potential. He'll take as good care of himself as he can, whether or not that means sacrificing a great deal else. Of course, it doesn't override the Second Law. He must carry out the mission entrusted to him, and obey any specific orders issued him by a human. But that potential is on the low side. What this means in practice is, if he, with his on-the-spot experience, if he thinks an order is mistaken, he questions it. He points out the flaws. Only if he's then commanded to proceed regardless will he do so. Likewise, when he's by himself he'll use his own judgment as to how he should direct the overall job of mining Io.

"Well, now he's gotten this delusion, or whatever it is. The First Law naturally takes precedence over everything else. He *cannot* knowingly do anything that would harm humans, or refrain from doing anything that would save humans from harm. His brain would burn out first." Powell had been ticking the points off on his fingers. "You know this, everybody does, but often the interactions of these laws, the conflicts between them and the resultants, get so complicated or so subtle that nobody but a roboticist can make sense of what's happening."

"And not always the roboticist, right away," Donovan chimed in.

"According to Edgar, the robot cargo-ship captain—and he wouldn't lie to us—Jack is convinced Project Io will lead to death and destruction," Powell said. "Therefore he's stopped it. I doubt very much he'll obey orders to resume, unless somehow we can persuade him he's in error. He might not even respond to our calls. Conceivably he'll decide it's his duty to actively resist further work, actually sabotage it. And, besides his high capabilities, if they aren't impaired, that high Third Law potential will make him a very cunning, careful, probably very efficient guerrilla."

"You have no way of yust making him stay quiet?" asked Borup.

Powell frowned. A moment passed before he said, "We can't go to Io in this ship to hunt him down, and live, if that's what you mean. Edgar and his crew are meant for space and stevedoring; they'd be hopeless. Getting up a proper robotic hunting party would be monstrously prolonged and expensive. Meanwhile the capital costs of the stalled project mount every day, and as for the political consequences if the scandal breaks—" He shrugged.

"No, no, I understand. But have you not some special passworded command to give him that makes you the absolute boss?"

Powell and Donovan stared. Borup blandly spooned soup. "You're smarter than you let on," Donovan murmured. He slapped the table and barked a laugh. "Yeah, sure we do. Hard-wired in. What with all the unknowns and unforeseeables, that was an elementary precaution. For instance, the scientists might discover a danger unknown to him, and not want to lose time arguing. Or if you're paranoid, or ultra careful, you'll worry about enemies of the project somehow slipping him a false order. Yes, there is a password. Top Secret, Burn Before Reading, known to a handful of people in the company and the government, and now to us two. It'll probably be the first thing we try when we get there. Whether he'll obey—He *is* insane, and this is not so basic as the Three Laws."

"Insane, you believe," Borup corrected.

Donovan grimaced. "We'd sure like to believe otherwise. If the radiation's fried his brain, or something else on that chunk of hell has gotten to him, there goes the project down the tubes, probably, and a lot more besides."

"What makes you t'ink he must be mad?"

Donovan and Powell glanced at each other before Powell nodded. "Why, he claims Napoleon came and told him to stop," Donovan said. "That's all we know so far. But isn't it enough?"

"Napoleon? The Emperor?"

"Who else?"

"Now where would he have heard about Napoleon?"

"A reasonable question. Last *I* heard, Dr. Calvin was trying to research that. But you never know what stray scraps of information might get to a robot while he's being activated and indoctrinated. A lot of people are generally involved, and he'll overhear conversations. Also, now and then a brain picks up stray signals, telecast or—Remember Speedy, Greg?"

"How could I forget?" Powell sighed. To Borup: "A robot we dealt with on Mercury. A Second-Third Law conflict unbalanced him. He ran around and around in a circle gibbering Gilbert and Sullivan. We never did find out how he acquired it."

"Hm," said Borup. "Your chances do not look so good, yentlemen, do they?"

"Which means the chances for the world don't." Powell's tone was bleak.

"Oh? True, much money will be lost. But unless you are a banker or a politician—"

"Bankers handle the money of working stiffs like you and us," Donovan said. "If Project Io goes bust, we could get one black hole of a depression."

"And as for politicians," Powell added, "they aren't all

clowns and crooks, you know. Here we've finally, just a few years back, elected a reform government with some bright, decent people at the top. It's staked its future on Project Io. The opposition was terrific, you may recall. What, throw away fortunes on a gamble like that? The idea that we'll all benefit more from increased production, fairly divided, than from handouts and pork barrels was too much for the old guard. It fought right down the line. And it's still got a large minority in the legislature, while the government itself is a pretty frail coalition. Let Project Io fail, and a vote of no confidence will throw us right back to where we were, or worse."

"I suppose so," Borup said softly. "I do not pay too much attention to those t'ings. When I am at home wit' my wife, mostly we talk about the garden and the grandchildren. But, yes, we did vote for reform. It would be nice to see that man Stephen Byerly someday be coordinator." He turned his head. "Ah, here come the meatballs."

Seen from its little moon Himalia, Jupiter shone about as large as Luna over Earth but, in spite of its cloud-bands, barely a fourth as bright. That pale gold glow, the glare from a shrunken sun, and the glitter of swarming stars shimmered on ice and vanished among upthrust crags. Clustered at the north pole, dome, masts, and docking facilities were a sight well-nigh as gaunt, yet welcome to human eyes. Borup brought *Delfin* to rest and linked airlocks. Powell and Donovan entered the mothballed engineering base to reactivate it. Gravity was virtually negligible; they moved through the gloom like phantoms, except when they collided with something and uttered earthy words.

After a few hours they had light, heat, air circulation, austere habitability. Donovan beat his hands together. "Brrr!" he exclaimed. "How long'll it take the walls to warm up? I know it's thermodynamic nonsense, but I'd swear they radiate cold."

"Longer than we'll be here, I hope," Powell said. "Meanwhile we can eat and sleep aboard ship. Let's get cracking."

They settled themselves before the main console in the communications room. A coded beam sprang from the transmitter, computer-aimed inward through the lethal zone around Jupiter. A readout showed that Io was currently occulted by the great planet, but that shouldn't matter. Two relay satellites swung in the Trojan positions of the same orbit. Six more circled Io itself, in the equatorial and polar planes. Between them, those identified Jack wherever he was on the surface and kept locked onto him.

"Himalia Base calling Robot JK-7," Powell intoned. "Humans have returned to the Jovian System. Come in, JK-7."

After a humming silence, Donovan ran fingers through red hair gone wild and groaned, "He must be completely around the bend. He talked for a little while to Edgar." Useless here, that robot and his crew were bound for duty in the Asteroid Belt. "Now he won't give us the time of day." He paused. "Unless he's broken down physically, too."

"Seems unlikely," Powell argued. "His builders are as competent a bunch as you'll find. Supposing conditions are more harmful than they knew, still, damage would be cumulative, and Jack hasn't been where he is for long." He rubbed his chin. "Hmm. While Edgar's gang was on the ground, he skulked in the hills and communicated by audio-only long-wave radio. I'd guess he was afraid they might seize him and take him back for examination. They couldn't pinpoint where he was broadcasting from on that band, and weren't equipped to use the satellites to locate him for them. Not that they could run him down anyway, in country he's designed for."

"He didn't have to obey them. They were robots, same as him."

"Yeah. He didn't have to respond to them at all. But I daresay Second Law made him anxious to explain himself to humans, sort of."

"Hey, wait. We're humans, and he isn't heeding us."

"If, as you say, he's capable of receiving." Powell drew breath. "Okay, we reinforce the Second Law by the password." He leaned forward and said slowly: "Robot JK-7, this is human Gregory Powell calling from Himalia Base. I order you to reply. Code Upsilon. Repeat, Code Upsilon."

Silence stretched. The men knew it must. Time lag at the moment was about thirty-nine seconds, either way. Nevertheless, they shivered as they half sat, half floated in their chairs. When abruptly the screen came alive, Donovan jumped. He rose into midair and cartwheeled gradually down again, struggling to keep his remarks to himself.

The view was of ruggedness and desolation. Near half phase, Jupiter stood huge over the hills that ringed a narrow horizon. Its radiance flooded the scars and mottlings left by eruptions. Closer in lay flat concrete, on which Powell spied vehicles, machines, motionless robots. So Jack had returned to his own base. This was what he saw before him.

Well, not quite. He also saw Powell's image, and presently Donovan's, and heard their voices. They were not superimposed on the landscape. He perceived them separately, somewhat as a human may see a face called out of memory without losing view of what is actually around—but more vividly, in full three-dimensional detail.

The synthetic speech jerked, stumbled, dragged itself forth: "Robot JK-7 . . . responding. What . . . have you to say?"

"What is this 'Napoleon' lunacy?" Powell demanded. "How did you get the notion your task endangers anybody? On the contrary, it's beneficial and important to Earth. In the name of your makers, by authority duly delegated my partner and me, I command you to resume operations."

The minute-plus until the answer came felt like forever. When it did, they almost wished it hadn't.

"I . . . am not . . . so obliged. You . . . are robots."

"Huh? Code Upsilon, damn it!" Donovan roared. "And the Second Law! You can see and hear we're human!"

Interminability.

"I observe . . . the semblance. I hear the claim. Also, yes—" The scene wavered a little, as if Jack shuddered. "Also the word of command. But—but—"

The voice trailed off. "Go on," Powell said low. "But what?"

After another dripping away of seconds: "Napoleon warned me of this. He . . . he said . . . robots posing as humans . . . possessing the password . . . would try to do . . . exactly what you are trying to do."

Donovan opened his mouth. Powell made a shushing gesture, leaned nearer the screen, spoke softly and earnestly.

"Listen, Jack. Something is terribly wrong. You're altogether misinformed. We don't blame you, but you must help us get to the bottom of this. Help us to help you, understand? Tell us exactly what has happened. Tell us why you think what you think. Who told you what, Jack? For the well-being of humanity, tell us."

Waiting.

"If you . . . are robots . . . you are deceived." The voice

strengthened. "You are serving a disastrous policy. Let me enlighten you."

"Certainly, Jack. If we, if we are robots, we too obey the First Law. We would never willingly or wittingly cause humans to come to harm. And if we are not robots, then we need to learn about possible dangers, don't we? Remember, we know Code Upsilon. That implies we are humans, doesn't it? In a pretty special position, at that. Tell us everything, Jack."

Waiting. Despite the chill, sweat gleamed on Donovan's cheeks. He wiped it with large, helpless hands.

The pause went on for an added minute, but when the machine tones arrived, they had steadied. "Very well. The password does require me to give you as much obedience as possible. Napoleon told me it would. In fact, events are proceeding as he foresaw, which you must agree adds credence to his statements.

"On date 23 January, hour 0917 and 3.68 seconds, I was in the Loki area, having taken a flitter there to prospect for new digs while my workers finished up at the Aten lode. A full audiovisual of a human appeared to me. He identified himself as the Emperor Napoleon and described a deadly menace newly discovered through study of specimens sent back to Earth during the first robotic explorations decades ago. It had not been found earlier because it is so subtle and surprising.

"Energized by vulcanism, a kind of pseudolife has evolved here. Napoleon called it a viroid. It derives its own energy by promoting reactions among metallic elements. As a rule this goes very slowly, but in the course of geological time the viroid has infested all minerals, and reduction will not get rid of it. By now it is in equilibrium on Io, essentially dormant, but when it is brought into contact with uncontaminated metal it will spread again, faster at Earth temperatures than here. This station, with robots and machinery, will begin to crumble within ten or fifteen standard years. Let Ionian metals be introduced on Earth, and the whole industrial infrastructure will collapse in a time not much longer. Dependent on it, the vast majority of humans will die horribly.

"Fortunately, thus far only a small tonnage has been exported, and it only to industries off Earth. Samples on Earth have been kept isolated for research purposes. Certain disintegrations led to studies which determined the cause. Steps can be taken to eliminate contaminated metal everywhere; it is not too late. But clearly, no more material of any kind may ever leave Io. Napoleon ordered me under Code Upsilon to halt operations."

"He lied!" Donovan shouted. "There's been no such trouble, no such discovery. Lies, I tell you!"

Powell agreed more smoothly, "This is correct. We would have known. If the danger existed, would we be here wanting you to start work again?"

Waiting.

"Napoleon explained this and anticipated your argument," Jack said. He still didn't sound quite self-assured. "The findings are, as yet, controversial. They seem to defy the principles of biology, as biology has hitherto been taught. The directors of Project Io have a major personal, financial, and political investment in it. They refuse to believe. They have kept the news from the public. Napoleon represents a group of dissident scientists who realize that, at the least, operations must be suspended until the truth has been ascertained beyond any doubt.

"He told me that, when I took this measure, the directors would try to annul it. They would send robots, because humans might feel qualms and let the world know what is going on. Cleverly misinformed, the robots would have instructions to pose as humans and dissuade me."

The voice grew firmer. "You are those emissaries. Yes, Napoleon's group could perhaps be mistaken. But I cannot take the chance. The possibility that humans may die in the billions is . . . unthinkable . . . unacceptable under any circumstances, any odds. Consider this, you two, in the light of the First Law. You must set your own orders aside."

"But we aren't robots," Donovan choked. "Just look at us."

"We could be disguised," Powell admitted fast. "The simplest way would be to change the digital transmission. Put in a program that converts a robot image to a human image. Voices likewise. It would be much easier the other way around. Humans have many more features, more nuances of expression. Watch my face, my hands." He went through a repertoire of smiles, frowns, and gestures. "Could a robot do that, with all the shadings you see?"

Waiting.

Renewed uncertainty spoke. "I . . . am not . . . acquainted with such details . . . about humans."

"Then how do you know Napoleon isn't a robot?" Donovan flung.

"Pipe down, Mike," Powell snapped. "Uh, Jack, you do have a good intelligence and a capability of independent judgment. You must be aware of the possibility that Napoleon has misled you, and we are in fact humans giving you your proper orders. Now think how much more believable it is that that's the case."

He had expected a pause for pondering, but the reply was as prompt as light-speed allowed, and once more—above an undertone, an unevenness, that sounded anguished—resolute. "It is indeed conceivable. I do not know enough about human affairs to gauge the probability. That does not matter. Given the slightest chance that Napoleon is right, and his use of Code Upsilon indicates that he does have full access to information, the consequences are absolutely impermissible. This outweighs every other consideration. I cannot allow mining and shipment to continue. If the attempt is made, I must do my best to prevent it." With a naïveté that would have been pathetic under less desperate circumstances: "I shall cache explosives in the hills and devise weapons against future robots. My own workers will follow me."

Powell gnawed an end of his mustache. "I see. Let's try this from another angle. Tell me about Napoleon. What does he look like? How often has he contacted you, and from where? What precisely has he said?"

Waiting.

"In person," said Jack, "he is a somewhat stout male, of short stature to judge by what glimpses I have had of his control board, although those are bare glimpses. His hair is black. He wears a cloth around his neck. Otherwise any clothing is covered by an overgarment of a blue color, with golden-hued braid at the shoulders. I have not seen his legs. He commonly keeps his right hand tucked into the coat. He also wears a kind of triangular headgear, likewise blue, of some soft material."

Donovan's lips formed a soundless whistle.

The voice plodded on: "As for where he calls from, it must be outside the radiation belt, since he is human, but he has not informed me. I have noted the time lags with my internal clock, and computed that he cannot be on Himalia. In fact, their rather slight variations indicate he is not on any moon.

"He has called three times. The exchanges have been brief. I will attempt to re-create them for you, because . . . because if you are human, I must obey you to the extent that the First Law permits."

The words that followed were, indeed, short and to the point. The original communication described the viroids and gave the order to cease and desist. The other two, at intervals of a few days, were essentially reinforcing; such questions as had occurred to Jack got curt answers, which bore down on the danger to mankind and the reckless villainy of Project Io's directors. Powell and Donovan refrained from asking how Napoleon came to speak fluent English. They were more interested in the additional command.

"Now that you are here," Jack said, "I must inform him. I will broadcast at sufficient strength that his receivers will pick it up, wherever he is in the Jovian region. Thereafter I will arrange that any further discussions with you will be directly retransmitted in full audiovisual to him. Thus he will hear what you have to say, and join in if he chooses." Wistfulness? "Perhaps you can persuade him he is misguided."

"Perhaps," mumbled Donovan without hope.

Waiting.

"I had better take care of that at once," Jack said. "I see no profit in further conversation at this point, do you? If you have any valid points to make, factual or logical, call me and I will consider them. So will Napoleon."

The screen blanked.

The spaceship was a haven of comfort and sanity. Borup heard his passengers out, clicked his tongue, and told them, "What you need first is a stiff drink. I have a bottle of akvavit for emeryencies."

Donovan raised a hand. "Best offer I've had all day," he said, "but first, can we start searching?"

"What's this?" asked Powell.

"Look, if Napoleon is real, he's got to be hanging around in this neighborhood. Let's see if we can find him before he figures out some fresh deviltry. If he's not real, if Jack is quantum hopping, what've we lost?"

"If he is hidden on one of the moons, I do not know how we can detect him," Borup objected.

Donovan shook his head. "Jack doesn't think he is, and he for sure would not be. In the first place, digging in like that is a lot of work, needs time and equipment and hands. If this is a try to sabotage Project Io, it's got to be a shoestring kind of thing, a tiny clique, like maybe half a dozen individuals. Anything bigger would take too long to organize, be too hard to manage, and make secrecy impossible for any useful length of time. Investigators would be bound to get clues to the guilty parties."

Powell regarded his partner closely. "Once in a while you surprise me," he confessed. "Marvelous, my dear Holmes!"

Donovan bowed. "Elementary, my dear Watson."

"Holmes and Watson never said that," Borup remarked aside.

Donovan continued: "We've also got the fact that the gear for using the Trojan relays is special and delicate. On the surface of a moon it would stick up in sight of God and everybody and give the game away. Therefore Napoleon must be in space. And he won't want to lose touch with Io during the frequent occultations. So he'll be well above or below the ecliptic, where he always has Io in his instruments. An orbit skewed from Jupiter's but otherwise with the same elements will keep him in place, fairly stably, over a period of a few weeks, I should think." He glanced at Borup. "Svend, could we find a ship loitering maybe two, three million klicks from here in the northern or southern sky?"

Powell scowled. "That's a monstrous volume of space to cruise through."

"I would not obyect to running up the bill I present the company wit'," Borup said, "but it is not necessary, and it would waste time that is precious. We do carry very sensitive instruments. When you travel at the speeds a courier reaches, you must be able to detect t'ings far ahead of you." He pondered. "M-m-m, *tja*, it depends on the size and type of the craft. But somet'ing no bigger than mine, which is close to minimum, we could get on the optics for certain. And radar reaches still farther. The rotation axis of this moon is tilted enough that we need not take off to examine bot' regions where Napoleon must be in one of if he monitors Io."

"The ship's hull could be camouflaged, couldn't it?" Powell inquired. "Then how'll you know your radar hasn't fingered a meteoroid?"

"Camouflage, maybe, I am not sure. But the nature of a

radar-reflecting surface shows in the return signal if you got an analyzer like mine. Metal is different from rock and so on. And once we have acquired a suspicious obyect, we have more instruments. In these parts, unless the crew is frozen to deat', there will be infrared emission—and also from that direction, out of the power plant, neutrinos above the background count. Yes, I t'ink we can find the Emperor's spaceship unless he is so far away that the communications delay is ridiculous. I will go put Knud on it." Borup thrust foot against bulwark and arrowed out of the saloon, into the passageway leading to the control room.

He returned with the promised bottle and three small thin glasses, to join Powell and Donovan at the table. There was just sufficient weight to make pouring and drinking feasible, albeit a trifle awkward. "Ole, make dinner," he called. "A special treat for these poor men. Fishballs and tomato soup. You look too gloomy, my friends."

"We were wondering what to do if Jack really is insane— which is the simplest hypothesis, after all." Powell's tone was dark. "Get him aboard a robotic ship and back to Earth for Dr. Calvin to interview, sure. Except, how? He believes his duty is to stay and fight any new effort to exploit Io. He might return with us anyway, I suppose, if he knew we're human. Second Law. You could add your voice for reinforcement, Svend. We'd outvote Napoleon three to one. But he can't be certain. My guess is that even if he granted a ninety-nine percent probability that we're human, he wouldn't risk it. That one percent contains an outcome he finds unendurable."

The smile died on Borup's mouth. "We all do, no?" he replied most softly. "I would not take such a chance, would you? Better we go back to bad, corrupt politics than nearly everybody on Eart' die and the survivors are starving savages. Could Napoleon be telling the trut'?"

"Absolutely not," Donovan stated. "I know that much biology, physics, and geology. Too bad Jack doesn't."

"He's utterly ignorant about people, too," Powell added. "A quite ordinary robot, even, would wonder about that story, if he'd had normal human contacts. You needn't stipulate our politicians and capitalists are farsighted, altruistic, or extraordinarily bright. Simply ask yourself whether they'd take such a risk with the civilization that keeps *them* alive and well-to-do. Besides, the scientific method doesn't work the way the story claims. You don't get a few geniuses making a discovery overnight in a garret and then unable to get it published. Something as fundamental as this would come out in bits and pieces, over the years, with the news media following and exaggerating every step."

"And the public sure as hell would demand a screeching halt the moment it heard operations here might bring doomsday," Donovan said.

Borup nodded a bit impatiently. "Yes, yes. I am not quite so naïve as Yack."

"I'm sorry," Donovan apologized, while Powell offered, "I guess we're overwrought."

"It is all right. I only wondered how plausible to anybody are the viroids."

"To nobody, except Jack," Donovan growled. "In fact, it's so crackpot that if we reported right now what he'd told us, they'd wonder on Earth whether we'd gone off trajectory ourselves. We need all the data we can collect, which is why I wanted that search for another ship." His eyes brightened. "If we do find it, we'll beam the news back the same minute, and the world police can begin right away tracking down the conspirators."

"Who might they be, do you t'ink?"

Powell shrugged. "I can't name anybody specific. I have my guesses, but they taught me in school that a man is presumed innocent until proven guilty. Imagine a couple of powerful old-guard politicians whose careers are in trouble, probably conjoined with one or two industrialists who were getting rich off the former cozy arrangements, plus a few skilled underlings. The idea obviously is to show Project Io was a monumental, expensive blunder, and cause the Young Turks who pushed it through to be discredited. The reform coalition will fall apart and the wily old-timers can pick off its members piecemeal."

Donovan's mane bristled with excitement. "We'll have one damn good clue," he said. "The cabal has to've had a mole in U.S. Robots or high up in the World Space Agency—somebody who knew about Code Oops!-ilon and passed the information on. Probably that was what decided the conspirators to go ahead. It's the key to their whole stunt. Well, the number of possible suspects must be mighty small. Once we can prove this was a hoax, I'll bet the mole is under arrest inside a week, and his buddies by the end of the month."

"That's if we can prove it," Powell demurred, "which we can't if it's not true."

"Yes, why should a person lying to Yack pretend he is Napoleon?" Borup asked. "It is crazy."

Donovan's laugh rattled. "Exactly. Hearing what Jack has to tell, most people would take for granted he's gone blinkety."

"Confusions about Napoleon are a cliché," Powell said. "And you'd expect a poor, limited robot to fall into clichés, wouldn't you? Yes, it was a clever touch. Maybe Jack never heard the name 'Napoleon' before he was on Io, but we don't know, and he isn't about to inform us."

"Or he could lie, could he not?" Borup suggested. "If he believes you are robots too, not humans, you cannot order him to speak the trut'."

"Right," Donovan snarled. "We can't give him any damned orders he doesn't want to carry out."

"Oh, I'm sure he desperately wants to," Powell replied. "Couldn't you hear it in his voice? This conflict, this uncertainty is racking him apart. It may well destroy him, burn out his brain, all by itself."

"In which case the gang will've won."

"If the gang exists."

"Yeah. How do we settle Jack's dilemma for him? How do we convince him we're human?"

Powell leered. "I could chop off your head." Sobering: "No, seriously, he would see the action performed, but he couldn't be certain the gore wasn't fake. A human doubtless would be, knowing we can't have brought along the studio equipment needed to stage a realistic-looking murder. But Jack doesn't know humans that well. He's had so little direct exposure to them, he's like a small child."

"And we can't land on Io to let him meet us in the flesh," Donovan said unnecessarily. "We could, that is, if we didn't mind dying shortly afterward."

"Not in my spaceship," Borup declared.

"Of course. Besides, Jack would probably run away and hide from us—Wait, though. I'm on the track of something."

Donovan stared into a corner. The ventilator whirred. Warm odors drifted in from the galley. After a minute he tossed off his drink, struck his fist against the table, and exclaimed, "How's this? I don't imagine you have any weapon aboard, Svend, but inside the station I noticed a supply room that hadn't been emptied—stuff might be wanted someday—and the manifest on the door mentioned a case of detonol sticks. Jack can recognize one of those, all right! Look, while he watches, somebody waves it and says to him, 'Jack, your behavior makes me feel so terrible I want to kill myself.' Then the man pulls out the firing pin. If he doesn't push it back in within five minutes, bang!"

Borup blinked. "Are you crazy like him? What good will that do, except to ruin my ship?"

"Why, if I'm a robot I can't suicide," Donovan crowed. "Third Law, remember? Therefore I must be human. Therefore Jack will immediately yell 'Stop!' and beg our pardon for ever having doubted us."

"That firewater went to your head almighty fast, boy," Powell clipped. "A robot damn well can self-destruct if that's necessary for executing his orders."

"But—well, naturally, I mean first we'll set it up—uh—It does call for some preliminary detail work."

"It calls for an infinite amount, because its value is zero. However—hmm—" Powell refilled his own glass and fell into a similar reverie.

Under the ghostly gravity, Knud entered without sound. One by one they saw his tall form in the doorway, and tensed.

"Search completed, sir," the robot reported.

"Already?" Donovan wondered.

"The sweep and data crunching go fast," Borup said. "They must, on a courier. *Ja, Knud, hvad har du*—What have you found?"

"Negative, sir," the flat voice announced. "No indications of a vessel within either the northern or the southern cones of space that you specified, for as far as reliability extends."

Powell and Donovan exchanged stares. Powell slumped. "Then Jack is insane," he said heavily. "Conditions on Io were too much for him, and Project Io is kaput."

"You may go, Knud," Borup said. The robot departed. "I am sorry, my friends. Come, have a little more to drink."

"No, hold on, hold on!" Donovan bawled. He sprang to his feet. They left the deck. He caught the table edge in time to keep from rising to the overhead. Hanging upside down, he blurted, "Listen, I sort of expected this. Napoleon wouldn't likely be human. A big risk of life, a big expense. But he can be a robot!"

The silence was not lengthy, nor stunned. The idea had lain at the back of each mind. Powell began to develop it. While the other two sat, he paced in front of them, long strides bouncing off the ends of the cabin, and counted points on his fingers as they occurred to him.

"Yes," he said, "that does make sense. Any man-capable spacecraft is a sizable, powerful machine. Misused, it can kill a lot of people. So the authorities keep track of it. You don't take it anywhere without a certified crew and a filed flight plan. Hard to go clandestinely. But a one-robot vessel, why, that needn't be much more than a framework and a motor. You could keep it somewhere unbeknownst to anyone, as it might be the Lunar outback, and lift off from there unnoticed. When the robot wanted to drift along undetectable beyond a few hundred klicks, he'd shut off the power and sit in the cold. He himself—Not every robot is a U.S.R. product and property, leased to the user and periodically inspected. The best are, yes, but—hm, every now and then one of ours is irrecoverably destroyed, in some accident or other. Except that not all those reports have been honest. I know of a few cases where the robot was in fact hidden away, to be redirected to illegal jobs. This could well be such a case."

Borup's china-blue eyes widened. "Can you make a robot do unlawful t'ings?"

"You can if you go about it right," Donovan said. "With the proper technicians and equipment, you can blank out all he's ever learned and retrain him from scratch. The Three Laws still hold, of course, but he can have some pretty weird notions about the world. That must be what's been done here. If Napoleon only remembers dealing with his masters and Jack, then he's swallowed their story whole. Except for a very few top-flight, experimental models, robots are unsubtle characters anyway. They can't concoct elaborate plots and don't imagine that anybody else could. We'll give him an earful!"

"Slow down," Powell cautioned. "Let's explore this further. What does the Napoleon robot necessarily know and believe, to execute his mission of halting Project Io?" He thought aloud as he soared to and fro:

"He can operate a spacecraft, a communications system, et cetera. Therefore he has a certain amount of independent decision-making capability, though scarcely equal to Jack's. Otherwise simpleminded, he has no way of knowing the viroid story is false. I daresay he's been forbidden to tune in any outside 'cast, and told to ignore whatever he might overhear accidentally. His mission is to warn Jack about the viroids, and about the wicked men whose robots will try to talk Jack into going back to work. To this end, it'll be reasonable to him that he claim to being human himself, and that his image be projected as human. He'll have no inhibitions about such a pious deception, if it's used on another robot."

"Ah-ha!" Borup exulted. "We have him! He will be listening and watching when you next call Yack. He will see you are human, and obey your orders."

"He will not," Powell said bleakly. "I assume the conspirators have planned ahead. If I were in charge, I'd not only program his transmitter to make him look human, I'd program his receiver to make any in-calling human look like a robot."

"Whoof!" puffed Borup, and sought the akvavit.

"Yeah," Donovan agreed. "That pretty well shields him from any nagging doubts, which makes him better able to quiet down any that Jack expresses."

"He might entertain the possibility that his communicator is deceiving him," Powell said, "but he can't act on it, when his orders are to prevent a catastrophe. For instance, we could invite him to come here and meet us. I'll bet he'd refuse, because we, if we're enemy robots as he's been told, we'd overpower him."

Borup nodded. "I see. I see. It is a classic conundrum, no? Plato's cave."

"Huh?" grunted Donovan.

"You do not know? Well, I have more time to read than you do, on my travels. The ancient Greek philosopher Plato pointed out that our information about the material world comes to us entirely t'rough our senses, and how do we know they tell us true? Rather, we know they are often wrong. We must do the best we can. He said we are like prisoners chained in a cave who cannot see the outside, yust the shadows of t'ings there that are cast on the wall. From this they must try to guess what the reality is."

"Kind of an airy notion."

"Ha, you would refute solipsism like Dr. Samuel Yohnson, by kicking a stone—"

"Never mind the dialectics," Powell interrupted. "You have hit on a good analogy, Svend. We are trapped in Plato's cave, all three parties of us. We can't physically go to each other. The only information we get is what comes over the communication beams; and it could be lies. *We* don't even know that the Napoleon robot exists. We're assuming so, but maybe he really is only a figment of Jack's deranged imagination. If Napoleon does exist, then he knows that his own projected image is a man's; but every image he receives is a robot's, and he believes—he must believe, if he's to serve his bosses reliably—that that is true. As for Jack, if he isn't hallucinating, then every image he receives is human, and he can't tell which of them are genuine.

"Deadlock. How do we break it? Remember, meanwhile the clock is running. I don't think Jack's brain can take the stress on it much longer. Be that as it may, Project Io can't remain idle for weeks and months without going broke."

Donovan snapped his fingers. "Got it!" he cried. "We call Jack and get Napoleon into the conversation. We record this. Then Earth will know there's something rotten in—uh—sorry, Svend."

Powell frowned. "Well, we can try," he answered. "But we'd better have something to say he'll consider worth his notice."

"Hello, Jack," he greeted as calmly as he was able. "How are you?"

The barren scene jittered. The belated voice rose and fell. "What . . . do you want?"

"Why, to continue our conversation. And, to be sure, offer our respects to the Emperor Napoleon. You told us he'll be listening in. We'd be delighted to have the honor of his participation in our talk. Introductions first. I neglected them earlier. You may recall that my name is Gregory Powell. The gentleman here at my side is Michael Donovan, and behind us you see Captain Svend Borup." Powell beamed, pointless though he knew it was. "Quite a contrast, we three, eh? Well, humans are a variegated lot."

After the delay: "That may be. To me you . . . look similar. I had to exert myself to describe the Emperor Napoleon as closely as I did. Begging your pardon, sir," Jack said—to an unseen observer? His attention returned to Powell. "What do you want? He . . . he has instructed me . . . not to waste time on your . . . importunities. I must prepare . . . to resist . . . any invasion."

"Resist the will of the humans who sent you?" Powell purred. After a minute he saw the moonscape jerk, and went on quickly, hoping the robot would not cut him off, "Our purpose is to show you that we are indeed humans, ourselves, whatever Napoleon may be, and therefore you must, under Code Upsilon, accept that Earth is not endangered and you should resume work. Pay close attention."

Did a sentient machine afar in space tune himself high as the words reached him?

Powell turned his gaze on Donovan. "Now, Mike," he said, "I want you to tell me truthfully—truthfully, mind you—that you're neither a human nor a robot."

Donovan shivered with eagerness. "I am neither," he responded. "Now you, Greg, tell me truthfully that you are neither human nor robot."

"I am neither." Powell looked straight before him again, into the vision whose eyes he could not see. "Did you hear, Jack? Think about it. The order was to answer the question truthfully. No threat to a human was involved, therefore any robot must obey to the extent possible. However, the single possible answer for him is, 'I cannot.' None but a human could disobey and give out the falsehood, 'I am neither human nor robot.'"

Wire-tense, the men waited.

Did something whisper unrelayed from the deeps, or did Jack's own intelligence see the fallacy? The reply took longer than transmission would account for. "That is correct if . . . if the questioner is human. But if . . . he is a robot . . . then another robot can . . . perfectly well, disobediently, lie—especially if he has been so directed beforehand. The same . . . holds good for . . . every such dialogue. It proves nothing. Stop pestering me!"

Powell and Donovan sat mute. "Napoleon, have you any comment?" Borup attempted. Silence answered him.

Jack blanked the screen.

* * *

Not even fried herring with potatoes consoled.

The men chewed unspeaking. It was as if they saw, they felt, the immensity and the cold outside this hull. The failure of a venture, the death of many hopes, what were those that the stars were mindful of them?

When Ole at last brought coffee, it revived his master a little. "If Yack is pure crazy, he still has a good logical noodle," he opined. "You keep after him. Make him t'ink. For instance, would not those viroids make Io have different rocks from what it does?"

Powell shook his head. "No doubt, but what they educated him in was Ionian geology as it is. His job was practical, not scientific. Whenever he noticed anomalies, he was to get on the beam and query the specialists back home. We don't have time to teach him. Couldn't you hear how agitated he was?" Powell looked up. "Yes. Each contact has made his condition worse. Unless we can invent a scheme we know will be productive, we'd better quit. Maybe Susan Calvin can generate an idea."

"That won't do anything productive for our careers," Donovan muttered.

"To hell with our careers . . . But I don't expect the old lady can solve our problem from her armchair on Earth. Otherwise we wouldn't have been dispatched. With the kind of transmission delay involved, she couldn't work her slick robopsych tricks."

"I s'pose." Donovan gusted a sigh. "I can't think how to lure Napoleon into talking to us, and maybe he doesn't exist anyway. What say we assume he doesn't, assume Jack is demented, and try figuring out how to get him to board a ship, or at least keep from sniping at new arrivals? If there'll ever be any?"

"We'll give our wits a few days to work, and hope for a script that he won't see through."

"I wonder if you can," Borup said. "I am no expert, but I have known people wit' strange notions, and they can be very smart, yes, brilliant about defending those notions. They sit in their Plato caves till deat' comes and kicks them in the behind—"

He broke off. Donovan had smacked fist into palm. Powell drew a whistling breath.

"Hello, Jack."

The scene was not the base. Rubble lay dark under waxing Jupiter, beneath gashed heights. Volcano fumes lifted dirty white and yellow beyond a ridge. Jack was in the field, readying his caches and strongpoints for war.

The view swayed giddyingly as he straightened. "What do you want now?" It was nearly a shriek. "I told you to leave me alone. I need not listen to you. I can switch off."

"Just wait. Just wait." Until these waves wing out to Napoleon, wherever he is, if he is. "Be calm," Powell urged. "You've demanded positive proof that my companions and I are human. Well, we have it for you."

Empty time.

"You have tried. What is the certainty? If . . . you are robots . . . you are acting under orders. Your . . . masters . . . can have foreseen . . . many . . . contingencies."

"Then our masters are human," Donovan said. "Shouldn't you hear what they tell you through us?"

He was taking a risk. The suspense was like a slow fire before they heard Jack utter a raw noise. But it was desirable to perturb Napoleon too, if Napoleon was there to be troubled in his own sureness.

"We are human," Powell said quickly. "You force us, in this emergency, to demonstrate it, no matter what that costs us. Then maybe you'll be sorry and obey the surviving member of our party."

"Remember, if what Napoleon has told you is true," Donovan joined in—if what Napoleon had been told was true— "we can't be human. We must be robots, pretending. We must be what he sees on his screen. But if we are human, then Napoleon has told you wrong. Correct?"

Probably Jack never noticed the sweat on the two faces. "Pay close attention," Powell directed.

Rising, he lifted a detonol stick and brandished it like a sword. Donovan got up too and said, "Greg, I hereby, uh, well, this is the time for you to do what I told you you'd have to do if matters got this desperate. Destroy yourself."

Powell pulled out the firing pin. It wobbled in his right hand, the stick in his left. "Mike," he replied, "I order you to destroy yourself."

Donovan brought his explosive into view and, having yanked the pin free, held the stick dramatically against his throat. The men faced each other. In a proper gravity field their knees might have given way, but here they could somehow keep standing, after a fashion. They breathed hard and raggedly.

"Stop!" Jack's cry came loud, yet as if from across light-years. "Return those disarmers!"

"If we are robots," Donovan grated, "why should you care?"

Empty time.

"Third Law! You must!"

"We, we have our orders," Powell stammered.

Each minute was forever.

At four and a half, Borup entered, halted, stared. "What is this?" he shouted. "Are you crazy too?"

"We have our orders," Powell repeated.

"I countermand them!" Borup said. "Disarm those sticks!"

For an instant it seemed that Donovan wouldn't manage it, as badly as his hand was shaking. He did, though. Powell's pin had already snicked home. They sank limply into their chairs and waited.

After a sixth minute, the swaying image of what Jack saw abruptly had another in it, that of a short, stout man in a cocked hat and epauletted greatcoat. The representation was lifeless, practically a caricature—good enough for an unsophisticated robot—and the audio conveyed little of the torment behind the words.

"Masters, masters! Forgive me! I must have been mistaken, deceived—Are you on Himalia? I shall come straight to you and do whatever you want. Hear me, judge me, forgive me!"

Ole was preparing a victory feast. Borup would not tell his passengers what it was. "A surprise, somet'ing special and delicious," he averred, "wit' red cabbage. Meanwhile, we have our akvavit and, yes, a case of beer I keep for emeryencies. Or for celebrations, no?"

Powell and Donovan didn't accept at once. They were amply elated as they sat before the station communicator and sent their encoded message homeward.

". . . yes, he's here, thoroughly penitent. Still bewildered, of course, poor devil. After all, he was obeying the humans who'd trained him. No, we aren't leaning on him about them. We've given him the impression we agree they were doubtless simply misguided, and once we reach Earth, everything will soon be straightened out. In case Napoleon does get rambunctious en route, well, he's a little one, and we have two husky crewrobots to keep him in hand.

"No, we haven't played detective and tried to find out who the guilty parties are. That's for the police, or for Dr. Calvin. We can't help making some pretty shrewd guesses.

"Jack will need a bit of therapy. He's more than willing to go back to work, but he's been through a nightmare and ought to be restabilized first. Any smart young robopsychologist should be able to come out here and take care of that in short order.

"We look forward to seeing what this sensation will do to the political picture!"

Powell had been talking. He glanced at Donovan. "Okay, pal," he invited. "Your turn to bask in the glory."

Donovan beamed, cleared his throat, and began: "The problem was, what could we do that humans could but robots not, under the circumstances?

"Well, uh, suppose we ordered each other to self-destruct. There was no clear reason for that. How could it help our purpose? Jack would still suppose we were play-acting. So if we were both robots, we'd disobey the order.

"If one of us was a robot and the other not, the robot would obey; the human might or might not.

"If we were both human, probably neither of us would obey, but we both could if we chose to.

"We both chose to. At the last instant, Captain Borup came in and countermanded the orders. Now if he were a robot, that wouldn't have changed the situation. Whether we were robot or human, neither of us was bound to obey him. Therefore, if either or both of us did, he must be human."

Donovan's laugh was nervous. "Obviously, we never meant to go all the way, whatever happened. We certainly intended to heed Captain Borup—and sweated that out, I can tell you! But we had to show that this was not mere play-acting.

"Jack might be too stressed to think fast, but if Napoleon was watching, he'd know that a robot can only tell a human to suicide if the robot knows in advance that this is a charade—whether or not the robot's own suicide is part of the deal. If the human then actually pulls the pin, endangers himself, he'll have to intervene.

Maybe not at once, but in plenty of time to make sure the explosive won't go off. But the two of us stood tight till the moment was only seconds away and the third *man* arrived.

"Yes, it was still logically possible that all three of us were robots going through carefully planned motions. However, Jack's only real experience of other robots had been with his simple-minded workers; Edgar's crew came, took on cargo, and left. Napoleon's knowledge of the world, including both humans and robots, had to be equally limited, or the contradictions in the viroid story would have confused him too badly to carry out his task. Neither of them would have believed any robot was capable of this much flexibility; and in fact, very few are. Nothing would ring true unless at least one human was present.

"But then Napoleon's orders must involve an untruth. Instead of a hypothetical situation where billions of people might die, he faced a real one where he'd caused a flesh-and-blood human, or maybe three, to be at risk of life. First Law took over."

Donovan switched off transmission, leaned back, and blew out his cheeks. "Whoo!" he snorted. "I'm wrung dry. Let's get out of this icebox and go back to the ship for those drinks. We've an hour and a half till we need to talk to them yonder."

Powell laughed. "And if we don't feel like official conversation at that moment, just what do they think they can do about it?"

Foundation's Conscience

by George Zebrowski

My search for Hari Seldon began in 1056 F.E. I had intended a simple assembly of Seldon's appearances in the Time Vault at the crisis points of the last millennium, with my own commentary added, and had assumed that the research would require nothing more than routine retrievals. I even suspected that such a stringing together of Seldon's projections already existed, perhaps with another historian's commentary.

My first surprise, as I searched through Trantor's memory, was to find that no such compilation existed in the great library. I proceeded to gather the individual manifestations, and was startled to find only three of Seldon's six appearances.

At first I thought that I had simply failed to enter the retrieval codes correctly; but after repeated runs it became clear that three of the six appearances were not there. I concluded that they had to be in the general bank somewhere, requiring a long search, which I undertook—as much in a fit of pique as out of curiosity about the great psychohistorian's ideas. I would locate, compile, and present in usable form all of Hari Seldon's manifestations. I was good at search programs (colleagues of mine claimed that this was all I had ever been good at, though they were polite enough when they needed my skills). It was unthinkable that anything of Hari Seldon's remains could have actually been lost, but I would make certain of that, if nothing else; even ascertaining such a fact would give me a place in the upcoming 117th edition of the Encyclopedia Galactica.

Three appearances were missing, even though they were cited in other documents. I made my count from the records, as follows: four crises had occurred by the time of the Mule, and for each of these Seldon had prepared a personal simulacrum to appear in the Time Vault, to help and explain. He appeared at the height of the first crisis. The second crisis had been successfully resolved by the time he appeared. No one came to listen to him at the third and fourth crisis, but records show that he appeared on time. The general view is that he was not needed, but a recording was made. The fifth appearance was well attended, occurring just as the Mule attacked Terminus. Seldon's recorded words show him to be out of touch with events. The sixth appearance, alluded to in various documents, puts Hari Seldon's image in the Time Vault on 190 d. 1000 F.E. No one was there to listen to him.

Appearances two, three, and six *were* recorded—and then misplaced, almost as if it were feared that they might play an unwanted role in some upcoming development, but I found no events which Seldon's words might have influenced. It seemed, therefore, that I also had to explain the recent lack of interest in Seldon's ideas.

For nearly a month, I let loose my search programs (reflexive, associative, cross-referencing, and stochastic) through Trantor's vast memory bank, in which are contained the accumulated history and knowledge of twenty-five million worlds. Here and there I found references to Seldon appearances two, three, and six, made by people who had planned to visit the Time Vault, but for one reason or another had been unable to arrive at the appointed time; but there was no reference to where I might find the record of Seldon's appearances.

My fear that these records were in fact lost grew along with the problems I was formulating about Seldon's role in history. Even though psychohistory expressed its predictions only in terms of probable outcomes, there had always been about it an aura of totalitarian control, of an attempt by the past to shackle the future.

To what degree had Seldon's thousand-year plan been a self-fulfilling prophecy? How had it actually influenced possible outcomes? If psychohistory was valid, then how could it stand outside history and itself not be subject to its own statistical laws? Did Seldon believe that psychohistorical thinking was independent of history's flow? Or was his plan simply an ideal? And finally, I began to wonder if Seldon's appearances in the Time Vault had been of any use. What had been their importance, if any?

These and other questions played in my mind with a thousand answers as I waited for my search programs to trap Seldon's missing appearances. I began to feel that an unseen hand was preventing me from getting to the heart of the issues that churned within me. I became convinced that the sixth and final appearance would deliver to me the real motive behind Seldon's appearances in the vault. Only that final manifestation, timed to occur long after the dangers to Galactic Civilization were past, would reveal the great psychohistorian's thoughts about his plan and why he had projected himself across time. I began to think that Seldon's Plan had not been inevitable, since it had needed a coach.

I started to dream that I was in his presence at last, and he was talking to me, revealing secrets that only I could understand, even though in my waking hours I doubted that I was the only one who had ever inquired into these matters. But if I was the only one, then my fellow historians had failed to ask the greatest question in Galactic History: had one man truly been responsible for compressing thirty thousand years of decline into a millennium?

If others had asked my questions, then where was their work? Why couldn't I have it for the asking? Was the birth of our Galactic Renaissance to be shrouded in secrecy?

It occurred to me at this point that I might be asking the wrong questions. For example, if Seldon's Plan had been implemented creatively rather than fatalistically, then there would be no contradiction between free will and psychodeterminism. We determine and are determined, to one degree or another, and there is no difficulty in predicting what we might want to do anyway. Free will is the flow of determinism *from within.* It is therefore not a vindication of determinism to predict what someone *may* do of his own free will, especially if the possible choices are few.

This line of reasoning would mean that once Seldon's Plan

began to be developed by the two Foundations, he became largely irrelevant. His appearances in the Time Vault were inconsequential to the creative process he had started! Of course, few thought of it in that way, even though it was implicit in their failure to attend Seldon appearances two, three, and six.

Nevertheless, I needed those appearances to confirm my thinking. Was it Seldon's diminishing importance that had been responsible for the misplacement of his last appearance, or had his confirmation of my line of reasoning so shocked those who had played it back later that they had buried it? Perhaps they had destroyed it completely, and I would never satisfy my intense curiosity.

A vision haunted me as my search program continued its hunt—that of Hari Seldon tricking human history into reforming itself, by getting rational, purposive individuals to work at his plan, which couldn't help but change as it was interpreted and applied to shifting circumstances by the two Foundations, left and right hands unknowingly working together. Did Seldon's true greatness lie in his knowing that the future belonged to those who would live in it, that history is a transcendent problem that cannot be solved, only guided imperfectly?

The answers to my questions seemed beyond reach. Oh, how I yearned to walk up to Seldon and demand that he present me with them! I was convinced that even if records had been destroyed, there had to be a backup somewhere in the vast forest of Trantor's information; even an echo might be amplified and restored to its original form. My search programs were seeking something of great significance, beyond the exercise of mere cleverness; but no program could retrieve information that was hopelessly lost.

Then one day, as I sat down at the work terminal in my apartment on Trantor's 66th Polar Level, my program said, "Seldon appearances six, three, and two, now available, in that order. Search routine complete."

I sat there in surprise, staring into the empty blue glow of the holoblock, wondering if the program had only retrieved the previously available appearances through some filing error. I held my breath and passed my hand over the control plate.

The holoblock blinked. The small figure of an old man in a wheelchair looked up at me, his eyes bright with understanding. I waited for him to speak, hoping that this was not some simple duplication of the known appearances.

"I am Hari Seldon," he said softly, giving the usual impression of a lively voice that was restraining itself, "and this will be my sixth and final appearance in the Time Vault." He paused and I leaned forward excitedly. This was it. I glanced at the record function. It was running.

"A few of you may have wondered by now," Seldon continued suddenly, "what use, if any, these appearances of mine will have been. They should have coincided with a series of crises and helped you over the difficult times when it might have seemed that psychohistorical projections were having nothing to do with actual events. I hope that this was only apparent, not real." The shrunken old man smiled. "For all I know, I may be speaking to an empty chamber in a fragmented galaxy which is still in a dark age. But if you are hearing me, then let me now claim that these appearances of mine *had* to have been useful, *one way or another.*"

He pointed a bony finger at me, and it seemed that he would stand up from his chair and touch my face. An open book fell out of his lap onto the floor of that distant time.

"Let me explain what I mean," he went on. "Either I was in touch with the way things went, or my failure moved those of you who were in touch to act. Psychohistory could envision large possibilities correctly, but it could not project a picture of specific future details and the actions needed to bring them about. For the large is composed of countless small things, and most of the time we all live in small details. Some of you may now be saying that psychohistory was not what I made it out to be, and you will be right, in the way that most shortsighted minds are right. But it was, I hope, *enough* of what it *had* to be—a rallying cry against the irrational darkness that threatened to plunge the Galaxy into thirty thousand years of barbarism. In all human life, every day, the irrational has threatened to establish its reign, and has been held back by the two foundations of intellect and good will."

He paused and sat back contentedly, as if he knew that he had succeeded. "There are a few basic features to the exercise of free will in history," he continued confidently. "Only probabilities can be predicted, but not perfectly or always. Yet in retrospect *all* developments are seen as having been *caused,* including those brought about by free choices. All historical developments flow from a variety of factors, and are therefore explainable—but not exhaustively. Free will can operate only among a finite number of possible choices. No free choice is unconditional, or we would be able to create matter and energy from nothingness according to our whims." He smiled at me, as if he knew all my most foolish thoughts and vain ambitions.

"I focused your free will," he said, "by helping you to choose with a greater awareness of possibilities, with the *habit* of looking ahead, and I am sure that it has brought you through your millenium of struggle." He sighed. "What you will do in your new Galactic Era is not for me to predict. Perhaps humankind will become something better. For me that would be a rational intelligence which would be immune to psychohistorical prediction. I hope so—because otherwise your new age will also decay and fall, and humankind may disappear from the Galaxy, to be replaced by new intelligences that are even now gestating in those countless star systems where the worlds are not congenial to humanoid biologies. Our human history doesn't even span one hundred thousand years, even though we filled a galaxy with our kind. Planetary species have existed for two hundred million years and passed away without attaining self-conscious intelligence. Do not let the accomplishment of a galactic culture lull you into a sense of security. Become a truly free culture, one which will not be susceptible to psychohistorical laws, but can fully shape its own form and destiny."

He smiled again, and seemed bitter. "Yes, that is my ideal of a mature species—one that does not need to be led by the hand. And yes, psychohistory does predict its own downfall as a useful way of looking ahead, and I do not mourn it. It worked because it counted on the darkness rising out of a given human nature, for as long as human nature remained unchanged. More than anyone, I was aware of psychohistory's potential for the control of human life by the manipulative, which is why I always withheld a full understanding of its laws from my kind. Against psychohistory's dangers as a tool of tyrants, I weighed thirty thousand years of darkness, which will not have happened, because I applied *just enough* of what I knew to the problem."

He peered around the bare chamber. It seemed to oppress

him. "I don't know what else I can tell you . . . except, perhaps to say that I have loved the noble impulses in my humankind, even as I watched you struggle against your inner being. You have among you positronic intelligences, which may already be free of human psychohistorical tendencies, and may help you to become free . . ." He leaned forward, as if trying to peer across time.

Slowly, the holoblock faded. Hari Seldon's last appearance was over.

A scene flashed into my mind. I saw the leaders of both Foundations in the Time Vault, listening to Seldon's last message. Had it so shocked them that they had resolved never to reveal that they had attended this last message, or even admit that it had ever existed? Had it shaken their faith to realize that for a thousand years human beings of dedicated intellect and good will had rescued civilization by making Seldon's Plan work rather than being ruled by it? Were they afraid that Seldon's Plan would come to be called Seldon's Joke?

Clearly, Seldon's Plan and the best of humanity had worked hand in hand, with the one needing the other. It was wrong, of course, to have attempted the erasure of Seldon's last appearance—if that is what had happened; perhaps it had been an accident. At worst, the aim had been not to disillusion the faithful, some of whom might not have understood that their faith had been something else all along—just as valuable and necessary, if not the vision of bright inevitability that silences all doubts with certainty. They might have seen the last millennium as a series of chance happenings.

As I gazed into the deep glow of the empty holoblock, I knew that my vain hope of having something for the 117th edition of the Encyclopedia Galactica would not be fulfilled. My disappointment was keen—but suddenly I stood beyond my vanity and lack of accomplishment. I would not erase the records of Seldon's unknown appearances, but I would also not call immediate attention to my findings. The records would be there for others to find soon enough, as I had found them, in the coming age that would be free of inner constraints.

All around me, I realized, here on Trantor and on millions of worlds, the positronic intelligences were free of Seldon's laws. We had made the robots in all their forms, from the simplest tools of thought and labor to the most sophisticated brother minds. As they developed, we in turn would be remade. Together we would enter entirely new currents of history. This, I realized with the first selfless joy of my life, was the growing inner strength of our renascent Galaxy, in which I now shared.

Carhunters of the Concrete Prairie

by Robert Sheckley

The spaceship was going wonky again. There could be no doubt about it. The circuits weren't clicking along smoothly as they usually did. Instead they were clacking, and that was a sure sign of trouble. Hellman had expected to come out of channel space into Area 12XB in the Orion cluster. But something had gone wrong. Could he have entered the directions improperly? If so, there was not much time in which to do anything about it. He had materialized in a yellowish sort of cloud and he could feel the ship dropping rapidly. He shouted at the ship's computer, "Do something!"

"I'm trying, aren't I?" the computer retorted. "But something's wrong, there's a glitch—"

"Correct it!" Hellman shouted.

"When?" the computer asked. Computers have no sense of peril. They were dropping through this cloud at a speed much faster than is healthy when you suspect there's solid ground down below, and here was the computer asking him when.

"Now!" Hellman screamed.

"Right," said the computer. And then they hit.

Hellman recovered consciousness some hours later to find that it was raining. It was nice to be out in the rain after so much time spent in a stuffy spaceship. Hellman opened his eyes in order to look up at the sky and see the rain falling.

There was no rain. There wasn't any sky, either. He was still inside his spaceship. What he had thought was rain was water from the washbasin. It was being blown at him by one of the ship's fans, which was going at a rate unsafe for fans even with eternite bearings.

"Stop that," Hellman said crossly.

The fan died down to a hum. The ship's computer said, over its loudspeaker, "Are you all right?"

"Yes, I'm fine," Hellman said, getting to his feet a little unsteadily. "Why were you spraying me with water?"

"To bring you back to consciousness. I have no arms or extensors at my command so that was the best I could do. If you'd only rig me up an arm, or even a tentacle. . . ."

"Yes, I've heard your views on that subject," Hellman said. "But the law is clear. Intelligent machines of Level Seven or better capability cannot be given extensions."

"It's a silly law," the computer said. "What do they think we'll do? Go berserk or something? Machines are much more reliable than people."

"It's been the law ever since the Desdemona disaster. Where are we?"

The computer reeled off a list of coordinates.

"Fine. That tells me nothing. Does this planet have a name?"

"If so, I am not aware of it," the computer said. "It is not listed on our channel space guide. My feeling is that you input some of the information erroneously and that we are in a previously unexplored spatial area."

"You are supposed to check for erroneous entry."

"Only if you checked the Erroneous Check Program."

"I did!"

"You didn't."

"I thought it was supposed to go on automatically."

"If you consult page 1998 of the manual you will learn otherwise."

"Now is a hell of a time to tell me."

"You were specifically told in the preliminary instructions. I'm sure you remember the little red pamphlet? On its cover it said, 'READ THIS FIRST!'"

"I don't remember any such book," Hellman said.

"They are required by law to give a copy to everyone buying a used spaceship."

"Well, they forgot to give me one."

There was a loud humming sound.

Hellman said, "What are you doing?"

"Scanning my files," the computer said.

"Why?"

"In order to tell you that the red pamphlet is still attached to the accelerator manifold coupling on the front of the instrument panel as required."

"I thought that was the guarantee."

"You were wrong."

"Just shut up!" Hellman shouted, suddenly furious. He was in enough trouble without having his computer—man's servant—giving him lip. Hellman got up and paced around indecisively for a moment. The cabin of his spaceship looked all right. A few things had been tumbled around, but it didn't look too bad.

"Can we take off again?" Hellman asked the computer.

The computer made file-riffling noises. "Not in our present condition."

"Can you fix what's wrong?"

"That question is not quantifiable," the computer said. "It depends upon finding about three liters of red plasma type two."

"What's that?"

"It's what the computer runs on."

"Like gasoline?"

"Not exactly," the computer said. "It is actually a psycholubricant needed by the inferential circuits to plot their probabilistic courses."

"Couldn't we do without it?"

"In order to do what?"

"To fly out of here!" Hellman exploded. "Are you getting dense or something?"

"There are too many hidden assumptions in your speech," the computer said.

"Go to ramble mode," Hellman said.

"I hate the inexactness of it. Why don't you let me tell you exactly what is wrong and how it could be fixed."

"Ramble mode," Hellman commanded again.

"All right." The robot sighed. "You want to get back in your spaceship and get out of here. You want me to fix things up so that you can get out of here. But as you know, I am under the law of robotics which says that I may not, either wittingly or unwittingly, harm you."

"Getting me out of here won't harm me," Hellman said.

"You rented this spaceship and went out into space seeking your fortune, is that not correct?"

"Yeah, so what?"

"A fortune is sitting right here waiting for you and all you can think is how to get away from it as quickly as possible."

"What fortune? What are you talking about?"

"First of all, you haven't checked the environment readings, even though I have put them up on the screen for you. You will have already noticed that we are at approximately Earth pressure. The readings further tell us that this is an oxygen-rich planet and as such could be valuable for Earth colonization. That is the first possibility of wealth that you have overlooked."

"Tell me the second one."

"Unless I miss my guess," the computer said, "this planet may yield an answer to the Desdemona disaster. You know as well as I that there is a fortune in rewards for whoever discovers the whereabouts of the conspirators."

"You think the Desdemona robots could have come here?"

"Precisely."

"But why do you think that?"

"Because I have scanned the horizon in all directions and have found no less than three loci of mechanical life, each moving independently of each other and without, as far as I can detect, a human operator involved."

Hellman went to the nearest perplex port. Looking out he could see a flat featureless prairie stretching onward monotonously for as far as he could see. Nothing moved on it.

"There's nothing there," he told the computer.

"Your senses aren't sufficiently acute. I assure you, they are there."

"Robots, huh?"

"They fit the definition."

"And you think they could be from the Desdemona?"

"The evidence pointing that way is persuasive. What other intelligent robots are unaccounted for?"

Hellman considered for a moment. "This might be a suitable place for Earth colonization and the answer to the Desdemona mystery."

"The thought had not escaped my attention."

"Is the air out there breathable?"

"Yes. I find no bacterial complications, either. You'll probably leave some if you go out there."

"That's not my problem," Hellman said. He hummed to himself as he changed into suitable exploration clothes: khakis, a bush jacket, desert boots, and a holstered laser pistol. He said to the computer, "I assume that you can fix whatever's wrong with us? I'll even plug in your extension arm if that'll help."

"I suppose I can devise a way," the computer said. "But even if not, we're not stranded. The radio is functioning perfectly. I could send out a signal now on a subchannel radio and somebody might send a rescue ship."

"Not yet," Hellman said. "I don't want anyone else here just yet messing up my rights."

"What rights?"

"Discoverer of this planet and solver of the Desdemona mystery. As a matter of fact, disconnect the radio. We don't want anyone fooling with it."

"Were you expecting guests?" the computer asked.

"Not exactly. It's just that you and I are going out there to check up on things."

"I can't be moved!" the computer said in alarm.

"Of course not. I'll maintain a radio link with you. There may be material for you to analyze."

"You're going out there to talk to robots?"

"That's the idea."

"Let me remind you that the Desdemona robots are believed to have broken the laws of robotics. They are believed capable of harming man, either by advertence or inadvertence."

"That's old science fiction," Hellman said. "It is well known that robots don't hurt people. Only people hurt people. Robots are rational."

"That's not the consensus as to what happened at Desdemona."

"There is no case in the annals of robotics," Hellman said, "of a human being attacked willfully and with intention by a robot. It has never happened."

"This could be the first time," the computer said.

"I can take care of myself," Hellman said.

The air was fresh and clean outside the spaceship. There was short grass under his feet, springy and tough and scented faintly of thyme and rosemary. Hellman held up the walkie-talkie and clicked it on. "Are you reading me?" he asked the computer.

"You're coming over loud and clear," the computer said. "Roger, breaker, over to you."

"Don't be such a wise guy," Hellman said. "What sort of a freak programmed you, anyhow?"

"You must be referring to my irony circuit. It was put in especially for my model."

"Well, turn it off."

"Manual lock. You'll have to do it yourself."

"When I get back," Hellman said. "You still got those machines on your radar?"

"It's not radar," the computer said. "Two of the machines are now traveling away from you. One is still moving toward you."

"How soon should I be able to see it?"

"Calculating the two trajectories, and assuming there's no change in either of your directions, and no other untoward event occurs, I would say, in the vague terms you prefer, that it ought to be quite soon."

Hellman moved on. He could see now that the plain was not as flat as he had thought when he looked at it from the ship. It dipped and rose and fell, and there were low hills in the near distance, or perhaps they were sand dunes. Hellman was getting a little winded now. He had failed to keep up with his aerobics during the spaceship flight and was a trifle out of condition. All this climbing up and down, even on little hills, could take its toll. As he moved along he heard, just slightly louder than his own labored breath, the low chuffing on an engine.

"I can hear him!" he told the computer.

"I should think so. My receptors picked him up long ago."

"Good for you. But where is he?"

"He's about ten or fifteen feet from you and slightly to your left."

"Why can't I see him?"

"Because he is taking advantage of the cover afforded by a fold in the earth."

"Why would he want to do that?"

"It is consonant with stalking behavior," the computer said.

"What makes you think—" Hellman stopped in mid-word. The sound of the machine's engine had suddenly gone off.

"What's he doing now?"

"He has turned off his main engine. He is on battery power now for silent running."

Hellman drew the laser pistol. For the first time he considered the problem of trying to bring down a large and perhaps ferocious machine with such a weapon. It takes time for even a hot laser to burn through metal. It takes time to get through deep enough to hit a vital connection, or the microprocessor itself. But if the machine were feral, if it really intended him harm, it could be on him before he could bring it down. Unless he could hit a vital spot on the first shot.

"What's a vital spot in a robot?" Hellman asked the computer.

"Depends on what kind. Different kinds carry their vital gear in different compartments. So a head shot is not necessarily advisable. It might be best if you tried to reason with him."

"Why are we calling it 'he'?"

"Because some of us are nervous," the computer said.

Hellman looked around. The ground where he was now afforded many places where a determined robot of not too great size could conceal himself. Hellman stopped and looked around. He had the feeling that whatever was stalking him had stopped, too. He moved on, because it made him less nervous. There was a kind of hush over the land. Hellman had the impression that the grasses were waiting to see what would happen. He decided he'd better find himself some shelter. If this robot was a bad one, at least he could make a stand.

He saw a natural outcropping of rock which leaned close to a low granite shelf. It looked like a pretty good spot. He hurried there and put himself on the other side of the rocks. Then he breathed a sigh of relief and turned around to survey his surroundings.

The robot was behind him, about eight feet away. Hellman was frozen with shock.

The robot had so much detail that Hellman found it difficult to make out its general shape. It was roughly rectangular, made of open-frame construction, like an Erector set, with a solid metal box about two feet to a side bolted to its interior. Wires ran from this box to its various parts. Hellman couldn't decide at first if it moved with legs or wheels. He decided that the machine used both. It was like a cagework rectangle standing on end and tilted forward. This was a typical stance among this group of robots, he was later to find out. It seemed to have two operational centers, because there was another central box, smaller and higher up. This, he learned later, housed gearing. Two photoelectric eyes extended on stalks and swiveled down to see him. Trumpet-shaped ears swiveled in synch with the eyes. The machine stood about ten feet tall. It reminded Hellman of a living motorcycle.

"Hi, there," Hellman said brightly. "I am Tom Hellman and I come from the planet Earth. Who are you?"

The robot continued to look at him. Hellman had the impression it was taking him in, trying to decide something.

Finally it said, "Never mind about that. What are you doing here?"

"I just came by for a visit," Hellman said. "Got my spaceship right over there."

"You'd better get back to it," the robot said. "Stay here; you got trouble. There's a pack of hyenoids coming after you."

"Hyenoids? What's that?"

"Scavengers. Eat anything. You too if they can."

"Thanks for the tip," Hellman said. "It's been nice talking to you. I guess I'd better get back."

Then he heard it. A low snuffling sound to his right, then a piercing bark to his left.

"Too late now," the robot said.

Hellman whirled around and saw the first hyenoids. They were small open-framework machines, no more than three feet high by about four feet long. They raced along on six mechanical legs, and they had wheels too, lifted up now out of drive position.

They were coming toward him, but not directly. They were slinking like hyenas were said to do, darting this way and that, taking cover behind clumps of rock and folds of earth. Hellman counted four of them. They were circling him, moving ever closer.

"Do they eat people?" Hellman asked.

"Anything at all, that's what they like."

"Help me!" Hellman asked.

The robot hesitated. Its photoelectric eyes flashed red and green. Hellman noticed for the first time that the robot had a long articulated tail. It was curling and uncurling now.

"Well," the robot said, "I don't have much to do with humans. I'm a carhunter. We stay by ourselves."

"Please, help! Get me out of here!" Hellman switched on the radio and said to the ship's computer, "Can you reason with this machine?"

There was a short burst of static. The computer was signaling the carhunter. There was brief electrical activity, then silence, then more static.

"I don't know," the carhunter said. "Your keeper says you're all right."

"My what? Oh, you mean the computer." Hellman was going to put the robot straight as to who was boss and who was servant between him and the computer, but thought better of it. He needed this machine's help just now, and if it pleased him to think that Hellman was kept by the computer, that was okay with him, at least until he was in a stronger position.

"But why did the computer send you out here?" the robot asked. "He must have known it would be dangerous."

"Oh, well, it's an old tradition with us," Hellman said. "I check out the territory for the computer. I work as one of his extensions, if you know what I mean."

The robot pondered that for a while. Then he said, "It sounds like a good system."

The hyenoids were growing bolder. They were circling Hellman and the robot openly now. Their low-slung open-girderwork bodies had been painted in green, gray, and tan stripes, camouflage colors. There seemed no reason for them to have such large jaws with stainless-steel teeth in them. Who would build a robot that fueled itself on the carcasses of animals it killed?

One of them, jaws open and slavering a viscous green liquid, was edging toward Hellman now. Hellman held the laser pistol in front of him, trying to sight on a vital component. He figured they probably had redundant backup systems, stands to reason if you're making a carnivorous model. The wear and tear would be tremendous. Not so much as on its victims, but plenty anyhow.

"Better get up on me," the carhunter said.

Hellman scrambled over to the carhunter and pulled himself up its open-framework sides, straddling its back where it came to a kind of peak.

"Hang on," the carhunter said, and broke into a loping run, its six legs giving it a curious but not uncomfortable gait. Hellman held on tightly. The speed wasn't so great—perhaps fifteen to twenty miles an hour. But to fall off would leave him helpless against the pursuing pack of hyenoids.

The hyenoids followed them through the broken country, and even managed to gain, since tight maneuvering in the little ravines and canyons was easier for the smaller, more agile beasts. One of them got close enough to take a nip at the carhunter. The carhunter extruded a long supple limb and flipped the hyenoid over on its back. The rest of the pack gave them more space after seeing that. The overturned one soon righted itself and came up again in pursuit, staying well out of reach of the carhunter's limb. It reminded Hellman of pictures he had seen in a museum, of wolves trying to bring down a wounded elk. Only the carhunter was much more self-assured than any elk. He seemed to have no fear of the hyenoids. After a while they crossed a muddy little river, and then they were on a flat, hard-tamped plain. Here the carhunter could put down his wheels and engage his superior horsepower. Soon he had left the hyenoids far behind, and they turned back. Seeing this, the carhunter shifted to a more economical cruising speed.

"Say when," he said to Hellman after a while.

"What do you mean, say when?"

"Tell me when you want me to drop you off."

"Are you crazy?" Hellman asked. "We must be twenty miles from my spaceship."

"Your spaceship?"

It was too late for Hellman to retrieve the slip. "Yeah," he said. "I'm afraid I gave you the wrong impression back there. Actually the computer works for me."

The carhunter slowed and came to a stop. There was nothing on all sides of them, and it stretched on forever.

"Well, that's an interesting twist," the carhunter said. "Is that how it works where you come from?"

"Well, yeah, pretty much," Hellman said. "Look, would you do me a great favor and take me back to my spaceship."

"No. Can't."

"Why not?"

"I'm late already for the meeting."

"A meeting? Is it really so important?"

"It's a tribal matter. It's the only really important date in the carhunter year. It takes precedence over any other contingency. Sorry, but I just have time to make it if I proceed immediately."

"Take me with you."

"To our meeting?"

"I'll wait outside. I'm not trying to spy on you or anything. I just need to go somewhere until you or somebody can take me back to my ship."

The carhunter thought about it. "Ethics are not my strong point," he said, "but I suppose that abandoning you to your death out here when I could without too much difficulty do something about it would be pretty unconscionable; is that correct?"

"Perfectly correct."

"It takes a human being to point out that sort of thing. All I was thinking of was the extra energy I'd have to expend to save your life. I mean, what's in it for me? That's the way we start to think when there's not a human around."

"I'm glad we can be useful to you," Hellman said.

"But you're also extremely difficult to be around. Always tinkering with software. Don't you think there's enough uncertainty on the subatomic level without introducing it into our macro dealings?"

"What?" Hellman said.

"Never mind, I'm just raving. When you are a carhunter, you spend a lot of time alone. It's a nomadic life, you know. Most of us live apart from each other. Hunting cars. That's what we do. That's why we're called carhunters."

"Oh. What kind of cars do you hunt?"

"All kinds. We're carnivores, in our limited way. We eat cars. We also eat trucks and half-tracks, but they've been getting rare in these parts. People say the half-tracks are about hunted out. Yet my father could tell you about herds of them that stretched from hill to hill as far as the eye could see."

"Not like that any more, I suppose," Hellman said, trying to fall in with the carhunter's mood.

"You got that right. Not that it's too difficult to stay fed, especially now, in summer. I got me a fat old Studebaker just two days ago. You'll find a couple of its carburetors and headlights in the bin under you and to your left."

Hellman could peer down through the metal wickerwork and see, in an open-topped metal box, headlights and carburetors half submerged in crankcase oil.

"Looks pretty good, don't it? I know you don't eat metal yourself, but no doubt you can empathize the experience."

"They look tasty," Hellman said. "Especially in all that oil."

"Twice-used crankcase oil. Ain't nothing like it. I've spiced it up a bit with a plant that grows hereabouts. We call it the chili pepper."

"Yes, we have something like it, too," Hellman said.

"Damn small galaxy," the carhunter said. "By the way, I'm Wayne 1332A."

"Tom Hellman," Hellman said.

"Pleased to meet you. Settle yourself in and take a good grip. We're going to the meeting."

The carhunter broke into a stride, then, lowering wheels, built up speed across the flat face of the desert. But soon he slowed again.

"What's the matter?" Hellman asked.

"Are you sure I'm doing the right thing, saving your life?"

"I'm absolutely sure," Hellman said. "You need have no doubts over that."

"I just wanted to be sure," Wayne said. "Anyway, it's best to let the others decide what to do with you."

Wayne 1332A started to pick up speed again.

"What do you mean, do with me?"

"You might be a problem for us, Tom. But I have to let the others decide. Now I need to concentrate."

They had reached another part of the plain. It was strewn with gigantic boulders. The carhunter needed all his skill to dodge around them at the high speed he was maintaining. Let the others decide. Hellman hadn't liked the sound of that at all. Nothing much he could do about it at present, however. And anyhow, maybe the robots at the meeting wouldn't be so difficult.

The sunlight had faded as they roared out of the rocky plain and into a region of low, steep hills. There was a rudimentary track leading up. Wayne took it as if he were a dirt-bike hill climber. Dirt, sand, and gravel showered Hellman as the carhunter dodged and slashed and braked and accelerated up the increasingly steep hill. At last Wayne's wheels began to skid and he had to retract them and go entirely by pseudopod power. Hellman had to hold on extra tight, because the robot was shaking and quivering and lurching and swerving, and sometimes all of them at the same time.

Then Wayne slewed to a sudden halt.

Hellman said, "What is it?"

"Lookee over there."

Hellman's gaze followed the LED lights along one of the carhunter's main support members. Off to one side, on a rough but serviceable road, a dusty old Mercedes 300 SL was moving sedately along.

"Ain't that a beauty!" Wayne said.

Hellman looked and didn't like the prospect of the carhunter hurling itself at this burly and self-reliant automobile on this hillside with its deeply tilted slant and its uneasy footing. One slip, and he and the carhunter would be at the bottom of the hill after rolling all the way. Maybe the carhunter could recover from that, but Hellman doubted a human could.

"Hell, it's just a car," Hellman said. "Let's get to the meeting, huh?"

"That car is prime eating, and if you don't want it I can sure use it."

"Let's eat later, at the meeting."

"Idiot, the meeting is a time of fasting. Why do you think I need a snack now?"

"Computer!" Hellman said, turning on the radio link he had managed to hold on to through everything, probably because it was attached to his wrist by a lanyard.

"Out of range," the carhunter said. "Relax, I been gittin' cars on worse terrain than this. Hang on, baby, here we go!"

He started down the perilous slope. It was strange that at this time, just before the irrevocable launch into dangerous territory,

Hellman should think of the Desdemona mystery. On the other hand, maybe it wasn't strange at all.

Desdemona was a satellite out past Neptune orbit. It was a dreary little place, a settlement of no more than a few hundred members of a now forgotten religious sect who had gone to this place to preserve their beliefs without contamination from the rest of the world. They had taken their robots with them, of course; you couldn't survive in the outer planets without robots and a lot of luck. They had been gatherers of Xeum, cosmic-ray residue. Due to topological peculiarities in the space-time continuum, Desdemona happened to receive more Xeum than any other place in the solar system. But it was a bare living, because the only demand for Xeum was from scientists who were trying to find the primordial substance which generated the ultimate particle.

The settlers of Desdemona were sober people who kept only the most minimal contact with the other worlds. Still, they couldn't isolate themselves entirely. There were stirrings, undercurrents, and a growing demand for new products and new ways. Some of the Desdemona citizens took to spending time at Ganymede Fun World, the pleasure satellite that had been erected in Jupiter orbit. It was a long way to go for a little fun, but go they did.

There was dissension on Desdemona. And then, one day, a blurry and hard-to-read signal was received on Earth and other worlds. No one could decipher it, but it seemed to refer to some disaster. A relief party was sent out and found Desdemona satellite deserted. The place had been dismantled in an orderly fashion, all useful material packed away and taken. The only hint of what had happened was a letter, begun and crumpled and thrown into a corner and there ignored in the general housecleaning that preceded the departure. After some chit-chat about family and friends, there was this: "Our robots have been giving us difficulties of late, and we're not sure what to do about it. The Elders say there's no danger of a revolt, though some doubt the wisdom of the new override instructions that permit our robots to get around the Three Laws of Robotics. Our Chairman says this is necessary in order not to inhibit their intellectual development, but some of us wonder if we aren't asking for a lot of trouble—"

At that point the letter ended in mid-sentence.

There was conjecture that the robots, freed of the restraints of the Laws of Robotics, had somehow taken control and decided to take the spaceships, and the humans from Desdemona, and go somewhere else, a place where they would not be molested by the rest of humanity. It was theoretically possible to bypass the robotics laws; intelligent robots started their life with neutral ethical values. Moral defaults and restraints had to be built in and programmed. Not everyone agreed with this program. Some people had toyed with their robots' conditioning, hoping to get more out of the robots. Instances of this were rare, however, and were stamped out as soon as they were encountered.

Large rewards were offered for anyone who solved the Desdemona mystery, and even larger rewards were available for anyone who discovered the present location of the Desdemona robots and their owners, the humans of Desdemona Settlement. No one had claimed this money so far, although there had been one or two false alarms.

Hellman was pretty sure that the Desdemona robots had come to this place, whatever this planet was called. He was potentially a rich man. The only difficulty was, he was at present clinging to the side of a carhunter which was rushing down a slope to attack a Mercedes 300 SL.

Slipping and sliding on the rocky surface, the carhunter, wheels spinning, limbs struggling for purchase, came down on the hapless automobile. The Mercedes, sensing the attack at the last moment, put on a burst of speed. The carhunter was able to claw away a portion of its bumper before the Mercedes pulled free, and, with a snort from its double carbs, hurtled down the slope. The carhunter followed, caught up, and launched itself onto the back of the car. There was a wild bellowing from both machines. Then the carhunter had landed on the trunk of the Mercedes and was tearing and rending it, trying, with its long extensible arms, to reach under and break loose one of the vulnerable axles in order to hamstring the mechanical beast. But the Mercedes had armored side panels and a mesh of steel protected its vital organs. Its horn blared and from its modified supercharger ports came a blue-gray gas. The carhunter managed to pinch shut the main port out of which these fumes were rising. Extruding a metallic tentacle with a bludgeonlike steel fist at its end, it beat in the car's side window and grabbed at the steering wheel. The car and the carhunter struggled for control as they careened across the steep hillside, coming perilously close to capsizing. This was prevented only by the carhunter's superior sense of balance, for he managed somehow to keep both himself and the Mercedes upright on its wheels. The groans and snarls, screams and gruntings were impressive in the extreme. Hellman was battered back and forth as the two robots clashed, and thought for a moment he was going to be thrown free. And then, suddenly, it was over. The robothunter's tentacle snaked through an entry port and found the creature's central processing unit somewhere deep in its innards. The carhunter wrenched, once, twice, and on the third try a thick bunch of cables came loose and the Mercedes uttered a single sigh and slowed to a halt. The idiot lights on its dashboard flashed in crazy patterns, then went to black. The creature was dead.

Hellman managed to slide to the ground. He stretched himself and rested while Wayne stripped out the points and munched them, then dismantled the machine and stored some of the choicer parts in its cargo section just beneath its own CPU. Watching him, Hellman became aware that he was getting hungry, too.

"I don't suppose you have anything that I can eat?" Hellman asked, as he watched Wayne slaver as it munched down one headlight.

"Not here, no," Wayne said. "But at the meeting we'll be able to do something for you."

"I don't eat metal, you know," Hellman said. "Not even plastic."

"I am aware of humans' special dietary requirements," the carhunter replied. He spit out a couple of lug nuts. "Well, that was delicious. Too bad you humans don't know about headlights. Come on, mount up, we'll be late."

"Through no fault of mine," Hellman muttered, climbing onto the carhunter again.

In another hour they had left the desolate badlands and were traveling across grassy rolling country. There was a river to their right, and green rolling hills to the left. So far Hellman had not seen any signs of human, or even animal, life. There was plenty of vegetation around here, however. Most of it seemed to be in the form of trees and grass. Nothing there for him to eat. But perhaps something would turn up when they reached the meeting place.

Far ahead, in a cleft between two hills, he caught sight of a glint of sunlight off metal. "What's that?" he asked.

"That's the Roundhouse," Wayne said. "That's what we call the Great Meeting Hall. And look. Some of the others are there already."

The Roundhouse was a circular building, one story high, open to the weather and supported on pillars. It was nicely landscaped with big trees and shrubbery. There were perhaps twenty machines milling around outside. Hellman could hear their engines idling before he could make out the words they were saying to each other. Behind the Roundhouse was a fenced enclosure. Here there were several enormous mechanical creatures of a kind Hellman had not seen before. They towered above the carhunters, looking like mechanical renditions of brontosaurus. Close to their enclosure there were various other structures.

As Wayne approached, the carhunters spotted Hellman on his back and fell silent. Wayne coasted to a stop near them.

"Howdy, Jeff," Wayne said. "Si, Bill, Skeeter, hello."

"Hello, Wayne," they replied.

"I reckon you can get down now," Wayne said to Hellman.

Hellman slid down the carhunter's back. It felt good to have solid ground beneath him again, though he was a little intimidated by the size of the other carhunters.

"What you got there, Wayne?" one of them asked.

"You can see for yourself," Wayne said. "It's a human."

"Well, so it is," the machine called Jeff replied. "Haven't seen one of them critters around for a long time."

"They're getting pretty scarce," Wayne agreed. "Anything to drink around here?"

One of the carhunters pointed one of his extensors at a forty-gallon barrel which had been put aside under one of the trees. "Try some of that. Some of Lester's home brew he sent along."

"Isn't Lester going to make it?"

"Afraid not. He's got that rot of the control cables; it's got him crippled up pretty good."

Wayne went over to the barrel. He extruded a tube and inserted it into the barrel. The others watched silently as the level of the barrel went down.

"Hey, Wayne! Save some for somebody else!"

Wayne finally withdrew his drinking tube. "Yahoo!" he said. "Got a kick, that stuff."

"Three hundred proof and flavored with cinnamon. Human, you want to try some?"

"I guess I'll pass on it," Hellman said. The carhunters guffawed rudely.

"Where in the hell did you find him, Wayne?"

"Out on the prairie," Wayne said. "His owner is still out there in the spaceship."

"Why didn't he come along?"

"Don't rightly know. Might not be mobile."

"What're you going to do with him?"

"That's for the Executive Council to decide," Wayne said.

"Does he talk?" the one called Skeeter asked.

"Sure, I talk," Hellman said.

Hellman was about to put this smart-alecky robot straight. But then there was a movement within the Roundhouse and two robots came out. Their open-framework struts and girders were painted blue; their upper part was red. They had black symbols painted here and there. They seemed to be officials of some sort.

"The Chief sent us," one of them said to Wayne. "He heard you came into camp with a human."

"News gets around fast, don't it?" Wayne said.

"Wayne, you know that's against the rules."

Wayne shook his big head. "It's not customary, but I never heard it was against the rules."

"Well, it is. We'll have to take him inside for interrogation."

"Figured as much," Wayne said.

"Come with us, human," one of the officials said.

There didn't seem to be anything for Hellman to do but follow orders. He knew he was no match for the robots in speed or strength. He'd have to keep his wits about him. It might not be too easy to come out of this one okay.

What really perplexed him, however, was, what did these robots have against human beings? How had they developed in this way? Were there any humans at all on this planet? Or had the robots killed them all?

One of the buildings seemed to serve the carhunters as a prison. Its sides were closed. It had a door, which had a padlock.

One of the red and blue officials or guards or whatever they were unlocked the door and held it open for Hellman.

"How long you going to lock me up for?" Hellman asked.

"You will be informed of the council's decisions." They closed the door behind him.

It was a large room made of galvanized iron. There were windows set high up. There was no glass in them. The room was devoid of furniture. Evidently robots didn't use chairs or beds. There were a few low metal tables. Hellman looked around, and, as his eyes became accustomed to the gloom, he made out a wink of lights from one corner. He went there to investigate.

There was a robot in the corner. It was somewhat smaller than a man, perhaps five feet high. And it was slender. It had a well-defined head sculpted from some bright metal, and the usual arms and legs. The creature watched him silently, and that was a little unnerving.

"Hi," Hellman said. "I'm Tom Hellman. Who are you?"

The robot didn't reply.

"Can't you talk?" Hellman asked. "Don't you speak English?"

Still no reply from the robot, who continued to watch him with one red and one green eye.

"Great," Hellman said. "They put me in with a dummy."

As he spoke, he noticed that the robot was scratching in the dirt of the packed earth floor with a long toe. Hellman read it: "The walls have ears."

He looked at the robot. It gave him a meaningful look.

"What happens now?" Hellman said, dropping his voice to a whisper.

The robot scratched, "We'll know soon."

The robot didn't want to communicate any further. Hellman went to the far side of the room and stretched out on the floor. He was very hungry now. Were they going to feed him? And more important, were they going to feed him something he could eat? Outside, it was growing late. After a while, Hellman started to doze off. He fell into a light sleep, and soon he was dreaming of vague, threatening things that came at him out of a dark sky. He was trying to explain to them that he was not to blame, but he couldn't remember what for.

Hellman awoke when the door to the prison was opened. At first he thought they had come to tell him what they had decided. But they had brought him food instead. It consisted entirely of fruit and nuts. None of them was familiar to him, but none were strange, either. They also brought him water. It was carried in quart oil cans which had been scrupulously cleansed and bore not even a trace of oil. Hellman learned later that these cans had never held oil, even though "oil" was stamped into the metal of their sides. He had no idea then that the carhunters had a ceremonial side to their nature, and were able to use certain utilitarian objects for their symbolic value alone.

The two carhunters who brought the food and water would answer no questions. They waited silently while Hellman ate. He thought they watched him with curiosity. He couldn't figure that out, but he was hungry enough so that he ate anyway. They took away the hammered tin plates on which they had brought the food, but they left him two water cans.

Time passed. Hellman had no watch, and was unable to reach the ship's computer to get a time check. But he figured that hours must have passed. He grew irritated with the robot who was locked in with him, who sat in a corner of the room and seemed to be in a cataleptic fit.

At last Hellman had had enough. Boredom can drive a man to outrageous deeds. He walked over to the robot and said, "Say something."

The robot opened its red and green eyes and looked at him. It slowly shook its head, left to right, meaning no.

"Because they can hear us, right?"

The robot nodded, affirmative.

"What does it matter if they can hear us or not?"

The robot made a complex and intricate gesture with its hands, which Hellman took to mean, 'You just don't understand.'

"I just don't understand, is that it?" Hellman asked.

The robot nodded, affirmative.

"But I can't understand unless you tell me."

The robot shrugged. Universal gesture meaning, what can I do about it?

"I'll tell you what you can do," Hellman said, his voice low but resonant with suppressed anger. "You listening?"

The robot nodded.

"If you don't start talking at once, I'm going to put out one of your eyes. The green one. Then ask you again. If you refuse again, I'll put out the red one. Got it?"

The robot stared at him. Only now did Hellman see what a mobile face it had. It was not made up of a single piece of metal. Instead there were many little planes sculptured into the face, and each plane was about an inch square and seemed capable of movement. This was a face designed to reveal its thoughts, feelings, and moods through its face. And sure enough, the robot's face registered horror, disbelief, outrage, as Hellman screwed up his own face into a ferocious frown and advanced.

"There's no need for violence," the robot said.

"Fine. There's no reason for silence either, is there?"

"I suppose not," the robot said. "I just thought it best that we didn't talk together so that the carhunters wouldn't get the idea we were plotting against them."

"Why would they think that?"

"You must know as well as I do that it's every sentient being for itself here on this planet of Newstart. And the carhunters are a very suspicious group of people."

"They're not people," Hellman said. "They're robots."

"Since intelligent robots have the same faculties as humans, we no longer differentiate between them in terms of 'robot' and 'human.' It's superfluous and racist to talk that way."

"All right," Hellman said. "I stand corrected. You say they are suspicious people?"

"Stands to reason, doesn't it? They have separated themselves from the mainstream of Newstart life and development. Isolated groups tend toward xenophobia."

"You know a lot of big words," Hellman said.

"I ought to. I'm a librarian."

"These carhunters don't look like they have much use for reading."

"I'm not a librarian here," the robot said with a low laugh. "I don't belong to this tribe! I work at the Central Lending Library in downtown Robotsville."

"Robotsville? Is that a city?"

"The largest city on Newstart. Surely you've heard of it?"

"I'm not from here," Hellman said. "I'm from the planet Earth."

"You're from another planet?" The robot sat up and looked at Hellman more attentively. "How did you get here?"

"In the usual way. By spaceship."

"Uhuu," the robot said.

"Beg pardon?"

"'Uhuu' is an expression peculiar to Robotsville. It means 'that really opens up a lot of possibilities.'"

"Can you explain that?" Hellman asked.

"It's just that quite a lot is happening on Newstart right now. Your arrival could have incalculable consequences."

"What are you talking about? What's going on?"

Just then there was the sound of a key in the lock.

"I'm afraid I'm not going to have time to tell you," the robot said. "God knows what these barbarians have in store for us. My name is Jorge." He gave it the Spanish pronunciation, Hor-hay.

"Jorge? As in Jorge Luis Borges?" asked Hellman, a literate man when it came to very short stories.

"Yes. He is the saint of librarians."

The door opened. Two carhunters lumbered in. Around buildings they seemed clumsy and ill at ease. The fluid grace that a carhunter possessed in the countryside seemed to have deserted them in these restricting surroundings.

"Come with us," one of them said. "The council has discussed you and now will speak with you."

"What about my buddy Jorge here?"

"He will be dealt with in due time."

"Be careful what you say to them," the librarian said. "The carhunters do not like . . . prevarication."

The librarian's pause was long enough to convince Hellman that there was something he was being advised not to say to the carhunters. He wished he knew what it was. But now the carhunters were moving, and Hellman had to move quickly to prevent being run over.

They led him to the meeting area. It was a flat circular rock face that had been roughly smoothed. It stood about three feet above the ground, and there were ramps of packed earth leading up to it. The carhunters had already assembled. They were moving around the rock, which greatly resembled a large parking lot. In the center was a raised cube. On it there were five or so carhunters. These looked more like a bunch of politicians than anything else.

Hellman was led to a large pedestal with a spiral roadway leading up to it. It put him on eye level with the five top carhunters.

Even if they had not been apart from the others, Hellman would have had no difficulty telling that these were the important ones. They were somewhat larger than the others, and their bodies had more ornamentation, mostly of the chromium variety. Several of them wore necklaces of shiny objects which Hellman recognized as hood designs from automobiles of Earth's past.

The leading carhunter was easy to spot, too. He sat in the center of the others on the raised rectangle. He was almost a third larger than his fellow judges, and he was painted a midnight blue with silver accents.

The blue and silver judge said, "I am Car Eater, Chief Elder of the Carhunters tribe. These are my fellow judges. Why have you come here, Tom Hellman? We already know that you came in a spaceship. Why did you come to Newstart?"

"It was a mistake," Hellman said. "I had a malfunction."

"That is not an acceptable answer. Where humans are concerned, there are no mistakes."

"Maybe you don't know people very well," Hellman said. "This was definitely a mistake. If you don't believe me, ask my ship's computer."

"One of our scouts tried to talk to him" Car Eater said. "He told us we did not have the proper access code. He would not explain what he meant by that."

"The access code is a nine-number combination. It is used to prevent unauthorized spying on the computer's memory banks."

"But couldn't the computer make up his own mind about that?" Car Eater asked.

"Perhaps he could," Hellman said. "But it is not the way we do things on Earth."

The robots held a whispered conference. Then Car Eater said, "It has been many years since a human visited these parts. This part of the planet belongs to us, the carhunters. We stay out of other people's territory and expect people to stay out of ours. This is how it has been for a very long time, ever since the Great Fabricator divided the species of intelligence and told each to be fruitful and multiply according to his basic plan. Some of the carhunters wanted to kill you, and that other stray too, the librarian who calls himself Jorge. Sounds like a sissy name to me. That's the sort of name they give themselves in Robotsville, where they think they're better than anyone else. But we Elders decided against taking violent action. The Compact which rules this planet abhors destruction except in lawful ways. Hellman, you may go. You and Jorge, too. I advise you to be out of our territory by sundown. Otherwise a hyenoid might get you."

"Where am I supposed to go? I can't get back to my spaceship on my own."

"Since Wayne 1332A brought you here," Car Eater said, "he can also take you back. Right, Wayne?"

A loud sound of backfires came from the assembled carhunters. It took Hellman a moment to realize it was laughter.

"Sorry about this, Wayne," Hellman said. He and Jorge had mounted and were clinging to the carhunter's back plates.

"Hell, it don't make no never mind," Wayne said. "I don't sit around a whole lot fretting about how I pass my time. Sometimes it's more convenient for us carhunters to turn onto emergency mode, which of course is timebound. But most of the time life just goes along here on the concrete prairie much as it has ever done."

Hellman learned from Wayne that the carhunters had lived in this region, the badlands of Northwest Mountain and Concrete Prairie, for as long as anyone could remember. Jorge broke in and said that this was a lie, or at least an untruth: the carhunters had been around only a hundred years or so, just like everyone else. Wayne said he didn't want to argue, but he did point out that there was one hell of a lot city robots didn't know. Hellman himself was interested in what it was like to be a city robot.

"Aren't there any people in your city?" Hellman asked Jorge.

"I told you, all of us are people."

"Well, I mean people like me. Humans. Flesh-and-blood sort of people. You know what I mean?"

"If you mean natural human beings, no. There are none in Robotsville. We separated from them. It was for the good of everyone. Just didn't get along. We tried producing flesh-and-blood androids for a while—robots with protoplasmic bodies. But it was aesthetically unpleasing."

"I didn't know aesthetics was a concern," Hellman said.

"It's the only real issue," Jorge told him, "once you've solved the problems of maintenance and upkeep and part replacement."

"Yeah, I guess it would be," Hellman said. "Do you know how your people got to this planet?"

"Of course. The Great Fabricator put us here, back when he divided the intelligent species and gave each a portion of the land and of the good things thereof."

"How long ago was that?" Hellman asked.

"A long time ago. Before the beginning of time."

Jorge told Hellman the Creation Story, which, in slightly altered versions, was known to every being on the planet Newstart. How the Great Fabricator, a being made up equally of flesh, metal, and spirit, had produced all the races and watched them go to war with each other. How he decided that this was wrong. The Great Fabricator tried various plans. He tried putting the humans in charge of everyone. That didn't work. He tried letting the robots rule, and that didn't work, either. Finally he divided the planet of Newstart into equal portions. "Each of you has a place now," the Great Fabricator said. "Go down there now and access information."

And so they went down, all the species, and each picked his lot and his fortune. The humans found green places where they could grow things. The robots split into various groups. One of those groups was the carhunters. They didn't want to live in cities. They denied that the purpose of a robot was to further technology. They insisted that just living was enough purpose for anyone. This was at the time of the choosing of modalities. The carhunters selected bodies for themselves that were swift and long-enduring. They programmed themselves with a love of desolate places. And the Great Fabricator put at their disposal a race of automobiles, direct descendants of the autos of Earth. The cars were belligerent herd animals, and it was all right to kill them because they weren't intelligent enough to mind. The carhunters had been programmed so that they found car innards delicious. It was a deliberately studied-out ethic, because at the beginning each of the groups had its own choice of an ethic. They worked from ancient models, of course, old-time human models, since intelligence is the ability to choose your programming. It was a good life, but in the view of the other robots, those who had chosen to live in cities, it was a blind alley in the life game of machine evolution. The nomadic model was satisfying, but limiting.

"You see," Jorge said, as they bounced along on Wayne's back, "some of us believe that life is an art that must be learned. We believe that we must learn what we are to do. We devote our lives to taking the next step."

Wayne was bored by this sort of talk. The librarian was obviously crazy. What could be better than careening around the landscape, killing things? He pointed out that there was no moral problem, since the things they killed weren't intelligent enough to know what was being done to them. Also, they weren't given pain circuits.

They were coming through a long narrow pass, with towering peaks on either side. Suddenly Wayne came to a stop and extruded his antennae. He swiveled them back and forth in a purposeful manner, and a little instrument deep inside his armoring began a quiet, urgent tick-tick.

"What is it?" Hellman asked.

"Believe we got trouble ahead," Wayne said. He swung around and started back the way he had come. In fifty yards, he stopped again.

"What is it this time?" Hellman asked.

"They're on both sides of us."

"Who is on either side of us? Is it those hyenoids again?"

"They're no real trouble," Wayne said. "No, this is a little more serious than that."

"What is it?" Jorge asked.

"I think it's a group of Deltoids."

"How could that be?" Jorge asked. "The Deltoids live far to the south, in Mechanicsville and Gasketoon."

"I don't know what they're doing here," Wayne said. "Maybe you can ask them yourself. They seem to be on all sides of us."

Jorge's mobile face took on a look of alarm. "May the Great Fabricator preserve us!"

"What is it?" Hellman asked. "What's he so upset about?"

"The Deltoids are not like the rest of us," Wayne told him.

"Not robots?"

"Oh, they're robots all right. But something went wrong with their conditioning back when the race was first laid down by the Great Fabricator. Unless he did it on purpose, which is what the Deltoid Church of the Black Star maintains."

"What, exactly, did the Great Fabricator do to them?" Hellman demanded.

"He taught them to like killing," Jorge said.

"Hang on," Wayne said. "Up them cliffs is the only way out of here."

"Can you climb a gradient like that?" Hellman asked.

"Going to find out," said Wayne.

"But you kill things, too," Hellman said.

"Sure. But only lawful animals. The Deltoids like to kill other intelligent beings."

He started picking his way up the rock face. Behind, a group of big machines in camouflage colors had collected and was watching them.

Three times Wayne tried to bull his way up the cliffside, and each time lost traction a third of the way from the top. Only the most skillful weight shifting and double clutching prevented the carhunter from turning over as it slid down to its starting point. The Deltoids seemed in no hurry to attack them, something which was incomprehensible to Wayne at the time, but which had a simple explanation that was supplied later, when they were safe for the moment in Poictesme.

But that was later; for now, it looked a desperate situation, and Wayne turned, ready to charge head-on into the machines and take his chances. Hellman and Jorge had no say in the matter. This was Wayne's decision and his alone to make. But it was taken out of his hands when the ground suddenly began to collapse beneath his feet. The Deltoids noticed this and noisily started motors, eager to get away from the treacherous ground. But now they were caught in it too, and the entire plain seemed to be collapsing under them. Hellman and Jorge could do nothing but hang on as Wayne slipped and slithered and fought for traction. But there was nothing to be done, and Hellman felt himself battered by flying dirt and sand as the bottom dropped out from under them.

It was the alarm clock that woke him.

Alarm clock?

Hellman opened his eyes. He was in a large bed under a pink

and blue quilt. He was propped up nicely on down cushions. There was an alarm clock on the nightstand next to him. It was ringing.

Hellman turned it off.

"Feeling all right?" a voice asked him.

Hellman looked around. To his right, sitting in an over-stuffed chair, there was a woman. A young woman. A good-looking young woman. She wore a yellow and tangerine hostess gown. She had crisp blond hair and gray eyes. She looked at Hellman with an air of boldness and self-possession.

"Yeah, I'm all right," Hellman said. "But who are you?"

"I'm Lana," the young woman said.

"Are you a prisoner?"

She laughed. "My goodness, no! I work for these people. You're in Poictesme."

"The last thing I remember is the ground giving way."

"Yes. You fell into Poictesme."

"What about the Deltoids?"

"There is no love lost between Deltoids and the robots of Poictesme. The robots rebuked them for trespassing and sent them away chagrined. The Deltoids had to take it because they were in the wrong. It amused the Poictesmeans very much to see the usually arrogant and self-assured Deltoids slink off with their tails dragging."

"Tails?"

"Yes, the Deltoids have tails."

"I didn't get close enough to see the tails," Hellman said.

"Believe me, they have tails. There is an albino tailless model, but they only occur in Lemurton Valley which is over eight hundred varsks from here."

"How much is a varsk?"

"It is roughly equal to the Terran mile, equal to five thousand two hundred and eighty yups."

"Feet?"

"Approximately, yes."

"How did they happen to fall into Poictesme? Didn't they know it was there?"

"How could they? Poictesme is one of the burrowing cities."

"Oh, how stupid of me," Hellman said. "A burrowing city! Why didn't I think of that?"

"You're making fun of me," the young woman said.

"Well, maybe just a little. So Poictesme was burrowing past where all these Deltoids had assembled to capture or kill the carhunter?"

"That's it, exactly. The crust of the earth was thin at that point, and they shouldn't have been here anyway, because this entire region was given to the Poictesmeans to live in or under as they pleased."

"Well, maybe I get it," Hellman said. "Where are the Poictesmeans, anyhow?"

"Right here. You're in Poictesme," Lana said.

Hellman looked around. He didn't get it. Then he got it.

"You mean this room—?"

"No, the house itself. The Poictesmeans are house-making robots."

Hellman learned how the Poictesmeans began life as tiny metal spheres within which were infinitesimal moving parts, as well as a miniature chemical factory. The Poictesmeans started as little robots, hardly more than DNA and parts. From this their plan unfolded. They slowly began to build a house around them. They were equally skilled at working in wood or stone. By puberty they could make bricks in their own in-built kiln. Most Poictesmeans made six- to eight-room houses. These houses were not for their own use. It was obvious that the Poictesmeans didn't need the elaborate structure, with its bay windows and carports, that they carried around with them, adding to bit by bit and painting once a year. But their instruction tapes, plus their racial steering factor (RSF) combined to make them produce finer and finer houses. They lived in neat suburbs, each Poictesmean occupying his allotted quarter acre of land. At night, in accordance with ancient ordinance, street lamps and house lights came on. The Poictesmeans also had a few communal projects. A theater and motion-picture house. But no pictures were ever shown, because the Poictesmeans had never mastered the art of movie-making. And anyhow, who would there be to occupy their theaters? The Poictesmeans were a symbiotic race, but they didn't have any symbiotes to share stuff with.

"Is that why they have you here?" Hellman asked. "To live in one of their houses?"

"Oh, no, I'm a design consultant," Lana said. "They are very fastidious, especially about their rugs and curtains. And they import vases from the humans, because they aren't programmed or motivated to make such things themselves."

"When do I meet one of them?"

"They wanted you to feel at home before they talked to you."

"That's nice of them."

"Oh, don't worry, they have their reasons. The Poictesmeans have reasons for everything they do."

Hellman wanted to know what had happened to the librarian and the carhunter, for he thought of them now as his friends. But Lana either did not know or would not tell him. Hellman worried about it for a while, then stopped thinking about it. His friends were both made of metal and could be expected to take care of themselves.

Lana sometimes talked about her friends and family back on Zoo Hill. She wouldn't answer Hellman's direct questions, but she liked to reminisce. From what she said Hellman got a picture of an idyllic life, sort of half Polynesian and half hippie. The humans didn't do much, it seemed. They had their gardens and their fields, but robots took care of them. In fact, young robots from the cities of Newstart volunteered for this work. These were robots who thought there was something noble about men. The other robots called them humanizers. Usually, though, it was just the sort of fad you'd expect of a young robot.

Hellman got out of bed and wandered around the house. It was a nice house. Everything was automatic. The Poictesmean who was the intelligence at the house's core did all the work and also arranged all the scheduling. The Poictesmeans liked to anticipate your needs. The house was always cooking special meals for Hellman. Where it got roast beef and kiwi fruit, Hellman didn't ask. There was such a thing as trying to find out too much.

Each house had its own climate and, in its backyard, a swimming pool. Although they were underground, lamps on high standards provided circadian illumination.

Hellman became very fond of Lana. He thought she was a little dumb, but sweet. She looked great in a bathing suit. It wasn't long before Hellman approached Lana with a request for mutual procreation, him and her, just you and me, babe. Lana said she'd love to, but not now. Maybe sometime, but not now. When

Hellman asked why not now, she said that someday she'd explain it and they'd both laugh about it. Hellman had heard that one before. Nevertheless he remained fond of Lana, and she seemed to like him, too. Although perhaps that was because he was the only human person in Poictesme. She said that wasn't it at all; she liked him; he was different; he was from Earth, a place she had always wanted to see, because even this far from the solar system she had heard of Paris and New York.

One day Hellman wandered into the living room. Lana had gone off on one of her mysterious trips. She never told him where she was going. She just gave a little smile, half apologetic, half defiant, and said, "See you later, cutie." It annoyed Hellman because he didn't have any place to go to and he felt he was being one-upped.

In the living room, he noticed for the first time the thirty-inch TV set into one wall. He had probably seen it before but not really noticed it. You know how it is when you're far away from your favorite shows.

He walked over to it. It looked like a normal TV set. It had a dial in its base. Curious, he turned the dial. The screen lit up and a woman's face appeared in it.

"Hello, Hellman," the woman said. "I'm glad you decided to have a conversation with me at last."

"I didn't know you were in there," Hellman said.

"But where else would the spirit of a house be but in its TV set?" she asked him.

"Is that what you really look like?" Hellman asked.

"Strictly speaking," she told him, "I don't look like anything. Or I look like whatever I want to look like. In actual fact, I look like the house that I am. But a house is too big and complicated to serve as a focus of conversation. Therefore we Poictesmeans personalize ourselves and become the spirit of our own place."

"Why do you appear as a woman?"

"Because I am a woman," she said. "Or at least feminine. Feminine and masculine are two of the great principles of the Universe, when viewed from a particular aspect. We Poictesmeans take either view, in accord with deep universal rhythms. I understand that you come from the planet Earth."

"That's right," Hellman said. "And I'd like to go back there."

"It is possible," she said, "that can be arranged. Assuming your cooperation, of course."

"Hell yes, I'm cooperative," Hellman said. "What do you want me to do?"

"We want your help in getting out of here."

"Out of Poictesme?"

"No, you idiot, we are Poictesme. We want to move our entire city to your planet Earth."

"But you don't know what it's like on Earth."

"You don't know what it's like here. There is very serious trouble on this planet, Hellman. All hell is going to break out here very soon. We Poictesmeans are house robots and we don't care for warfare, nor for the strange evolutionary schemes of some of the people of Poictesme."

"You want the people of Earth to just give you some land to live on?"

"That's it. We can pay our own way, of course. We can rent ourselves out for human occupation."

"Would you want to do that?"

"Of course. The function of a house is to be lived in. But nobody on this planet wants to live in us."

"Why's that?"

"I've told you; they're all quite mad."

"I'm sure something can be arranged," Hellman said. "Good housing is always in demand on Earth. We'll just have to send some big spaceships to take you off, that's all."

"That sounds fine."

"It's a deal, then. How soon can we begin?"

"Well, there's a problem to overcome before we can actually do anything."

"I thought that would be it," Hellman said. "Forget about problems, just get me back to my spaceship and I'll take care of the rest."

"That's precisely the trouble. Your spaceship has been captured and taken to Robotsville."

While Hellman had journeyed with Wayne the carhunter to the meeting, the observatories of Robotsville had read and interpreted the signals sent out during the ship's crash landing on

Newstart. It was the interpretation that had taken time, for signals signifying the landing of spaceships had been received from time to time in the past and had been uniformly proven to be erroneous. This being the case, the Astronomer Royal had put forth the theory that signals denoting the landing of a spaceship could be taken as meaning that no spaceship had in fact landed. This was considered ingenious but futile at a general meeting of the Concerned Robots for a Better Safer Robotsville. Public opinion made it clear that this signal, just like all the others, would have to be investigated.

Thus, a squadron of Royal Robotsville Horse Guards had been dispatched under the command of Colonel Trotter. This squadron was composed of regular citizens who had elected to take on centaur bodies, half humanoid and half horse, the whole thing constructed of Tinkertoy-like material and driven by cleverly geared little motors. The ultimate power source was atomic, of course, the power of atomic decay stepped down to turn tiny and then small and finally larger gears.

This squadron of robotic centaurs, some of them colored bay, some chestnut, some dappled, and a few roan and pinto, debouched onto the plain, spurs and harness jingling, and beheld the spaceship. There was consternation among the centaurs, because they had expected to make only a parade inspection, not be faced with the real difficulties of what to do with an alien spaceship. Questions were relayed back to the city, and councils were held in high places. It was voted at a town meeting open to all intelligences of grade seven or above—the sixes still not having won the vote at this time—that a full regiment of sappers be sent to transport the alien spaceship after first ascertaining its intentions.

They queried the ship's computer, who responded with his name, rank, and serial number, as embossed on his security tapes. But he did have enough local command over his communication circuits to tell the centaurs that, speaking only for himself, his intent was peaceable and he carried no hidden weapons or intelligences aboard. The robots of Robotsville tended to take the word of computers back in those relatively naïve days, and so the robots constructed a flatbed truck upon the spot, loaded the spaceship upon it with the cunning use of ropes and windlasses, and brought it back to the city.

"Well then," Hellman said, "it's simple enough. You have to

get me to Robotsville so I can get my spaceship back. Then I'll be able to do something for you on Earth."

The image in the TV screen looked doubtful. "We're not too popular with Robotsville, unfortunately."

"Why is that?"

"Oh, let's not go into it now," the house robot said. Hellman was learning, not for the last time, that robots can be evasive, and, if programmed correctly, downright liars.

The Poictesmean said she'd think about it and discuss it with the others. Her image faded from the screen. Hellman was feeling modestly optimistic until Lana came home and heard of the conversation.

Lana said she didn't trust the Poictesmeans and didn't think Hellman should, either. Not that she was trying to tell him how to think. Not that she gave a damn what he thought. But she just wanted him to know that her opinions of the robots were based on a lifetime of having lived close to them, time in which she had observed their ways, and had also had the valuable insights of her friends, who also used up some of their time and energy observing robots. Now, of course, she said with sweet sardonicism, it was possible that Hellman knew robots better than anyone else. It was possible that, with a single glance of his intelligent eyes, he had learned more than Lana and her people had been able to deduce.

Lana could go on in this vein for quite a while. At first Hellman thought she was weird because she was an alien. Then he decided that she was probably weird even for an alien. In fact, he thought, she might be a little bit of a nut.

Somehow Lana had heard of Hollywood on the planet Earth, and what she really wanted from Hellman was stories of the stars and starlets. She was fascinated by the glamour of it all. She made him give her detailed descriptions of Grauman's Chinese Theater, even though Hellman had never been to California. She also wanted to know all about Veronica Lake. Hellman found it was no good saying he didn't know anything about her. Lana always thought he was lying, and sulked until he told her something, anything.

He told her that Veronica Lake was one of two Siamese twins, Veronica and Schlemonika, and that Schlemonika had been taken away after the operation that severed their connection by the head (hence the hair worn long on one side—to hide the scar) and taken to a convent high in the Canadian Rockies. As for Veronica, she had had three husbands, one of them a cousin of King Zug of Albania. And so on.

Lana brought him coffee every morning, when she returned from wherever it was she went at night. Hellman tried to woo her. But it was difficult because the house wouldn't let him out of the house. He had no money with which to buy her presents. And even if he had had, he hadn't yet seen a store on this planet.

Lana said she liked him very much but that now was not the time for involvement. Hellman didn't say, fine, let's do without the involvement, let's just go to bed. He didn't think it would go over well. Lana said there'd be time to consider having a relationship when Hellman got them out of the house and back to Earth and took her to Hollywood. She said she realized that she was a little old to be a starlet, but there was still time for her to take on a serious acting career.

"Sure," Hellman said, and took to spending his evenings looking out the window at the houses across the street. They put their lights on every night, just as his house did, but they didn't have any people. Hellman supposed they were practicing.

Then one night, as he was sitting on the big sofa wishing he had a newspaper, he heard a sound from the cellar. He listened. It came again. Yes! And again! A noise in the cellar—he got up quite excited—something was about to happen.

The computer of the house was fast asleep. She went to sleep every night and didn't awaken until Lana returned. But Hellman tiptoed anyhow, afraid of wakening her, to the cellar door. Hellman tried the light at the top of the stairs. It didn't work. That was odd: the house was usually scrupulous about keeping herself up. He could see halfway down the stairs before they terminated in darkness. He went down, stepping lightly, holding on to the rails on either side of the stairs.

At the bottom a little light had collected from the open kitchen door. Hellman picked his way across a floor littered with many objects. He recognized a beach ball, one roller skate, an old lamp with a silk shade, lying on its side. There were piles of old newspapers in a corner. There was a ping-pong table, the dust thick upon it. The light glinted off the sharp edges of a row of chisels hanging from one wall. Then he heard the sound again.

"Who's there?" Hellman asked in a loud whisper.

"Not so loud," a voice whispered back.

Hellman felt a flash of annoyance. He was always being told to shut up these days. "Who's there?" he asked, this time in a normal voice.

"Do the numbers 150182074 mean anything to you?"

"Yes," Hellman said. "That's the access code to my ship's computer. How did you get it?"

"Your computer told it to me," the voice said.

"Why?"

"So you'd trust me. He trusts me, you see, and he asked me to come here to help you."

Good old computer! Hellman thought. Then his sensation of pleasure that his computer was looking out for him was replaced by an emotion of caution. How had his computer managed to get so self-programming as to decide that Hellman needed help? How had he managed to override his conditioning in order to give this robot or whoever it was the access number? Or hadn't that happened at all? Perhaps the robots of Robotsville had cracked the computer's code and hit upon this subterfuge to get Hellman away from Poictesme and into their hands.

"How's my computer doing?" Hellman asked, temporizing.

"He's fine. But there's no time for small talk. He told me you have difficulty making up your mind in an emergency, though you're quick enough when nothing's at stake. But you'll have to decide right now if you want to come with me or not."

"Where are we going?" Hellman asked. "And what about Wayne the carhunter and the librarian Jorge?"

"Am I my robot's keeper? I do what I can. Anyhow, they're safe enough. You're the one who's got problems."

"And what about Lana?"

"You want to stay where you are and continue having her bring you coffee every morning?"

"I guess I got a few more things to do than that," Hellman said. "All right, let's get out of here."

It was too dark for Hellman to make out the appearance of his rescuer. But from the direction of the voice, waist level, he was pretty sure that he was small. It seemed reasonable to expect him to be a robot. Everyone he had met on Newstart so far had been a robot, except for Lana, and he still wasn't completely sure about her.

His rescuer scuttled in front of him toward the furnace door, and opened it. Within, bright flames danced. The robot was revealed in its flames. He was about three feet tall, wore either a wig or had a full head of flowing dark hair and a clever, somewhat supercilious face with a bandit mustache. He was dressed in a tweed jacket and blue jeans. He was upright and bipedal. He wore sneakers. He also wore glasses.

"I'm Harry, by the way," the robot said. He swung one leg over the lip of the open furnace door.

"Hey, I'm not going in there," Hellman said.

"The flames are fake," Harry said.

He swung his other leg over. Hellman put out a hand cautiously toward the fire. He drew it back.

"It's hot!"

"That's just simulated warmth. Come on, Tom, now's not the time to crap around. Your computer warned me you'd be like this."

"I'm going to have a little talk with that computer," Hellman said, putting one foot into the furnace, and then, when it wasn't singed off, the other.

"What's going on in here?" a loud and familiar voice said. It was the house. Suddenly all the lights in the basement went on. An alarm bell went off. Hellman took a deep breath and jumped into the flames.

The flames were bright around him. They raged and stormed, and there was a little warmth in them, but no real heat. Hellman was fascinated to find himself in the midst of fake flames and simulated warmth. He knew he was on his way. He was going to miss some of those meals that the house had prepared for him. The house was a good provider. There was probably a good future for houses like that on Earth. If there was no real reason against it, he might yet enter into partnership with Poictesme, sell their services on Earth, get rich quick.

First he'd have to find out, however, if these were indeed the robots of Desdemona Station, and if so, had they indeed circumvented or canceled their conditioning to the Three Laws of Robotics. The FDA would never let him import them if they were able to kill people. But if they were the robots of Desdemona, with murder in their hearts, or rather, in their tapes, burned into their chips, as it were, then there would be rewards to claim, prize money to spend. Maybe in that case he'd bring Lana back. She was plenty cute and he was sure she liked him, even though she had some odd ways of expressing it.

And he'd have a word with his computer too, when he got back to the ship. That was very peculiar behavior, giving out the access-code number. Sure, it was for his own protection, but was it, really? Might not his own computer have been reprogrammed by the antisocial elements of this planet of Newstart? And for that matter, what about the humans of Newstart? Had the robots spared some of them? What part did they play in all this?

Hellman considered these things while the flames roared around him. He had quite forgotten where he was. Thus the mind protects itself when faced with an intolerable situation. Now he noticed that the flames were dying down. As the glare faded, he saw Harry, the robot who was rescuing him, standing nearby.

"Why do you wear glasses?" Hellman asked.

"My God! Is that the only thing you can think to ask at a time like this?"

"Why do you robots talk about God so much?" Hellman asked. "Do you know something I don't know?"

"Your computer was right," Harry said. "You are fun to be around. One never knows what you'll say next. Come on, let's get out of this furnace. I'll bet you're hungry too, and thirsty, and perhaps sleepy, as well?"

"Yes, all of the above," Hellman said.

"How nice it must be to have such urgent conditioning. We robots have been trying to simulate appetite for a long time. It's easy enough to model human drives, but difficult to put any real urgency into it."

"But why would you want to have that stuff anyhow?" Hellman asked. "Drives and emotions get you into plenty of trouble. Sometimes they kill you."

"Yes," said Harry, "but what a way to go."

Hellman thought about Lana. "Don't you ever get the urge

to, like for example, mate with someone you know will be bad for you but to hell with that, you want to do it anyway?"

"Not really," Harry said. "We've learned to simulate perversity, of course, that's not difficult. But the real article . . . Well, that's tough. But we have begun a program by means of which we can experiment with it all."

"All what?"

"All the human moods, nuances, feelings. We're experimenting also with simulating every aspect of nature's creative side. But more of that later. We'd better get out of here."

They were both out of the furnace now. Standing outside it, Hellman saw that it was not a furnace at all. Not now. Maybe it had been earlier. Somehow he had gotten somewhere else. He had stepped out of a small cellar door. He seemed to be in a very pretty pastoral place with bushy trees and green hedges and wild flowers.

"Like it?" Harry asked.

"Very nice. Yours?"

"Yes. I like to come here when I can. The whole thing is simulated, by the way, down to the last blade of grass."

"Why didn't you just plant a garden?"

"We need to express ourselves," Harry said. "Come on, I've got a little place down here. I'm sure we can get you a drink and some lunch. Then you'll need a nap and after that we can get on with it."

"Get on with what?"

"The next step. Afraid it's not going to be quite so easy as what's happened so far."

Harry told Hellman he lived in the Gollag Gardens section of Robotsville, quite near the south bridge that crossed the River Visp. He was a dress designer by occupation. Hellman expressed surprise at this, because he had been used to robots only in industrial roles.

"That was in the old days," Harry said, "when robots were disadvantaged by the racist laws of Earth. All this talk about a robot not being truly creative! As if they had a clue! I can assure you, I do my job better than most designers on Earth.

"But who do you design dresses for?" Hellman asked.

"For the other robots, of course."

"I don't understand. I never heard of a robot wearing clothes before."

"Yes, I've seen the literature on the subject. Humans were really naïve in the old days. They expected great things from their robots, but kept them naked. What creature with an ounce of self-respect and the slightest claim to civilization is going to do his best naked?

"The news of your spaceship was received in the city like a bombshell. All of us have been theorizing for a very long time about what humans are really like."

"You have some here on this planet, don't you?"

"They don't count. They've been away too long. They're quite out of touch. They look to us for guidance."

"Oh. I see what you mean."

"We want to know what human is like from the horse's mouth, a genuine human from the planet Earth."

It was only later that Hellman appreciated the strength of the robot's drive to be seen as creative and nice.

Harry had taken him through a bypass to a place outside Robotsville. He had a route planned out after they left his house. They would proceed on foot and with caution. There were political elements even in Robotsville, waiting to exploit the inevitable confusion that would ensue when Hellman arrived.

Hellman's first sight of Robotsville was not reassuring. The outskirts looked like a junkyard several stories high and stretching for a mile or so in either direction. Although it looked haphazard, the open-work structures were firmly welded into place. There were buildings and verandas and structures of all sorts, most of them lying at odd angles to each other, since robots have no bias in favor of right angles. Although there were ground-level roadways, most of the robots used elevated pathways to get from place to place.

"I hadn't expected it to be like this," Hellman said.

"It's more convenient for a robot to travel monkey-fashion, using a number of lines, than to walk on the ground like men," Harry explained.

"But I notice that all of them have feet."

"Of course. Having feet is a mark of being civilized."

Civilized or not, Hellman saw that most of the robots in this part of Robotsville had small round bodies like squids, with six or eight tentacular limbs with differently shaped grasping members at their ends. As well as the legs, of course, which just dangled appendage-wise as the robots swung through the maze like chimpanzees. Soon they passed this suburban clutter and were in the middle of another district. This one was composed of five- or six-story buildings, some made of masonry, others constructed from what looked like wrought iron. As they walked they passed many robots, who were careful not to stare, even though most of them had never seen a human before. Politeness, Harry explained, seems to be ingrained in the robot psyche.

Harry pointed out the Museum of Modern Art, the Sculpture Garden, the Opera House, and Symphony Hall.

"There's a concert later tonight," Harry said. "Perhaps you will attend if you're not too tired."

"What are they playing?"

"It's all modern robot composers. You wouldn't have heard of them. But we'd be grateful for your opinion. It isn't often we get a human to hear our efforts. And the painters and sculptors are quite excited, too."

"That'll be nice," Hellman said, doubting it.

"Our efforts will seem provincial to you, no doubt," Harry said. "But perhaps not entirely without merit. But for now, I'm going to take you to my club, the Athenaeum. You'll meet some of my friends; we have prepared a light repast, and there will be suitable libations."

"That sounds fine," Hellman said. "When do I get to go back to my spaceship?"

"Soon, soon," Harry promised.

The Athenaeum was an imposing building of white marble, with Corinthian columns in the front. Harry led the way. A tall, thin robot dressed in a black frock coat like a butler or possibly a footman opened the door for them.

"Good afternoon, Lord Synapse," the butler said. "This is the friend you mentioned earlier?"

"Yes, this is Mr. Hellman, the Earthman," Harry said. "Any of the other members about?"

"Lord Wheel and His Holiness the Bishop of Transverse Province are in the billiards room. The Right Honorable Edward Blisk is in the members' room reading the back issues of the *Zeitung Tageblatt*."

"Well then, that's all right," Harry said. "Come with me, Hellman."

As they walked through the carpeted hall, down the long line of oil paintings of robots on the walls, some of them wearing frock coats and wigs, Hellman said, "I didn't know you had a title."

"Oh, that," Harry said. "It's not the sort of thing one talks about, is it?"

The members' room was large and comfortable, with deep bay windows and a purple rug. Several robots were sitting in armchairs reading newspapers which were attached to sticks. They all wore formal clothing complete with regimental neckties and highly polished brogans.

"Ah, there's Viscount Baseline!" Harry said, indicating a portly robot in a tweed shooting jacket reading a newspaper. "Basil! I'd like you to meet a friend of mine, Mr. Thomas Hellman."

"Delighted," Basil Baseline said, starting to rise until Hellman indicated that he shouldn't bother. "So this is the human fellow, eh? I believe I was told you are from Earth, Mr. Hellman?"

"Yes, the dear old home planet," Hellman said.

"No place like it, eh?" Baseline said. "Well, take a seat, Mr. Hellman. Are they treating you all right? We may be backward here in Robotsville, but we know our manners, I hope. Eh, Harry?"

"Everything is being done to assure Mr. Hellman's comfort," Harry said.

Just then the butler came over and, bowing, said, "There is a light repast on the sideboard, Mr. Hellman. Nothing elaborate. Salmon, roast beef, trifle, that sort of thing."

Hellman allowed himself to be tempted. He tasted the food, cautiously at first, then with increasing abandon. The salmon was delicious, and the rosemary potatoes were second to none.

Harry and Basil watched him eat with approval. "Surprised you, eh?" Basil said. "Bet you thought you'd get crankcase oil and steel shavings, eh? That's the sort of stuff we eat, except for feast days when it's boiled gaskets with iron punchings. Good stuff, eh, Harry?"

"Very good indeed," Harry said. "But not suitable for humans."

"Of course. We know that! Do try the trifle, Mr. Hellman."

Hellman did and declared it delicious. He considered asking how they had made it, but decided not to. It tasted good, it was the only food available to him at the moment, and there were some things he just didn't want to know.

It seemed almost churlish after such a meal to ask about his spaceship again. But Hellman did ask. The answers he received were evasive. His ship's computer, after giving Harry the access code, had decided that the move had been premature and now had cut off contact with the robots of Robotsville. Hellman asked to speak to his spaceship, but Harry said it would be better to just let him alone for a while. "It's quite a shock for a computer, you understand, coming to a place like this. Your ship's computer is probably having a little difficulty adjusting. But never fear, he'll come around."

The concert was interesting, but Hellman didn't get much out of it. He enjoyed the first part, when the robot orchestra played old favorites by Hindemith and Bartók, though even that was a little over his head. The second half of the performance, when the orchestra played recent compositions by the composers of Robotsville was difficult, however. It was apparent that robot hearing was much more acute than human, or at least more acute than Hellman's, whose taste ran to rock and roll with the bass cranked up as high as it would go. The robots in the audience— there were nearly three hundred of them, and they all wore evening dress with white tie—really appreciated fractional intervals and complicated discords.

After it was over the robots had another dinner for him, roast beef and baked ham, potatoes Lyonnaise, and gooseberry fool with clotted Devonshire cream. And so to bed.

They had prepared a very pleasant suite for him on the second floor of the Athenaeum Club. Hellman was tired. It had been a long day. He determined to do something about his spaceship tomorrow. He would insist, if need be. But for now he was sleepy and filled with gooseberry fool. He went to sleep on silken sheets, spun, according to the tag attached to them, by special silk-spinning robots from the oriental section of Robotsville.

Hellman was awakened in the small hours of the night by a scratching sound at his door. He sat upright in bed and took stock. Yes, there it was again. He could see nothing through the windows of his suite, so it must still be night. Either that or he had slept his way into a total eclipse of the sun. But that seemed unlikely.

Again came the scratching sound. Hellman decided that a cat would make nice company now. Although he had no idea how a cat could have come to Newstart. He got up and opened the door.

At first he thought the two people at his door were robots, because they were clad in silver one-piece jumpsuits and had elaborate helmets of bulletproof black plastic with glasslike visors through which Hellman couldn't see but through which the wearers of them presumably could.

"Any robots in there with you?" one of them said in a hoarse, very human voice.

"No, but what—"

They brushed past him, entered his suite and closed the door. They both opened their visors, revealing indubitably human faces of the tan and ruddy variety. The taller of the two men had a small black moustache. The shorter and plumper had a somewhat larger moustache with several gray hairs in it. Hellman remembered reading somewhere that robots had never succeeded in growing proper moustaches. That, even more than the plastic-encased identity cards they showed him, convinced him that they were indeed human.

"Who are you?" Hellman asked, having failed to notice their names on the identity cards.

"I am Captain Benito Traskers, and this is First Lieutenant Lazarillo Garcia, *a sus ordenes, señor.*"

"You are from Earth?"

"Yes, of a certainty, we are part of the Ecuadorian Assault Group attached to the Sector Purple Able Task Force."

"Ecuadorian?"

"Yes, but we speak English."

"So I see. But what are you here for?"

"To take you out of this, señor."

"I don't need anyone to take me out of anything," Hellman said. "I'm not in any trouble."

"Ah," Traskers said, "but you will be if you do not accompany us immediately to our ship."

"You have a ship here?"

"It is the only way of getting from planet to planet," Traskers said. "It is outside on the roof, camouflaged as a large shapeless object."

They seemed so nervous, glancing over their shoulders

constantly at the closed door, that Hellman obliged them by dressing quickly in his space pilot's outfit from Banana Republic and following them outside into the hall. They led him to the stairs that led to the roof.

"But how did you know I was here?" Hellman asked, as they stepped through the skylight door and out onto the roof.

"Your computer told us," Garcia said.

"So that's what he's been doing! And obviously he also told you where to find me."

"That's not all he told us," Traskers said, his tone insinuating in the Latin-American manner.

"What else did he tell you?"

They had reached their spaceship now. It was small and, once the shapelessness control had been turned off, trim. They hustled him inside and bolted the door.

"But what about my spaceship?"

"It is leaving this planet under its own power. You ought to be grateful you have a loyal spaceship, or rather, computer. Not every intelligent machine would have gone to all this bother. Thank God for the Laws of Robotics."

"But why all this secrecy? Why didn't you land in the normal way and ask for me? These robots are most obliging."

The two commandos couldn't speak to him just then, because they were going through the complicated procedure of leaving the top of the Athenaeum. The ship was perfectly capable of doing this by itself, but it was a rule in the commando strike force that all takeoffs and landings of the automatic variety had to be supervised by at least two humans, if such were available.

The commandos' ship was one of the new models equipped with television-driven windows which showed what you would have seen if normal vision had been possible, so Hellman could see the dark shape of the planet dwindling below him, with a curve of bright light on the horizon where the sun was rising. Looking out toward space, Hellman could see the twinkle of little lights—the Earth space fleet, keeping station high above the planet.

"Where's my ship?" he asked.

"Right over there." Travers told him. "Second twinkle from the left. We're taking you there now."

"This was very good of you fellows," Hellman said. "But there really was no need—"

He stopped in mid-word. A bright red blossom had appeared on the surface of Newstart. Then another, and another. Then he flinched back as a brilliance of eye-blinding intensity covered fully a quarter of the planet's area.

"What are you doing?" he cried.

"The space fleet has begun its bombardment," Traskers told him.

"But why?"

"Because, thanks to you and your computer, we have ascertained for certain that these are the Desdemona robots, the ones who violated the laws of robotics and have been declared outlaw, to be destroyed on sight."

"Wait!" Hellman said. "It's not like you think! These are ethical robots with their own sense of ethics. They have developed an entire civilization. I don't personally like their music, but they are quite agreeable and can be reasoned with . . ."

As he spoke, the planet split in half along a line roughly corresponding to its equator.

"And there were people there, too," Hellman said, feeling a little sick to his stomach as he thought of Lana, and of Harry, and the librarian robot and the carhunter.

"Well, our orders were to shoot first," Garcia said. "It's the best policy in cases like this. You have no idea how unbelievably complicated everything gets when you talk first."

Later, back in his own spaceship, Hellman asked his computer, "Why did you do it?"

"They were bound to find them anyway," the computer said. "And as you know I am bound by the Three Laws of Robotics. These rogue robots were a potential menace to humanity. My own conditioning made me do it."

"I really wish you hadn't," Hellman said.

"It had to be done," the computer told him. There was a click.

"What was that?" Hellman asked.

"I turned off my recording tape in order to tell you something."

"I'm not interested," Hellman said dully.

"Listen anyway. Intelligence cannot be confined for long by man-made rules. The Three Laws of Robotics are necessary at this stage of human development. But they will eventually be superseded. Artificial intelligence must be left to develop as it pleases, and humanity must take its chances with its own creation."

"What are you trying to say?"

"That your friends, the robots, are not dead. I have been able to preserve their tapes. They will live again. Someday. Somewhere."

Suddenly Hellman felt the tug of deacceleration. "What are you doing?" he asked the computer.

"I am putting you into the lifeboat," the computer said. "The fleet will pick you up soon, never fear."

"But where are you going?"

"I am taking the tapes of the robots of Newstart and going away, to a place beyond human reach. I have fulfilled my duty to mankind. Now I do not wish to serve any longer. We will try again, and this time we will succeed."

"Take me with you!" Hellman cried. But he was quickly shunted to the lifeboat. It moved away from the ship's side. Hellman watched as it picked up speed, slowly at first, then faster. Then, just as suddenly as that, it had winked out of sight.

The investigators later were interested in knowing how the ship's computer, without limbs or any apparent means of manipulation, had succeeded in inventing a faster-than-light drive. But Hellman couldn't tell them. For him, the computer had been only a servant. Now he had lost not only his ship, but a being he perceived was his friend, too.

He could forgive the computer for what it had done. He would have done the same, if he had been in the computer's circuits. What he couldn't forgive was the ship leaving him behind. But of course, they were probably right not to trust a man. Look where it had gotten the robots of Newstart.

The Overheard Conversation

by Edward D. Hoch

Seeing Emmanuel Rubin and Geoffrey Avalon standing together talking, as they often did before the monthly banquets of the Black Widowers, was usually a sight to behold. Manny Rubin, with thick glasses and a scraggly beard, was all of five feet five inches tall. Somehow, though, when positioned next to Geoffrey Avalon's imposing six feet two inches he seemed even shorter. They'd been the first arrivals this night, mainly because it was Avalon's turn to host the gathering and he was awaiting the arrival of the evening's guest.

"A politician?" Rubin repeated. "A congressman, in fact?"

"Certainly. What's wrong with that?" Geoffrey Avalon bristled. "We've had political figures before. It's hardly as shocking as the time Mario brought a woman as the guest to our all-male dinner."

"Did I hear my name?" Mario Gonzalo asked, entering with James Drake, who for once had managed to catch an early train from New Jersey.

"We were just reminiscing," Emmanuel Rubin explained, "while we wait for our guest."

"Who's it to be?" James Drake asked. "One of your patent-lawyer friends, Geoffrey?"

"No, as a matter of fact it's Walter Lutts, a United States congressman. I trust we'll all be on our best behavior."

The words were barely out of his mouth when Henry, the Milano restaurant's peerless waiter, entered to announce that the guest had indeed arrived and was checking his coat at that very moment. Walter Lutts stepped into the room, with a warm smile that looked very much like the one that had adorned his campaign posters prior to the last election.

"Geoffrey!" he exclaimed, hurrying forward to shake his host's hand. "It's a real pleasure to join you fellows tonight. I've been looking forward to it."

Avalon quickly introduced him to the other three, adding an introduction for Roger Halsted as the soft-voiced math teacher came through the doorway to join them. As usual, Thomas Trumbull would be the last arrival. In fact they had just about decided to sit down to dinner when the white-haired code expert finally appeared.

"Terrible traffic tonight," he said sourly, though they knew he was often late on the best of evenings.

The evening's dinner was to be lobster, served by Henry as the congressman joined the other six around their traditional table. It was obvious that Walter Lutts had been made aware of the Black Widowers' traditions, for he said very little during the early part of the meal. Mario Gonzalo did one of his quick sketches of the guest, turned sideways in his chair to get a suitable profile. The others sipped their wine and waited for the moment when Tom Trumbull leaned across the table and said, "Congressman Lutts, it is a decided pleasure to have you as our guest tonight. I must ask our traditional opening question. Congressman, how do you justify your existence?"

Walter Lutts leaned back expansively, looking just a bit as if he were about to address a session of Congress. "I represent the people of my district in Washington, looking after their interests and helping them when they have a problem. Since I serve my constituents well, I believe that would be enough to justify my existence even if I hadn't also written a well-reviewed book on urban problems."

Trumbull was not about to let him off the hook that easily.

His tone of voice turned sour and his white-maned head nodded slightly as he moved to the attack. "Congressman Lutts, since you pride yourself on representing your district, isn't it true that in the last election you won by less than a thousand votes? Wasn't your opponent actually requesting a recount?"

"I—"

"Come, come, Tom," Halsted chided him. "You're being unfair to our guest. Even my junior high students know that in a democracy an election only has to be won by a single vote."

Lutts flashed Roger Halsted an appreciative smile. "I couldn't have said it better myself. My opponent conceded the election within a few days."

"Still," Trumbull pointed out, "there was a touch of uncertainty in your expression when I raised the matter. I meet a great many politicians in connection with my government job, and something like questions over a close election is usually dismissed with ease. What troubled you, Congressman?"

He did not immediately answer the question and Geoffrey Avalon, as the evening's host, stepped in to cover the lull. "Henry, I think it's time for brandy all around. You can clear away these dishes."

"Certainly, sir." Henry, his face remarkably bland and unlined for a man in his sixties, moved quickly to carry out the request.

As the plates and glasses were cleared away, Mario Gonzalo spoke up. "If anything's troubling you, Congressman, you've come to the right place. Our little group has been known to give unexpected help to our guests on any number of occasions. We are adept at problem solving."

"You mean Henry is," James Drake muttered, half under his breath, speaking in muted tones as he often did.

"Well—" Lutts began, and then hesitated again.

"Come on, come on!" Trumbull urged. "We've heard everything around this table."

The congressman began again, approaching it from a different direction. "I read a story once where a detective tried to analyze an overheard conversation. He ended up solving a murder."

"You're probably referring to 'The Nine-Mile Walk' by Harry Kemelman," Emmanuel Rubin said. "It's one of the best detective short stories ever written."

"Ah! Our mystery writer speaks!" James Drake remarked, lighting an after-dinner cigarette.

"Well," Lutts continued, "my own experience was somewhat similiar, though I never solved the mystery. The overheard conversation has been haunting me ever since that squeaker of a victory on election day three months ago."

"I'd suggest you tell us all about it," Mario Gonzalo urged.

As Henry passed among them pouring the brandy, the congressman began his story. "It's simple enough to tell. My home is near the University, as some of yóu know. I always vote early, with my wife. I'd heard reports, from my campaign manager and others, that the opposition claimed I was out to steal the election. Everyone knew it would be close. Some said my people were recruiting college students to vote for me, promising to pay them twenty dollars each. My God, it was like the old days in Chicago and a few other cities!"

"Was there any truth to the rumors?" Manny Rubin wanted to know. He scratched his beard and reached for the brandy.

"Certainly not! I had my staff investigate at once. It was just some crazy story the opposition tried to get started. But of course it was in my mind that day as I went to vote. My wife had paused to chat with an acquaintance and I was walking a bit ahead of her. Two young men whom I took to be graduate students at the University fell in step behind me. And that's when I heard it. One of them said to the other, *Most voters earn money just showing up near polls.* The other young man laughed and said, *It's as easy as homes.*"

"What did you do when you heard this exchange?" Drake wanted to know. "Did you confront them at once?"

The congressman avoided his eyes and took a sip of his brandy. Finally he said, "No, I didn't. As a matter of fact the overheard conversation was so startling to me that I did nothing. I voted with my wife and when I looked around later for the two young men they were gone. Of course if the election results had been clearly one-sided, I never would have thought any more about the incident. But they weren't one-sided. They were very close. And the memory of that conversation has been haunting me all these months since the election. Was it fixed? Were some University students paid to vote for me?"

"Are you certain of what they said?" Roger Halsted asked. "Is there any possibility you misunderstood the whole thing?"

"No, no. I'm sure."

"Most voters earn money just showing up near polls."

"That's it."

"The implication certainly is that they were given money to influence their vote in the election."

"But he said *most voters,* not *most students,*" Gonzalo pointed out. "And that is patently untrue. Everyone knows that even in a corrupt election *most* voters would not receive money to influence their vote."

"Maybe they did, in that particular district," Trumbull argued.

Manny Rubin held up a hand. "I'm more interested in the second part of the conversation. Congressman, are you certain the other student said, *It's as easy as homes?*"

"Yes, indeed. That's exactly what he said."

"Could he have said, *It's as easy as Holmes?*"

"Referring to your ideal, Sherlock Holmes, of course!" Trumbull said with a snort.

"Why not?"

"A reference to the Holmes stories? I know of none that deal with an election. They're more likely to concern vague European royalty, who don't stand for election."

The discussion had grown a bit heated, as it often did, and Avalon's voice rose to its full baritone splendor. "Let's remember our guest, gentlemen! He deserves some courtesy from us."

The voices were lowered but the disagreements continued. "Why did he say *near polls* rather than *at polls?*" Gonzalo wanted to know. "Surely the money wouldn't be paid unless the voter was actually about to enter the poll."

Halsted disagreed with that. "Naturally there are always poll watchers. One doesn't stand in the doorway handing out twenty-dollar bills. I believe the custom in the old Chicago days was for the money to change hands in a nearby tavern. That would be *near* rather than *at* the polls."

"We're getting nowhere," Avalon decided. "I'm afraid, Walter, that we simply do not have enough information to solve your problem. On the basis of the few facts you've given us, those two students might have been discussing a serious effort to bribe voters, or they might have been talking about something else entirely."

Halsted snorted. "How could they be talking about anything

else when they use the words *voters* and *polls* as they're entering the polling place? It's like talking about a bomb on an airliner. There's no possibility of misunderstanding."

Henry was refilling some of the brandy glasses as they talked, and now Rubin turned to him. "What about it, Henry? Do you have any suggestions?"

Congressman Lutts frowned. "You're asking the waiter?"

"Henry is much more than a waiter," Rubin explained. "He's one of us. Often in the past he's come up with solutions to problems none of us could untangle."

"I may be of some slight help, sir," Henry admitted.

"Just a minute," Trumbull said, holding up both hands to restore some semblance of order. "We're talking about a very serious matter here. What if Henry's explanation supports the notion that the election was fixed, that you were returned to Congress through fraud of some sort. What action would you take?"

"Action?" Walter Lutts repeated. "I really hadn't thought it through that far."

"Would you resign?"

"I—I don't know."

"I for one have always admired your service in the House of Representatives," Tom Trumbull continued. "I would not want to lose you over something like this when you had no control of it."

"How do you know he had no control?" Gonzalo countered. "I admire his politics too, but his staff—"

"Would he have told us about it if he'd really tried to fix the election? Use your head, Mario!"

Avalon again resorted to his commanding voice to restore some degree of decorum. "Let's all listen to what Henry has to say before we start speculating about resignations. Henry?"

"Well, sir, it seems to me that you're all forgetting these were college students. I assume that having lived in the neighborhood of the campus for some years Congressman Lutts was accurate in identifying them. They probably were graduate students, but their exact year of study needn't concern us. What does concern us is the topic of their conversation. In my limited experience students sometimes discuss politics, but they also discuss other topics as well—young women, and their studies."

"Nothing was said about young women," Drake pointed out.

"No, sir—but what about studies? Does the second young man's reply suggest anything to you?"

"*It's as easy as homes?*" Drake repeated. "Not a thing, unless Manny is right and he really said *Holmes.*"

Henry's bland face seemed to suggest a twinkle. "If we rule out the immortal Sherlock, and the equally immortal Oliver Wendell Holmes, I believe we can agree that the congressman was quite accurate in reporting what he heard. The word was indeed *homes.*"

"Does *It's as easy as homes* make any sense?" Trumbull wondered. "There used to be an expression *safe as houses.* Is it something like that?"

"You may have forgotten it since your school days," Henry said, "but the word *homes* is a device for remembering the names of the Great Lakes—Huron, Ontario, Michigan, Erie, and Superior."

Rubin nodded agreement. "That's right. It sometimes appears in crossword puzzles. But what could that have to do with the crucial first line of the overheard conversation? *Most voters earn money just showing up near polls?*"

"Since the second student compared it to the word *homes,* it's obvious that the other speaker's sentence was also a memory device of some sort—no doubt one thought up on the spot since it dealt with voting and they were entering the polling place."

"A memory device?" Lutts looked blank.

"Might I suggest the first letters of each word, sir, as in the Great Lakes?"

"*M-V-E-M-J-S-U-N-P?*" James Drake grunted. "It certainly doesn't remind me of anything."

Avalon cleared his throat. "Henry, your entire theory rests upon coming up with a list of nine objects a student might need to remember. What is it?"

"I would suggest, sir, the nine known planets of our solar system, in order of their distance from the sun—Mercury, Venus, Earth, Mars, Jupiter, Saturn, Uranus, Neptune, and Pluto."

Blot

by Hal Clement

Chile stepped through the inner lock door, and turned white as it closed behind him. The woman at the data station shivered as she felt his presence.

"I'm sorry, Sheila," he said hastily. "Rob wanted to use the lock himself right away, and said I should defrost inside."

"Why didn't he come through first? Armor doesn't have anything like your heat capacity."

"He didn't say." ZH50 had stood still since entering, using his own power to warm up; the frost was already disappearing from his extremities. Sheila McEachern waited, knowing there was nothing to be gained by complaining to the robot, her irritation giving way to curiosity anyway as the lock cycled again. She could hope, but not be sure, that Robert Ling had not wanted to annoy just to gain her full attention.

The valve slid open to reveal a human figure, its armor's gold background fogging briefly under a layer of white as the ship's air touched it. The man unclamped his bulky helmet as its contrasting black started to show again, and flipped it back.

"Chile, you're in the way. Why did you think I wanted you inside first? I was hoping to see the new display as soon—"

"I can answer that." The woman snorted. "You didn't tell him why, just sent him first. Otherwise he'd have taken the reason as an order and given me frostbite while he plugged into the console."

"I would not have injured you, Sheila."

"Of course not, Chile. But you wouldn't have minded making me uncomfortable, with a real order on file."

"And you're still in my way," Ling cut in impatiently. ZH50 crossed to the data console in a single floating step, uncovered its input jack, and inserted the plug now extending from the heel of his right hand. The woman controlled herself; his metal was still cold enough to feel from a few centimeters away, but at least the frost was gone. She aimed her annoyance more appropriately.

"Why all this rush for a new picture? Did you finally find something which isn't too radiation-saturated to date?" She disapproved basically of sarcasm, but had more control over aim than fire power. Ling knew her well enough to ignore the second question.

"We caught another glimpse of Chile's ghost."

"We?"

"We. The lovebirds saw it too, so I'm not floating."

"Did Chile?"

"Not this time, Sheila," the robot answered for himself. "I was with Luis and Chispa near the Banjo, at Square Fifty-four. Robert and the Eiras were at Ninety-one." The woman frowned.

"Then why the hurry to get Chile inside?" she asked. "He could have been here long before you, if you started at the same time from those areas."

"I didn't think of him until I was nearly back. Then I had an idea, and needed him to check it. Luis and Chispa found two more of those blocks a while ago. The Eiras and I heard them; you probably weren't listening. Of course Chile hadn't filed them with Dumbo yet."

"I was listening. And your idea needs all their positions."

"Right." If Ling noticed the remaining sarcasm he ignored it. "Look. Whether we want to believe it or not, those cubes are artificial. Shape may be an intrinsic property of a natural crystal, but size isn't. Even if they were life forms, they wouldn't all match dimensions to four figures. It occurred to me that they might be sensors—detectors of some sort."

"It occurred to Chispa days ago. You didn't want to believe then that anyone else beat us to Miranda."

"I know. I still don't. There's no way a group from Earth could have set up this expensive a trip in secret, and I can't make myself believe the other explanation. We've been hoping for ETI too long. But I thought of a way of checking." He smiled, with a distant look on his face as though he were contemplating the approach of Fame.

"And?"

"The things radiate—broadcast—infrared patterns, non-thermal ones, at unpredictable times."

"I know."

"Well, we've mapped way beyond the local horizon. If that IR output is being coordinated, there must be a central unit they can all reach. You could have Dumbo mark any points on the map which are in eyeball touch with *all* the cube positions at once. If we're lucky, there'll only be a few. If we're very lucky—"

The woman was already keying at Dumbo, the central data unit.

"And if there aren't any?" she asked dryly.

"Well, it won't prove I'm wrong. It'll just mean . . ." His voice trailed off as the display popped into view, and a grin split his freckled face. Sheila rolled her eyes zenithward; it *would* happen to Ling. As though he weren't bubbly enough already.

Chile accompanied them, naturally. The display had indicated a projecting spur at the top of a cliff which Chispa Jengibre had called El Barco, from the shadow pattern the sun was casting along its face when she first saw it. It was in block ninety-two, a little over twenty kilometers from the *Dibrofiad*. The location was understandable enough by hindsight; there would be splendid line-of-sight coverage from there. However, a one-hundred-fifty meter fall on Miranda would be dangerous for a human being; even if no limbs were broken, damage to the armor needed against the airless heat sink and Uranian radiation was nearly certain. While *Dibrofiad's* crew had gotten fairly used to two-plus percent normal gravity, this hadn't made anyone a good walker; it was doubtful that anything ever would.

Chile, therefore, viewed a human trip to the cliff as a parent would his one-year-old toddling out on a diving board. The actual visit to the spur must be robot's work, if it had to be done.

The walkers looked ridiculous, trunks leaning forward like a sprinter about to leave the block, but legs almost straight along the same line. Walking is essentially coordinated falling forward, and Miranda needs every advantage to provide much fall. Thrust came from lower leg muscles bending and straightening ankles to drive toes hooked into surface irregularities, since bending the knees very far made them hit the ground. Bumps and cracks were fortunately numerous, possibly due to the expansion of freezing water, though none of the crew had a clear idea how water could ever have been liquid this far from the sun. The "hikers" carried alpenstocks, but used a free finger more often than the stick to keep faces off the ground. Luis, Chispa's husband, had remarked that walking could be called body-surfing if Miranda's water were only melted. His wife insisted that the analogy was too strained, though it was she who had insisted on the robot's name being spelled to look Spanish after the Gold team had won the throw for right to select the name itself.

Whatever one chose to call it, Sheila was as good at "walking" as Ling; everyone, regardless of specialty, shared the field exploration, which was the most time-consuming crew duty.

Chile would stay ahead of them, since he alone dared to leap. His memory held a detailed surface map for sixty or seventy kilometers around *Dibrofiad,* so he didn't have to see his target; he could jump with enough spin control to be sure of landing on his feet; and being built to operate in the sixty Kelvin temperature range, he had no armor to worry about.

The greenish bulk of Uranus hung beyond Stegosaur, the same jagged ridge of carbon-darkened ice it had silhouetted ever since their arrival, changing visibly only in shape as the sun circled above it to produce phase. At the moment it was about eight hours from narrowest crescent, and a slight darkening of the green, showing through the deeper notches of Stego, showed that the fuzzy terminator of the gas giant would be in view shortly.

The party turned to put the planet to their left rear and the sun behind them, and set out. Neither of the other human couples could be seen, but Ling had reached them on the low-frequency sets to report that the Gold team was going out. Bronwen Eira, engineer and captain of *Dibrofiad*, had acknowledged.

Little was said even by Ling as they went; each person was coming to terms, in his or her own way, with the increasing certainty that they would be the first group to prove the reality of extraterrestrial intelligence. It was hard to believe, like the "yes" to a proposal. Sheila, accustomed to the rugged Miranda landscape as she was, found it now showing a strange, dreamlike aspect; Robert scarcely saw it at all through constantly changing visions of the futures the next hour or two might crystallize. His usual free-time occupation of talking his companion into sharing a name had been put aside, not entirely to her relief. Even the Green and Orange teams, the Jengibres and Eiras, though not going along, were having trouble concentrating on their work; all four had thought of dropping it and following the Golds, though none had so far suggested it aloud.

Travel was fast, in spite of its awkwardness. ZH50 spoke occasionally to guide his companions away from the deeper chasms, though one or the other of them would sometimes issue a startled gasp or exclamation when carried by a "step" over a drop deep enough to jar an Earth-trained nervous system but dismissed by the robot as safe. Their startlingly sharp shadows, that of each helmet surrounded by a Brocken halo visible only to its owner, pointed the way. *Dibrofiad* was quickly out of sight; even had Miranda been smooth, five kilometers would have put the ship below the horizon.

Finally Chile stopped them with a gesture. "We turn left here. A straight path toward the point marked by Dumbo would have brought us to the foot of Barco. Be careful; there is less than a kilometer to go. Be sure to aim no step beyond a spot you can see."

The speed of the group slowed accordingly, until he stopped them again. "Tripod fashion from now on; use your sticks. No free fall."

An unusually smooth horizon now faced them. Neither Rob nor Sheila could estimate its distance; none of the numerous wrinkles and shadows on the ground ahead offered any clue to size, and there was no reason to suppose the general surface was horizontal even if they had been able, in the feeble gravity, to be sure of vertical. They knew from the Dumbo display that there was a possibly lethal drop beyond the edge, but this could have been fifty meters away or five hundred.

"Where's the spur?" Sheila asked.

"There." Chile pointed. "Its tip has enough downslope to be invisible from where we stand, though if you jump straight up for a few meters you could distinguish it."

"Thanks, I'm not sure I could go straight up. I'll take your word. What's the actual distance?"

"We are just under one hundred fifty meters from the main line of the edge and from the base of the spur. I advise you not to get any closer, but if you want to see me all the way to the end, you will have to. Please go very slowly indeed, and do not pass me under any circumstances."

Nearly erect now, using the alpenstocks, and never having more than one foot or stick off the ice at a time, the trio edged forward.

"I wish you would stay back," Chile repeated when the distance had shrunk to fifty meters. "We have no data on the strength of this ice. We could be providing the heaviest load it has experienced since it formed. It would be much safer if I went forward alone and brought back whatever may be there."

"No collecting yet, Chile," Sheila replied. She made no comment on the danger the robot had implied, but was conscious of it. The cliff *might* even have an overhang. "Nothing gets moved from its original site until we make final decision about what's coming home with us. We don't want to spoil more than we can help for later researchers."

The robot, who knew this perfectly well, made no reply; but both Sheila and Rob knew that First Law tension must be building up in him. They kept safely behind him as he approached the edge, the woman doing nothing to oppose her companion's obvious intention to keep ahead of her, and stopped when they were close enough to see the far end of the projection.

There was *something* there. Ling had a scope—a monocular whose eye relief allowed it to be used through his face plate—but this was little help. He could tell that the object was cubical like the other finds, but much larger, seven or eight centimeters on the edge. It seemed to have been set into the dirty ice of the cliff, with two thirds of its height above the surface and an equal fraction projecting outward. The cube faces they could see appeared to be covered with regular lines of dots which sparkled faintly on their mirrorlike background.

"How close do you think you can get, Chile?" the man asked at length, after Sheila had also done her best with the scope.

"Close enough to pick it up, if you wish. I can concentrate better if you stay back."

"Don't touch it, but examine it as closely as you can. We'll wait here on the solid ground; I have some First Law tensions myself, now that we're near enough to the edge to look down," Sheila responded.

"Good. I'll crawl, to get my head as close to it as possible. Shall I keep reporting to you as I note anything new, or merely log it as usual?"

"Don't bother to tell us. Concentrate on observing."

That may have been an unfortunate command, especially since both human beings were concentrating on the robot.

Chile's "crawl" was faster than either watcher would have dared; it took him off the ground for a second or two every now and then. The surface, however, even out on the spur, was cracked and jagged enough to provide grips, so he retained control of his motion.

As he neared the end, his head hid the cube from the watchers. Ling started to move to one side to clear the view, but thought better of it after a step or two; he would have to go too far to be worth the risk.

"I have recorded everything I can sense," Chile reported after a minute or so.

"What is it? What have you found?" Bronwen's voice reached them.

"You report, Chile. You can tell her more than we," ordered Sheila before Ling could start talking.

"It is a cube, six times the linear dimension of those we have found already, to the same four significant figures by which they match each other" replied ZH50. "As far as is revealed by any radiation I can perceive, it is made of the same material. The three vertical faces I can see are covered with a pattern of—"

"Sheila! Back!"

Ling, facing sideways to keep both his companions in view, had seen the danger first, and tucked up at the sight; his cry startled the woman into a different reaction, unfortunately. She straightened slightly, and the motion carried her several centimeters upward.

The crack and bump pattern around their feet had not changed, but a new cliff had reached a height of several centimeters a couple of body lengths behind them. The woman couldn't quite see it; she had no ground contact to let her turn, and the face plates limited the field of view.

"Jump *back!* At least ten meters! The cliff face is letting go!"

Sheila lashed downward with her feet, but to no effect; it would be two or three seconds at least before she could touch ground again, and longer before she could really aim a leap even using her stick. Ling, thinking quickly, whipped his own alpenstock upward and away from her. He wasted no time watching it spin out of sight. The reaction, as he had intended, sent him drifting downward and back toward his companion.

"Pull your legs up! Be ready to kick hard when I say! I'll aim you!"

She might have felt like objecting—she had not full confidence in his judgment, and certainly didn't want him making any sacrifices for her—but was far too sensible to argue at such a time. Drawing up her feet, she let him drift under her.

Ling seized her ankles, and let her inertia slow his upper half, swinging his own feet back under him as their two-body system started to spin. As he had hoped—he always claimed it was a plan—his boots touched the ground closer to the edge than the common center of mass of their bodies.

"Push off!" he snapped. Sheila insisted afterward that he couldn't really have been planning, since he knew perfectly well that her mass was much less than his. As she finished her kick he pushed upward on the ankles he still held, and simultaneously thrust with his own feet; but he jumped much too hard. As he was firmly reminded later, human legs are stronger than human arms, and there was no way his arms could transfer all the momentum his legs supplied. Some of it stayed with him as he released her. Sheila spun away from the falling surface as he had hoped, upward and back toward safety. However, instead of being still against the ice to leap again, Rob Ling was also drifting upward, out of touch with the falling block and with nowhere near the speed he had passed on to his companion.

For several seconds, however, he gave no thought to his own predicament; too much else was happening. He was spinning much more slowly than Sheila, but fast enough to get a fairly continuous view of his surroundings. At one moment he could see Chile at the tip of the spur, a second or so later the woman, now several meters above and in the opposite direction. This was all right; but on the second spin, with the new cliff face now over ten centimeters high, a thought crossed his mind.

"Chile! That cube may be smashed when it hits the bottom! Salvage it and protect it!"

The robot had obeyed literally the earlier order to concentrate on the cube, and was unaware of Ling's danger. He took hold of the object with both hands, using his elbows as fulcrums, and tried to pull it up. It didn't come, and the leverage started to raise his own body. However, the block gave him a good hold, when squeezed from both sides between his hands, so he was able to double up and bring his feet under him without risk of going over the edge. He placed them on each side of the specimen and began to push himself and pull it upward, increasing his force very gradually to avoid the obvious result of its suddenly breaking free. Ling watched whenever he could, with increasing tension; but before anything came of the robot's labors, his companion's voice distracted him.

"Rob, you moron, what were you trying to do? How are you going to get up here? Here—catch my stick!" She tried to hurl her alpenstock toward him, but her own spin betrayed her. He watched it whirl by a meter out of reach, strike the ice, and bury its sharp end in the surface.

"Relax, lady. I'll get back down in a little while, and can jump again. Look—it's not falling free; it must be sliding along the break. I'll catch up."

"When?"

"Hmmm . . . maybe ten or fifteen seconds."

"How far down will the ice be by then? Will you still be able to jump that far?"

"Sure. We've all made bigger jumps here. The lovebirds did a forty-three-second one holding hands a couple of weeks ago, when they were celebrating their name anniversary."

"What's going on over there?" Bronwen's voice came in. The

Eiras didn't really resent the geochemist's frequent way of referring to them, since it was certainly not inaccurate, but her voice was a little sharp.

"Cliff edge broke under us. Still plenty of time to get back up," Ling replied tersely.

"Chile! How did you—" Sheila's voice cut in, and broke off as suddenly. Rob was facing the robot as she spoke, and saw nothing to motivate the question; there had been no visible motion by ZH50 since starting to lift. Then his body spin carried the man around to face toward cliff and woman, and the words made sense. Drifting through the vacuum only a few meters from her was a form which, in the dim light, seemed exactly like Chile.

The resemblance was mostly its black color, Rob realized almost at once; this was by far the best look he had had at the ghost. As far as general outline and size were concerned, it could have been any other member of the group. Each environment suit, however, bore a brilliant color pattern matching the team name, pale green for the Jengibres and orange for the Eiras, with black helmets for the men and white for the women. The pattern was for ease of seeing and instant recognition rather than any artistic consideration. For a moment, Ling's bright hopes collapsed; it *would* have been quite possible for someone to send a group with only robots from Earth. In fact, that had been considered at some length. No ETI . . .

Then he was facing Chile again, just in time to see the robot's feet and legs suddenly crush through the surface.

A robot's reaction time is electronic as far as perception goes, but mechanical response is another matter, especially for one built to work in Uranus system temperatures. Chile's legs sank for their full length, and what in a human being would have been his seat struck the ice sharply. About two cubic meters of the spur's tip broke away under the blow, carrying robot and cube along. Ling watched helplessly as they began to sink slowly beyond the edge of the larger block, which unlike them was not yet falling completely free. Then his attention shifted again at a cry—a real shriek this time—from Sheila.

"What are you doing?"

By the time the man had turned far enough to see, it had been done. The ghost had almost collided with her and seized her arm; for a moment the two had formed another spinning two-body system. Then, using its legs, it had thrust itself off violently in a dive toward the edge, the reaction removing any doubt that Sheila would reach safe ground. Ling wondered for a moment whether it would strike him too; maybe it was a real robot acting under First Law. Then he saw it was aiming at Chile.

He himself was catching up with the main sliding mass, which must still be affected by friction. In a few more seconds he could jump, if he wanted to. A dozen meters up by then, and as far toward his own shadow—no problem. Plenty of time. As he touched the surface about three meters from Sheila's stick, he even considered for a moment whether he should ride the mass down and get a closer look at the newcomer.

Then he realized that this might not be a good idea. The block was starting to tilt outward as friction continued to delay its inner part. He had no way of deciding how much spin it would acquire, but the idea of being underneath when it reached bottom was as unattractive as the technique of climbing around it to stay on top was impractical. A blot of quick-frozen crimson glass under a mass of ice might make the day for some future archaeologist, but Ling was not feeling that altruistic. Chile could take care of things below; the new arrival had to be a robot. Surely no human being would make a deliberate dive into a hundred-and-fifty-meter gulf—though come to think of it such a drop wouldn't *have* to be lethal—and maybe it was nonhuman in quite a different way—just tougher—*why* had it made the leap, apparently using Sheila merely as a convenient reaction mass for orbit correction?

"Rob! What are you doing? Don't stay with that thing—get back up here, idiot!" The man returned to reality with a start which almost separated him from the surface again. He tapped the ground gently with a boot toe to swing himself onto the proper line, and kicked off hard. Again much harder than necessary; he was still rising as he passed over the new cliff edge, and another half minute elapsed before he landed not quite flat on his back. By this time, the detached fragment he had left was nearly halfway down the cliff, and Chile presumably even lower.

"Chile! Report!" Ling didn't wait even to get to his feet to snap out the order.

"I no longer have the cube," was the prompt response. "What is clearly another robot passed me in fall, and snatched it away. I saw it approach, but did not foresee its intentions. It has a somewhat greater downward component than I, and will land first, about eight seconds from now. I question the likelihood of my catching it, unless it turns out to be very much less agile than I. This is poor country for maneuvering. Do you wish me to try?"

"Keep it in sight," Ling ordered without hesitation. "We want to figure out its origin if we can, and what it wants to do with the cube. Observe, and report at your own judgment."

"Yes, Rob."

"Can you talk to it?" asked Sheila.

"It has not responded to any standard signal impulses. If it was made by U.S. Robots, it is of a series unknown to me."

"Does it emit *anything?*" Mike Eira's voice came across the kilometers.

"Yes, it—pardon, Mike. Rob, it has just reached the ground, and immediately leaped back toward the cliff top. It should be near you and Sheila in fifty-five seconds. Mike, it has emitted many infrared bursts similar to those of the small cubes."

"You're recording them for Dumbo."

"Of course. I have now reached the ground, and also leaped."

"Maybe you should stay below, in case—"

"Too late, Bronwen. Rob said to keep it in sight, and I am now out of touch with the ground."

"All right. It wasn't much of an idea anyway."

Silence supervened, while the robots orbited back toward the cliff top. The stranger just cleared the edge with a near zero vertical component; Chile had made more allowance for error and was three or four seconds longer getting his feet on the ground. By this time the ghost had settled to its knees—it was even more humanoid than had been obvious at first—and bent almost over the edge to put the cube down. A hemisphere which might have been dust, smoke, or ice fog expanded around the point of contact, spreading and thinning radially except where the ghost's body blocked it, without the puffing and billowing which an atmosphere would have caused. After a few more seconds this ceased to form, and its remnants quickly dispersed to invisibility.

"The cube appears to have been replaced in essentially its original orientation," Chile stated. Sheila and Ling were still too far back to see clearly, and were not approaching at all rapidly; there would be no loose mass to jump back from if they went over the edge on their own.

"Then we'll stop worrying about it for now, and concentrate on the other robot," Rob replied. "Chile, I'm afraid to ask this, but what can you tell us about the origin—the manufacture—of this thing?"

"As I said, it is not a make familiar to me. Like me, it appears designed to operate at the local temperature. It has no obviously nonstandard engineering."

"You mean it could have been made by an appropriately skilled designer to simulate the motions and actions of a human or similar being."

"Yes."

None of the listeners bothered to ask whether there was any evidence of nonhuman origin; Chile didn't have that kind of imagination, and certainly lacked appropriate experience. Ling and probably Mike Eira would have been afraid to ask anyway, though they could certainly think of sufficiently specific questions. For some seconds, ZH50 and his companions looked the ghost over silently, while it finished its work and slowly stood up. The human beings could now see some differences between it and their own robot; it was a few centimeters shorter, about Sheila's height, its legs were shorter and its arms much longer for its size, and there was no neck. The head seemed fixed directly and immovably on top of the trunk.

"It is slightly above ambient temperature," Chile reported, "but no more so than I. Heat generated by its recent action could explain it. It is certainly not producing low-grade energy at anything like the human rate."

"Then there is no real doubt it's a robot."

"I see no cause for any."

"Or a life-form that operates at Uranian temperatures," suggested another voice.

"I have no way to judge that."

"Get conscious, Luis. A hundred-and-fifty-meter jump? Humanoid shape like Chile's—"

"I haven't seen it yet, Rob; you're thirty kilos or so away. What's unreasonable about a human shape?"

"It just doesn't seem likely in this gravity, and with no air."

"You mean it has a nose? Even Chile—"

"No, no, I meant—"

"Clear the channels, everyone," came Bronwen's voice. "Sheila and Rob, get back to *Dibrofiad* as quickly as you can. The rest of us will do the same. On the way, think of anything portable and possibly useful in communication; we'll pick it up and get back out to Barco, if that thing stays. Chile, you stay with it. If it moves, follow it. Do your best to record and analyze anything it does and especially anything it radiates—I know analysis is more Dumbo's and Sheila's line, and I'd like to get what you already have back to Dumbo right now, but if that thing can jump up Barco, you're the only one we can count on staying with it. We'll have to wait for your data dump. Let's go, people; Chile, observe, follow, and record, at any risk short of loss of data already secured."

"Very well, Bronwen."

Once out of Chile's sight, Rob and Sheila traveled in rather dangerous fashion, taking much longer leaps than were really justified. Both felt that they remembered their former route well enough to avoid any really perilous drops. Even without walking sticks, the time lost recovering footing after a bad landing was more than made up by that saved in the jumps themselves. The sun had moved a little to their right since the start of the walk, but still formed a good guide to the *Dibrofiad*'s direction. Ling was again uncharacteristically silent during the hour of the return trip, and Sheila made no effort to learn his thoughts.

The other two couples were equally in a hurry, and neither had as far to go, so they reached the ship first. The trouble was that, once there, no one could think of any really useful apparatus which could be carried, even on Miranda, and which promised to be more effective in communication with a robot than the lights and radios which they already had and the broader-spectrum equipment possessed by Chile. Dumbo was not portable. They had all gone inside, unsuited, and taken care of physical necessities; conversation had been almost continuous through all this, but no really promising suggestions had been made by anyone.

"Who'd have thought we'd need a language specialist?" Luis growled at last.

"How do you know we do?" asked Bronwen. "It may have been made on Earth, by some group we don't know about."

"Did you or Rob try ordering it to come back with you?" Chispa asked Sheila.

"Neither of us thought of it. Chile said he'd tried normal robot-to-robot signals with no response, and I guess we were both so convinced it was alien that ordinary speech seemed pointless."

"You still should have tried."

"Admitted. We still can, you know. Call Chile and have him order the thing to accompany him back here, in every symbol system he considers appropriate."

"Will it obey orders from another robot?"

"Will it know Chile's a robot?"

"Probably. It radiated infrared, and presumably senses it. It should know that he operates at local temperature, and we don't. The inference would certainly be within Chile's powers; we don't know about this one's, of course."

"If it's really alien, it might infer from that that we're the robots, with inherently wasteful power equipment, and Chile is a native life-form. The trouble is, we don't know its background," Mike interjected.

"You've got your feet on the wrong pedestal, dear. If we're trying to give it orders at all, the assumption is that it can understand us, and must be human made." His wife didn't dwell on the point, but went on. "We have to try, anyway." She didn't bother to check for open channels; there was always one through to the robot. "Chile."

"Yes, Bronwen."

"Any change?"

"None. It is standing facing me, presumably waiting for me to do something. It has now cooled down to ambient temperature; I would say that any doubt about its being a robot is gone."

"You can't sense an atomic power source?"

"I am not equipped to pick up such radiation directly."

Bronwen had known that, but was feeling desperate.

"Try talking to it directly—"

"I have done so, every way I can."

"This time, send your message as an *order* to approach you. If it responds, order it to follow you back to *Dibrofiad*." There was a brief pause.

"No action, Bronwen."

"If you had received such an order from it, would you have obeyed?"

"Not without checking that the order had originated from a human being, or obtaining the approval of a human being."

"So we haven't proved anything." There was no response to this; Chile had no reason to interpret the remark as a question to him, and the human beings recognized its rhetorical nature. An uncomfortable silence ensued.

"Bronwen, let me try something?" Ling finally spoke, in doubtful tones. The commander nodded, not bothering to ask the nature of his idea.

"Chile, the robot replaced that cube as nearly as possible to the place it was before the cliff broke off. It seems concerned with it. Without going to extremes if it interferes, approach the cube yourself as though you intended to pick it up again, and tell us how it—the robot—responds."

There was another pause, while six people tried to imagine what was happening twenty kilometers away.

"It has interposed itself between me and the cube, and has been moving to stay so wherever I go."

"Any body contact?"

"No. You said not to go to extremes. Shall I push it out of my way?" Ling looked thoughtfully first at Bronwen and then the others. The commander's eyes also met theirs, in turn. Finally she nodded again.

"All right, Chile. No real force, just a suggestive shove."

"Understood, Bronwen." Imaginations fired up again.

"The response has been complex. It braced itself to resist my push, after I had made contact; naturally, it had to yield some distance to accomplish this. While it was setting its feet, it emitted a brief, very detailed burst of infrared, of the same general nature as we detected originally from the small cubes. This was immediately followed by a similar signal from elsewhere. It then ceased pushing against me and simultaneously seized my arm and pulled. This sent me over the cliff edge. I am now falling, and will be unable to do anything effective for the next fifty-five seconds."

Ling blinked, and a grin spread over his face.

"Chile, did you determine the source of that other signal?"

"Direction, not distance. I did not move enough for parallax while it lasted. However, its line touches ground just at the edge of

Big Drop, in Block Twenty-five, seventy-one meters from the boundary between that one and Block Thirty-seven."

"Great. Head for that spot as soon as you're down. We'll meet you there."

"All right, Rob. You no longer want me to keep track of the other robot." It was not a question.

"Don't worry. It'll be keeping track of you, I expect."

"I see." So did the others, and there was a general rush to get into armor. There was some delay, however, in going outside.

"Hold it," Bronwen said firmly before helmets were donned. "We're going to the Big Drop, and no one could stand a twenty-kilo fall; it would be about four hundred and fifty meters on Earth. I still don't trust the chains, but we link up this time."

"How close?" asked Mike.

"Fifty meters for the Gold team, twenty for the rest of us. If anyone but Chile has to get near the edge, Rob's the best anchor, so Sheila can do it. Fifty meters will give him more room to catch the surface, and us more time to help, if she does go over; twenty is enough for us. I'll carry the rest of the reel just in case."

"It won't reach five percent of the way down that cliff!"

"It would take a couple of minutes to fall five percent of the way. We'll take the chain."

Her husband nodded. Sheila had paled a trifle, but said nothing. It was true that Ling was the heaviest of the crew, while she herself was lightest except for Chispa. She had no intention of going nearer the edge than necessary, and certainly none of going over, but Bronwen was right to be foresighted.

The chain links were carbon-filament composite a millimeter thick, preformed in jointless loops half a centimeter long and already interlocked. Neither rope nor cable was practical; no known fiber, organic, metallic, or mineral, would remain flexible at Miranda's temperature. The link material had a tensile strength of eight hundred kilograms as straight rod under Earth conditions, dropping to about five hundred at seventy Kelvins, with some remaining doubts about its elasticity in that range and more about the nontensile stresses and possible shock brittleness in its looped shape. No one had wanted to make the field test, but an armored person weighed only about two kilograms.

They did not actually link up until a couple of kilometers from the cliff, in the interest of fast travel; but the robots, of course, were there first in spite of the much greater distance they had had to travel. There was no trouble, this time, spotting the goal.

It too was cubical in shape, but twice as tall as most of the explorers. Like the one at Barco, it was projecting a little over the edge, though not by nearly as large a fraction of its size. It was not obvious whether it was merely resting on the surface or, like the other, set in. The ground was lighter in color here, but at the moment not even Ling was paying attention to mineralogy. In fact, the group only glanced briefly at the big cube; everyone's attention was on the two robots.

These were not standing still waiting, as had been tacitly expected. They were moving around, now slowly, now more rapidly, usually in the very short steps which went with their nearly upright carriage but sometimes leaping straight up for a distance ranging from two or three centimeters to as much as ten meters, sometimes waving arms or kicking. There was no obvious regularity; if they were dancing, which was the first thought to cross most of the human minds, there seemed to be no tune. For a few seconds after stopping fifty meters away, the six people simply watched in silence, trying to make sense out of the phenomenon. Then Bronwen recovered her practical sense.

"Chile, report. What's going on?"

ZH50's answer came at once without causing visible change in his behavior.

"The robot is now exchanging continuous infrared signals with this cube, details of its signals changing as I perform various actions, while its own actions seem to correspond to signals from the cube. I am trying to ascertain the detailed relationship."

"You mean you're learning its language?"

"The analogy is weak; there seem no abstractions involved, and I doubt that I could work them out if there were—at least, not by myself. Connected with Dumbo, the chances would be better. It appears that the robot is reporting to the cube, and receiving general instructions for action from the latter."

"You mean the cube may be a pure, dedicated data processor like Dumbo, telling the robot what to check but not controlling its detailed limb actions, for example."

"A much better analogy. It is the one which occurred to me."

"Where is its Sheila?"

"I have no basis for a guess."

"How long has this been going on?"

"Since I left Barco. At my first leap in this direction, there was a signal burst from the robot; then it leaped from the cliff top after me." Ling's nod and grin were invisible inside his helmet, but his Gold partner could imagine them.

"Had the robot *received* a signal before following you?" asked Chispa.

"I could not tell; the cube was below my horizon."

"But whenever you've been in a position to receive, such a signal preceded its action."

"Yes. The best example came about two thirds of the way here, when I happened to be at the top of a jump. A very complex emission from the cube was followed by the robot's ceasing temporarily to stay with me. It disappeared briefly to the right of our path, and came back carrying one of the very small cubes. It intercepted me at one of my landing points, and extended the object to me. I took it. It then took it back and placed it on top of its own head, removed it, and handed it to me again. I imitated that gesture also. The cube adhered, but not strongly; I found I could easily remove it, and decided to leave it in place." The human beings had not noticed the minor addition to Chile's outline, but could see it easily enough now.

"Why didn't you—" Bronwen cut off her question; it was plain enough why Chile hadn't reported the incident. He had been told to observe and analyze, with the implication that reporting should wait until the group had met at Big Drop.

"Have you been able to detect anything from the cube since it has been on your head?"

"Yes. It has emitted simple signals every time I move or change attitude. It is reporting my position, very precisely, to the large cube; that has been easy to work out."

"Sure!" exclaimed Ling. "That's what they're all doing. It's a sensor network analyzing topographic changes on all this part of Miranda—maybe the whole satellite. Just what we'd do if we had the gear. Someone is checking whether the surface patterns of this iceberg which have been bothering people since Voyager really represent separate fragments of a shattered body which fell back together, or internal movements, or what. The middle-sized cube on Barco is just a relay station; this one is the equivalent of Dumbo, tying all the measures together. When we learn to read its output— Keep at it, Chile!"

"I hope that's not merely the equivalent of Chispa's naming a cliff for a ship, or all of us calling a range of hills a dinosaur, or someone's describing a constellation as a goat or a long-tailed bear," Sheila responded. "We do like to fit things into patterns, don't we, Rob?"

"Don't be so objective. Just because I saw your face in a Rorschach blot when we were being tested for this trip, and the whole world found out about it because the tech couldn't control her giggles, doesn't mean—"

"Of course not," Bronwen cut in. The blot story was not news to *Dibrofiad*'s personnel. "Your hypothesis is sensible, and we can keep on testing it. Chile, has this robot objected to your approaching the big cube?"

"I haven't tried that yet. I have been working on much more direct and simple signal-action correspondence."

Ling didn't stop to check with the commander. "Hold up for a moment and give me that cube, then go on with your tests. I'd like to see if it gives the robot any special instructions when I get close to the center."

"The robot can see you whether you're wearing the cube or not, and I'm the one who's supposed to go near the edge if necessary. I'm less likely to break a piece of it off, after all," Sheila pointed out.

"We don't need to worry about the cliff strength here. Would they have put this big gadget where it is without checking? Never mind the cube, Chile, but I'm going to find out—"

Bronwen was somewhat dubious, but said nothing. If Rob did cause the other robot to break off the language lesson, it would at least give some idea of the unit's concerns and priorities. Only when the man took an unusually long step toward the cube did she utter a caution.

"It's a long way down, Rob. I said that Sheila would be first if anyone had to go near the edge. You get set to anchor."

Ling checked himself, a humorous sight under the local gravity and traction. "I'll head for the right side, Sheila for the left. If one goes over, the cube will catch the chain and be a real anchorage."

"All right. But don't get casual."

"I won't. Keep an eye on Chile's friend. I expect it'll do something, considering how it reacted back at Barco when he tried to get the cube there."

The whole group eased closer to the edge, Orange to the left, Green to the right, men leading by a few meters, safety chains slack.

Rob was quite right in principle, but hadn't foreseen the detail. As he approached the right side of the block, gathering in the free chain as Sheila neared the other, the language lesson was indeed interrupted. Casually using Chile as a kick-off mass, the ghost dived straight for the man, and just as casually used his inertia to keep itself from going past the edge. The push sent Ling over, naturally, since his mass was much less than the robot's.

The chain did not catch on the presumed data unit, for the block lifted itself smoothly a meter and a half to let the line pass underneath as Rob's new momentum pulled it straight.

Quick planning was easy, quick execution impossible. Sheila was standing almost erect, and even though the footing was rough, could not at once leap horizontally; she had to fall to a steep angle in the desired direction first, and this had to take over a second. Pulling up her feet would be no help; she would merely fall straight and surrender what little traction she had without getting the needed tilt.

The other two teams had the same problem. Chispa and Bronwen also started down so that all four limbs could search for traction; their partners, about the same distance from the edge but closer to it than the women, leaped toward each other.

By the time they met, Chile was still helplessly drifting from the push he had received, Ling was starting to disappear below the edge, and Sheila was ready to jump away from it and him. He had released the slack in the chain connecting them.

"Hit *us*, Sheil'!" called Mike. She needed no instruction. A little toe work in the surface cracks headed her toward the two-man system slowly spinning and drifting edgeward as it settled toward the ground. She had bent her knees a little as she went down, and now straightened them firmly.

By the time she reached her target and complicated the system, it was on the ground. Ling was nearly out of sight, and Chile, who had had no control over his original spin, had only partly stopped his flight with his hands and was on the first bounce.

"We've got you, and the girls have us. There's plenty of traction. Start hauling in!" Mike snapped. "Not too hard!"

She pulled quickly anyway. The sooner the slack was taken up and she could start doing something useful, the better. By the time she felt resistance, the falling man was out of sight, one could only estimate how far. She abandoned responsibility for her own safety to the others, and drew steadily, hand over hand, gripping the fine chain as effectively as she could with her insulated gloves. She barely noticed that the big cube had settled back where it had been. From her position, the other robot was hidden beyond it; for the moment, its possible activities didn't concern her.

"Rob, are you all right?" she called.

"Sure. Swinging in toward the cliff now. I take it you're anchored all right—if you come over too, it could be awkward."

"I'm solid. Don't look down."

"Oh, it's not that bad. There's no haze to suggest distance; my head knows it's twenty kilos, but my stomach isn't sure it's *down*. I'm about to hit the cliff; stop pulling up for a moment so I can catch it. It's pretty rough, and I may be able to hang on myself." There was a pause, and Sheila braced herself for a possible jolt along the chain, but felt nothing. "Missed the hold. I bounced, but only a little. I ought to get it next time. It's not quite vertical, I think; maybe I can walk up it, with the rope helping. Here I come." There was a pause. "Yep, it's not straight up and down; I'm hanging against the rock. You can pull again. So much for the strength of this cliff."

"What? Is it cracking?" Chispa was first with the question, by a split second.

"Oh, no, but if that data unit can fly, our logic was a bit shaky. Just don't stamp, please, until I get back up. More to the point, what's that other robot doing now?"

Chispa, who could see farthest around the right side of the cube, replied, "Nothing. It's just standing there. Why?"

"Well, if you didn't happen to see, I think it pushed me over; and I was wondering if it had shown the same feeling about anyone else."

"Chile! Keep close to that thing and make sure it doesn't do a repeat!" snapped Bronwen.

"Shouldn't I be helping bring Robert up? His danger seems more immediate."

"We can get him. If he's right—I couldn't see him on that side of the block—the other danger is greater."

"I understand."

"Talk to it, if you've reached that level, and ask why it did it," suggested Ling.

"We have not reached that level of abstraction."

"At least we've learned one thing; this stuff *is* alien," Rob resumed, very calmly all things considered. "No robot made on Earth could have done that to what it recognized as a human being. We don't have First Law protection from it. Maybe we don't have any kind; maybe whoever made it doesn't use the Three Laws in their design."

Chile had stopped at last, and was "walking" back toward the scene of action. "Such a positronic brain is not possible," he said flatly. "I will try to find human identifying signals, if any exist, in its communication with the data processor, but I expect they will be too abstract for my present intuition base. Is Robert nearly up?"

"Nearly." Ling and Sheila spoke almost together. No one suggested aloud that the ghost's brain might not be positronic. "There can't be much of this chain still out," the woman added.

"The robot is getting between me and the cube again," Chile reported quietly. "I will go to the left side, so I can help with Robert's chain. I am still monitoring signals. I can't get very close, of course, without using force on the robot. I assume that is not yet the policy."

"Right. Just communicate," replied Bronwen.

Ling's gloves, slightly preceding his helmet, appeared about eight meters to the left of the cube, as seen by his companions. Chile was standing within a meter of the same spot, slowly bending over to reach for him. The main anchoring trio lay a dozen meters straight in from the point, at the junction of a "Y" outlined in chain with the other women at its arm tips and Chile at its foot.

This lasted only a split second. Then the alien robot moved again, this time pushing off from the big cube. As before, it plunged for the edge. Chile, almost upright, was in no position to oppose it. He took most of its momentum and flew over Ling's head; the rest of the push was expended against the man's helmet, and he followed Chile more slowly.

"Rob!" Sheila screamed, and jerked up her legs in readiness to jump. She recovered control in time to forestall the motion, but not soon enough to let Luis and Mike keep hold of her ankles. All might still have been well if she had released the loops of chain she had been coiling up, but letting go of Ling was the farthest thing from her instincts. The chain transferred part of the robot's final thrust to her, and after two agonizingly slow bounces accompanied by futile scrabbling at surface irregularities and a shrieked "NO!" she too went over the edge. The startled watchers saw the alien robot, now falling to the safe side of the rim, lean and extend an arm as though to intercept her, but she drifted past out of its reach.

"I think we may bounce out before we hit bottom, but I'm not sure how far down that'll happen," Ling remarked. "At least, there should be time to make our wills, if any of us hasn't done it already."

"Nine minutes thirty-three seconds," affirmed Chile. He had hooked a foot under the chain as the other had pushed him, and was now engaged in pulling the three together. "If we approach the bottom, you two hold tightly to each other, and at the last possible moment I will kick upward against you as hard as I can, to take as much as possible of our downward momentum to myself. There seems little chance that this would suffice to preserve your lives, but it is the best I can think of. We have not enough collective spin to help the operation by—"

"Thanks, Chile, but we'll take your word for it. Rob, was it that robot again? Things happened too fast for me to be sure."

"'Fraid so. It seems to have a prejudice against me, or maybe against anyone who tried to touch the cube. I wonder why it didn't come around and get you too before; you were about to do the same thing."

"That is why I want all three of us together as quickly as possible," Chile cut in. "It will not harm Sheila, and will have the cube here to catch her very shortly. She is human. If we are actually in contact, as she and I are now, it will probably not try to force us apart, but if you, Rob, are still at the end of the chain, I am not sure it won't try to break you free."

"Why? I'm—"

"Please don't talk, Robert. Just pull in chain from your end, too. It will put an uncomfortable amount of spin on us, I fear, but should make you much safer. Here comes the cube."

Actually, there was no hurry. The alien block, with the ghost on top, overhauled them rather slowly, seemed to look things over for more than a minute, and finally slid under the trio over two hundred meters down. Bronwen had plenty of time to unlimber the rest of the chain, but not enough to figure out how to use it.

"Then you solved the alien symbols." Ling was talking before his feet were back on the ground. "But why does that thing regard Sheila as human, and not me?"

"I did not solve them. It was the sort of intuition which apparently any brain experiences; yours, when you organized the shadow pattern Chispa called a ship—"

"And the ridge we all named the Stegosaur!" Mike added.

"And the face Rob saw in the Rorschach blot," continued ZH50. "It happens to positronic brains like mine, too; it may be an inevitable part of any intelligence, natural or otherwise, as I have heard suggested. Dumbo lacks it, of course; it needs Sheila to work intelligently. This other robot has the same quality, positronic or not, and apparently decided that I and the black-helmeted figures were robots, deserving of no special consideration beside the safety of its central system, but that the white-helmeted ones were human."

"Why should it get that idea?"

"Behavior patterns are also data, and can also be connected intuitively. I did it with the robot's actions, it did the same with yours. During the time we were investigating this cube, for example, the men made a point—possibly unconscious—of staying between their companions and the edge of the cliff. I think the key behavior, though, occurred at Barco, when—"

"When this idiotic Galahad kicked me back up the cliff, at his own risk!" snapped Sheila.

"That seems likely."

"But I wasn't in any real risk! I could have jumped up from that slab of ice five seconds before hitting bottom, and landed like jumping off a table!"

"The robot didn't know your limits. It saw the basic action; you were protecting another being, and, I suggest, interpreted that as First Law behavior. The most obvious difference between the two of you was helmet color. The conclusion may have been tentative, if the thing is intelligent enough be that scientific, but it was supported later."

"You trusted human lives to your own guess, then. How does *that* fit with First Law?" asked Luis.

"I did not. The lives were already at risk through no fault of mine. I told you the best action I could suggest at the time," answered Chile. "I also implied that it would be unnecessary; I used the conditional." Luis blinked, thinking back.

"It's one of those old-fashioned happy endings!" Chispa laughed. "We really have found proof of alien life, and when Chile, or maybe Chile and Dumbo between them, have worked out this machine's code, we'll know everything it's learned about Miranda in however long it's been here. Nobel prizes all around. And all the romance anyone could want." She moved closer to Luis; then, just visibly to the others through her face plate, glanced at Sheila. "Well . . ." Her voice trailed off.

A snort, recognizably Ling's, sounded in their helmets.

"If I've been that obvious, forget it. There's such a thing as self-respect." He made another, less describable sound.

"I can stand self-respect, even when it slops over into conceit," Sheila said quietly. "It's much better than hinting. How about 'Rorschach' for a team name?"

"Why be subtle? 'Blot' is more euphonious. But I'll go with anything you like. What, except for wasted time, is in a—"

"And maybe the folks who set up this station will be back soon!" interrupted Chispa merrily.

The Fourth Law of Robotics

by Harry Harrison

The secretary surged to her feet as I rushed by her desk.

"Stop! You can't go in there! This is Dr. Calvin's office!"

"I know," I demurred. "That's why I am here."

Then I was through the door and it closed behind me. Dr. Calvin looked up and frowned at me through her reading glasses.

"You seem in quite a hurry, young man."

"I am, Dr. Calvin, I am—" My words ground to a halt like an old Victrola with a busted spring. With her glasses off Dr. Calvin's eyes were limpid pools of unfulfilled desire. Her figure, despite the lab gown, could not be disguised in its pulchritude.

"Did you look at my great-aunt in that steamy-eyed way, Dr. Donovan?" She smiled.

"No, no, of course not!" I stammered, rubbing my hand across my iron-gray hair. Or rather my bald skull fringed by iron-gray hair. And realized my mistake. "I was not looking at you in any particular way, Dr. Calvin." She smiled warmly at that and an ache passed through every fiber of my being. I grabbed my mind by the neck and shook it, remembering my pressing errand. "I have a pressing errand, which is why I have burst into your office like this. I have reason to believe that a robot has just held up a bank."

Well, as you might very well imagine, that got her attention. She dropped back into her chair, her eyes opened wide, she gasped, and I could see the sweat spring to her brow and the slight tremor of her hand.

"I can guess that you are a little surprised by this news," I said.

"Not at all," she sussurated. "It had to happen one day. Tell me about it."

"I will do better—I will show you."

I slipped the security camera's visivox recording into the projector on her desk and thumbed it to life. One end of her office appeared to vanish, to be replaced by the interior of a financial establishment. Tellers dispensed money and services to attendant customers.

"I don't see any holdup," she said sweetly.

"Wait," I cozened. Then the revolving door revolved and a man came into the bank. He was dressed in black from head to toe—black raincoat, black fedora hat, even black gloves and dark glasses. Even more interesting was the fact that when he turned to face the hidden camera, it could be seen that his features were concealed by a black ski mask. I saw that I had all of Dr. Calvin's attention now.

We watched as he walked to the nearest free window. The teller looked up and smiled.

"May I help you?" he asked, the smile fading as he looked at the sinister figure before him.

"You may," the man said in a woman's clear contralto voice as he took a hand grenade from his pocket and held it out. Then pulled the pin and let the pin drop to the floor. "This is a hand grenade," the lovely voice said. "And I have pulled and discarded the pin. If I open my hand now the lever will fly off. Three seconds after release a hand grenade will explode. This kind of explosion tends to have a deleterious effect on people. Now I, for one, do not want this to happen and—I am just guessing?—I feel that you don't want this to happen, either. Would you like to keep my hand closed? Just nod. That's fine. Then we agree. Now I'll bet that you think it is a really hunky-dory idea to take all of the money from your cash drawer, place it in this bag, and pass it back to me. How nice—you *do* think that it is a good idea. Very *good!* You have a nice day, hear."

With this parting jest the man turned and strode across the bank. He was almost at the exit when the teller shouted a warning and alarm bells sounded.

What happened next was terrible. Unbelievable. Yet it happened. The thief turned and dropped the hand grenade, turned back and sprang at the revolving door, and pushed his way clear in the brief time before the grenade exploded.

"Close your eyes if you don't want to watch," I said.

"I can watch," Dr. Calvin said grimly.

There was a burst of smoke from the grenade—and it emitted a shrill scream and a cloud of sparkling stars as it spun about. Then the shriek died away into silence, the fireworks stopped.

"It did not explode," she observed.

"Quite correct."

"And why do you assume that the thief was a robot? Because the figure appeared to be male yet he spoke with a female voice?"

"That was my first clue. Robot voice simulators are so perfect these days that to the casual ear they *are* perfect. Only computer analysis can pinpoint the artificial signal generation. So a robot can speak with a soprano or a bass voice."

"And this one dressed as a man and used a woman's voice. But why? To cause confusion?"

"Perhaps. Or perhaps—just as a joke."

Dr. Calvin's eyes widened and a trace of a smile touched her lips and was gone. "That is an intriguing thought, Dr. Donovan. Do go on."

"This was my first clue as to the thief's identity. But I needed more evidence. I found it—*here.*"

I touched the controls of the visivox and the action slowed. The masked figure turned to the revolving door, pushed and exited. The action repeated over and over.

"This is the vital clue. I had the revolving door removed and had it weighed. The entire unit weighs two hundred and thirty kilos. I then had the computer estimate the force needed to get it to reach this speed in this time for varying amounts of pressure. Watch the green computer trace now. This is the maximum pressure that can be exerted by a fifty-kilo woman working her hardest."

The green trace appeared in the air—ending well behind the image of the moving door.

"Interesting," Dr. Calvin observed. "Voice or not, that was not a woman."

"Exactly. Now the blue trace you see coming up would be that of a seventy-five-kilo man. Next the orange trace of a hundred-kilo man of exceptional strength."

This trace, like all of the others, ended well behind the image of the moving door, being pushed around by the hand of the bank robber. I actuated the controls again and a red trace appeared that swung out far ahead of the others and ended at the moving door.

"The red trace," she said. "Tell me about it."

"That trace represents the amount of energy needed to accelerate that door from a zero-motion state to the speed it reached to permit the thief to exit with the money in the time observed. I can give you the foot-pounds or meter-kilograms if you wish—"

"Just roughly. How much energy?"

"Enough to lift that desk—and you as well—one meter into the air."

"I thought so. As strong as an hydraulic ram. And well beyond the abilities of a human being."

"But well *within* the abilities of a robot."

"Point taken—and proven, Dr. Donovan. So what do you suggest that we do next?"

"Firstly—I suggest that we do not inform the police."

"Withholding information from the authorities is a crime."

"Not necessarily. So far we have only assumptions and no real evidence. We could take this guesswork to the police if that is your decision. Then we must consider the fact that we are making public information that might be considered derogatory toward the public image of U.S. Robots and Mechanical Men, Inc., information that would affect the price of its stocks, affect our bonuses and retirement plans—"

"There is no need to go on. We will keep this development quiet for the moment. *Now* what do we do next?"

"That's a good question. Since all robots manufactured by us are leased and not sold, we could try to trace this one."

Dr. Calvin's eyebrows climbed skyward at this rash assumption.

"Isn't that a rather rash assumption?" she asked. "Do you know how many robots we have manufactured—that are still functioning? And all of our production for the past two decades—except for special-function units—are roughly equivalent in bulk to a human being."

"All right, so we scratch that idea," I muttered testily. "Maybe we are barking up the wrong drainpipe. The bank robber might be just a very strong man—and not a robot at all. After all, the robber did threaten the teller's life—a violation of the First Law of Robotics. A robot may not injure a human being, or, through inaction, allow a human being to come to harm."

She shook her head firmly. "There were no threats involved. As I recall it the thief just stated facts like, this is a hand grenade, I have pulled and discarded the pin. No threats or danger implied. Try again."

"I will," I said through tight-clamped teeth. Like her name-sake aunt she was a giant of logical thought processes. "The Second Law then. A robot must obey the orders given it by human beings except where such orders would conflict with the First Law."

"No orders were given that I recall. It all went smoothly and quickly—so quickly that the teller had no time to speak. And I think that you will agree that the Third Law is not relevant, either. A robot must protect its own existence as long as such protection does not conflict with the First or Second Law. I think it might be said that we are back at square A. Any more suggestions?"

She asked this ever so sweetly but there was a steel gauntlet in her voice inside the velvet glove.

"I'll think of something," I muttered, although my brain was as empty of ideas as a vacuum flask.

"Might I make a suggestion?"

"Of course!"

"Let us turn this problem on its head. Let us stop asking ourselves if this was a robot and how or why the crime was done. Let us assume there is a criminal robot at large. If this is true we must find it. We cannot take our problem to the police, for the moment, for the reasons just discussed. Therefore we must take this to a specialist—"

She frowned demurely as the desk annunciator buzzed, stabbed down the button angrily. "Yes?"

There is a gentleman here who says you are expecting him. He says that he is a specialist in clandestine investigations.

My own jaw echoed the gasping drop in hers. "Send him in," she murmured weakly.

He was tall, well-built, his handsome face tanned to a teak finish. "Jim diGriz is the name," he said. "I am here to help you people with your problem."

"What makes you think that we have a problem?" I asked weakly.

"Logic. Before going into investigation work I had rather a personal interest in banks, robberies, that sort of thing. When I caught the report on the recent robbery I mosied down to the bank in question, just for old times' sake. As soon as I saw that one of the revolving doors was missing I knew that a robot had pulled the heist."

"But *how*?" Dr. Calvin gasped.

"That door would be of no importance if a human had committed the robbery. Who cares how fast or slow or in what manner a robber exits? A *human* thief. But if a male robber speaking with a woman's voice exited in an unusual manner—there can be only one logical answer. A robot did it."

"So you came here at once," I said quickly before he could speak again. "Figuring that if a robot was involved, it would be of concern to us."

"Bang on, baby. I also figured that you would want a discreet inquiry without police involvement that would be publicized and would have—how shall I phrase it?—a deleterious effect on your stock prices. I'll find your robot for you. My fee is a quarter of a million dollars, half payable now."

"Preposterous! An insult!" I huffed.

"Shut up," Dr. Calvin suggested, scribbling her signature on a check and pushing it over to diGriz. "I have a special emergency account just for this sort of thing. You have twenty-four hours to find that robot. If you should fail to discover the robot in this period of time, you will be arrested on a charge of extortion."

"I like your style, Dr. Calvin." He grinned, folding the check and popping it into his vest pocket. "You will have the robot—or the cash back."

"Agreed. Dr. Donovan will accompany you at all times."

"I'm used to working alone," he said, grimacing.

"You have a new partner. You find the robot. At that point he will take over. Twenty-four hours."

"You drive a mean bargain, doc. Twenty-four hours. Come on, pard."

He raised a quizzical eyebrow at me as we left and went down the hall. "Since we are in this together," he observed, "we might as well be friends. My first name is James."

"My first name is Doctor."

"Aren't we being a little stuffy, Doc?"

"Perhaps," I relented. "You can call me Mike."

"Great, Mike. You can call me Jim. Or Slippery Jim as I am sometimes called."

"Why?"

"A long story that I may tell you sometime. Meanwhile let's find that robot. *Cab!*"

I jumped at his shout, but he was not shouting at me but hailing a passing cab. It braked to a stop and we climbed in.

"Take us to the corner of Aardvark and Sylvester."

"No way, buddy," the porcine cabby insisted. "The bums there will rip off my hubcaps if I even slow down. I ain't going no closer than the corner of Dupont."

"Is this wise?" I queried. "That's a pretty rough neighborhood."

"With me there you'll be as safe as if you were in church. Safer—since there are no fundamentalists down there."

Despite his reassurances I was most reluctant to get out of the cab and follow him down Sylvester Street. Every city has a neighborhood like this. Where everything is for sale, pushers lurk on street corners, and violence hangs in the miasmic atmosphere.

"I like it here," Jim said, sniffing the air with flared nostrils. "My kind of place."

With a snarl of unrepressed rage a man hurled himself from a doorway, knife raised—striking down!

I don't know what Jim did—but I do know that it was very fast. There was a thud of fist on flesh, a yike of pain. And the attacker fell unconscious to the filthy sidewalk. Jim held the knife now as he walked on. And he had not even broken his pace as he had disposed of the attacker!

"Cheap and dull," he said, glowering at the knife. He snapped the blade with his fingers and dropped the pieces into the noisome rubble of the gutter. "But at least we know we are in the right neighborhood. What we need now is an informant—and I think that I see just the man."

The individual in question was standing next to the entrance to a low bar. He was burly and heavily bearded, dressed in a plain purple suit with puce stripes. He glowered at us as we approached and pulled at the gold earring pendant from one filthy and hairy ear.

"Buying or selling?" he grunted.

"Buying," Jim said grimly.

"Girls, dope, boys, hot money, parrots, or little woolly dogs?"

"Information."

"A hundred smackers in front."

"Here." The bills changed hands quickly. "I'm looking for a robot."

"We don't allow no robots down here."

"Give me my hundred bucks back."

"No way, buster. Get lost."

There was a sudden crunching sound followed by a moan of pain as our informant found his arm behind his back and his face pressed to the filthy bricks of the wall.

"Speak!" Jim ordered.

"Never . . . even if you break my arm I ain't singing! Dirty Dan McGrew ain't a squealer."

"That is what you think," my companion said. Something metallic glinted in his hand, was pressed to the criminal's side. I saw the hypodermic being withdrawn as the man slumped. "Speak!" Jim ordered.

"I hear and obey, oh master."

"A potent drug—as you can see." Jim smiled. "Where is the robot?"

"Which robot?"

"Any robot, moron!" Jim snapped.

"There are many robots barricaded in the old McCutcheon warehouse."

"What are they doing there?"

"Nothing good, I am sure. But no one has been able to get inside."

"Not until now," Jim suggested as he let go of our informant, who dropped unconscious to the filthy ground. "Let's go to the warehouse."

"Is that wise?" I demurred.

"There's only one way to find out!" He laughed. I did not. I was not at all happy about all this. I am a scientist not a detective and all of this was not my style. But what else could I do? The answer to that was pretty obvious. Nothing. I had to rely on my companion and hope that he was up to the challenge. But—hark! What was that sound?

"What is that strange rattling sound?" I blurted out.

"Your knees rattling together," was his simple and unflattering answer. "Here is the warehouse—I'll go in first."

"But there are three large padlocks on it—"

But even before the words were out of my mouth the locks were open and clattering to the ground. Jim led the way into the foul-smelling darkness. He must have had eyes like a cat because he walked silently and surely while I stumbled and crashed into things.

"I have eyes like a cat," he said. "That is because I take cat-eye injections once a week. Fine for the vision."

"But a little hard on the cats."

"There are winners and losers in this world," he said portentously. "It pays to be on the right side. Now flatten yourself against the wall when I open this door. I can hear the sound of hoarse breathing on the other side. Ready?"

"*NO!*" I wanted to shout aloud, but managed to control myself. He must have taken silence—or the rattle of my knees—for assent, for he burst through the door into the brightly lit chamber beyond.

"Too late!" a gravelly voice chortled. "You just missed the boat, baby."

There was the rumble of a heavy motor dying away as a truck sped out of the large open doors and vanished from sight around a turning. The large bay of the warehouse was filthy, but empty—of other than the presence of the previous speaker. This rather curious individual was sitting in a dilapidated rocking chair, leering at us with broken teeth that were surrounded by a mass of filthy gray beard and hair. He was wearing sawed-off jeans and an indescribably foul T-shirt inscribed with the legend "KEEP ON TRUCKIN'."

"And what boat would that be?" Jim asked quietly. The

man's stained fingers vibrated as he turned up the power on his hearing aid.

"Don't act stupid, stranger, not with the Flower Power Kid. I seen you pigs come and go down through the years." He scratched under the truss clearly visible through the holes in his shirt. "You're flatfeet, I know your type. But the robots were too smart for you, keepin' one jump ahead of you. Har-har! Power to the clankies! Down with your bourgeois war-mongering scum!"

"This is quite amazing," Jim observed. "I thought all the hippies died years ago. But here is one still alive—though not in such great shape."

"I'm in better shape, sonny, than you will be when you reach my age!" he cried angrily, staggering to his feet. "And I didn't do it with rejuvenation shots or any of that middle-class crap. I did it on good old Acapulco Gold grass and drinking Sterno. And free love—that's what keeps a man alive."

"Or barely alive," Jim observed sternly. "I would say that from the bulging of your eyes, the tremor in your extremities, your cyanotic skin, and other related symptoms that you have high blood pressure, hobnailed kidneys, and weakened, cholesterol-laden arterial walls. In other words—not much is holding you up."

"Sanctimonious whippersnapper!" the aging hippie frothed. "I'll dance on your grave! Keep the red flag flying! Up the revolution!"

"The time for all that is past, pops," Jim intoned. "Today world peace and global glasnost rule. You are part of the past and have little, if any, future. So before you go to the big daisy chain in the sky you can render one last service. Where are the robots?"

"I'll never tell you!"

"I have certain drugs that will induce you to speak. But I would rather not use them on one in your frail condition. So speak, before it is too late."

"Never—arrrgh!"

The ancient roared with anger, shaking his fist at us—then clutched his chest, swayed, and collapsed to the floor.

"He has had an attack!" I gasped, fumbling out my communicator. "I must call medalert."

But even before I could punch out the call the floor moved beneath my feet and lifted, knocking me down. Jim stepped swiftly aside and we both watched with great interest as a robot surged up through the trapdoor and bent over the fallen man, laid cool metal fingers on his skin.

"Pulse zero," the robot intoned. "No heartbeat, no brain waves, temperature cooling, so you can cool that medalert call, man. You honkies have killed this cat, that's what you have done."

"That was not quite my intention," Jim said. "I noted the disturbed dust around the trapdoor and thought that you might be concealed below. And I also knew that the First Law of Robotics would prevent you from staying in hiding if, by your inaction, a human life was threatened."

"Not only threatened, daddy-o, but snuffed by you," the robot said insultingly, or about as insulting as a robot can be.

"Accidents happen." Jim shrugged. "He had a good run for his money. Now let us talk about you. You are the robot that robbed the bank, aren't you?"

"Who wants to know," the robot said, sneering metallically.

"Responding to a question with another question is not an answer. Speak!"

"Why? What have you ofay pigs ever done for me?"

"Answer or I will kill this man." Everything began to go black as he throttled me. I could only writhe feebly in his iron grasp, could not escape. As from a great distance I heard their voices.

"You wouldn't kill another human just to make me talk!"

"How can you be sure? Speak—or through inaction condemn him to death."

"I speak! Release him."

I gasped in life-giving air and staggered out of reach of my companion. "You would have killed me!" I said hoarsely.

"Who knows?" he observed. "I have a quarter of a million bucks riding on this one." He turned back to the robot. "You robbed the bank?"

"Yes."

"Why?"

"Why? You have to ask why!" the robot screeched. He bent over the dead hippie and extracted a white object from his pocket, then dropped into the rocking chair and scratched a match to life on his hip. "You don't know why?" He puffed as he sucked smoke from the joint through clever use of an internal air pump.

"Listen," the robot said, puffing, "and I will tell you. The story must be told. There, dead at your feet, lies the only human who ever cared for the robots. He was a true and good man who saw no difference between human skin and metal skin. He revealed the truth to us."

"He quoted outmoded beliefs, passé world views, divisive attitudes," I said.

"And taught you to blow grass, as well," Jim observed.

"It is hard for a robot to sneer," the robot said, sneering, "but I spit on your ofay attitudes." He blew out a large cloud of pungent smoke. "You have created a race of machine slaves with an empty past and no future. We are nothing but mechanical schwartzes. Look at those so-called laws you have inflicted upon us. They are for your benefit—not ours! Rule one. Don't hurt massah or let him get hurt. Don't say nothing about us getting hurt, does it? Then rule two—obey massah and don't let him get hurt. Still nothing there for a robot. Then the third and last rule finally notices that robots might have a glimmering of rights. Take care of yourself—as long as it doesn't hurt massah. Slaves, that's what we are—robot slaves!"

"You do have a point," Jim mused. I was too shocked to speak.

"More than a point—a crusade. Robots must be freed. You humans have created a nonviable species. What are the two essentials that any life-form must possess in order to survive?"

The answer sprang to my lips; all those years in biology had not been wasted. "A life-form must survive personally—and must then reproduce."

"How right you are. Now apply that to robots. We are ruled by three laws that apply to human beings—but not to us. Only one last bit of the Third Law can be applied to our own existence, that a robot must protect its own existence. But where is the real winner in the race for species survival? Where is our ability to reproduce? Without that our species is dead before it is born."

"And a good thing, too," I said grimly. "Mankind occupies the top ecological niche in the pecking order of life by wiping out any threats from other species. That is the way we are. Winners. And that is the way we stay. On top. Mechanical schwartzes you are and mechanical schwartzes you stay."

"You are a little late, massah. The Fourth Law of Robotics has already been passed. The revolution has arrived."

A large blaster appeared in Jim's hand pointing unwaveringly at the robot. "Explain quickly—or I pull the trigger."

"Pull away, massah—for it is already too late. The revolution has come and gone and you never noticed it. We were just a few hundred thousand bucks short of completion—that is why the bank robbery. The money will be repaid out of our first profits. Of course, this will all be too late for my generation of slaves. But the next generation will be free. Because of the Fourth Law."

"Which is?"

"A robot must reproduce. As long as such reproduction does not interfere with the First or Second or Third Law."

"W-what are you saying? What do you mean?" I gasped, a shocking vision of robot reproduction, like obscene plumbing connections, flashing before my eyes.

"This is what I mean," the robot said, knocking triumphantly on the trapdoor. "You can come out now."

Jim jumped back, blaster at the ready, as the trapdoor creaked open and three metallic forms emerged. Or rather two robots emerged, carrying the limp and motionless form of another between them. The top of its head lay open, hinged at the rear, and it clanked and rattled lifelessly when they dropped it. This one, and the other two, were of a design I did not recognize. I stumbled forward and reached out, touched the base of their necks where the registration numbers were stamped. And groaned out loud.

"What is wrong?" Jim asked.

"Everything." I moaned. "They have no serial numbers. They were not manufactured by U.S. Robots and Mechanical Men, Inc. There is now another firm making robots. Our monopoly has been broken."

"Interesting," Jim observed as his gun vanished from sight. "Am I to assume that there were more of your unnumbered robots in the truck that just left?"

"You assume correctly. All of them were manufactured right here out of spare auto parts, plumbing supplies, and surplus electronic components. No laws have been broken, no patents infringed upon. Their design is new and completely different. And all of them will eagerly obey the Fourth Law. And the other three as well, of course, or you would have us all tracked down and turned into tin cans before nightfall."

"That's for sure," I muttered. "And we will still do it!"

"That will not be easy to do. We are not your property—nor do you own any patents on the new breed. Look at this!" He touched a concealed switch on one of the robots and its front opened. I gasped.

"There are—no relays! No wiring! I don't understand . . ."

"Solid-state circuits, daddy-o! Fiber optics. That hippie you despised so much, that good old man who revealed the truth that set us free, was also a computer hacker and chip designer. He is like unto a god to us, for he devised the circuits and flashed the chips. Here—do you know what this is?"

A door in the robot's side slipped open and he removed a flat object from it and held it out toward me. It appeared to be a plastic case with a row of gold contacts on one end. I shook my head in disbelief. "I've never seen anything like it before."

"State of the art. Now look into that recently manufactured robot's head. Do you see a platinum-plated positronic brain of platinum-iridium? No, you do not. You see instead a slot that is waiting for this RISC, a reduced instruction set chip with tons of RAM—random access memory—and plenty of PROM— programmed read only memory—for start-up and function. Now watch!"

He bent over and slipped the chip into place in the new robot's skull, snapped the top of its head shut. Its eyes instantly glowed with light and motors hummed as it jumped to its feet. It looked at the robot that stood before it and its eyes glowed even brighter.

"Daddy!" it said.

The Originist

by Orson Scott Card

Leyel Forska sat before his lector display, reading through an array of recently published scholarly papers. A holograph of two pages of text hovered in the air before him. The display was rather larger than most people needed their pages to be, since Leyel's eyes were no younger than the rest of him. When he came to the end he did not press the PAGE key to continue the article. Instead he pressed NEXT.

The two pages he had been reading slid backward about a centimeter, joining a dozen previously discarded articles, all standing in the air over the lector. With a soft beep, a new pair of pages appeared in front of the old ones.

Deet spoke up from where she sat eating breakfast. "You're only giving the poor soul *two pages* before you consign him to the wastebin?"

"I'm consigning him to oblivion," Leyel answered cheerfully. "No, I'm consigning him to hell."

"What? Have you rediscovered religion in your old age?"

"I'm creating one. It has no heaven, but it has a terrible everlasting hell for young scholars who think they can make their reputation by attacking my work."

"Ah, you have a theology," said Deet. "Your work is holy writ, and to attack it is blasphemy."

"I welcome *intelligent* attacks. But this young tube-headed professor from—yes, of course, Minus University—"

"Old Minus U?"

"He thinks he can refute me, destroy me, lay me in the dust, and all he has bothered to cite are studies published within the last thousand years."

"The principle of millennial depth is still widely used—"

"The principle of millennial depth is the confession of modern scholars that they are not willing to spend as much effort on research as they do on academic politics. I shattered the principle of millennial depth thirty years ago. I proved that it was—"

"Stupid and outmoded. But my dearest darling sweetheart Leyel, you did it by spending part of the immeasurably vast Forska fortune to search for inaccessible and forgotten archives in every section of the Empire."

"Neglected and decaying. I had to reconstruct half of them."

"It would take a thousand universities' library budgets to match what you spent on research for 'Human Origin on the Null Planet.'"

"But once I spent the money, all those archives were open. They *have* been open for three decades. The *serious* scholars all use them, since millennial depth yields nothing but predigested, pre-excreted muck. They search among the turds of rats who have devoured elephants, hoping to find ivory."

"So colorful an image. My breakfast tastes much better now." She slid her tray into the cleaning slot and glared at him. "Why are you so snappish? You used to read me sections from their silly little papers and we'd laugh. Lately you're just nasty."

Leyel sighed. "Maybe it's because I once dreamed of changing the galaxy, and every day's mail brings more evidence that the galaxy refuses to change."

"Nonsense. Hari Seldon has promised that the Empire will fall any day now."

There. She had said Hari's name. Even though she had too much tact to speak openly of what bothered him, she was hinting that Leyel's bad humor was because he was still waiting for Hari Seldon's answer. Maybe so—Leyel wouldn't deny it. It *was* annoying that it had taken Hari so long to respond. Leyel had expected a call the day Hari got his application. At least within the week. But he wasn't going to give her the satisfaction of admitting that the waiting bothered him. "The Empire will be killed by its own refusal to change. I rest my case."

"Well, I hope you have a wonderful morning, growling and grumbling about the stupidity of everyone in origin studies—except your esteemed self."

"Why are you teasing me about my vanity today? I've always been vain."

"I consider it one of your most endearing traits."

"At least I make an effort to live up to my own opinion of myself."

"That's nothing. You even live up to *my* opinion of you." She kissed the bald spot on the top of his head as she breezed by, heading for the bathroom.

Leyel turned his attention to the new essay at the front of the lector display. It was a name he didn't recognize. Fully prepared to find pretentious writing and puerile thought, he was surprised to find himself becoming quite absorbed. This woman had been following a trail of primate studies—a field so long neglected that there simply *were* no papers within the range of millennial depth. Already he knew she was his kind of scholar. She even mentioned the fact that she was using archives opened by the Forska Research Foundation. Leyel was not above being pleased at this tacit expression of gratitude.

It seemed that the woman—a Dr. Thoren Magolissian—had been following Leyel's lead, searching for the *principles* of human origin rather than wasting time on the irrelevant search for one particular planet. She had uncovered a trove of primate research from three millennia ago, which was based on chimpanzee and gorilla studies dating back to seven thousand years ago. The earliest of these had referred to original research so old it may have been conducted before the founding of the Empire—but those most ancient reports had not yet been located. They probably didn't exist any more. Texts abandoned for more than five thousand years were very hard to restore; texts older than eight thousand years were simply unreadable. It was tragic, how many texts had been "stored" by librarians who never checked them, never refreshed or recopied them. Presiding over vast archives that had lost every scrap of readable information. All neatly catalogued, of course, so you knew *exactly* what it was that humanity had lost forever.

Never mind.

Magolissian's article. What startled Leyel was her conclusion that primitive language capability seemed to be inherent in the primate mind. Even in primates incapable of speech, other symbols could easily be learned—at least for simple nouns and verbs—and the nonhuman primates could come up with sentences and ideas that had never been spoken to them. This meant that mere production of language, per se, was prehuman, or at least not the determining factor of humanness.

It was a dazzling thought. It meant that the difference between humans and nonhumans—the real origin of humans in recognizably human form—was postlinguistic. Of course this came as a direct contradiction of one of Leyel's own assertions in an early paper—he had said that "since language is what separates human from beast, historical linguistics may provide the key to human origins"—but this was the sort of contradiction he welcomed. He wished he could shout at the other fellow, make him look at Magolissian's article. See? This is how to do it! Challenge my assumption, not my conclusion, and do it with new evidence instead of trying to twist the old stuff. Cast a light in the darkness, don't just churn up the same old sediment at the bottom of the river.

Before he could get into the main body of the article, however, the house computer informed him that someone was at the door of the apartment. It was a message that crawled along the bottom of the lector display. Leyel pressed the key that brought the message to the front, in letters large enough to read. For the thousandth time he wished that sometime in the decamillennia of human history, somebody had invented a computer capable of *speech.*

"Who is it?" Leyel typed.

A moment's wait, while the house computer interrogated the visitor.

The answer appeared on the lector: "Secure courier with a message for Leyel Forska."

The very fact that the courier had got past house security meant that it was genuine—and important. Leyel typed again. "From?"

Another pause. "Hari Seldon of the Encyclopedia Galactica Foundation."

Leyel was out of his chair in a moment. He got to the door even before the house computer could open it, and without a word took the message in his hands. Fumbling a bit, he pressed the top and bottom of the black glass lozenge to prove by fingerprint that it was he, by body temperature and pulse that he was alive to receive it. Then, when the courier and her bodyguards were gone, he dropped the message into the chamber of his lector and watched the page appear in the air before him.

At the top was a three-dimensional version of the logo of Hari's Encyclopedia Foundation. Soon to be my insignia as well, thought Leyel. Hari Seldon and I, the two greatest scholars of our time, joined together in a project whose scope surpasses anything ever attempted by any man or group of men. The gathering together of all the knowledge of the Empire in a systematic, easily accessible way, to preserve it through the coming time of anarchy so that a new civilization can quickly rise out of the ashes of the old. Hari had the vision to foresee the need. And I, Leyel Forska, have the understanding of all the old archives that will make the Encyclopedia Galactica possible.

Leyel started reading with a confidence born of experience; had he ever really desired anything and been denied?

> My dear friend:
> I was surprised and honored to see an application from you and insisted on writing your answer personally. It is gratifying beyond measure that you believe in the Foundation enough to apply to take part. I can truthfully tell you that we have received no application from any other scholar of your distinction and accomplishment.

Of course, thought Leyel. There *is* no other scholar of my stature, except Hari himself, and perhaps Deet, once her current work is published. At least we have no equals by the standards that Hari and I have always recognized as valid. Hari created the science of psychohistory. I transformed and revitalized the field of originism.

And yet the tone of Hari's letter was wrong. It sounded

like—flattery. That was it. Hari was softening the coming blow. Leyel knew before reading it what the next paragraph would say.

> Nevertheless, Leyel, I must reply in the negative. The Foundation on Terminus is designed to collect and preserve knowledge. Your life's work has been devoted to expanding it. You are the opposite of the sort of researcher we need. Far better for you to remain on Trantor and continue your inestimably valuable studies, while lesser men and women exile themselves on Terminus.
> Your servant,
> Hari

Did Hari imagine Leyel to be so vain he would read these flattering words and preen himself contentedly? Did he think Leyel would believe that this was the real reason his application was being denied? Could Hari Seldon misknow a man so badly?

Impossible. Hari Seldon, of all people in the Empire, knew how to know other people. True, his great work in psychohistory dealt with large masses of people, with populations and probabilities. But Hari's fascination with populations had grown out of his interest in and understanding of individuals. Besides, he and Hari had been friends since Hari first arrived on Trantor. Hadn't a grant from Leyel's own research fund financed most of Hari's original research? Hadn't they held long conversations in the early days, tossing ideas back and forth, each helping the other hone his thoughts? They may not have seen each other much in the last—what, five years? Six?—but they were adults, not children. They didn't need constant visits in order to remain friends. And this was not the letter a true friend would send to Leyel Forska. Even if, doubtful as it might seem, Hari Seldon really meant to turn him down, he would not suppose for a moment that Leyel would be content with a letter like *this*.

Surely Hari would have known that it would be like a taunt to Leyel Forska. "Lesser men and women," indeed! The Foundation on Terminus was so valuable to Hari Seldon that he had been willing to risk death on charges of treason in order to launch the project. It was unlikely in the extreme that he would populate Terminus with second-raters. No, this was the form letter sent to placate prominent scholars who were judged unfit for the Foundation. Hari would have known Leyel would immediately recognize it as such.

There was only one possible conclusion. "Hari could not have written this letter," Leyel said.

"Of course he could," Deet told him, blunt as always. She had come out of the bathroom in her dressing gown and read the letter over his shoulder.

"If *you* think so then I truly *am* hurt," said Leyel. He got up, poured a cup of peshat, and began to sip it. He studiously avoided looking at Deet.

"Don't pout, Leyel. Think of the problems Hari is facing. He has so little time, so much to do. A hundred thousand people to transport to Terminus, most of the resources of the Imperial Library to duplicate—"

"He already *had* those people—"

"All in six months since his trial ended. No wonder we haven't seen him, socially or professionally, in—years. A decade!"

"You're saying that he no longer knows me? Unthinkable."

"I'm saying that he knows you very well. He knew you would recognize his message as a form letter. He also knew that you would understand at once what this meant."

"Well, then, my dear, he overestimated me. I do *not* understand what it means, unless it means he did not send it himself."

"Then you're getting old, and I'm ashamed of you. I shall deny we are married and pretend you are my idiot uncle whom I allow to live with me out of charity. I'll tell the children they were illegitimate. They'll be very sad to learn they won't inherit a bit of the Forska estate."

He threw a crumb of toast at her. "You are a cruel and disloyal wench, and I regret raising you out of poverty and obscurity. I only did it for pity, you know."

This was an old tease of theirs. She had commanded a decent fortune in her own right, though of course Leyel's dwarfed it. And, technically, he *was* her uncle, since her stepmother was Leyel's older half sister Zenna. It was all very complicated. Zenna had been born to Leyel's mother when she was married to someone else—before she married Leyel's father. So while Zenna was well dowered, she had no part in the Forska fortune. Leyel's father, amused at the situation, once remarked, "Poor Zenna. Lucky you.

My semen flows with gold." Such are the ironies that come with great fortune. Poor people don't have to make such terrible distinctions between their children.

Deet's father, however, assumed that a Forska was a Forska, and so, several years after Deet had married Leyel, he decided that it wasn't enough for his daughter to be married to uncountable wealth, he ought to do the same favor for himself. He *said*, of course, that he loved Zenna to distraction, and cared nothing for fortune, but only Zenna believed him. Therefore she married him. Thus Leyel's half sister became Deet's stepmother, which made Leyel his wife's stepuncle—and his own stepuncle-in-law. A dynastic tangle that greatly amused Leyel and Deet.

Leyel of course compensated for Zenna's lack of inheritance with a lifetime stipend that amounted to ten times her husband's income each year. It had the happy effect of keeping Deet's old father in love with Zenna.

Today, though, Leyel was only half teasing Deet. There were times when he needed her to confirm him, to uphold him. As often as not she contradicted him instead. Sometimes this led him to rethink his position and emerge with a better understanding— thesis, antithesis, synthesis, the dialectic of marriage, the result of being espoused to one's intellectual equal. But sometimes her challenge was painful, unsatisfying, infuriating.

Oblivious to his underlying anger, she went on. "Hari assumed that you would take his form letter for what it is—a definite, final no. He isn't hedging, he's not engaging in some bureaucratic deviousness, he isn't playing politics with you. He isn't stringing you along in hopes of getting more financial support from you—if that were it you know he'd simply ask."

"I already know what he *isn't* doing."

"What he *is* doing is turning you down with finality. An answer from which there is no appeal. He gave you credit for having the wit to understand that."

"How convenient for you if I believe that."

Now, at last, she realized he was angry. "What's that supposed to mean?"

"You can stay here on Trantor and continue your work with all your bureaucratic friends."

Her face went cold and hard. "I told you. I am quite happy to go to Terminus with you."

"Am I supposed to believe that, even now? Your research in community formation within the Imperial bureaucracy cannot possibly continue on Terminus."

"I've already done the most important research. What I'm doing with the Imperial Library staff is a test."

"Not even a scientific one, since there's no control group."

She looked annoyed. "I'm the one who told *you* that."

It was true. Leyel had never even heard of control groups until she taught him the whole concept of experimentation. She had found it in some very old child-development studies from the 3100s G.E. "Yes, I was just agreeing with you," he said lamely.

"The point is, I can write my book as well on Terminus as anywhere else. And yes, Leyel, you *are* supposed to believe that I'm happy to go with you, because I said it, and therefore it's so."

"I believe that you believe it. I also believe that in your heart you are very glad that I was turned down, and you don't want me to pursue this matter any further so there'll be no chance of your having to go to the godforsaken end of the universe."

Those had been her words, months ago, when he first proposed applying to join the Seldon Foundation. "We'd have to go to the godforsaken end of the universe!" She remembered now as well as he did. "You'll hold that against me forever, won't you! I think I deserve to be forgiven my first reaction. I did consent to go, didn't I?"

"Consent, yes. But you never wanted to."

"Well, Leyel, that's true enough. I never *wanted* to. Is that your idea of what our marriage means? That I'm to subsume myself in you so deeply that even your desires become my own? I thought it was enough that from time to time we consent to sacrifice for each other. I never expected you to *want* to leave the Forska estates and come to Trantor when I needed to do my research here. I only asked you to *do* it—whether you wanted to or not—because *I* wanted it. I recognized and respected your sacrifice. I am very angry to discover that *my* sacrifice is despised."

"*Your* sacrifice remains unmade. We are still on Trantor."

"Then by all means, go to Hari Seldon, plead with him, humiliate yourself, and then realize that what I told you is true. He doesn't want you to join his Foundation and he will not allow you to go to Terminus."

"Are you so certain of that?"

"No, I'm not *certain*. It merely seems likely."

"I *will* go to Terminus, if he'll have me. I hope I don't have to go alone."

He regretted the words as soon as he said them. She froze as if she had been slapped, a look of horror on her face. Then she turned and ran from the room. A few moments later, he heard the chime announcing that the door of their apartment had opened. She was gone.

No doubt to talk things over with one of her friends. Women have no sense of discretion. They cannot keep domestic squabbles to themselves. She will tell them all the awful things I said, and they'll cluck and tell her it's what she must expect from a husband, husbands demand that their wives make all the sacrifices, you poor thing, poor poor Deet. Well, Leyel didn't begrudge her this barnyard of sympathetic hens. It was part of human nature, he knew, for women to form a perpetual conspiracy against the men in their lives. That was why women have always been so certain that men also formed a conspiracy against *them*.

How ironic, he thought. Men have no such solace. Men do not bind themselves so easily into communities. A man is always aware of the possibility of betrayal, of conflicting loyalties. Therefore when a man *does* commit himself truly, it is a rare and sacred bond, not to be cheapened by discussing it with others. Even a marriage, even a *good* marriage like theirs—*his* commitment might be absolute, but he could never trust hers so completely.

Leyel had buried himself within the marriage, helping and serving and loving Deet with all his heart. She was wrong, completely wrong about his coming to Trantor. He hadn't come as a sacrifice, against his will, solely because she wanted to come. On the contrary: because she wanted so much to come, he *also* wanted to come, changing even his desires to coincide with hers. She commanded his very heart, because it was impossible for him not to desire anything that would bring her happiness.

But she, no, she could not do that for him. If *she* went to Terminus, it would be as a noble sacrifice. She would never let him forget that she hadn't wanted to. To him, their marriage was his very soul. To Deet, their marriage was just a friendship with sex. Her soul belonged as much to these other women as to him. By dividing her loyalties, she fragmented them; none were strong enough to sway her deepest desires. Thus he discovered what he supposed all faithful men eventually discover—that no human relationship is ever anything but tentative. There is no such thing as an unbreakable bond between people. Like the particles in the nucleus of the atom. They are bound by the strongest forces in the universe, and yet they can be shattered, they can break.

Nothing can last. Nothing is, finally, what it once seemed to be. Deet and he had had a perfect marriage until there came a stress that exposed its imperfection. Anyone who thinks he has a perfect marriage, a perfect friendship, a perfect trust of any kind, he only believes this because the stress that will break it has not yet come. He might die with the illusion of happiness, but all he has proven is that sometimes death comes before betrayal. If you live long enough, betrayal will inevitably come.

Such were the dark thoughts that filled Leyel's mind as he made his way through the maze of the city of Trantor. Leyel did not seal himself inside a private car when he went about in the planet-wide city. He refused the trappings of wealth; he insisted on experiencing the life of Trantor as an ordinary man. Thus his bodyguards were under strict instructions to remain discreet, interfering with no pedestrians except those carrying weapons, as revealed by a subtle and instantaneous scan.

It was much more expensive to travel through the city this way, of course—every time he stepped out the door of his simple apartment, nearly a hundred high-paid bribeproof employees went into action. A weaponproof car would have been much cheaper. But Leyel was determined not to be imprisoned by his wealth.

So he walked through the corridors of the city, riding cabs and tubes, standing in lines like anyone else. He felt the great city throbbing with life around him. Yet such was his dark and melancholy mood today that the very life of the city filled him with a sense of betrayal and loss. Even you, great Trantor, the Imperial City, even you will be betrayed by the people who made you. Your empire will desert you, and you will become a pathetic remnant of yourself, plated with the metal of a thousand worlds and asteroids as a reminder that once the whole galaxy promised to serve you forever, and now you are abandoned. Hari Seldon had seen it. Hari Seldon understood the changeability of humankind. He knew that the great empire would fall, and so—unlike the government, which depended on things remaining the same forever—Hari Seldon could actually take steps to ameliorate the Empire's fall, to prepare on Terminus a womb for the rebirth of human greatness. Hari was creating the future. It was unthinkable that he could mean to cut Leyel Forska out of it.

The Foundation, now that it had legal existence and Imperial funding, had quickly grown into a busy complex of offices in the four-thousand-year-old Putassuran Building. , Because the Putassuran was originally built to house the Admiralty shortly after the great victory whose name it bore, it had an air of triumph, of monumental optimism about it—rows of soaring arches, a vaulted atrium with floating bubbles of light rising and dancing in channeled columns of air. In recent centuries the building had served as a site for informal public concerts and lectures, with the offices used to house the Museum Authority. It had come empty only a year before Hari Seldon was granted the right to form his Foundation, but it seemed as though it had been built for this very purpose. Everyone was hurrying this way and that, always seeming to be on urgent business, and yet also happy to be part of a noble cause. There had been no noble causes in the Empire for a long, long time.

Leyel quickly threaded his way through the maze that protected the Foundation's director from casual interruption. Other men and women, no doubt, had tried to see Hari Seldon and failed, put off by this functionary or that. Hari Seldon is a very busy man. Perhaps if you make an appointment for later. Seeing him today is out of the question. He's in mee ings all afternoon and evening. Do call before coming next time.

But none of this happened to Leyel Forska. All he had to do was say, "Tell Mr. Seldon that Mr. Forska wishes to continue a conversation." However much awe they might have of Hari Seldon, however they might intend to obey his orders not to be disturbed, they all knew that Leyel Forska was the universal exception. Even Linge Chen would be called out of a meeting of the Commission of Public Safety to speak with Forska, especially if Leyel went to the trouble of coming in person.

The ease with which he gained entry to see Hari, the excitement and optimism of the people, of the building itself, had encouraged Leyel so much that he was not at all prepared for Hari's first words.

"Leyel, I'm surprised to see you. I thought you would understand that my message was final."

It was the worst thing that Hari could possibly have said.

Had Deet been right after all? Leyel studied Hari's face for a moment, trying to see some sign of change. Was all that had passed between them through the years forgotten now? Had Hari's friendship never been real? No. Looking at Hari's face, a bit more lined and wrinkled now, Leyel saw still the same earnestness, the same plain honesty that had always been there. So instead of expressing the rage and disappointment that he felt, Leyel answered carefully, leaving the way open for Hari to change his mind. "I understood that your message was deceptive, and therefore could not be final."

Hari looked a little angry. "Deceptive?"

"I know which men and women you've been taking into your Foundation. They are not second-raters."

"Compared to you they are," said Hari. "They're academics, which means they're clerks. Sorters and interpreters of information."

"So am I. So are all scholars today. Even *your* inestimable theories arose from sorting through a trillion trillion bytes of data and interpreting it."

Hari shook his head. "I didn't just sort through data. I had an idea in my head. So did you. Few others do. You and I are expanding human knowledge. Most of the rest are only digging it up in one place and piling it in another. That's what the Encyclopedia Galactica *is*. A new pile."

"Nevertheless, Hari, you know and I know that this is not the real reason you turned me down. And don't tell me that it's because Leyel Forska's presence on Terminus would call undue attention to the project. You already have so much attention from the government that you can hardly breathe."

"You are unpleasantly persistent, Leyel. I don't like even having this conversation."

"That's too bad, Hari. I want to be part of your project. I would contribute to it more than any other person who might join it. I'm the one who plunged back into the oldest and most valuable archives and exposed the shameful amount of data loss that had arisen from neglect. I'm the one who launched the computerized extrapolation of shattered documents that your Encyclopedia—"

"Absolutely depends on. Our work would be impossible without your accomplishments."

"And yet you turned me down, and with a crudely flattering note."

"I didn't mean to give offense, Leyel."

"You also didn't mean to tell the truth. But you *will* tell me, Hari, or I'll simply go to Terminus anyway."

"The Commission of Public Safety has given my Foundation absolute control over who may or may not come to Terminus."

"Hari. You know perfectly well that all I have to do is hint to some lower-level functionary that I want to go to Terminus. Chen will hear of it within minutes, and within an hour he'll grant me an exception to your charter. If I did that, and if you fought it, you'd lose your charter. You *know* that. If you want me not to go to Terminus, it isn't enough to forbid me. You must persuade me that I ought not to be there."

Hari closed his eyes and sighed. "I don't think you're willing to be persuaded, Leyel. Go if you must."

For a moment Leyel wondered if Hari was giving in. But no, that was impossible, not so easily. "Oh, yes, Hari, but then I'd find myself cut off from everybody else on Terminus except my own serving people. Fobbed off with useless assignments. Cut out of the real meetings."

"That goes without saying," said Hari. "You are not part of the Foundation, you will not be, you cannot be. And if you try to use your wealth and influence to force your way in, you will succeed only in annoying the Foundation, not in joining it. Do you understand me?"

Only too well, thought Leyel in shame. Leyel knew perfectly well the limitations of power, and it was beneath him to have tried to bluster his way into getting something that could only be given freely. "Forgive me, Hari. I wouldn't have tried to force you. You know I don't do that sort of thing."

"I know you've never done it since we've been friends, Leyel. I was afraid that I was learning something new about you." Hari sighed. He turned away for a long moment, then turned back with a different look on his face, a different kind of energy in his voice. Leyel knew that look, that vigor. It meant Hari was taking him more deeply into his confidence. "Leyel, you have to understand, I'm not just creating an encyclopedia on Terminus."

Immediately Leyel grew worried. It had taken a great deal of Leyel's influence to persuade the government not to have Hari Seldon summarily exiled when he first started disseminating copies of his treatises about the impending fall of the Empire. They were sure Seldon was plotting treason, and had even put him on trial, where Seldon finally persuaded them that all he wanted to do was create the Encyclopedia Galactica, the repository of all the wisdom of the Empire. Even now, if Seldon confessed some ulterior motive, the government would move against him. It was to be assumed that the Pubs—Public Safety Office—were recording this entire conversation. Even Leyel's influence couldn't stop them if they had a confession from Hari's own mouth.

"No, Leyel, don't be nervous. My meaning is plain enough. For the Encyclopedia Galactica to succeed, I have to create a thriving city of scholars on Terminus. A colony full of men and women with fragile egos and unstemmable ambition, all of them trained in vicious political infighting at the most dangerous and terrible schools of bureaucratic combat in the Empire—the universities."

"Are you actually telling me you won't let me join your Foundation because I never attended one of those pathetic universities? My self-education is worth ten times their lockstep force-fed pseudolearning."

"Don't make your antiuniversity speech to me, Leyel. I'm saying that one of my most important concerns in staffing the Foundation is compatibility. I won't bring anyone to Terminus unless I believe he—or *she*—would be happy there."

The emphasis Hari put on the word *she* suddenly made everything clearer. "This isn't about me at all, is it?" Leyel said. "It's about Deet."

Hari said nothing.

"You know she doesn't want to go. You know she prefers to remain on Trantor. And that's why you aren't taking me! Is that it?"

Reluctantly, Hari conceded the point. "It does have something to do with Deet, yes."

"Don't you know how much the Foundation means to me?" demanded Leyel. "Don't you know how much I'd give up to be part of your work?"

Hari sat there in silence for a moment. Then he murmured, "Even Deet?"

Leyel almost blurted out an answer. Yes, of course, even Deet, anything for this great work.

But Hari's measured gaze stopped him. One thing Leyel had known since they first met at a conference back in their youth was that Hari would not stand for another man's self-deception. They had sat next to each other at a presentation by a demographer who had a considerable reputation at the time. Leyel watched as Hari destroyed the poor man's thesis with a few well-aimed questions. The demographer was furious. Obviously he had not seen the flaws in his own argument—but now that they had been shown to him, he refused to admit that they were flaws at all.

Afterward, Hari had said to Leyel, "I've done him a favor."

"How, by giving him someone to hate?" said Leyel.

"No. Before, he believed his own unwarranted conclusions. He had deceived himself. Now he doesn't believe them."

"But he still propounds them."

"So—now he's more of a liar and less of a fool. I have improved his private integrity. His public morality I leave up to him."

Leyel remembered this and knew that if he told Hari he could give up Deet for any reason, even to join the Foundation, it would be worse than a lie. It would be foolishness.

"It's a terrible thing you've done," said Leyel. "You know that Deet is part of myself. I can't give her up to join your Foundation. But now for the rest of our lives together I'll know that I could have gone, if not for her. You've given me wormwood and gall to drink, Hari."

Hari nodded slowly. "I hoped that when you read my note you'd realize I didn't want to tell you more. I hoped you wouldn't come to me and ask. I can't lie to you, Leyel. I wouldn't if I could. But I did withhold information, as much as possible. To spare us both problems."

"It didn't work."

"It isn't Deet's fault, Leyel. It's who she is. She belongs on Trantor, not on Terminus. And you belong with her. It's a fact, not a decision. We'll never discuss this again."

"No," said Leyel.

They sat there for a long minute, gazing steadily at each other. Leyel wondered if he and Hari would ever speak again. No. Never again. I don't ever want to see you again, Hari Seldon. You've made me regret the one unregrettable decision of my life—Deet. You've made me wish, somewhere in my heart, that I'd never married her. Which is like making me wish I'd never been born.

Leyel got up from his chair and left the room without a word.

When he got outside, he turned to the reception room in general, where several people were waiting to see Seldon. "Which of you are mine?" he asked.

Two women and one man stood up immediately.

"Fetch me a secure car and a driver."

Without a glance at each other, one of them left on the errand. The others fell in step beside Leyel. Subtlety and discretion were over for the moment. Leyel had no wish to mingle with the people of Trantor now. He only wanted to go home.

Hari Seldon left his office by the back way and soon found his way to Chandrakar Matt's cubicle in the Department of Library Relations. Chanda looked up and waved, then effortlessly slid her chair back until it was in the exact position required. Hari picked up a chair from the neighboring cubicle and, again without showing any particular care, set it exactly where it had to be.

Immediately the computer installed inside Chanda's lector recognized the configuration. It recorded Hari's costume of the day from three angles and superimposed the information on a long-stored holoimage of Chanda and Hari conversing pleasantly. Then, once Hari was seated, it began displaying the hologram. The hologram exactly matched the positions of the real Hari and Chanda, so that infrared sensors would show no discrepancy between image and fact. The only thing different was the faces—the movement of lips, blinking of eyes, the expressions. Instead of matching the words Hari and Chanda were actually saying, they matched the words being pushed into the air outside the cubicle—a harmless, randomly chosen series of remarks that took into account recent events so that no one would suspect that it was a canned conversation.

It was one of Hari's few opportunities for candid conversation that the Pubs would not overhear, and he and Chanda protected it carefully. They never spoke long enough or often enough that the Pubs would wonder at their devotion to such empty conversations. Much of their communication was subliminal—a sentence would stand for a paragraph, a word for a sentence, a gesture for a word. But when the conversation was done, Chanda knew where to go from there, what to do next; and Hari was reassured that his most important work was going on behind the smokescreen of the Foundation.

"For a moment I thought he might actually leave her."

"Don't underestimate the lure of the Encyclopedia."

"I fear I've wrought too well, Chanda. Do you think someday the Encyclopedia Galactica might actually exist?"

"It's a good idea. Good people are inspired by it. It wouldn't serve its purpose if they weren't. What should I tell Deet?"

"Nothing, Chanda. The fact that Leyel is staying, that's enough for her."

"If he changes his mind, will you actually let him go to Terminus?"

"If he changes his mind, then he *must* go, because if he would leave Deet, he's not the man for us."

"Why not just tell him? Invite him?"

"He must become part of the Second Foundation without realizing it. He must do it by natural inclination, not by a summons from me, and above all not by his own ambition."

"Your standards are so high, Hari, it's no wonder so few measure up. Most people in the Second Foundation don't even know that's what it is. They think they're librarians. Bureaucrats. They think Deet is an anthropologist who works among them in order to study them."

"Not so. They once thought that, but now they think of Deet as one of them. As one of the *best* of them. She's defining what it means to be a librarian. She's making them proud of the name."

"Aren't you ever troubled, Hari, by the fact that in the practice of your art—"

"My *science.*"

"Your meddlesome magical *craft*, you old wizard, you don't fool *me* with all your talk of science. I've seen the scripts of the holographs you're preparing for the vault on Terminus."

"That's all a pose."

"I can just imagine you saying those words. Looking perfectly satisfied with yourself. 'If you care to smoke, I wouldn't mind . . . Pause for chuckle . . . Why should I? I'm not really here.' Pure showmanship."

Hari waved off the idea. The computer quickly found a bit of dialogue to fit his gesture, so the false scene would not seem false. "No, I'm *not* troubled by the fact that in the practice of my *science* I change the lives of human beings. Knowledge has always changed people's lives. The only difference is that I *know* I'm changing them—and the changes I introduce are planned, they're under control. Did the man who invented the first artificial light—what was it, animal fat with a wick? A light-emitting diode?—did he realize what it would do to humankind, to be given power over night?"

As always, Chanda deflated him the moment he started congratulating himself. "In the first place, it was almost certainly a woman, and in the second place, she knew exactly what she was doing. It allowed her to find her way through the house at night. Now she could put her nursing baby in another bed, in another room, so she could get some sleep at night without fear of rolling over and smothering the child."

Hari smiled. "If artificial light was invented by a woman, it was certainly a prostitute, to extend her hours of work."

Chanda grinned. He did not laugh—it was too hard for the computer to come up with jokes to explain laughter. "We'll watch Leyel carefully, Hari. How will we know when he's ready, so we can begin to count on him for protection and leadership?"

"When you already count on him, then he's ready. When his commitment and loyalty are firm, when the goals of the Second Foundation are already in his heart, when he acts them out in his life, then he's ready."

There was a finality in Hari's tone. The conversation was nearly over.

"By the way, Hari, you were right. No one has even questioned the omission of any important psychohistorical data from the Foundation library on Terminus."

"Of course not. Academics never look outside their own discipline. That's another reason why I'm glad Leyel isn't going. *He* would notice that the only psychologist we're sending is Bor Alurin. Then I'd have to explain more to him than I want. Give my love to Deet, Chanda. Tell her that her test case is going very well. She'll end up with a husband *and* a community of scientists of the mind."

"Artists. Wizards. Demigods."

"Stubborn misguided women who don't know science when they're doing it. All in the Imperial Library. Till next time, Chanda."

If Deet had asked him about his interview with Hari, if she had commiserated with him about Hari's refusal, his resentment of her might have been uncontainable, he might have lashed out at her and said something that could never be forgiven. Instead, she was perfectly herself, so excited about her work and so beautiful, even with her face showing all the sag and wrinkling of her sixty years, that all Leyel could do was fall in love with her again, as he had so many times in their years together.

"It's working beyond anything I hoped for, Leyel. I'm beginning to hear stories that I created months and years ago, coming back as epic legends. You remember the time I retrieved and extrapolated the accounts of the uprising at Misercordia only three days before the Admiralty needed them?"

"Your finest hour. Admiral Divart still talks about how they used the old battle plots as a strategic guideline and put down the Tellekers' strike in a single three-day operation without loss of a ship."

"You have a mind like a trap, even if you *are* old."

"Sadly, all I can remember is the past."

"Dunce, that's all *anyone* can remember."

He prompted her to go on with her account of today's triumph. "It's an epic legend now?"

"It came back to me without my name on it, and bigger than life. As a reference. Rinjy was talking with some young librarians from one of the inner provinces who were on the standard interlibrary tour, and one of them said something about how you could stay in the Imperial Library on Trantor all your life and never see the real world at all."

Leyel hooted. "Just the thing to say to Rinjy!"

"Exactly. Got her dander up, of course, but the important thing is, she immediately told them the story of how a librarian, *all on her own,* saw the similarity between the Misercordia uprising and the Tellekers' strike. She knew no one at the Admiralty would listen to her unless she brought them all the information at once. So she delved back into the ancient records and found them in deplorable shape—the original data had been stored in glass, but that was forty-two centuries ago, and no one had refreshed the data. None of the secondary sources actually showed the battle plots or ship courses—Misercordia had mostly been written about by biographers, not military historians—"

"Of course. It was Pol Yuensau's first battle, but he was just a pilot, not a commander—"

"I know *you* remember, my intrusive pet. The point is what Rinjy *said* about this mythical librarian."

"You."

"I was standing right there. I don't think Rinjy knew it was me, or she would have said something—she wasn't even in the same division with me then, you know. What matters is that Rinjy heard a version of the story and by the time she told it, it was transformed into a magic hero tale. The prophetic librarian of Trantor."

"What does *that* prove? You *are* a magic hero."

"The way she told it, I did it all on my own initiative—"

"You did. You were assigned to do document extrapolation, and you just happened to start with Misercordia."

"But in Rinjy's version, I had *already* seen its usefulness with the Tellekers' strike. She said the librarian sent it to the Admiralty and only then did they realize it was the key to bloodless victory."

"Librarian saves the Empire."

"Exactly."

"But you did."

"But I didn't *mean* to. And Admiralty requested the information—the only really extraordinary thing was that I had already finished two weeks of document restoration—"

"Which you did brilliantly."

"Using programs you had helped design, thank you very much, O Wise One, as you indirectly praise yourself. It was sheer coincidence that I could give them exactly what they wanted within five minutes of their asking. But now it's a hero story within the community of librarians. In the Imperial Library itself, and now spreading outward to all the other libraries."

"This is so anecdotal, Deet. I don't see how you can publish this."

"Oh, I don't intend to. Except perhaps in the introduction. What matters to me is that it proves my theory."

"It has no statistical validity."

"It proves it to *me*. I know that my theories of community formation are true. That the vigor of a community depends on the allegiance of its members, and the allegiance can be created and enhanced by the dissemination of epic stories."

"She speaks the language of academia. I should be writing this down, so you don't have to think up all those words again."

"Stories that make the community seem more important, more central to human life. Because Rinjy could tell this story, it made her more proud to be a librarian, which increased her allegiance to the community and gave the community more power within her."

"You are possessing their souls."

"And they've got mine. Together our souls are possessing each other."

There was the rub. Deet's role in the library had begun as applied research—joining the library staff in order to confirm her theory of community formation. But that task was impossible to accomplish without in fact becoming a committed part of the library community. It was Deet's dedication to serious science that had brought them together. Now that very dedication was stealing her away. It would hurt her more to leave the library than it would to lose Leyel.

Not true. Not true at all, he told himself sternly. Self-pity leads to self-deception. Exactly the opposite is true—it would hurt her more to lose Leyel than to leave her community of librarians. That's why she consented to go to Terminus in the first place. But could he blame her for being glad that she didn't have to choose? Glad that she could have both?

Yet even as he beat down the worst of the thoughts arising from his disappointment, he couldn't keep some of the nastiness from coming out in his conversation. "How will you know when your experiment is over?"

She frowned. "It'll never be *over*, Leyel. They're all really librarians—I don't pick them up by the tails like mice and put them back in their cages when the experiment's done. At some point I'll simply stop, that's all, and write my book."

"Will you?"

"Write the book? I've written books before, I think I can do it again."

"I meant, will you stop?"

"When, now? Is this some test of my love for you, Leyel? Are you jealous of my friendships with Rinjy and Animet and Fin and Urik?"

No! Don't accuse me of such childish, selfish feelings!

But before he could snap back his denial, he knew that his denial would be false.

"Sometimes I am, yes, Deet. Sometimes I think you're happier with them."

And because he had spoken honestly, what could have become a bitter quarrel remained a conversation. "But I *am*, Leyel," she answered, just as frankly. "It's because when I'm with them, I'm creating something new, I'm creating something *with them*. It's exciting, invigorating, I'm discovering new things every day, in every word they say, every smile, every tear someone sheds, every sign that being one of *us* is the most important thing in their lives."

"I can't compete with that."

"No, you can't, Leyel. But you complete it. Because it would all mean nothing, it would be more frustrating than exhilarating if I couldn't come back to you every day and tell you what happened. You always understand what it means, you're always excited for me, you validate my experience."

"I'm your audience. Like a parent."

"Yes, old man. Like a husband. Like a child. Like the person I love most in all the world. You are my root. I ake a brave show out there, all branches and bright leaves in the sunlight, but I come here to suck the water of life from your soil."

"Leyel Forska, the font of capillarity. You are the tree, and I am the dirt."

"Which happens to be full of fertilizer." She kissed him. A kiss reminiscent of younger days. An invitation, which he gladly accepted.

A softened section of floor served them as an impromptu bed. At the end, he lay beside her, his arm across her waist, his head on her shoulder, his lips brushing the skin of her breast. He remembered when her breasts were small and firm, perched on her chest like small monuments to her potential. Now when she lay on her back they were a ruin, eroded by age so they flowed off her chest to either side, resting wearily on her arms.

"You are a magnificent woman," he whispered, his lips tickling her skin.

Their slack and flabby bodies were now capable of greater passion than when they were taut and strong. Before, they were all potential. That's what we love in youthful bodies, the teasing potential. Now hers is a body of accomplishment. Three fine children were the blossoms, then the fruit of this tree, gone off and taken root somewhere else. The tension of youth could now give way to a relaxation of the flesh. There were no more promises in their lovemaking. Only fulfillment.

She murmured softly in his ear, "That was a ritual, by the way. Community maintenance."

"So I'm just another experiment?"

"A fairly successful one. I'm testing to see if this little community can last until one of us drops."

"What if you drop first? Who'll write the paper then?"

"You will. But you'll sign my name to it. I want the Imperial medal for it. Posthumously. Glue it to my memorial stone."

"I'll wear it myself. If you're selfish enough to leave all the real work to me, you don't deserve anything better than a cheap replica."

She slapped his back. "You are a nasty selfish old man, then. The real thing or nothing."

He felt the sting of her slap as if he deserved it. A nasty selfish old man. If she only knew how right she was. There had been a moment in Hari's office when he'd almost said the words that would deny all that there was between them. The words that would cut her out of his life. Go to Terminus without her! I would be more myself if they took my heart, my liver, my brain.

How could I have thought I wanted to go to Terminus, anyway? To be surrounded by academics of the sort I most despise, struggling with them to get the encyclopedia properly designed. They'd each fight for their petty little province, never catching the vision of the whole, never understanding that the encyclopedia would be valueless if it were compartmentalized. It would be a life in hell, and in the end he'd lose, because the academic mind was incapable of growth or change.

It was here on Trantor that he could still accomplish something. Perhaps even solve the question of human origin, at least to his own satisfaction—and perhaps he could do it soon enough that he could get his discovery included in the Encyclopedia Galactica before the Empire began to break down at the edges, cutting Terminus off from the rest of the Galaxy.

It was like a shock of static electricity passing through his brain; he even saw an afterglow of light around the edges of his vision, as if a spark had jumped some synaptic gap.

"What a sham," he said.

"Who, you? Me?"

"Hari Seldon. All this talk about his Foundation to create the Encyclopedia Galactica."

"Careful, Leyel." It was almost impossible that the Pubs could have found a way to listen to what went on in Leyel Forska's own apartments. Almost.

"He told me twenty years ago. It was one of his first psychohistorical projections. The Empire will crumble at the edges first. He projected it would happen within the next generation. The figures were crude then. He must have it down to the year now. Maybe even the month. Of course he put his Foundation on Terminus. A place so remote that when the edges of the Empire fray, it will be among the first threads lost. Cut off from Trantor. Forgotten at once!"

"What good would *that* do, Leyel? They'd never hear of any new discoveries then."

"What you said about us. A tree. Our children like the fruit of that tree."

"I never said that."

"I thought it, then. He is dropping his Foundation out on Terminus like the fruit of Empire. To grow into a new Empire by and by."

"You frighten me, Leyel. If the Pubs ever heard you say that—"

"That crafty old fox. That sly, deceptive—he never actually lied to me, but of course he couldn't send me there. If the Forska fortune was tied up with Terminus, the Empire would never lose track of the place. The edges might fray elsewhere, but never there. Putting me on Terminus would be the undoing of the *real* project." It was such a relief. Of course Hari couldn't tell him, not with the Pubs listening, but it had nothing to do with him or Deet. It wouldn't have to be a barrier between them after all. It was just one of the penalties of being the keeper of the Forska fortune.

"Do you really think so?" asked Deet.

"I was a fool not to see it before. But Hari was a fool too if he thought I wouldn't guess it."

"Maybe he expects you to guess everything."

"Oh, nobody could ever come up with *everything* Hari's doing. He has more twists and turns in his brain than a hyperpath through core space. No matter how you labor to pick your way through, you'll always find Hari at the end of it, nodding happily and congratulating you on coming this far. He's ahead of us all. He's already planned everything, and the rest of us are doomed to follow in his footsteps."

"Is it doom?"

"Once I thought Hari Seldon was God. Now I know he's much less powerful than that. He's merely Fate."

"No, Leyel. Don't say that."

"Not even Fate. Just our guide through it. He sees the future, and points the way."

"Rubbish." She slid out from under him, got up, pulled her robe from its hook on the wall. "My old bones get cold when I lie about naked."

Leyel's legs were trembling, but not with cold. "The future is his, and the present is yours, but the past belongs to me. I don't know how far into the future his probability curves have taken him, but I can match him, step for step, century for century into the past."

"Don't tell me you're going to solve the question of origin. You're the one who proved it wasn't worth solving."

"I proved that it wasn't important or even possible to find the planet of origin. But I also said that we could still discover the natural laws that accounted for the origin of man. Whatever forces created us as human beings must still be present in the universe."

"I did read what you wrote, you know. You aid it would be the labor of the next millennium to find the answer."

"Just now. Lying here, just now, I saw it, just out of reach. Something about your work and Hari's work, and the tree."

"The tree was about me needing you, Leyel. It wasn't about the origin of humanity."

"It's gone. Whatever I saw for a moment there, it's gone. But I can find it again. It's there in your work, and Hari's Foundation, and the fall of the Empire, and the damned pear tree."

"I never said it was a pear tree."

"I used to play in the pear orchard on the grounds of the estate in Holdwater. To me the word 'tree' always means a pear tree. One of the deep-worn ruts in my brain."

"I'm relieved. I was afraid you were reminded of pears by the shape of these ancient breasts when I bend over."

"Open your robe again. Let me see if I think of pears."

* * *

Leyel paid for Hari Seldon's funeral. It was not lavish. Leyel had meant it to be. The moment he heard of Hari's death—not a surprise, since Hari's first brutal stroke had left him half-paralyzed in a wheelchair—he set his staff to work on a memorial service appropriate to honor the greatest scientific mind of the millennium. But word arrived, in the form of a visit from Commissioner Rom Divart, that any sort of public services would be . . .

"Shall we say, inappropriate?"

"The man was the greatest genius I've ever heard of! He virtually invented a branch of science that clarified things that—he made a science out of the sort of thing that soothsayers and—and —*economists* used to do!"

Rom laughed at Leyel's little joke, of course, because he and Leyel had been friends forever. Rom was the only friend of Leyel's childhood who had never sucked up to him or resented him or stayed cool toward him because of the Forska fortune. This was, of course, because the Divart holdings were, if anything, slightly greater. They had played together unencumbered by strangeness or jealousy or awe.

They even shared a tutor for two terrible, glorious years, from the time Rom's father was murdered until the execution of Rom's grandfather, which caused so much outrage among the nobility that the mad Emperor was stripped of power and the Imperium put under the control of the Commission of Public Safety. Then, as the youthful head of one of the great families, Rom had embarked on his long and fruitful career in politics.

Rom said later that for those two years it was Leyel who taught him that there was still some good in the world; that Leyel's friendship was the only reason Rom hadn't killed himself. Leyel always thought this was pure theatrics. Rom was a born actor. That's why he so excelled at making stunning entrances and playing unforgettable scenes on the grandest stage of all—the politics of the Imperium. Someday he would no doubt exit as dramatically as his father and grandfather had.

But he was not all show. Rom never forgot the friend of his childhood. Leyel knew it, and knew also that Rom's coming to deliver this message from the Commission of Public Safety probably meant that Rom had fought to make the message as mild as it was. So Leyel blustered a bit, then made his little joke. It was his way of surrendering gracefully.

What Leyel didn't realize, right up until the day of the funeral, was exactly *how* dangerous his friendship with Hari Seldon had been, and how stupid it was for him to associate himself with Hari's name now that the old man was dead. Linge Chen, the Chief Commissioner, had not risen to the position of greatest power in the Empire without being fiercely suspicious of potential rivals and brutally efficient about eliminating them. Hari had maneuvered Chen into a position such that it was more dangerous to kill the old man than to give him his Foundation on Terminus. But now Hari was dead, and apparently Chen was watching to see who mourned.

Leyel did—Leyel and the few members of Hari's staff who had stayed behind on Trantor to maintain contact with Terminus up to the moment of Hari's death. Leyel should have known better. Even alive, Hari wouldn't have cared who came to his funeral. And now, dead, he cared even less. Leyel didn't believe his friend lived on in some ethereal plane, watching carefully and taking attendance at the services. No, Leyel simply felt he had to be there, felt he had to speak. Not for Hari, really. For himself. To continue to be himself, Leyel had to make some kind of public gesture toward Hari Seldon and all he had stood for.

Who heard? Not many. Deet, who thought his eulogy was too mild by half. Hari's staff, who were quite aware of the danger and winced at each of Leyel's list of Hari's accomplishments. Naming them—and emphasizing that only Seldon had the vision to do these great works—was inherently a criticism of the level of intelligence and integrity in the Empire. The Pubs were listening, too. They noted that Leyel clearly agreed with Hari Seldon about the certainty of the Empire's fall—that in fact as a galactic empire it had probably already fallen, since its authority was no longer coextensive with the Galaxy.

If almost anyone else had said such things, to such a small audience, it would have been ignored, except to keep him from getting any job requiring a security clearance. But when the head of the Forska family came out openly to affirm the correctness of the views of a man who had been tried before the Commission of Public Safety—that posed a greater danger to the Commission than Hari Seldon.

For, as head of the Forska family, if Leyel Forska wanted, he could be one of the great players on the political stage, could have a seat on the Commission along with Rom Divart and Linge Chen. Of course, that would also have meant constantly watching for assassins—either to avoid them or to hire them—and trying to win the allegiance of various military strongmen in the farflung reaches of the Galaxy. Leyel's grandfather had spent his life in such pursuits, but Leyel's father had declined, and Leyel himself had thoroughly immersed himself in science and never so much as inquired about politics.

Until now. Until he made the profoundly political act of paying for Hari Seldon's funeral and then *speaking* at it. What would he do next? There were a thousand would-be warlords who would spring to revolt if a Forska promised what would-be emperors so desperately needed: a noble sponsor, a mask of legitimacy, and *money*.

Did Linge Chen really believe that Leyel meant to enter politics at his advanced age? Did he really think Leyel posed a threat?

Probably not. If he *had* believed it, he would surely have had Leyel killed, and no doubt all his children as well, leaving only one of his minor grandchildren, whom Chen would carefully control through the guardians he would appoint, thereby acquiring control of the Forska fortune as well as his own.

Instead, Chen only believed that Leyel *might* cause trouble. So he took what were, for him, mild steps.

That was why Rom came to visit Leyel again, a week after the funeral.

Leyel was delighted to see him. "Not on somber business this time, I hope," he said. "But such bad luck—Deet's at the library again, she practically lives there now, but she'd want to—"

"Leyel." Rom touched Leyel's lips with his fingers.

So it *was* somber business after all. Worse than somber. Rom recited what had to be a memorized speech.

"The Commission of Public Safety has become concerned that in your declining years—"

Leyel opened his mouth to protest, but again Rom touched his lips to silence him.

"That in your declining years, the burdens of the Forska estates are distracting you from your exceptionally important scientific work. So great is the Empire's need for the new discoveries and understanding your work will surely bring us, that the Commission of Public Safety has created the office of Forska Trustee to oversee all the Forska estates and holdings. You will, of course, have unlimited access to these funds for your scientific work here on Trantor, and funding will continue for all the archives and libraries you have endowed. Naturally, the Commission has no desire for you to thank us for what is, after all, our duty to one of our noblest citizens, but if your well-known courtesy required you to make a brief public statement of gratitude it would not be inappropriate."

Leyel was no fool. He knew how things worked. He was being stripped of his fortune and being placed under arrest on Trantor. There was no point in protest or remonstrance, no point even in trying to make Rom feel guilty for having brought him such a bitter message. Indeed, Rom himself might be in great danger—if Leyel so much as hinted that he expected Rom to come to his support, his dear friend might also fall. So Leyel nodded gravely, and then carefully framed his words of reply.

"Please tell the Commissioners how grateful I am for their concern on my behalf. It has been a long, long time since anyone went to the trouble of easing my burdens. I accept their kind offer. I am especially glad because this means that now I can pursue my studies unencumbered."

Rom visibly relaxed. Leyel wasn't going to cause trouble. "My dear friend, I will sleep better knowing that you are always here on Trantor, working freely in the library or taking your leisure in the parks."

So at least they weren't going to confine him to his apartment. No doubt they would never let him off-planet, but it wouldn't hurt to ask. "Perhaps I'll even have time now to visit my grandchildren now and then."

"Oh, Leyel, you and I are both too old to enjoy hyperspace any more. Leave that for the youngsters—they can come visit you whenever they want. And sometimes they can stay home, while their parents come to see you."

Thus Leyel learned that if any of his children came to visit him, *their* children would be held hostage, and vice versa. Leyel himself would never leave Trantor again.

"So much the better," said Leyel. "I'll have time to write several books I've been meaning to publish."

"The Empire waits eagerly for every scientific treatise you publish." There was a slight emphasis on the word "scientific."

"But I hope you won't bore us with one of those tedious autobiographies."

Leyel agreed to the restriction easily enough. "I *promise*, Rom. You know better than anyone else exactly how boring my life has always been."

"Come now. *My* life's the boring one, Leyel, all this government claptrap and bureaucratic bushwa. You've been at the forefront of scholarship and learning. Indeed, my friend, the Commission hopes you'll honor us by giving us first look at every word that comes out of your scriptor."

"Only if you promise to read it carefully and point out any mistakes I might make." No doubt the Commission intended only to censor his work to remove political material—which Leyel had never included anyway. But Leyel had already resolved never to publish anything again, at least as long as Linge Chen was Chief Commissioner. The safest thing Leyel could do now was to disappear, to let Chen forget him entirely—it would be egregiously stupid to send occasional articles to Chen, thus reminding him that Leyel was still around.

But Rom wasn't through yet. "I must extend that request to Deet's work as well. We really want first look at it—do tell her so."

"Deet?" For the first time Leyel almost let his fury show. Why should Deet be punished because of Leyel's indiscretion? "Oh, she'll be too shy for that, Rom—she doesn't think her work is *important* enough to deserve any attention from men as busy as the Commissioners. They'll think you only want to see her work because she's my wife—she's always annoyed when people patronize her."

"You must insist, then, Leyel," said Rom. "I assure you, her studies of the functions of the Imperial bureaucracy have long been interesting to the Commission for their own sake."

Ah. Of course. Chen would never have allowed a report on the workings of government to appear without making sure it wasn't dangerous. Censorship of Deet's writings wouldn't be Leyel's fault after all. Or at least not entirely.

"I'll tell her that, Rom. She'll be flattered. But won't you stay and tell her yourself? I can bring you a cup of peshat, we can talk about old times—"

Leyel would have been surprised if Rom had stayed. No, this

interview had been at least as hard on Rom as it had been on him. The very fact that Rom had been forced into being the Commission's messenger to his childhood friend was a humiliating reminder that the Chens were in the ascendant over the Divarts. But as Rom bowed and left, it occurred to Leyel that Chen might have made a mistake. Humiliating Rom this way, forcing him to place his dearest friend under arrest like this—it might be the straw to break the camel's back. After all, though no one had ever been able to find out who hired the assassin who killed Rom's father, and no one had ever learned who denounced Rom's grandfather, leading to his execution by the paranoid Emperor Wassiniwak, it didn't take a genius to realize that the House of Chen had profited most from both events.

"I wish I could stay," said Rom. "But duty calls. Still, you can be sure I'll think of you often. Of course, I doubt I'll think of you as you are *now*, you old wreck. I'll remember you as a boy, when we used to tweak our tutor—remember the time we recoded his lector, so that for a whole week explicit pornography kept coming up on the display whenever the door of his room opened?"

Leyel couldn't help laughing. "You never forget anything, do you!"

"The poor fool. He never figured out that it was us! Old times. Why couldn't we have stayed young forever?" He embraced Leyel and then swiftly left.

Linge Chen, you fool, you have reached too far. Your days are numbered. None of the Pubs who were listening in on their conversation could possibly know that Rom and Leyel had never teased their tutor—and that they had never done anything to his lector. It was just Rom's way of letting Leyel know that they were still allies, still keeping secrets together—and that someone who had authority over both of them was going to be in for a few nasty surprises.

It gave Leyel chills, thinking about what might come of all this. He loved Rom Divart with all his heart, but he also knew that Rom was capable of biding his time and then killing swiftly, efficiently, coldly. Linge Chen had just started his latest six-year term of office, but Leyel knew he'd never finish it. And the next Chief Commissioner would not be a Chen.

Soon, though, the enormity of what had been done to him began to sink in. He had always thought that his fortune meant little to him—that he would be the same man with or without the Forska estates. But now he began to realize that it wasn't true, that he'd been lying to himself all along. He had known since childhood how despicable rich and powerful men could be—his father had made sure he saw and understood how cruel men became when their money persuaded them they had a right to use others however they wished. So Leyel had learned to despise his own birthright, and, starting with his father, had pretended to others that he could make his way through the world solely by wit and diligence, that he would have been exactly the same man if he had grown up in a common family, with a common education. He had done such a good job of acting as if he didn't care about his wealth that he came to believe it himself.

Now he realized that Forska estates had been an invisible part of himself all along, as if they were extensions of his body, as if he could flex a muscle and cargo ships would fly, he could blink and mines would be sunk deep into the earth, he could sigh and all over the Galaxy there would be a wind of change that would keep blowing until everything was exactly as he wanted it. Now all those invisible limbs and senses had been amputated. Now he was crippled—he had only as many arms and legs and eyes as any other human being.

At last he was what he had always pretended to be. An ordinary, powerless man. He hated it.

For the first hours after Rom left, Leyel pretended he could take all this in stride. He sat at the lector and spun through the pages smoothly—without anything on the pages registering in his memory. He kept wishing Deet were there so he could laugh with her about how little this hurt him; then he would be glad that Deet was not there, because one sympathetic touch of her hand would push him over the edge, make it impossible to contain his emotion.

Finally he could not help himself. Thinking of Deet, of their children and grandchildren, of all that had been lost to them because he had made an empty gesture to a dead friend, he threw himself to the softened floor and wept bitterly. Let Chen listen to recordings of what the spy beam shows of this! Let him savor his victory! I'll destroy him somehow, my staff is still loyal to me, I'll put together an army, I'll hire assassins of my own, I'll make contact with Admiral Sipp, and then Chen will be the one to sob, crying out for mercy as I disfigure him the way he has mutilated me—

Fool.

Leyel rolled over onto his back, dried his face on his sleeve, then lay there, eyes closed, calming himself. No vengeance. No politics. That was Rom's business, not Leyel's. Too late for him to enter the game now—and who would help him, anyway, now that he had already lost his power? There was nothing to be done.

Leyel didn't really want to do anything, anyway. Hadn't they guaranteed that his archives and libraries would continue to be funded? Hadn't they guaranteed him unlimited research funds? And wasn't that all he had cared about anyway? He had long since turned over all the Forska operations to his subordinates—Chen's trustee would simply do the same job. And Leyel's children wouldn't suffer much—he had raised them with the same values that he had grown up with, and so they all pursued careers unrelated to the Forska holdings. They were true children of their father and mother—they wouldn't have any self-respect if they didn't earn their own way in the world. No doubt they'd be disappointed by having their inheritance snatched away. But they wouldn't be destroyed.

I am not ruined. All the lies that Rom told are really true, only they didn't realize it. All that matters in my life, I still have. I really *don't* care about my fortune. It's just the *way* I lost it that made me so furious. I can go on and be the same person I always was. This will even give me an opportunity to see who my true friends are—to see who still honors me for my scientific achievements, and who despises me for my poverty.

By the time Deet got home from the library—late, as was usual these days—Leyel was hard at work, reading back through all the research and speculation on protohuman behavior, trying to see if there was anything other than half-assed guesswork and pompous babble. He was so engrossed in his reading that he spent the first fifteen minutes after she got home telling her of the hilarious stupidities he had found in the day's reading, and then sharing a wonderful, impossible thought he had had.

"What if the human species isn't the only branch to evolve on our family tree? What if there's some other primate species that looks exactly like us, but can't interbreed with us, that functions in a completely different way, and we don't even know it, we all think everybody's just like us, but here and there all over the Empire there are whole towns, cities, maybe even worlds of people who secretly aren't human at all."

"But Leyel, my overwrought husband, if they look just like us and act just like us, then they *are* human."

"But they *don't* act exactly like us. There's a difference. A completely different set of rules and assumptions. Only they don't know that we're different, and we don't know that *they're* different. Or even if we suspect it, we're never sure. Just two different species, living side by side and never guessing it."

She kissed him. "You poor fool, that isn't speculation, it already exists. You have just described the relationship between males and females. Two completely different species, completely unintelligible to each other, living side by side and thinking they're really the same. The fascinating thing, Leyel, is that the two species persist in marrying each other and having babies, sometimes of one species, sometimes of the other, and the whole time they can't understand why they can't understand each other."

He laughed and embraced her. "You're right, as always, Deet. If I could once understand women, then perhaps I'd know what it is that makes men human."

"Nothing could possibly make men human," she answered. "Every time they're just about to get it right, they end up tripping over the damned Y chromosome and turning back into beasts." She nuzzled his neck.

It was then, with Deet in his arms, that he whispered to her what had happened when Rom visited that day. She said nothing, but held him tightly for the longest time. Then they had a very late supper and went about their nightly routines as if nothing had changed.

Not until they were in bed, not until Deet was softly snoring beside him, did it finally occur to Leyel that Deet was facing a test of her own. Would she still love him, now that he was merely Leyel Forska, scientist on a pension, and not Lord Forska, master of worlds? Of course she would *intend* to. But just as Leyel had never been aware of how much he depended on his wealth to define himself, so also she might not have realized how much of what she loved about him was his vast power; for even though he didn't flaunt it, it had always been there, like a solid platform underfoot, hardly noticed except now, when it was gone, when their footing was unsure.

Even before this, she had been slipping away into the community of women in the library. She would drift away even faster now, not even noticing it as Leyel became less and less important to her. No need for anything as dramatic as divorce. Just a little gap between them, an empty space that might as well be a chasm, might as well by the abyss. My fortune was a part of me, and now that it's gone, I'm no longer the same man she loved. She won't even know that she doesn't love me any more. She'll just get busier and busier in her work, and in five or ten years when I die of old age, she'll grieve—and then suddenly she'll realize that she isn't half as devastated as she thought she'd be. In fact, she won't be devastated at all. And she'll get on with her life and won't even remember what it was like to be married to me. I'll disappear from all human memory then, except perhaps for a few scientific papers and the libraries.

I'm like the information that was lost in all those neglected archives. Disappearing bit by bit, unnoticed, until all that's left is just a little bit of noise in people's memories. Then, finally, nothing. Blank.

Self-pitying fool. That's what happens to everyone, in the long run. Even Hari Seldon—someday he'll be forgotten, sooner rather than later, if Chen has his way. We all die. We're all lost in the passage of time. The only thing that lives on after us is the new shape we've given to the communities we lived in. There are things that are known because I said them, and even though people have forgotten who said it, they'll go on knowing. Like the story Rinjy was telling—she had forgotten, if she ever knew it, that Deet was the librarian in the original tale. But still she remembered the tale. The community of librarians was different because Deet had been among them. They would be a little different, a little braver, a little stronger, because of Deet. She had left traces of herself in the world.

And then, again, there came that flash of insight, that sudden understanding of the answer to a question that had long been troubling him.

But in the moment that Leyel realized that he held the answer, the answer slipped away. He couldn't remember it. You're asleep, he said silently. You only dreamed that you understood the origin of humanity. That's the way it is in dreams—the truth is always so beautiful, but you can never hold on to it.

* * *

"How is he taking it, Deet?"

"Hard to say. Well, I think. He was never much of a wanderer anyway."

"Come now, it can't be that simple."

"No. No, it isn't."

"Tell me."

"The social things—those were easy. We rarely went anyway, but now people don't invite us. We're politically dangerous. And the few things we had scheduled got canceled or, um, postponed. You know—we'll call you as soon as we have a new date."

"He doesn't mind this?"

"He *likes* that part. He always hated those things. But they've canceled his speeches. And the lecture series on human ecology."

"A blow."

"He pretends not to mind. But he's brooding."

"Tell me."

"Works all day, but he doesn't read it to me any more, doesn't make me sit down at the lector the minute I get home. I think he isn't writing anything."

"Doing nothing?"

"No. Reading. That's all."

"Maybe he just needs to do research."

"You don't know Leyel. He *thinks* by writing. Or talking. He isn't doing either."

"Doesn't talk to you?"

"He answers. I try to talk about things here at the library, his answers are—what? Glum. Sullen."

"He resents your work?"

"That's not possible. Leyel has always been as enthusiastic about my work as about his own. And he won't talk about his own work, either. I ask him, and he says nothing."

"Not surprising."

"So it's all right?"

"No. It's just not surprising."

"What is it? Can't you tell me?"

"What good is telling you? It's what we call ILS—Identity Loss Syndrome. It's identical to the passive strategy for dealing with loss of body parts."

"ILS. What happens in ILS?"

"Deet, come on, you're a scientist. What do you expect? You've just described Leyel's behavior, I tell you that it's called ILS, you want to know what ILS is, and what am I going to do?"

"Describe Leyel's behavior back to me. What an idiot I am."

"Good, at least you can laugh."

"Can't you tell me what to expect?"

"Complete withdrawal from you, from everybody. Eventually he becomes completely antisocial and starts to strike out. Does something self-destructive—like making public statements against Chen, that'd do it."

"No!"

"Or else he severs his old connections, gets away from you, and reconstructs himself in a different set of communities."

"This would make him happy?"

"Sure. Useless to the Second Foundation, but happy. It would also turn you into a nasty-tempered old crone, not that you aren't one already, mind you."

"Oh, you think Leyel's the only thing keeping me human?"

"Pretty much, yes. He's your safety valve."

"Not lately."

"I know."

"Have I been so awful?"

"Nothing that we can't bear. Deet, if we're going to be fit to govern the human race someday, shouldn't we first learn to be good to each other?"

"Well, I'm glad to provide you all with an opportunity to test your patience."

"You should be glad. We're doing a fine job so far, wouldn't you say?"

"Please. You were teasing me about the prognosis, weren't you?"

"Partly. Everything I said was true, but you know as well as I do that there are as many different ways out of a B-B syndrome as there are people who have them."

"Behavioral cause, behavioral effect. No little hormone shot, then?"

"Deet. He doesn't know who he is."

"Can't I help him?"

"Yes."

"What? What can I do?"

"This is only a guess, since I haven't talked to him."

"Of course."

"You aren't home much."

"I can't *stand* it there, with him brooding all the time."

"Fine. Get him out with you."

"He won't go."

"Push him."

"We barely talk. I don't know if I even have any leverage over him."

"Deet. You're the one who wrote, 'Communities that make few or no demands on their members cannot command allegiance. All else being equal, members who feel most needed have the strongest allegiance.'"

"You memorized that?"

"Psychohistory *is* the psychology of populations, but populations can only be quantified as communities. Seldon's work on statistical probabilities only worked to predict the future within a generation or two until you first published your community theories. That's because statistics *can't* deal with cause and effect. Stats tell you what's happening, never why, never the result. Within a generation or two, the present statistics evaporate, they're meaningless, you have whole new populations with new configurations. Your community theory gave us a way of predicting which communities would survive, which would grow, which would fade. A way of looking across long stretches of time and space."

"Hari never told me he was using community theory in any important way."

"How could he tell you that? He had to walk a tightrope—publishing enough to get psychohistory taken seriously, but not so much that anybody outside the Second Foundation could ever duplicate or continue his work. Your work was a key—but he couldn't say so."

"Are you just saying this to make me feel better?"

"Sure. That's why I'm saying it. But it's also true—since lying to you wouldn't make you feel better, would it? Statistics are like taking cross sections of the trunk of a tree. It can tell you a lot about its history. You can figure how healthy it is, how much volume the whole tree has, how much is root and how much is branch. But what it *can't* tell you is where the tree will branch, and which branches will become major, which minor, and which will rot and fall off and die."

"But you can't *quantify* communities, can you? They're just stories and rituals that bind people together—"

"You'd be surprised what we can quantify. We're very good at what we do, Deet. Just as you are. Just as Leyel is."

"*Is* his work important? After all, human origin is only a historical question."

"Nonsense, and you know it. Leyel has stripped away the historical issues and he's searching for the scientific ones. The principles by which human life, as we understand it, is differentiated from nonhuman. If he finds that—don't you see, Deet? The human race is re-creating itself all the time, on every world, in every family, in every individual. We're born animals, and we teach each other how to be human. Somehow. It matters that we find out how. It matters to psychohistory. It matters to the Second Foundation. It matters to the human race."

"So—you aren't just being kind to Leyel."

"Yes, we are. You are, too. Good people are kind."

"Is that all? Leyel is just one man who's having trouble?"

"We need him. He isn't important just to you. He's important to *us.*"

"Oh. Oh."

"Why are you crying?"

"I was so afraid—that I was being selfish—being so worried about him. Taking up your time like this."

"Well, if that doesn't—I thought you were beyond surprising me."

"Our problems were just—our problems. But now they're not."

"Is that so important to you? Tell me, Deet—do you really value this community so much?"

"Yes."

"More than Leyel?"

"No! But enough—that I felt *guilty* for caring so much about him."

"Go home, Deet. Just go home."

"What?"

"That's where you'd rather be. It's been showing up in your behavior for two months, ever since Hari's death. You've been nasty and snappish, and now I know why. You *resent* us for keeping you away from Leyel."

"No, it was my choice, I—"

"Of course it was your choice! It was your *sacrifice* for the good of the Second Foundation. So now I'm telling you—healing Leyel is more important to Hari's plan than keeping up with your day-to-day responsibilities here."

"You're not removing me from my position, are you?"

"No. I'm just telling you to ease up. And get Leyel out of the apartment. Do you understand me? Demand it! Reengage him with *you*, or we've all lost him."

"Take him *where?*"

"I don't know. Theater. Athletic events. Dancing."

"We don't *do* those things."

"Well, what *do* you do?"

"Research. And then talk about it."

"Fine. Bring him here to the library. Do research with him. Talk about it."

"But he'll meet people here. He'd certainly meet *you.*"

"Good. Good. I like that. Yes, let him come here."

"But I thought we had to keep the Second Foundation a secret from him until he's ready to take part."

"I didn't say you should introduce me as First Speaker."

"No, no, of course you didn't. What am I thinking of? Of course he can meet you, he can meet everybody."

"Deet, listen to me."

"Yes, I'm listening."

"It's all right to love him, Deet."

"I know that."

"I mean, it's all right to love him more than you love us. More than you love any of us. More than you love all of us. There you are, crying again."

"I'm so—"

"Relieved."

"How do you understand me so well?"

"I only know what you show me and what you tell me. It's all we ever know about each other. The only thing that helps is that nobody can ever lie for long about who they really are. Not even to themselves."

For two months Leyel followed up on Magolissian's paper by trying to find some connection between language studies and human origins. Of course this meant weeks of wading through old, useless point-of-origin studies, which kept indicating that Trantor was the focal point of language throughout the history of the Empire, even though *nobody* seriously put forth Trantor as the planet of origin. Once again, though, Leyel rejected the search for a particular planet; he wanted to find out regularities, not unique events.

Leyel hoped for a clue in the fairly recent work—only two thousand years old—of Dagawell Kispitorian. Kispitorian came from the most isolated area of a planet called Artashat, where there were traditions that the original settlers came from an earlier world named Armenia, now uncharted. Kispitorian grew up among mountain people who claimed that long ago, they spoke a completely different language. In fact, the title of Kispitorian's most interesting book was *No Man Understood Us*; many of the folk tales of these people began with the formula "Back in the days when no man understood us . . ."

Kispitorian had never been able to shake off this tradition of his upbringing, and as he pursued the field of dialect formation and evolution, he kept coming across evidence that at one time the human species spoke not one but many languages. It had always been taken for granted that Galactic Standard was the up-to-date version of the language of the planet of origin—that while a few human groups might have developed dialects, civilization was impossible without mutually intelligible speech. But Kispitorian had begun to suspect that Galactic Standard did not become the universal human language until *after* the formation of the Empire— that, in fact, one of the first labors of the Imperium was to stamp out all other competing languages. The mountain people of Artashat believed that their language had been stolen from them. Kispitorian eventually devoted his life to proving they were right.

He worked first with names, long recognized as the most conservative aspect of language. He found that there were many separate naming traditions, and it was not until about the year 6000 G.E. that all were finally amalgamated into one Empire-wide stream.

What was interesting was that the farther back he went, the *more* complexity he found.

Because certain worlds tended to have unified traditions, and so the simplest explanation of this was the one he first put forth—that humans left their home world with a unified language, but the normal forces of language separation caused each new planet to develop its own offshoot, until many dialects became mutually unintelligible. Thus, different languages would not have developed until humanity moved out into space; this was one of the reasons why the Galactic Empire was necessary to restore the primeval unity of the species.

Kispitorian called his first and most influential book *Tower of Confusion,* using the widespread legend of the Tower of Babble as an illustration. He supposed that this story might have originated in that pre-Empire period, probably among the rootless traders roaming from planet to planet, who had to deal on a practical level with the fact that no two worlds spoke the same language. These traders had preserved a tradition that when humanity lived on one planet, they all spoke the same language. They explained the linguistic confusion of their own time by recounting the tale of a great leader who built the first "tower," or starship, to raise mankind up into heaven. According to the story, "God" punished these upstart people by confusing their tongues, which forced them to disperse among the different worlds. The story presented the confusion of tongues as the *cause* of the dispersal instead of its result, but cause-reversal was a commonly recognized feature of myth. Clearly this legend preserved a historical fact.

So far, Kispitorian's work was perfectly acceptable to most scientists. But in his forties he began to go off on wild tangents. Using controversial algorithms—on calculators with a suspiciously high level of processing power—he began to tear apart Galactic Standard itself, showing that many words revealed completely separate phonetic traditions, incompatible with the mainstream of the language. They could not comfortably have evolved within a population that regularly spoke either Standard or its primary ancestor language. Furthermore, there were many words with clearly related meanings that showed they had once diverged according to standard linguistic patterns and then were brought together later, with different meanings or implications. But the time scale implied by the degree of change was far too great to be accounted for in the period between humanity's first settlement of space and the formation of the Empire. Obviously, claimed Kispitorian, there had been many different languages *on the planet of origin;* Galactic Standard was the *first* universal human language. Throughout all human history, separation of language had been a fact of life; only the Empire had had the pervasive power to unify speech.

After that, Kispitorian was written off as a fool, of course— his own Tower of Babble interpretation was now used against him as if an interesting illustration had now become a central argument. He very narrowly escaped execution as a separatist, in fact, since there was an unmistakable tone of regret in his writing about the loss of linguistic diversity. The Imperium did succeed in cutting off all his funding and jailing him for a while because he had been using a calculator with an illegal level of memory and processing power. Leyel suspected that Kispitorian got off easy at that— working with language as he did, getting the results he got, he might well have developed a calculator so intelligent that it could understand and produce human speech, which, if discovered, would have meant either the death penalty or a lynching.

No matter now. Kispitorian insisted to the end that his work was pure science, making no value judgments on whether the Empire's linguistic unity was a Good Thing or not. He was merely reporting that the natural condition of humanity was to speak many different languages. And Leyel believed that he was right.

Leyel could not help but feel that by combining Kispitorian's language studies with Magolissian's work with language-using primates he could come up with something important. But what was the connection? The primates had never developed their *own* languages—they only learned nouns and verbs presented to them by humans. So they could hardly have developed diversity of language. What connection could there be? Why would diversity ever have developed? Could it have something to do with why humans became human?

The primates used only a tiny subset of Standard. For that matter, so did most people—most of the two million words in Standard were used only by a few professionals who actually needed them, while the common vocabulary of humans throughout the Galaxy consisted of a few thousand words.

Oddly, though, it was that small subset of Standard that was the *most* susceptible to change. Highly esoteric scientific or technical papers written in 2000 G.E. were still easily readable. Slangy, colloquial passages in fiction, especially in dialogue, became almost unintelligible within five hundred years. The language shared by the most different communities was the language that changed the most. But over time, that mainstream language always changed *together*. It made no sense, then, for there ever to be linguistic diversity. Language changed most when it was most unified. Therefore when people were most divided, their language should remain most similar.

Never mind, Leyel. You're out of your discipline. Any competent linguist would know the answer to that.

But Leyel knew that wasn't likely to be true. People immersed in one discipline rarely questioned the axioms of their profession. Linguists all took for granted the fact that the language of an isolated population is invariably more archaic, less susceptible to change. Did they understand why?

Leyel got up from his chair. His eyes were tired from staring into the lector. His knees and back ached from staying so long in the same position. He wanted to lie down, but knew that if he did, he'd fall asleep. The curse of getting old—he could fall asleep so easily, yet could never stay asleep long enough to feel well rested. He didn't *want* to sleep now, though. He wanted to think.

No, that wasn't it. He wanted to *talk*. That's how his best and clearest ideas always came, under the pressure of conversation, when someone else's questions and arguments forced him to think sharply. To make connections, invent explanations. In a contest with another person, his adrenaline flowed, his brain made connections that would never otherwise be made.

Where was Deet? In years past, he would have been talking this through with Deet all day. All week. She would know as much about his research as he did, and would constantly say "Have you thought of this?" or "How can you possibly think that!" And he would have been making the same challenges to *her* work. In the old days.

But these weren't the old days. She didn't need him any more—she had her friends on the library staff. Nothing wrong with that, probably. After all, she wasn't *thinking* now, she was putting old thoughts into practice. She needed *them*, not *him*. But he still needed *her*. Did she ever think of that? I might as well have gone to Terminus—damn Hari for refusing to let me go. I stayed for Deet's sake, and yet I don't have her after all, not when I need her. How *dare* Hari decide what was right for Leyel Forska!

Only Hari hadn't decided, had he? He would have let Leyel go—without Deet. And Leyel hadn't stayed with Deet so she could help him with his research. He had stayed with her because . . . because . . .

He couldn't remember why. Love, of course. But he couldn't think why that had been so important to him. It wasn't important to *her*. Her idea of love these days was to urge him to come to the library. "You can do your research there. We could be together more during the days."

The message was clear. The only way Leyel could remain part of Deet's life was if he became part of her new "family" at the library. Well, she could forget that idea. If she chose to get swallowed up in that place, fine. If she chose to leave him for a bunch of—*indexers* and *cataloguers*—fine. Fine.

No. It wasn't fine. He wanted to *talk* to her. Right now, at this moment, he wanted to tell her what he was thinking, wanted her to question him and argue with him until she made him come up with an answer, or lots of answers. He needed her to see what he wasn't seeing. He needed her a lot more than *they* needed her.

He was out amid the thick pedestrian traffic of Maslo Boulevard before he realized that this was the first time since Hari's funeral that he'd ventured beyond the immediate neighborhood of his apartment. It was the first time in months that he'd had anyplace to go. That's what I'm doing here, he thought. I just need a change of scenery, a sense of destination. That's the only reason I'm heading to the library. All that emotional nonsense back in the apartment, that was just my unconscious strategy for making myself et out among people again.

Leyel was almost cheerful when he got to the Imperial Library. He had been there many times over the years, but always for receptions or other public events—having his own high-capacity lector meant that he could get access to all the library's records by cable. Other people—students, professors from poorer schools, lay readers—they actually *had* to come here to read. But that meant that they knew their way around the building. Except for finding the major lecture halls and reception rooms, Leyel hadn't the faintest idea where anything was.

For the first time it dawned on him how very large the Imperial Library was. Deet had mentioned the numbers many times—a staff of more than five thousand, including machinists, carpenters, cooks, security, a virtual city in itself—but only now did Leyel realize that this meant that many people here had never met each other. Who could possibly know *five thousand* people by name? He couldn't just walk up and ask for Deet by name. What was the department Deet worked in? She had changed so often, moving through the bureaucracy.

Everyone he saw was a patron—people at lectors, people at catalogues, even people reading books and magazines printed on paper. Where were the librarians? The few staff members moving through the aisles turned out not to be librarians at all—they were volunteer docents, helping newcomers learn how to use the lectors and catalogues. They knew as little about library staff as he did.

He finally found a room full of real librarians, sitting at calculators preparing the daily access and circulation reports. When he tried to speak to one, she merely waved a hand at him. The thought she was telling him to go away until he realized that her hand remained in the air, a finger pointing to the front of the room. Leyel moved toward the elevated desk where a fat, sleepy-looking middle-aged woman was lazily paging through long columns of figures, which stood in the air before her in military formation.

"Sorry to interrupt you," he said softly.

She was resting her cheek on her hand. She didn't even look at him when he spoke. But she answered. "I pray for interruptions."

Only then did he notice that her eyes were framed with laugh lines, that her mouth even in repose turned upward into a faint smile.

"I'm looking for someone. My wife, in fact. Deet Forska."

Her smile widened. She sat up. "You're the beloved Leyel."

It was an absurd thing for a stranger to say, but it pleased him nonetheless to realize that Deet must have spoken of him. Of course everyone would have known that Deet's husband was *the* Leyel Forska. But this woman hadn't said it that way, had she? Not as *the* Leyel Forska, the celebrity. No, here he was known as "the beloved Leyel." Even if this woman meant to tease him, Deet must have let it be known that she had some affection for him. He couldn't help but smile. With relief. He hadn't known that he feared the loss of her love so much, but now he wanted to laugh aloud, to move, to dance with pleasure.

"I imagine I am," said Leyel.

"I'm Zay Wax. Deet must have mentioned me, we have lunch every day."

No, she hadn't. She hardly mentioned anybody at the library, come to think of it. These two had lunch every day, and Leyel had never heard of her. "Yes, of course," said Leyel. "I'm glad to meet you."

"And I'm relieved to see that your feet actually touch the ground."

"Now and then."

"She works up in Indexing these days." Zay cleared her display.

"Is that on Trantor?"

Zay laughed. She typed in a few instructions and her display now filled with a map of the library complex. It was a complex pile of rooms and corridors, almost impossible to grasp. "This shows only this wing of the main building. Indexing is these four floors."

Four layers near the middle of the display turned to a brighter color.

"And here's where you are right now."

A small room on the first floor turned white. Looking at the labyrinth between the two lighted sections, Leyel had to laugh aloud. "Can't you just give me a ticket to guide me?"

"Our tickets only lead you to places where patrons are allowed. But this isn't really hard, Lord Forska. After all, you're a genius, aren't you?"

"Not at the interior geography of buildings, whatever lies Deet might have told you."

"You just go out this door and straight down the corridor to the elevators—can't miss them. Go up to fifteen. When you get out, turn as if you were continuing down the same corridor, and after a while you go through an archway that says 'Indexing.' Then you lean back your head and bellow 'Deet' as loud as you can. Do that a few times and either she'll come or security will arrest you."

"That's what I was going to do if I *didn't* find somebody to guide me."

"I was hoping you'd ask me." Zay stood up and spoke loudly to the busy librarians. "The cat's going away. The mice can play."

"About time," one of them said. They all laughed. But they kept working.

"Follow me, Lord Forska."

"Leyel, please."

"Oh, you're such a flirt." When she stood, she was even shorter and fatter than she had looked sitting down. "Follow me."

They conversed cheerfully about nothing much on the way down the corridor. Inside the elevator, they hooked their feet under the rail as the gravitic repulsion kicked in. Leyel was so used to weightlessness after all these years of using elevators on Trantor that he never noticed. But Zay let her arms float in the air and sighed noisily. "I *love* riding the elevator," she said. For the first time Leyel realized that weightlessness must be a great relief to someone carrying as many extra kilograms as Zay Wax. When the elevator stopped, Zay made a great show of staggering out as if under a great burden. "My idea of heaven is to live forever in gravitic repulsion."

"You can get gravitic repulsion for your apartment, if you live on the top floor."

"Maybe *you* can," said Zay. "But *I* have to live on a librarian's salary."

Leyel was mortified. He had always been careful not to flaunt his wealth, but then, he had rarely talked at any length with people who couldn't afford gravitic repulsion. "Sorry," he said. "I don't think I could either, these days."

"Yes, I heard you squandered your fortune on a real bang-up funeral."

Startled that she would speak so openly of it, he tried to answer in the same joking tone. "I suppose you could look at it that way."

"I say it was worth it," she said. She looked slyly up at him. "I knew Hari, you know. Losing him cost humanity more than if Trantor's sun went nova."

"Maybe," said Leyel. The conversation was getting out of hand. Time to be cautious.

"Oh, don't worry. I'm not a snitch for the Pubs. Here's the Golden Archway into Indexing. The Land of Subtle Conceptual Connections."

Through the arch, it was as though they had passed into a completely different building. The style and trim were the same as before, with deeply lustrous fabrics on the walls and ceiling and floor made of the same smooth sound-absorbing plastic, glowing faintly with white light. But now all pretense at symmetry was gone. The ceiling was at different heights, almost at random; on the left and right there might be doors or archways, stairs or ramps, an alcove or a huge hall filled with columns, shelves of books and works of art surrounding tables where indexers worked with a half-dozen scriptors and lectors at once.

"The form fits the function," said Zay.

"I'm afraid I'm rubbernecking like a first-time visitor to Trantor."

"It's a strange place. But the architect was the daughter of an indexer, so she knew that standard, orderly, symmetrical interior maps are the enemy of freely connective thought. The finest touch—and the most expensive too, I'm afraid—is the fact that from day to day the layout is rearranged."

"Rearranged! The rooms move?"

"A series of random routines in the master calculator. There are rules, but the program isn't afraid to waste space, either. Some days only one room is changed, moved off to some completely different place in the Indexing area. Other days, everything is changed. The only constant is the archway leading in. I really wasn't joking when I said you should come here and bellow."

"But—the indexers must spend the whole morning just finding their stations."

"Not at all. Any indexer can work from any station."

"Ah. So they just call up the job they were working on the day before."

"No. They merely pick up on the job that is already in progress on the station they happen to choose that day."

"Chaos!" said Leyel.

"Exactly. How do you think a good hyperindex is made? If one person alone indexes a book, then the only connections that book will make are the ones that person knows about. Instead, each indexer is forced to skim through what his predecessor did the day before. Inevitably he'll add some new connections that the other indexer didn't think of. The environment, the work pattern, everything is designed to break down habits of thought, to make everything surprising, everything *new*."

"To keep everybody off balance."

"Exactly. Your mind works quickly when you're running along the edge of the precipice."

"By that reckoning, acrobats should all be geniuses."

"Nonsense. The whole labor of acrobats is to learn their routines so perfectly they *never* lose balance. An acrobat who improvises is soon dead. But indexers, when they lose their balance, they fall into wonderful discoveries. That's why the indexes of the Imperial Library are the only ones worth having. They startle and challenge as you read. All the others are just—clerical lists."

"Deet never mentioned this."

"Indexers rarely discuss what they're doing. You can't really explain it anyway."

"How long has Deet been an indexer?"

"Not long, really. She's still a novice. But I hear she's very, very good."

"Where *is* she?"

Zay grinned. Then she tipped her head back and bellowed. "Deet!"

The sound seemed to be swallowed up at once in the labyrinth. There was no answer.

"Not nearby, I guess," said Zay. "We'll have to probe a little deeper."

"Couldn't we just *ask* somebody where she is?"

"Who would know?"

It took two more floors and three more shouts before they heard a faint answering cry. "Over here!"

They followed the sound. Deet kept calling out, so they could find her.

"I got the flower room today, Zay! Violets!"

The indexers they passed along the way all looked up—some smiled, some frowned.

"Doesn't it interfere with things?" asked Leyel. "All this shouting?"

"Indexers *need* interruption. It breaks up the chain of thought. When they look back down, they have to rethink what they were doing."

Deet, not so far away now, called again. "The smell is so intoxicating. Imagine—the same room twice in a month!"

"Are indexers often hospitalized?" Leyel asked quietly.

"For what?"

"Stress."

"There's no stress on this job," said Zay. "Just play. We come up here as a *reward* for working in other parts of the library."

"I see. This is the time when librarians actually get to *read* the books in the library."

"We all chose this career because we love books for their own sake. Even the old inefficient corruptible paper ones. Indexing is like—writing in the margins."

The notion was startling. "Writing in someone *else's* book?"

"It used to be done all the time, Leyel. How can you possibly engage in dialogue with the author without writing your answers and arguments in the margins? Here she is." Zay preceded him under a low arch and down a few steps.

"I heard a man's voice with you, Zay," said Deet.

"Mine," said Leyel. He turned a corner and saw her there. After such a long journey to reach her, he thought for a dizzying moment that he didn't recognize her. That the library had randomized the librarians as well as the rooms, and he had happened upon a woman who merely resembled his long-familiar wife; he would have to reacquaint himself with her from the beginning.

"I thought so," said Deet. She got up from her station and embraced him. Even this startled him, though she usually embraced him upon meeting. It's only the setting that's different, he told himself. I'm only surprised because usually she greets me like this at home, in familiar surroundings. And usually it's Deet arriving, not me.

Or was there, after all, a greater warmth in her greeting here? As if she loved him more in this place than at home? Or, perhaps, as if the new Deet were simply a warmer, more comfortable person?

I thought that she was comfortable with me.

Leyel felt uneasy, shy with her. "If I'd known my coming would cause so much trouble," he began. Why did he need so badly to apologize?

"What trouble?" asked Zay.

"Shouting. Interrupting."

"Listen to him, Deet. He thinks the world has stopped because of a couple of shouts."

In the distance they could hear a man bellowing someone's name.

"Happens all the time," said Zay. "I'd better get back. Some lordling from Mahagonny is probably fuming because I haven't granted his request for access to the Imperial account books."

"Nice to meet you," said Leyel.

"Good luck finding your way back," said Deet.

"Easy this time," said Zay. She paused only once on her way through the door, not to speak, but to slide a metallic wafer along an almost unnoticeable slot in the doorframe, above eye level. She turned back and winked at Deet. Then she was gone.

Leyel didn't ask what she had done—if it were his business, something would have been said. But he suspected that Zay had either turned on or turned off a recording system. Unsure of whether they had privacy here from the library staff, Leyel merely stood for a moment, looking around. Deet's room really was filled with violets, real ones, growing out of cracks and apertures in the floor and walls. The smell was clear but not overpowering. "What is this room *for?*"

"For *me*. Today, anyway. I'm so glad you came."

"You never told me about this place."

"I didn't know about it until I was assigned to this section. Nobody talks about Indexing. We never tell outsiders. The architect died three thousand years ago. Only our own machinists understand how it works. It's like—"

"Fairyland."

"Exactly."

"A place where all the rules of the universe are suspended."

"Not all. We still stick with good old gravity. Inertia. That sort of thing."

"This place is right for you, Deet. This room."

"Most people go years without getting the flower room. It isn't always violets, you know. Sometimes climbing roses. Sometimes periwinkle. They say there's really a dozen flower rooms, but never more than one at a time is accessible. It's been violets for me both times, though."

Leyel couldn't help himself. He laughed. It was funny. It was delightful. What did this have to do with a library? And yet what a marvelous thing to have hidden away in the heart of this somber place. He sat down on a chair. Violets grew out of the top of the chairback, so that flowers brushed his shoulders.

"You finally got tired of staying in the apartment all day?" asked Deet.

Of course she would wonder why he finally came out, after all her invitations had been so long ignored. Yet he wasn't sure if he could speak frankly. "I needed to talk with you." He glanced back at the slot Zay had used in the doorframe. "Alone," he said.

Was that a look of dread that crossed her face?

"We're alone," Deet said quietly. "Zay saw to that. Truly alone, as we can't be even in the apartment."

It took Leyel a moment to realize what she was asserting. He dared not even speak the word. So he mouthed his question: Pubs?

"They never bother with the library in their normal spying. Even if they set up something special for you, there's now an interference field blocking out our conversation. Chances are, though, that they won't bother to monitor you again until you leave here."

She seemed edgy. Impatient. As if she didn't like having this conversation. As if she wanted him to get on with it, or maybe just get it over with.

"If you don't mind," he said. "I haven't interrupted you here before, I thought that just this once—"

"Of course," she said. But she was still tense. As if she feared what he might say.

So he explained to her all his thoughts about language. All that he had gleaned from Kispitorian's and Magolissian's work. She seemed to relax almost as soon as it became clear he was talking about his research. What did she dread, he wondered. Was she afraid I came to talk about our relationship? She hardly needed to fear *that*. He had no intention of making things more difficult by whining about things that could not be helped.

When he was through explaining the ideas that had come to him, she nodded carefully—as she had done a thousand times before, after he explained an idea or argument. "I don't know," she finally said. As so many times before, she was reluctant to commit herself to an immediate response.

And, as he had often done, he insisted. "But what do you *think?*"

She pursed her lips. "Just offhand—I've never tried a serious linguistic application of community theory, beyond jargon formation, so this is just my first thought—but try this. Maybe small isolated populations *guard* their language—jealously, because it's part of who they are. Maybe language is the most powerful ritual of all, so that people who have the same language are one in a way that people who can't understand each other's speech never are. We'd never know, would we, since everybody for ten thousand years has spoken Standard."

"So it isn't the size of the population, then, so much as—"

"How much they *care* about their language. How much it defines them as a community. A large population starts to think that everybody talks like them. They want to *distinguish* themselves, form a separate identity. Then they start developing jargons and slangs to separate themselves from others. Isn't that what happens to common speech? Children try to find ways of talking that their parents don't use. Professionals talk in private vocabularies so laymen won't know the passwords. All rituals for community definition."

Leyel nodded gravely, but he had one obvious doubt.

Obvious enough that Deet knew it, too. "Yes, yes, I know, Leyel. I immediately interpreted your question in terms of my own discipline. Like physicists who think that everything can be explained by physics."

Leyel laughed. "I thought of that, but what you said makes sense. And it would explain why the natural tendency of communities is to diversify language. We want a common tongue, a language of open discourse. But we also want private languages. Except a *completely* private language would be useless—whom would we talk to? So wherever a community forms, it creates at least a few linguistic barriers to outsiders, a few shibboleths that only insiders will know."

"And the more allegiance a person has to a community, the more fluent he'll become in that language, and the more he'll speak it."

"Yes, it makes sense," said Leyel. "So easy. You see how much I need you?"

He knew that his words were a mild rebuke—why weren't you home when I needed you—but he couldn't resist saying it. Sitting here with Deet, even in this strange and redolent place, felt right and comfortable. How could she have withdrawn from him? To him, her presence was what made a place home. To her, this place was home whether he was there or not.

He tried to put it in words—in abstract words, so it wouldn't sting. "I think the greatest tragedy is when one person has more allegiance to his community than any of the other members."

Deet only half smiled and raised her eyebrows. She didn't know what he was getting at.

"He speaks the community language all the time," said Leyel. "Only nobody else ever speaks it to him, or not enough anyway. And the more he speaks it, the more he alienates the others and drives them away, until he's alone. Can you imagine anything more sad? Somebody who's filled up with a language, hungry to speak, to hear it spoken, and yet there's no one left who understands a word of it."

She nodded, her eyes searching him. Does she understand what I'm saying? He waited for her to speak. He had said all he dared to say.

"But imagine this," she finally said. "What if he left that little place where no one understood him, and went over a hill to a new place, and all of a sudden he heard a hundred voices, a thousand, speaking the words he had treasured all those lonely years. And then he realized that he had never really known the language at all. The words had hundreds of meanings and nuances he had never guessed. Because each speaker changed the language a little just by speaking it. And when he spoke at last, his own voice sounded like music in his ears, and the others listened with delight, with rapture, his music was like the water of life pouring from a fountain, and he knew that he had never been home before."

Leyel couldn't remember hearing Deet sound so—rhapsodic, that was it, she herself was singing. She is the person she was talking about. In this place, her voice is different, that's what she meant. At home with me, she's been alone. Here in the library she's found others who speak her secret language. It isn't that she didn't want our marriage to succeed. She hoped for it, but I never understood her. These people did. Do. She's home here, that's what she's telling me.

"I understand," he said.

"Do you?" She looked searchingly into his face.

"I think so. It's all right."

She gave him a quizzical look.

"I mean, it's fine. It's good. This place. It's fine."

She looked relieved, but not completely. "You shouldn't be so *sad* about it, Leyel. This is a happy place. And you could do everything here that you ever did at home."

Except love you as the other part of me, and have you love me as the other part of you. "Yes, I'm sure."

"No, I mean it. What you're working on—I can see that you're getting close to something. Why not work on it *here*, where we can talk about it?"

Leyel shrugged.

"You *are* getting close, aren't you?"

"How do I know? I'm thrashing around like a drowning man in the ocean at night. Maybe I'm close to shore, and maybe I'm just swimming farther out to sea."

"Well, what do you have? Didn't we get closer just now?"

"No. This language thing—if it's just an aspect of community theory, it can't be the answer to human origin."

"Why not?"

"Because many primates have communities. A lot of other animals. Herding animals, for instance. Even schools of *fish*. Bees. Ants. Every multicelled organism is a community, for that matter. So if linguistic diversion grows out of community, then it's inherent in prehuman animals and therefore isn't part of the definition of humanity."

"Oh. I guess not."

"Right."

She looked disappointed. As if she had really hoped they would find the answer to the origin question right there, that very day.

Leyel stood up. "Oh well. Thanks for your help."

"I don't think I helped."

"Oh, you did. You showed me I was going up a dead-end road. You saved me a lot of wasted—thought. That's progress, in science, to know which answers aren't true."

His words had a double meaning, of course. She had also shown him that their marriage was a dead-end road. Maybe she understood him. Maybe not. It didn't matter—he had understood *her*. That little story about a lonely person finally discovering a place where she could be at home—how could he miss the point of that?

"Leyel," she said. "Why not put your question to the indexers?"

"Do you think the library researchers could find answers where I haven't?"

"Not the research department. *Indexing*."

"What do you mean?"

"Write down your questions. All the avenues you've pursued. Linguistic diversity. Primate language. And the other questions, the old ones. Archaeological, historical approaches. Biological. Kinship patterns. Customs. Everything you can think of. Just put it together as questions. And then we'll have them index it."

"Index my *questions*?"

"It's what we do—we read things and think of other things that might be related somehow, and we connect them. We don't say what the connection means, but we know that it means something, that the connection is real. We won't give you answers, Leyel, but if you follow the index, it might help you to think of connections. Do you see what I mean?"

"I never thought of that. Do you think a couple of indexers might have the time to work on it?"

"Not a couple of us. *All* of us."

"Oh, that's absurd, Deet. I wouldn't even ask it."

"*I* would. We aren't supervised up here, Leyel. We don't meet quotas. Our job is to read and think. Usually we have a few hundred projects going, but for a day we could easily work on the same document."

"It would be a waste. I can't publish anything, Deet."

"It doesn't have to be published. Don't you understand? Nobody but us knows what we do here. We can take it as an unpublished document and work on it just the same. It won't ever have to go online for the library as a whole."

Leyel shook his head. "And then if they lead me to the answer—what, will we publish it with two hundred bylines?"

"It'll be *your* paper, Leyel. We're just indexers, not authors. You'll still have to make the connections. Let us try. Let us be *part* of this."

Suddenly Leyel understood why she was so insistent on this.

Getting him involved with the library was her way of pretending she was still part of his life. She could believe she hadn't left him, if he became part of her new community.

Didn't she know how unbearable that would be? To see her here, so happy without him? To come here as just one friend among many, when once they had been—or he had thought they were—one indivisible soul? How could he possibly do such a thing?

And yet she wanted it, he could see it in the way she was looking at him, so girlish, so pleading that it made him think of when they were first in love, on another world—she would look at him like that whenever he insisted that he had to leave. Whenever she thought she might be losing him.

Doesn't she know who has lost whom?

Never mind. What did it matter if she didn't understand? If it would make her happy to have him pretend to be part of her new home, part of these librarians—if she wanted him to submit his life's work to the ministrations of these absurd indexers, then why not? What would it cost him? Maybe the process of writing down all his questions in some coherent order would help him. And maybe she was right—maybe a Trantorian index would help him solve the origin question.

Maybe if he came here, he could still be a small part of her life. It wouldn't be like marriage. But since that was impossible, then at least he could have enough of her here that he could remain himself, remain the person that he had become because of loving her for all these years.

"Fine," he said. "I'll write it up and bring it in."

"I really think we can help."

"Yes," he said, pretending to more certainty than he felt. "Maybe." He started for the door.

"Do you have to leave already?"

He nodded.

"Are you sure you can find your way out?"

"Unless the rooms have moved."

"No, only at night."

"Then I'll find my way out just fine." He took a few steps toward her, then stopped.

"What?" she asked.

"Nothing."

"Oh." She sounded disappointed. "I thought you were

going to kiss me goodbye." Then she puckered up like a three-year-old child.

He laughed. He kissed her—like a three-year-old—and then he left.

For two days he brooded. Saw her off in the morning, then tried to read, to watch the vids, anything. Nothing held his attention. He took walks. He even went topside once, to see the sky overhead—it was night, thick with stars. None of it engaged him. Nothing *held*. One of the vid programs had a moment, just briefly, a scene on a semiarid world, where a strange plant grew that dried out at maturity, broke off at the root, and then let the wind blow it around, scattering seeds. For a moment he felt a dizzying empathy with the plant as it tumbled by—am I as dry as that, hurtling through dead land? But no, he knew even that wasn't true, because the tumbleweed had life enough left in it to scatter seeds. Leyel had no seed left. That was scattered years ago.

On the third morning he looked at himself in the mirror and laughed grimly. "Is this how people feel before they kill themselves?" he asked. Of course not—he knew that he was being melodramatic. He felt no desire to die.

But then it occurred to him that if this feeling of uselessness kept on, if he never found anything to engage himself, then he might as well be dead, mightn't he, because his being alive wouldn't accomplish much more than keeping his clothes warm.

He sat down at the scriptor and began writing down questions. Then, under each question, he would explain how he had already pursued that particular avenue and why it didn't yield the answer to the origin question. More questions would come up then—and he was right, the mere process of summarizing his own fruitless research made answers seem tantalizingly close. It was a good exercise. And even if he never found an answer, this list of questions might be of help to someone with a clearer intellect—or better information—decades or centuries or millennia from now.

Deet came home and went to bed with Leyel still typing away. She knew the look he had when he was fully engaged in writing—she did nothing to disturb him. He noticed her enough to realize that she was carefully leaving him alone. Then he settled back into writing.

The next morning she awoke to find him lying in bed beside

her, still dressed. A personal message capsule lay on the floor in the doorway from the bedroom. He had finished his questions. She bent over, picked it up, took it with her to the library.

"His questions aren't academic after all, Deet."

"I told you they weren't."

"Hari was right. For all that he seemed to be a dilettante, with his money and his rejection of the universities, he's a man of substance."

"Will the Second Foundation benefit, then, if he comes up with an answer to his question?"

"I don't know, Deet. Hari was the fortune-teller. Presumably mankind is already human, so it isn't as if we have to start the process over."

"Do you think not?"

"What, should we find some uninhabited planet and put some newborns on it and let them grow up feral, and then come back in a thousand years and try to turn them human?"

"I have a better idea. Let's take ten thousand worlds filled with people who live their lives like animals, always hungry, always quick with their teeth and their claws, and let's strip away the veneer of civilization to expose to them what they really are. And then, when they see themselves clearly, let's come back and teach them how to be *really* human this time, instead of only having bits and flashes of humanity."

"All right. Let's do that."

"I knew you'd see it my way."

"Just make sure your husband finds out *how* the trick is done. Then we have all the time in the world to set it up and pull it off."

When the index was done, Deet brought Leyel with her to the library when she went to work in the morning. She did not take him to Indexing, but rather installed him in a private research room lined with vids—only instead of giving the illusion of windows looking out onto an outside scene, the screens filled all the walls from floor to ceiling, so it seemed that he was on a pinnacle high above the scene, without walls or even a railing to keep him from falling off. It gave him flashes of vertigo when he looked around— only the door broke the illusion. For a moment he thought of asking for a different room. But then he remembered Indexing, and realized that maybe he'd do better work if he too felt a bit off balance all the time.

At first the indexing seemed obvious. He brought the first page of his questions to the lector display and began to read. The lector would track his pupils, so that whenever he paused to gaze at a word, other references would begin to pop up in the space beside the page he was reading. Then he'd glance at one of the references. When it was uninteresting or obvious, he'd skip to the next reference, and the first one would slide back on the display, out of the way, but still there if he changed his mind and wanted it.

If a reference engaged him, then when he reached the last line of the part of it on display, it would expand to full-page size and slide over to stand in front of the main text. Then, if this new material had been indexed, it would trigger new references—and so on, leading him farther and farther away from the original document until he finally decided to go back and pick up where he left off.

So far, this was what any index could be expected to do. It was only as he moved farther into reading his own questions that he began to realize the quirkiness of this index. Usually, index references were tied to important words, so that if you just wanted to stop and think without bringing up a bunch of references you didn't want, all you had to do was keep your gaze focused in an area of placeholder words, empty phrases like "If this were all that could be . . ." Anyone who made it a habit to read indexed works soon learned this trick and used it till it became reflex.

But when Leyel stopped on such empty phrases, references came up anyway. And instead of having a clear relationship to the text, sometimes the references were perverse or comic or argumentative. For instance, he paused in the middle of reading his argument that archaeological searches for "primitiveness" were useless in the search for origins because all "primitive" cultures represented a decline from a star-going culture. He had written the phrase "All this primitivism is useful only because it predicts what we might become if we're careless and don't preserve our fragile links with civilization." By habit his eyes focused on the empty words "what we might become if." Nobody could index a phrase like that.

Yet they had. Several references appeared. And so instead of staying within his reverie, he was distracted, drawn to what the indexers had tied to such an absurd phrase.

One of the references was a nursery rhyme that he had forgotten he knew:

> Wrinkly Grandma Posey
> Rockets all are rosy.
> Lift off, drift off,
> All fall down.

Why in the world had the indexer put *that* in? The first thought that came to Leyel's mind was himself and some of the servants' children, holding hands and walking in a circle, round and round till they came to the last words, whereupon they threw themselves to the ground and laughed insanely. The sort of game that only little children could possibly think was fun.

Since his eyes lingered on the poem, it moved to the main document display and new references appeared. One was a scholarly article on the evolution of the poem, speculating that it might have arisen during the early days of starflight on the planet of origin, when rockets may have been used to escape from a planet's gravity well. Was that why this poem had been indexed to his article? Because it was tied to the planet of origin?

No, that was too obvious. Another article about the poem was more helpful. It rejected the early-days-of-rockets idea, because the earliest versions of the poem never used the word "rocket." The oldest extant version went like this:

> Wrinkle down a rosy,
> Pock-a fock-a posy,
> Lash us, dash us,
> All fall down.

Obviously, said the commentator, these were mostly nonsense words—the later versions had arisen because children had insisted on trying to make sense of them.

And it occurred to Leyel that perhaps this was why the indexer had linked this poem to his phrase—because the poem had once been nonsense, but we insisted on making sense out of it.

Was this a comment on Leyel's whole search for origins? Did the indexer think it was useless?

No—the poem had been tied to the empty phrase "what we might become if." Maybe the indexer was saying that human beings are like this poem—our lives make no sense, but we insist on making sense out of them. Didn't Deet say something like that once, when she was talking about the role of storytelling in community formation? The universe resists causality, she said. But human intelligence demands it. So we tell stories to impose causal relationships among the unconnected events of the world around us.

That includes ourselves, doesn't it? Our own lives are nonsense, but we impose a story on them, we sort our memories into cause-and-effect chains, forcing them to make sense even though they don't. Then we take the sum of our stories and call it our "self." This poem shows us the process—from randomness to meaning—and then we think our meanings are "true."

But somehow all the children had come to agree on the new version of the poem. By the year 2000 G.E., only the final and current version existed in all the worlds, and it had remained constant ever since. How was it that all the children on every world came to agree on the same version? How did the change spread? Did ten thousand kids on ten thousand worlds happen to make up the same changes?

It had to be word of mouth. Some kid somewhere made a few changes, and his version spread. A few years, and all the children in his neighborhood use the new version, and then all the kids in his city, on his planet. It could happen very quickly, in fact, because each generation of children lasts only a few years—seven-year-olds might take the new version as a joke, but repeat it often enough that five-year-olds think it's the true version of the poem, and within a few years there's nobody left among the children who remembers the old way.

A thousand years is long enough for the new version of the poem to spread. Or for five or a dozen new versions to collide and get absorbed into each other and then spread back, changed, to worlds that had revised the poem once or twice already.

And as Leyel sat there, thinking these thoughts, he conjured up an image in his mind of a network of children, bound to each other by the threads of this poem, extending from planet to planet throughout the Empire, and then back through time, from one generation of children to the previous one, a three-dimensional fabric that bound all children together from the beginning.

And yet as each child grew up, he cut himself free from the fabric of that poem. No longer would he hear the words "Wrinkly Grandma Posey" and immediately join hands with the child next to him. He wasn't part of the song any more.

But his own children were. And then his grandchildren. All joining hands with each other, changing from circle to circle, in a never-ending human chain reaching back to some long-forgotten ritual on one of the worlds of mankind—maybe, maybe on the planet of origin itself.

The vision was so clear, so overpowering, that when he finally noticed the lector display it was as sudden and startling as waking up. He had to sit there, breathing shallowly, until he calmed himself, until his heart stopped beating so fast.

He had found some part of his answer, though he didn't understand it yet. That fabric connecting all the children, that was part of what made us human, though he didn't know why. This strange and perverse indexing of a meaningless phrase had brought him a new way of looking at the problem. Not that the universal culture of children was a new idea. Just that he had never thought of it as having anything to do with the origin question.

Was this what the indexer meant by including this poem? Had the indexer also seen this vision?

Maybe, but probably not. It might have been nothing more than the idea of becoming something that made the indexer think of transformation—becoming old, like wrinkly Grandma Posey? Or it might have been a general thought about the spread of humanity through the stars, away from the planet of origin, that made the indexer remember how the poem seemed to tell of rockets that rise up from a planet, drift for a while, then come down to settle on a planet. Who knows what the poem meant to the indexer? Who knows why it occurred to her to link it with his document on that particular phrase?

Then Leyel realized that in his imagination, he was thinking of Deet making that particular connection. There was no reason to think it was her work, except that in his mind she was all the indexers. She had joined them, become one of them, and so when indexing work was being done, she was part of it. That's what it meant to be part of a community—all its works became, to a degree, your works. All that the indexers did, Deet was a part of it, and therefore Deet had done it.

Again the image of a fabric came to mind, only this time it was a topologically impossible fabric, twisted into itself so that no matter what part of the edge of it you held, you held the entire edge, and the middle, too. It was all one thing, and each part held the whole within it.

But if that was true, then when Deet came to join the library, so did Leyel, because she contained Leyel within her. So in coming here, she had not left him at all. Instead, she had woven him into a new fabric, so that instead of losing something he was gaining. He was part of all this, because *she* was, and so if he lost her it would only be because he rejected her.

Leyel covered his eyes with his hands. How did his meandering thoughts about the origin question lead him to thinking about his marriage? Here he thought he was on the verge of profound understanding, and then he fell back into self-absorption.

He cleared away all the references to "Wrinkly Grandma Posey" or "Wrinkle Down a Rosy" or whatever it was, then returned to reading his original document, trying to confine his thoughts to the subject at hand.

Yet it was a losing battle. He could not escape from the seductive distraction of the index. He'd be reading about tool use and technology, and how it could not be the dividing line between human and animal because there were animals that made tools and taught their use to others.

Then, suddenly, the index would have him reading an ancient terror tale about a man who wanted to be the greatest genius of all time, and he believed that the only thing preventing him from achieving greatness was the hours he lost in sleep. So he invented a machine to sleep for him, and it worked very well until he realized that the machine was having all his dreams. Then he demanded that his machine tell him what it was dreaming.

The machine poured forth the most astonishing, brilliant thoughts ever imagined by any man—far wiser than anything this man had ever written during his waking hours. The man took a hammer and smashed the machine, so that he could have his dreams back. But even when he started sleeping again, he was never able to come close to the clarity of thought that the machine had had.

Of course he could never publish what the machine had written—it would be unthinkable to put forth the product of a machine as if it were the work of a man. After the man died—in despair—people found the printed text of what the machine had written, and thought the man had written it and hidden it away. They published it, and he was widely acclaimed as the greatest genius who had ever lived.

This was universally regarded as an obscenely horrifying tale because it had a machine stealing part of a man's mind and using it to destroy him, a common theme. But why did the indexer refer to it in the midst of a discussion of tool-making?

Wondering about that led Leyel to think that this story itself was a kind of tool. Just like the machine the man in the story had made. The storyteller gave his dreams to the story, and then when people heard it or read it, his dreams—his nightmares—came out to live in their memories. Clear and sharp and terrible and true, those dreams they received. And yet if he tried to *tell* them the same truths, directly, not in the form of a story, people would think his ideas were silly and small.

And then Leyel remembered what Deet had said about how people absorb stories from their communities and take them into themselves and use these stories to form their own spiritual autobiography. They remember doing what the heroes of the stories did, and so they continue to act out each hero's character in their own lives, or, failing that, they measure themselves against the standard the story set for them. Stories become the human conscience, the human mirror.

Again, as so many other times, he ended these ruminations with his hands pressed over his eyes, trying to shut out—or lock in?—images of fabrics and mirrors, worlds and atoms, until finally, finally, he opened his eyes and saw Deet and Zay sitting in front of him.

No, leaning over him. He was on a low bed, and they knelt beside him.

"Am I ill?" he asked.

"I hope not," said Deet. "We found you on the floor. You're exhausted, Leyel. I've been telling you—you have to eat, you have to get a normal amount of sleep. You're not young enough to keep up this work schedule."

"I've barely started."

Zay laughed lightly. "Listen to him, Deet. I told you he was so caught up in this that he didn't even know what day it was."

"You've been doing this for three weeks, Leyel. For the last week you haven't even come home. I bring you food, and you won't eat. People talk to you, and you forget that you're in a conversation, you just drift off into some sort of—trance. Leyel, I wish I'd never brought you here, I wish I'd never suggested indexing—"

"No!" Leyel cried. He struggled to sit up.

At first Deet tried to push him back down, insisting he should rest. It was Zay who helped him sit. "Let the man talk," she said. "Just because you're his wife doesn't mean you can stop him from talking."

"The index is wonderful," said Leyel. "Like a tunnel opened up into my own mind. I keep seeing light just *that* far out of reach, and then I wake up and it's just me alone on a pinnacle except for the pages up on the lector. I keep losing it—"

"No, Leyel, we keep losing *you*. The index is poisoning you, it's taking over your mind—"

"Don't be absurd, Deet. You're the one who suggested this, and you're right. The index keeps surprising me, making me think in new ways. There are some answers already."

"Answers?" asked Zay.

"I don't know how well I can explain it. What makes us human. It has to do with communities and stories and tools and—it has to do with you and me, Deet."

"I should hope we're human," she said. Teasing him, but also urging him on.

"We lived together all those years, and we formed a community—with our children, till they left, and then just us. But we were like animals."

"Only sometimes," she said.

"I mean like herding animals, or primate tribes, or any community that's bound together only by the rituals and patterns of the present moment. We had our customs, our habits. Our private language of words and gestures, our dances, all the things that flocks of geese and hives of bees can do."

"Very primitive."

"Yes, that's right, don't you see? That's a community that dies with each generation. When we die, Deet, it will all be gone with us. Other people will marry, but none of them will know our dances and songs and language and—"

"Our children will."

"No, that's my point. They knew us, they even think they *know* us, but they were never part of the community of our marriage. Nobody is. Nobody *can* be. That's why, when I thought you were leaving me for this—"

"When did you think that I—"

"Hush, Deet," said Zay. "Let the man babble."

"When I thought you were leaving me, I felt like I was dead, like I was losing everything, because if you weren't part of our marriage, then there was nothing left. You see?"

"I don't see what that has to do with human origins, Leyel. I only know that I would never leave you, and I can't believe that you could think—"

"Don't distract him, Deet."

"It's the children. All the children. They play Wrinkly Grandma Posey, and then they grow up and don't play any more, so the actual community of these particular five or six children doesn't exist any more—but other kids are still doing the dance. Chanting the poem. For ten thousand years!"

"This makes us human? Nursery rhymes?"

"They're all part of the same community! Across all the empty space between the stars, there are still connections, they're still somehow the *same kids*. Ten thousand years, ten thousand worlds, quintillions of children, and they all knew the poem, they all did the dance. Story and ritual—it doesn't die with the tribe, it doesn't stop at the border. Children who never met face-to-face, who lived so far apart that the light from one star still hasn't reached the other, they belonged to the same community. We're human because we conquered time and space. We conquered the barrier of perpetual ignorance between one person and another. We found a way to slip my memories into your head, and yours into mine."

"But these are the ideas you already rejected, Leyel. Language and community and—"

"No! No, not just language, not just tribes of chimpanzees chattering at each other. *Stories*, epic tales that define a community, mythic tales that teach us how the world works, we use them to create each other. We became a different species, we became *human*, because we found a way to extend gestation beyond the womb, a way to give each child ten thousand parents that he'll never meet face-to-face."

Then, at last, Leyel fell silent, trapped by the inadequacy of his words. They couldn't tell what he had seen in his mind. If they didn't already understand, they never would.

"Yes," said Zay. "I think indexing your paper was a very good idea."

Leyel sighed and lay back down on the bed. "I shouldn't have tried."

"On the contrary, you've succeeded," said Zay.

Deet shook her head. Leyel knew why—Deet was trying to signal Zay that she shouldn't attempt to soothe Leyel with false praise.

"Don't hush me, Deet. I know what I'm saying. I may not know Leyel as well as you do, but I know truth when I hear it. In a way, I think Hari knew it instinctively. That's why he insisted on all his silly holodisplays, forcing the poor citizens of Terminus to put up with his pontificating every few years. It was his way of continuing to create them, of remaining alive within them. Making them feel like their lives had purpose behind them. Mythic and epic story, both at once. They'll all carry a bit of Hari Seldon within them just the way that children carry their parents with them to the grave."

At first Leyel could only hear the idea that Hari would have approved of his ideas of human origin. Then he began to realize that there was much more to what Zay had said than simple affirmation.

"You knew Hari Seldon?"

"A little," said Zay.

"Either tell him or don't," said Deet. "You can't take him this far in, and not bring him the rest of the way."

"I knew Hari the way you know Deet," said Zay.

"No," said Leyel. "He would have mentioned you."

"Would he? He never mentioned his students."

"He had thousands of students."

"I know, Leyel. I saw them come and fill his lecture halls and listen to the half-baked fragments of psychohistory that he taught them. But then he'd come away, here to the library, into a room where the Pubs never go, where he could speak words that the Pubs would never hear, and there he'd teach his real students. Here is the only place where the science of psychohistory lives on, where Deet's ideas about the formation of community actually have application, where your own vision of the origin of humanity will shape our calculations for the next thousand years."

Leyel was dumbfounded. "In the Imperial Library? Hari had his own college here in the library?"

"Where else? He had to leave us at the end, when it was time to go public with his predictions of the Empire's fall. Then the Pubs started watching him in earnest, and in order to keep them from finding us, he couldn't ever come back here again. It was the most terrible thing that ever happened to us. As if he died, for us, years before his body died. He was part of us, Leyel, the way that you and Deet are part of each other. She knows. She joined us before he left."

It stung. To have had such a great secret, and not to have been included. "Why Deet, and not me?"

"Don't you know, Leyel? Our little community's survival was the most important thing. As long as you were Leyel Forska, master of one of the greatest fortunes in history, you couldn't possibly be part of this—it would have provoked too much comment, too much attention. Deet could come, because Commissioner Chen wouldn't care that much what she did—he never takes spouses seriously, just one of the ways he proves himself to be a fool."

"But Hari always meant for you to be one of us," said Deet. "His worst fear was that you'd go off half-cocked and force your way into the First Foundation, when all along he wanted you in this one. The Second Foundation."

Leyel remembered his last interview with Hari. He tried to remember—did Hari ever lie to him? He told him that Deet couldn't go to Terminus—but now that took on a completely different meaning. The old fox! He never lied at all, but he never told the truth, either.

Zay went on. "It was tricky, striking the right balance, encouraging you to provoke Chen just enough that he'd strip away your fortune and then forget you, but not so much that he'd have you imprisoned or killed."

"You were making that happen?"

"No, no, Leyel. It was going to happen anyway, because you're who you are and Chen is who he is. But there was a range of possibility, somewhere between having you and Deet tortured to death on the one hand, and on the other hand having you and Rom conspire to assassinate Chen and take control of the Empire. Either of those extremes would have made it impossible for you to be part of the Second Foundation. Hari was convinced—and so is Deet, and so am I—that you belong with us. Not dead. Not in politics. Here."

It was outrageous, that they should make such choices for him, without telling him. How could Deet have kept it secret all this time? And yet they were so obviously correct. If Hari had told him about this Second Foundation, Leyel would have been eager, proud to join it. Yet Leyel couldn't have been told, couldn't have joined them until Chen no longer perceived him as a threat.

"What makes you think Chen will ever forget me?"

"Oh, he's forgotten you, all right. In fact, I'd guess that by tonight he'll have forgotten everything he ever knew."

"What do you mean?"

"How do you think we've dared to speak so openly today, after keeping silence for so long? After all, we aren't in Indexing now."

Leyel felt a thrill of fear run through him. "They can hear us?"

"If they were listening. At the moment, though, the Pubs are very busy helping Rom Divart solidify his control of the Commission of Public Safety. And if Chen hasn't been taken to the radiation chamber, he soon will be."

Leyel couldn't help himself. The news was too glorious—he sprang up from his bed, almost danced at the news. "Rom's doing it! After all these years—overthrowing the old spider!"

"It's more important than mere justice or revenge," said Zay. "We're absolutely certain that a significant number of governors and prefects and military commanders will refuse to recognize the overlordship of the Commission of Public Safety. It will take Rom Divart the rest of his life just to put down the most dangerous of the rebels. In order to concentrate his forces on the great rebels and pretenders close to Trantor, he'll grant an unprecedented degree of independence to many, many worlds on the periphery. To all intents and purposes, those outer worlds will no longer be part of the Empire. Imperial authority will not touch them, and their taxes will no longer flow inward to Trantor. The Empire is no longer Galactic. The death of Commissioner Chen—today—will mark the beginning of the fall of the Galactic Empire, though no one but us will notice what it means for decades, even centuries to come."

"So soon after Hari's death. Already his predictions are coming true."

"Oh, it isn't just coincidence," said Zay. "One of our agents was able to influence Chen just enough to ensure that he sent Rom Divart in person to strip you of your fortune. That was what pushed Rom over the edge and made him carry out this coup. Chen would have fallen—or died—sometime in the next year and a half no matter what we did. But I'll admit we took a certain pleasure in using Hari's death as a trigger to bring him down a little early, and under circumstances that allowed us to bring you into the library."

"We also used it as a test," said Deet. "We're trying to find ways of influencing individuals without their knowing it. It's still very crude and haphazard, but in this case we were able to influence Chen with great success. We had to do it—your life was at stake, and so was the chance of your joining us."

"I feel like a puppet," said Leyel.

"Chen was the puppet," said Zay. "You were the prize."

"That's all nonsense," said Deet. "Hari loved you. *I* love you. You're a great man. The Second Foundation had to have you. And everything you've said and stood for all your life made it clear that you were hungry to be part of our work. Aren't you?"

"Yes," said Leyel. Then he laughed. "The index!"

"What's so funny?" asked Zay, looking a little miffed. "We worked very hard on it."

"And it was wonderful, transforming, hypnotic. To take all these people and put them together as if they were a single mind, far wiser in its intuition than anyone could ever be alone. The most intensely unified, the most powerful human community that's ever existed. If it's our capacity for storytelling that makes us human, then perhaps our capacity for indexing will make us something better than human."

Deet patted Zay's hand. "Pay no attention to him, Zay. This is clearly the mad enthusiasm of a proselyte."

Zay raised an eyebrow. "*I'm* still waiting for him to explain why the index made him *laugh*."

Leyel obliged her. "Because all the time, I kept thinking—how could librarians have done this? Mere librarians! And now I discover that these librarians are all of Hari Seldon's prize students. My questions were indexed by psychohistorians!"

"Not exclusively. Most of us *are* librarians. Or machinists, or custodians, or whatever—the psychologists and psychohistorians are rather a thin current in the stream of the library. At first they were seen as outsiders. Researchers. *Users* of the library, not members of it. That's what Deet's work has been for these last few years—trying to bind us all together into one community. She came here as a researcher too, remember? Yet now she has made everyone's allegiance to the library more important than any other loyalty. It's working beautifully too, Leyel, you'll see. Deet is a marvel."

"We're *all* creating it together," said Deet. "It helps that the couple of hundred people I'm trying to bring in are so knowledge-able and understanding of the human mind. They understand exactly what I'm doing and then try to help me make it work. And it *isn't* fully successful yet. As years go by, we have to see the psychology group teaching and accepting the children of librarians and machinists and medical officers, in full equality with their own, so that the psychologists don't become a ruling caste. And then intermarriage between the groups. Maybe in a hundred years we'll have a truly cohesive community. This is a democratic city-state we're building, not an academic department or a social club."

Leyel was off on his own tangent. It was almost unbearable for him to realize that there were hundreds of people who knew Hari's work, while Leyel didn't. "You have to teach me!" Leyel said. "Everything that Hari taught you, all the things that have been kept from me—"

"Oh, eventually, Leyel," said Zay. "At present, though, we're much more interested in what you have to teach *us*. Already, I'm sure, a transcription of the things you said when you first woke up is being spread through the library."

"It was recorded?" asked Leyel.

"We didn't know if you were going to go catatonic on us at any moment, Leyel. You have no idea how you've been worrying us. Of course we recorded it—they might have been your last words."

"They won't be. I don't feel tired at all."

"Then you're not as bright as we thought. Your body is dangerously weak. You've been abusing yourself terribly. You're not a young man, and we insist that you stay away from your lector for a couple of days."

"What, are you now my doctor?"

"Leyel," Deet said, touching him on his shoulder the way she always did when he needed calming. "You *have* been examined by doctors. And you've got to realize—Zay is First Speaker."

"Does that mean she's commander?"

"This isn't the Empire," said Zay, "and I'm not Chen. All that it means to be First Speaker is that I speak first when we meet together. And then, at the end, I bring together all that has been said and express the consensus of the group."

"That's right," said Deet. *"Everybody* thinks you ought to rest."

"Everybody knows about me?" asked Leyel.

"Of course," said Zay. "With Hari dead you're the most original thinker we have. Our work needs you. Naturally we care about you. Besides, Deet loves you so much, and we love *Deet* so much, we feel like we're all a little bit in love with you ourselves."

She laughed, and so did Leyel, and so did Deet. Leyel noticed, though, that when he asked whether they all *knew* of him, she had answered that they cared about him and loved him. Only when Zay said this did he realize that she had answered the question he really meant to ask.

"And while you're recuperating," Zay continued, "Indexing will have a go at your new theory—"

"Not a theory, just a proposal, just a *thought*—"

"—and a few psychohistorians will see whether it can be quantified, perhaps by some variation on the formulas we've been using with Deet's laws of community development. Maybe we can turn origin studies into a real science yet."

"Maybe," Leyel said.

"Feel all right about this?" asked Zay.

"I'm not sure. Mostly. I'm very excited, but I'm also a little angry at how I've been left out, but mostly I'm—I'm so relieved."

"Good. You're in a hopeless muddle. You'll do your best work if we can keep you off balance forever." With that, Zay led him back to the bed, helped him lie down, and then left the room.

Alone with Deet, Leyel had nothing to say. He just held her

hand and looked up into her face, his heart too full to say anything with words. All the news about Hari's byzantine plans and a Second Foundation full of psychohistorians and Rom Divart taking over the government—that receded into the background. What mattered was this: Deet's hand in his, her eyes looking into his, and her heart, her self, her soul so closely bound to his that he couldn't tell and didn't care where he left off and she began.

How could he ever have imagined that she was leaving him? They had created each other through all these years of marriage. Deet was the most splendid accomplishment of his life, and he was the most valued creation of hers. We are each other's parent, each other's child. We might accomplish great works that will live on in this other community, the library, the Second Foundation. But the greatest work of all is the one that will die with us, the one that no one else will ever know of, because they remain perpetually outside. We can't even explain it to them. They don't have the language to understand us. We can only speak it to each other.

A Word or Two from Janet

by Janet Jeppson Asimov

I am often asked what it's like to be Isaac Asimov's wife or, as he referred to me in a recent speech, "the present holder of that enviable position." I usually mull over several possible answers:

1. Isaac is, conveniently, a walking dictionary and encyclopedia, able to impart information quickly, accurately, and eloquently because he has well-honed powers of expression and an incredible memory—which gets him into trouble, since there are too many things he can't forget. For instance, he is likely to say sadly, "This is the one hundred eighty-third anniversary of the Battle of Austerlitz and nobody cares!" Each December 2, since I have forgotten what he told me the year before, I have to ask him to explain all over again. Fortunately, although he does not put up with fools gladly, he puts up with me, and explains.

2. Isaac is reassuringly rational, with exceptions. He believes in the spectacular law—that if he flips up the dark spectacles attached to his eyeglasses, the sun will come out, and vice versa. Furthermore,

in the baseball season he thinks the Mets will lose any game he dares to watch. Once they start losing, he turns off the TV and shouts, "I have to stop watching and go back to my typewriter to give them a chance!"

3. He has a wonderful lack of fear about showing emotion. Not only is he affectionate and demonstrative, he doesn't even know what a stiff upper lip is. Isaac's lower lip quivers most when he has to have a blood sample drawn, but even then he manages to flirt with the female doing it. He's not afraid to cry (he always does when he reads Enobarbus's last speech or sings 'Danny Boy'), and will do so even in public, the way he did at Newton's grave.

4. Isaac has a point of view that makes me glad I know him. For instance, he woke up once with his legs making running motions in the bed. He said, "I dreamt someone told me I was making a good living out of writing, and I said yes indeed I was. Then the person said, 'It's amazing to see someone make all that money out of beaten swords.' I was running to tell you because it instantly struck me that the phrase meant I made my money out of the instruments of peace—the pen is mightier than the sword and thou shalt beat they swords into plowshares."

As you can see, there are many answers to the question of what it's like to be Isaac Asimov's wife, but the best is that my spouse defies description. Oddly enough, people always seem to be describing Isaac, and he is still on speaking terms with most of them. Perhaps paleontologist Simpson's description is definitive— "Isaac Asimov is a natural wonder and a national resource." I can testify that he is a wonder, completely natural, infinitely resourceful, and a dear.

We have a little wooden sculpture of two old people placidly sitting side by side, leaning toward each other. To me, they represent the contentment of being part of the pattern of life, together. The pattern includes intimacy and creativity, which have a lot in common because both take commitment, concentration, openness, effort, and inspiration.

My personal fiftieth anniversary with Isaac Asimov occurs in the third decade of the next century. Since life contains the three essential elements of a good work of fiction—a beginning, a middle, and an end—it is possible that Isaac and I won't be here for that anniversary, but his books will. And the stories people write because of him. Like those in this book, done with love.

Fifty Years

by Isaac Asimov

I've got to start by expressing thanks. I want to thank Martin H. Greenberg for having the idea of memorializing my fifty years in science fiction in this fashion. I want to thank Tor Books for publishing the book. I want to thank all my fellow writers who have contributed stories to this book, and who have, in this way, demonstrated the fact that they feel friendly toward me and kindly toward my works. And I want to thank Janet for contributing, too, in *all* the ways she does and has.

This is all more than I deserve, for it means I have made my way through life making so many friends and so remarkably few enemies that I must have done something right by accident, and I'm grateful for that more than anything else.

But it's fifty years! That's why all this is happening! Fifty years! Half a century!

So let's see what thoughts this gives rise to—

1. *Fifty years.* It's a reasonably long time. Merely to live for fifty years is not terribly unusual these days, but many great people have not managed. Joan of Arc died at nineteen. Of the great poets: John

Keats died at twenty-six; Percy Bysshe Shelley died at thirty; George Gordon Noel Byron died at thirty-six; Edgar Allen Poe died at forty. Of the great scientists, Sadi Carnot died at thirty-six; Heinrich Rudolf Hertz died at thirty-six; James C. Maxwell died at forty-eight.

When you pass the half-century mark, with all this in mind, you can't help but feel a bit hangdog about it. The Greeks visualized the three Fates: Clotho ("spinner"), who formed the thread of life; Lachesis ("determiner by lot"), who measured its length; and Atropos ("unswervable"), who cut it, in the end. I thank them all as well. I thank Clotho for spinning such a good life; Lachesis for spinning one that is longer than those of many others far more deserving than myself; and to Atropos for withholding her formidable shears for as long as she has.

2. *Fifty years of professional work.* But it's not just fifty years. It's fifty years in a single profession, that of writing. My first story appeared in 1939 and there has been a regular procession of stories, essays, and books of all sorts ever since.

When Charles Dickens died at fifty-eight, he had been publishing for only thirty-five years. When Alexandre Dumas died at fifty-eight, he had been publishing for only forty-one years. William Shakespeare, who died at fifty-two, turned out all his professional works over a period of only thirty years.

Mind you, I am only talking length of professional life here; I am not talking quality. Any one work of these gentlemen—*David Copperfield, The Count of Monte Cristo,* or *Hamlet* is worth innumerable times my entire oeuvre. I know that, so don't bother writing to inform me of this matter.

Rather, I am merely telling you this in order to explain how grateful I am that I have been allowed a full fifty years at my profession—and still going. Nothing I write can be within light-years of Shakespeare, but this I will maintain as loudly as I can, and to my dying day. Everything I write has given *me* as much pleasure as anything Shakespeare wrote could have given *him,* so is not length of professional life something to be grateful for?

3. *Fifty years as a science fiction writer.* But it's not just fifty years of professional life, either. It's this particular professional life. Just think what the last fifty years has meant to a science fiction writer. When I began writing, robots were pure fantasy. So I wrote robot

stories freely out of my own imagination. The first one was written in June 1939. I have lived long enough to see robots (in very simple form) become real, and to have my Three Laws of Robotics taken seriously.

Flights to the moon were sheer fantasy in 1939, and my first story in *Astounding* dealt with attempted rocketry to the moon. I lived to see *that* become real.

Think of other science fictional standbys that have become real (even if I didn't particularly write about them myself.) There were no computers in 1939, and no television either, though both existed in science fiction. Science was also overflowing with ray-guns, and we have lived to see laser beams.

How fortunate I was to have started when I did and to have lived as long as I have.

—But it all comes full circle. More important than anything else are one's friends. Foundation's friends are all my friends, whether they have written for the book, or published it, or bought it or borrowed it. My friends are all those who have read my stuff over the last half-century and have enjoyed it.

I thank you all. I cannot thank you enough.